Praise for
New York Times and *USA TODAY*
bestselling author Brenda Jackson

"Brenda Jackson writes romance that sizzles and
characters you fall in love with."
—*New York Times* and *USA TODAY* bestselling author
Lori Foster

"Jackson's trademark ability to weave multiple
characters and side stories together makes shocking
truths all the more exciting."
—*Publishers Weekly*

"There is no getting away from the sex appeal
and charm of Jackson's Westmoreland family."
—*RT Book Reviews* on *Feeling the Heat*

"Jackson's characters are wonderful, strong, colorful
and hot enough to burn the pages."
—*RT Book Reviews* on *Westmoreland's Way*

"The kind of sizzling, heart-tugging story Brenda
Jackson is famous for."
—*RT Book Reviews* on *Spencer's Forbidden Passion*

"This is entertainment at its best."
—*RT Book Reviews* on *Star of His Heart*

Dear Readers,

I introduced Rico Claiborne in my seventh Westmoreland novel, *The Chase is On,* as the brother to my heroine, Jessica Claiborne. And you met him again in *A Durango Affair* as the brother of Savannah Claiborne, the heroine in that novel. Your emails began pouring in requesting that I write Rico's story. I put him on my "To Do" list until I thought I had the perfect heroine. Someone who was worthy of his heart.

I found her in Megan Westmoreland.

Texas Wild is Megan and Rico's story as they join forces in search of information about the patriarch of the Denver Westmorelands, Raphel. Their journey takes them from the mountains of Denver to the plains of Texas where the heat they encounter is blazing and wild—and is mainly for each other.

It's time to get to know Rico, up close and personal, in a love story that will leave you breathless and tempt you to get wild.

Happy reading!

Brenda Jackson

BRENDA JACKSON

TEXAS WILD

HARLEQUIN®
entertain, enrich, inspire™

To Gerald Jackson, Sr. My one and only. My everything.
Happy 40th Anniversary!!

To my readers who asked for Rico Claiborne's story,
Texas Wild is especially for you!

To my Heavenly Father. How Great Thou Art.

Though your beginning was small,
yet your latter end would increase abundantly.
—*Job* 8:7

ISBN-13: 978-0-373-73198-5

TEXAS WILD

Copyright © 2012 by Brenda Streater Jackson

PLEASE RECYCLE
THIS PRODUCT IS RECYCLABLE

Recycling programs
for this product may
not exist in your area.

www.Harlequin.com

Printed in U.S.A.

Selected Books by Brenda Jackson

Other titles by this author
are available in ebook format.

BRENDA JACKSON

is a die "heart" romantic who married her childhood sweetheart and still proudly wears the "going steady" ring he gave her when she was fifteen. Because she believes in the power of love, Brenda's stories always have happy endings. In her real-life love story, Brenda and her husband of forty years live in Jacksonville, Florida, and have two sons.

A *New York Times* bestselling author of more than seventy-five romance titles, Brenda is a recent retiree who now divides her time between family, writing and traveling with Gerald. You may write Brenda at P.O. Box 28267, Jacksonville, Florida 32226, by email at WriterBJackson@aol.com or visit her website, www.brendajackson.net.

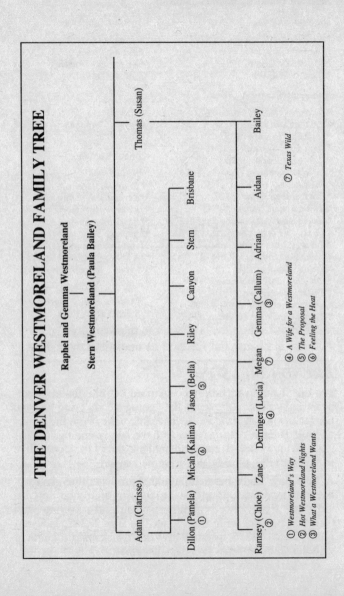

THE DENVER WESTMORELAND FAMILY TREE

Raphel and Gemma Westmoreland

Stern Westmoreland (Paula Bailey)

Adam (Clarisse)

Thomas (Susan)

Dillon (Pamela) ①

Micah (Kalina) ⑥   Jason (Bella) ⑤   Riley   Canyon   Stern   Brisbane

Ramsey (Chloe) ②

Zane   Derringer (Lucia) ④   Megan ⑦   Gemma (Callum) ③   Adrian   Aidan   Bailey

① Westmoreland's Way
② Hot Westmoreland Nights
③ What a Westmoreland Wants
④ A Wife for a Westmoreland
⑤ The Proposal
⑥ Feeling the Heat
⑦ Texas Wild

Prologue

A beautiful June day

"OMG, who's the latecomer to the wedding?"

"Don't know, but I'm glad he made it to the reception."

"Look at that body."

"Look at that walk."

"He should come with a warning sign that says Extremely Hot."

Several ladies in the wedding party whispered among themselves, and all eyes were trained on the tall, ultrahandsome man who'd approached the group of Westmoreland male cousins across the room. The reception for Micah Westmoreland's wedding to Kalina Daniels was in full swing on the grounds of Micah Manor, but every female in attendance was looking at one particular male.

The man who'd just arrived.

"For crying out loud, will someone please tell me who he is?" Vickie Morrow, a good friend of Kalina's, pleaded in a low voice. She looked over at Megan Westmoreland. "Most of the good-looking men here are related to you in some way, so tell us. Is he another Westmoreland cousin?"

Megan was checking out the man just as thoroughly as all the other women were. "No, he's no kin of mine. I've never seen him before," she said. She hadn't seen the full view yet, either, just his profile, but even that was impressive—he had handsome features, a deep tan and silky straight hair that brushed against the collar of his suit. He was both well dressed and good-looking.

"Yes, he definitely is one fine specimen of a man and is probably some Hollywood friend of my cousins, since he seems to know them."

"Well, I want to be around when the introductions are made," Marla Ford, another friend of Kalina's, leaned over and whispered in Megan's ear. "Make that happen."

Megan laughed. "I'll see what I can do."

"Hey, don't look now, ladies, but he's turned this way and is looking over here," Marla said. "In fact, Megan, your brother Zane is pointing out one of us to him…and I hope it's me." Seconds later, Marla said in a disappointed voice, "It's *you,* Megan."

Marla had to be mistaken. Why would Zane point her out to that man?

"Yeah, look how the hottie is checking you out," Vickie whispered to Megan. "It's like the rest of us don't even exist. *Lordy, I do declare*. I wish some man would look at me that way."

Megan met the stranger's gaze. Everyone was right.

He was concentrated solely on her. And the moment their eyes connected, something happened. It was as if heat transmitted from his look was burning her skin, flaming her blood, scorching her all over. She'd never felt anything so powerful in her life.

Instant attraction.

Her heart pounded like crazy, and she shivered as everything and everyone around her seemed to fade into the background…everything except for the sound of the soft music from the orchestra that pulled her and this stranger into a cocoon. It was as if no one existed but the two of them.

Her hand, which was holding a glass of wine, suddenly felt moist, and something fired up within her that had never been lit before. Desire. As potent as it could get. How could a stranger affect her this way? For the first time in her adult life, at the age of twenty-seven, Megan knew what it meant to be attracted to someone in a way that affected all her vital signs.

And, as an anesthesiologist, she knew all about the workings of the human body. But up until now she'd never given much thought to her own body or how it would react to a man. At least, not to how it would react to this particular man…whomever he was. She found her own reaction as interesting as she found it disconcerting.

"That guy's hot for you, Megan."

Vickie's words reminded Megan that she had an audience. Breaking eye contact with the stranger, she glanced over at Vickie, swallowing deeply. "No, he's not. He doesn't know me, and I don't know him."

"Doesn't matter who knows who. What just happened between you two is called instant sexual attraction. I felt it. We all did. You would have to be dead not to have felt it. That was some kind of heat emitting between the two of you just now."

Megan drew in a deep breath when the other women around her nodded and agreed with what Vickie had said. She glanced back over at the stranger. He was still staring and held her gaze until her cousin Riley tapped him on the shoulder to claim his attention. And when Savannah and Jessica, who were married to Megan's cousins Durango and Chase, respectively, walked up to him, she saw how his face split in a smile before he pulled both women into his arms for a huge hug.

That's when it hit her just who the stranger was. He was Jessica and Savannah's brother, the private investigator who lived in Philadelphia, Rico Claiborne. The man Megan had hired a few months ago to probe into her great-grandfather's past.

Rico Claiborne was glad to see his sisters, but the woman Zane had pointed out to him, the same one who had hired him over the phone a few months ago, was still holding his attention, although he was pretending otherwise.

Dr. Megan Westmoreland.

She had gone back to talking to her friends, not looking his way. That was fine for now since he needed to get his bearings. What in the hell had that been all about? What had made him concentrate solely on her as if all those other women standing with her didn't exist? There was something about her that made her stand out, even before Zane had told him the one in the pastel pink was his sister Megan.

The woman was hot, and when she had looked at him, every cell in his body had responded to that look. It wasn't one of those I'm-interested-in-you-too kind of looks. It was one of those looks that questioned the power of what was going on between them. It was quite obvious she was just as confused as he was. Never had he reacted so fiercely to a woman before. And the fact that she was the one who had hired him to research Raphel Westmoreland made things even more complicated.

That had been two months ago. He'd agreed to take the case, but had explained he couldn't begin until he'd wrapped up the other cases he was working on. She'd understood. Today, he'd figured he could kill two birds with one stone. He'd attend Micah's wedding and finally get to meet Micah's cousin Megan. But he hadn't counted on feeling such a strong attraction to her, one that still had heat thrumming all through him.

His sisters' husbands, as well as the newlyweds, walked up to join him. And as Rico listened to the conversations swirling around him, he couldn't help but steal glances over at Megan. He should have known it would be just a matter of time before one of his sisters noticed where his attention had strayed.

"You've met Megan, right? I know she hired you to investigate Raphel's history," Savannah said with a curious gleam in her eyes. He knew that look. If given the chance she would stick that pretty nose of hers where it didn't belong.

"No, Megan and I haven't officially met, although we've talked on the phone a number of times," he said, grabbing a drink off the tray of a passing waiter. He needed it to cool off. Megan Westmoreland was so freaking hot he could feel his toes beginning to burn. "But I know which one she is. Zane pointed her out to me a few minutes ago," he added, hoping that would appease his sister's curiosity.

He saw it didn't when she smiled and said, "Then let me introduce you."

Rico took a quick sip of his drink. He started to tell Savannah that he would rather be introduced to Megan later, but then decided he might as well get it over with. "All right."

As his sister led him over to where the group of women stood, all staring at him with interest in their eyes, his gaze was locked on just one. And he knew she felt the strong attraction flowing between them as much as he did. There was no way she could not.

It was a good thing they wouldn't be working together closely. His job was just to make sure she received periodic updates on how the investigation was going, which was simple enough.

Yes, he decided, as he got closer to her, with the way his entire body was reacting to her, the more distance he put between himself and Megan the better.

One

Three months later

"Dr. Westmoreland, there's someone here to see you."

Megan Westmoreland's brow arched as she glanced at her watch. She was due in surgery in an hour and had hoped to grab a sandwich and a drink from the deli downstairs before then. "Who is it, Grace?" she asked, speaking into the intercom system on her desk. Grace Elsberry was a student in the college's work-study program and worked part-time as an administrative assistant for the anesthesiology department at the University of Colorado Hospital.

"He's hot. A Brad Cooper look-alike with a dark tan," Grace whispered into the phone.

Megan's breath caught and warm sensations oozed through her bloodstream. She had an idea who her visitor was and braced herself for Grace to confirm her suspicions. "Says his name is Rico Claiborne." Lowering her voice even more, Grace added, "But I prefer calling him Mr. Yummy…if you know what I mean."

Yes, she knew exactly what Grace meant. The man was so incredibly handsome he should be arrested for being a menace to society. "Please send Mr. Claiborne in."

"Send him in? Are you kidding? I will take the pleasure of *escorting* him into your office, Dr. Westmoreland."

Megan shook her head. She couldn't remember the last time Grace had taken the time to escort anyone into her office. The door opened, and Grace, wearing the biggest of grins, escorted Rico Claiborne in. He moved with a masculine grace that exerted power, strength and confidence, and he looked like a model, even while wearing jeans and a pullover sweater.

Megan moved from behind her desk to properly greet him. Rico was tall, probably a good six-four, with dark brown hair and a gorgeous pair of hazel eyes. They had talked on the phone a number of times, but they had only met once, three months ago, at her cousin Micah's wedding. He had made such an impact on her feminine senses that she'd found it hard to stop thinking about him ever since. Now that he had completed that case he'd been working on, hopefully he was ready to start work on hers.

"Rico, good seeing you again," Megan said, smiling, extending her hand to him. Grace was right, he did look like Brad Cooper, and his interracial features made his skin tone appear as if he'd gotten the perfect tan.

"Good seeing you again as well, Megan," he said, taking her hand in his.

The warm sensation Megan had felt earlier intensified with the touch of his hand on hers, but she fought to ignore it. "So, what brings you to Denver?"

He placed his hands in the pockets of his jeans. "I arrived this morning to appear in court on a case I handled last year, and figured since I was here I'd give you an update. I actually started work on your case a few weeks ago. I don't like just dropping in like this, but I tried calling you when I first got to town and couldn't reach you on your cell phone."

"She was in surgery all morning."

They both turned to note Grace was still in the room. She stood in the doorway smiling, eyeing Rico up and down with a look of pure female appreciation on her face. Megan wouldn't have been surprised if Grace started licking her lips.

"Thanks, and that will be all Grace," Megan said.

Grace actually looked disappointed. "You sure?"

"Yes, I'm positive. I'll call you if I need you," Megan said, forcing back a grin.

"Oh, all right."

It was only when Grace had closed the door behind her that Megan glanced back at Rico to find him staring at her. A shiver of nervousness slithered down her spine. She shouldn't feel uncomfortable around him. But she had discovered upon meeting Rico that she had a strong attraction to him, something she'd never had for a man before. For the past three months, out of sight had meant out of mind where he was concerned—on her good days. But with him standing in the middle of her office she was forced to remember why she'd been so taken with him at her cousin's wedding.

The man was hot.

"Would you like to take a seat? This sounds important," she said, returning to the chair behind her desk, eager to hear what he had to say and just as anxious to downplay the emotional reaction he was causing.

A few years ago, her family had learned that her great-grandfather, Raphel Stern Westmoreland, who they'd assumed was an only child, had actually had a twin brother, Reginald Scott Westmoreland. It all started when an older man living in Atlanta by the name of James Westmoreland—a grandson of Reginald—began genealogy research on his family. His research revealed a connection to the Westmorelands living in Denver—her family. Once that information had been uncovered, her family had begun to wonder what else they didn't know about their ancestor.

They had discovered that Raphel, at twenty-two, had become the black sheep of the family after running off with the preacher's wife, never to be heard from again. He had passed through various states, including Texas, Wyoming, Kansas and Nebraska, before settling down in Colorado. It was found that he had taken up with a number of women along the way. Everyone was curious about what happened to those women, since it appeared he had been married to each one of them at some point. If that was true, there were possibly even more Westmorelands out there that Megan and her family didn't know about. That was why her oldest cousin, Dillon, had taken it upon himself to investigate her great-grandfather's other wives.

Dillon's investigation had led him to Gamble, Wyoming, where he'd not only met his future wife, but he'd also found out the first two women connected with Raphel hadn't been the man's wives, but were women he had helped out in some way. Since that first investigation, Dillon had married and was the father of one child, with another on the way. With a growing family, he was too busy to chase information about Raphel's third and fourth wives. Megan had decided to resume the search, which was the reason she had hired Rico, who had, of course, come highly recommended by her brothers and cousins.

Megan watched Rico take a seat, thinking the man was way too sexy for words. She was used to being surrounded by good-looking men. Case in point, her five brothers and slew of cousins were all gorgeous. But there was something about Rico that pulled at her in a way she found most troublesome.

"I think it's important, and it's the first break I've had," he responded. "I was finally able to find something on Clarice Riggins."

A glimmer of hope spread through Megan. Clarice was rumored to have been her great-grandfather's third wife. Megan leaned forward in her chair. "How? Where?"

"I was able to trace what I've pieced together to a small town in Texas, on the other side of Austin, called Forbes."

"Forbes, Texas?"

"Yes. I plan to leave Thursday morning. I had thought of leaving later today, after this meeting, but your brothers and cousins talked me out of it. They want me to hang out with them for a couple of days."

Megan wasn't surprised. Although the Westmorelands were mostly divided among four states—Colorado, Georgia, Montana and Texas—the males in the family usually got together often, either to go hunting, check on the various mutual business interests or just for a poker game getaway. Since Rico was the brother-in-law to two of her cousins, he often joined those trips.

"So you haven't been able to find out anything about her?" she asked.

"No, not yet, but I did discover something interesting."

Megan lifted a brow. "What?"

"It's recorded that she gave birth to a child. We can't say whether the baby was male or female, but it was a live birth."

Megan couldn't stop the flow of excitement that seeped into her veins. If Clarice had given birth, that could mean more Westmoreland cousins out there somewhere. Anyone living in Denver knew how important family was to the Westmorelands.

"That could be big. Really major," she said, thinking. "Have you mentioned it to anyone else?"

He shook his head, smiling. "No, you're the one who hired me, so anything I discover I bring to you first."

She nodded. "Don't say anything just yet. I don't want to get anyone's hopes up. You can say you're going to Texas on a lead, but nothing else for now."

Presently, there were fifteen Denver Westmorelands. Twelve males and three females. Megan's parents, as well as her aunt and uncle, had been killed in a plane crash years ago, leaving Dillon and her oldest brother, Ramsey, in charge. It hadn't been easy, but now all of the Westmorelands were self-supporting individuals. All of them had graduated from college except for the two youngest—Bane and Bailey. Bane was in the U.S. Navy, and Bailey, who'd fought the idea of any education past high school, was now in college with less than a year to go to get her degree.

There had never been any doubt in Megan's mind that she would go to college to become an anesthesiologist. She loved her job. She had known this was the career she wanted ever since she'd had her tonsils removed at six and had met the nice man who put her to sleep. He had come by to check on her after the surgery. He'd visited with her, ate ice cream with her and told her all about his job. At the time, she couldn't even pronounce it, but she'd known that was her calling.

Yet everyone needed a break from their job every once in a while, and she was getting burned out. Budget cuts required doing more with less, and she'd known for a while that it was time she went somewhere to chill. Bailey had left that morning for Charlotte to visit their cousin Quade, his wife Cheyenne and their triplets. Megan had been tempted to go with her, since she had a lot of vacation time that she rarely used. She also thought about going to Montana, where other Westmorelands lived. One nice thing about having a large family so spread out was that you always had somewhere to go.

Suddenly, a thought popped into Megan's head, and she glanced over at Rico again to find him staring at her. Their gazes held for a moment longer than necessary before she broke eye contact and looked down at the calendar on her desk while releasing a slow breath. For some reason she had a feeling he was on the verge of finding out something major. She wanted to be there when he did. More than anything she wanted to be present when he found out about Clarice's child. If she was in Denver while he was in Texas, she would go nuts waiting for him to contact her with any information he discovered. Once she'd gotten her thoughts and plans together, she glanced back up at him.

"You're leaving for Texas in two days, right?"

He lifted a brow. "Yes. That's my plan."

Megan leaned back in her chair. "I've just made a decision about something."

"About what?"

Megan smiled. "I've decided to go with you."

Rico figured there were a lot of things in life he didn't know. But the one thing he did know was that there was no way Megan Westmoreland was going anywhere with him. Being alone with her in this office was bad enough. The thought of them sitting together on a plane or in a car was too close for comfort. It was arousing him just thinking about it.

He was attracted to her big-time and had been from the moment he'd seen her at Micah's wedding. He had arrived late because of a case he'd been handling and had shown up at the reception just moments before the bride and groom were to leave for their honeymoon. Megan had hired him a month earlier, even though they'd never met in person. Because of that, the first thing Rico did when he arrived at the reception was to ask Zane to point her out.

The moment his and Megan's gazes locked he had felt desire rush through him to a degree that had never happened before. It had shocked the hell out of him. His gaze had moved over her, taking in every single thing he saw, every inch of what he'd liked. And he'd liked it all. Way too much. From the abundance of dark curls on her head to the creamy smoothness of her mahogany skin, from the shapely body in a bridesmaid gown to the pair of silver stilettos on her feet. She had looked totally beautiful.

At the age of thirty-six, he'd figured he was way too old to be *that* attracted to any woman. After all, he'd dated quite a few women in his day. And by just looking at Megan, he could tell she was young, that she hadn't turned thirty yet. But her age hadn't stopped him from staring and staring and staring…until one of her cousins had reclaimed his attention. But still, he had thought about her more than he should have since then.

"Well, with that settled, I'll notify my superiors so they can find a replacement for me while I'm gone," she said, breaking into his thoughts. "There are only a few surgeries scheduled for tomorrow, and I figure we'll be back in a week or so."

Evidently she thought that since he hadn't said anything, he was okay with the idea of her accompanying him to Texas. Boy, was she wrong. "Sorry, Megan, there's no way I'll let you come with me. I have a rule about working alone."

He could tell by the mutinous expression on her face that he was in for a fight. That didn't bother him. He had two younger sisters to deal with so he knew well how to handle a stubborn female.

"Surely you can break that rule this one time."

He shook his head. "Sorry, I can't."

She crossed her arms over her chest. "Other than the fact that you prefer working alone, give me another reason I can't go with you."

He crossed his arms over his own chest. "I don't need another reason. Like I said, I work alone." He did have a reason, but he wouldn't be sharing it with her. All he had to do was recall what had almost happened the last time he'd worked a case with a woman.

"Why are you being difficult?"

"Why are you?" he countered.

"I'm not," she said, throwing her head back and gritting out her words. "This is my great-grandfather we're talking about."

"I'm fully aware of who he was. You and I talked extensively before I agreed to take on this case, and I recall telling you that I would get you the information you wanted…doing things my way."

He watched as she began nibbling on her bottom lip. Okay, so now she was remembering. Good. For some reason, he couldn't stop looking into her eyes, meeting her fiery gaze head on, thinking her eyes resembled two beautiful dark orbs.

"As the client, I demand that you take me," she said, sharply interrupting his thoughts.

He narrowed his gaze. "You can demand all you want, but you're not going to Texas with me."

"And why not?"

"I've told you my reasons, now can we move on to something else, please?"

She stood up. "No, we can't move on to something else."

He stood, as well. "Now you're acting like a spoiled child."

Megan's jaw dropped. "A spoiled child? I've never acted like a spoiled child in my entire life. And as for going to Texas, I will be going since there's no reason that I shouldn't."

He didn't say anything for a moment. "Okay, there is another reason I won't take you with me. One that you'd do well to consider," he said in a calm, barely controlled tone. She had pushed him, and he didn't like being pushed.

"Fine, let's hear it," she snapped furiously.

He placed his hands in the pockets of his jeans, stood with his legs braced apart and leveled his gaze on her when he spoke in a deep, husky voice. "I want you,

Megan. Bad. And if you go anywhere with me, I'm
going to have you."

He then turned and walked out of her office.

Shocked, Megan dropped back down in her chair.
"Gracious!"

Three surgeries later, back in her office, Megan
paced the floor. Although Rico's parting statement
had taken her by surprise, she was still furious. Typi-
cal man. Why did they think everything began and
ended in the bedroom? So, he was attracted to her. Big
deal. Little did he know, but she was attracted to him
as well, and she had no qualms about going to Texas
with him. For crying out loud, hadn't he ever heard of
self-control?

She was sister to Zane and Derringer and cousin
to Riley and Canyon—three were womanizers to the
core. And before marrying Lucia, Derringer had all
but worn his penis on his sleeve and Zane, Lord help
him, wore his anywhere there was a free spot on his
body. She couldn't count the number of times she'd unexpectedly shown up at Zane's place at the wrong time
or how many pairs of panties she'd discovered left behind at Riley's. And wasn't it just yesterday she'd seen
a woman leave Canyon's place before dawn?

Besides that, Rico Claiborne honestly thought all he
had to do was decide he wanted her and he would have
her? Wouldn't she have some kind of say-so in the matter? Evidently he didn't think so, which meant he really
didn't know whom he was dealing with. The doctors at
the hospital, who thought she was cold and incapable
of being seduced, called her "Iceberg Megan."

So, okay, Rico had thawed her out a little when she'd
seen him at the wedding three months ago. And she

would admit he'd made her heart flutter upon seeing
him today. But he was definitely under a false assump-
tion if he thought all he had to do was snap his fingers,
strut that sexy walk and she would automatically fall
into any bed with him.

She scowled. The more she thought about it, the
madder she got. He should know from all the conversations they'd shared over the phone that this investigation was important to her. Family was everything to
her, and if there were other Westmorelands out there,
she wanted to know about them. She wanted to be in
the thick of things when he uncovered the truth as to
where those Westmorelands were and how quickly they
could be reached.

Megan moved to the window and looked out. September clouds were settling in, and the forecasters had
predicted the first snowfall of the year by the end of the
week. But that was fine since she had no intention of
being here in Denver when the snow started. Ignoring
what Rico had said about her not going to Texas with
him, she had cleared her calendar for not only the rest
of the week, but also for the next month. She had the
vacation time, and if she didn't use it by the end of the
year she would end up losing it anyway.

First, she would go to Texas. And then, before returning to work, she would take off for Australia and
spend time with her sister Gemma and her family.
Megan enjoyed international travel and recalled the
first time she'd left the country to visit her cousin Delaney in the Middle East. That had been quite an enjoyable experience.

But remembering the trip to visit her cousin couldn't
keep her thoughts from shifting back to Rico, and she
felt an unwelcoming jolt of desire as she recalled him

standing in her office, right in this very spot, and saying what he'd said, without as much as blinking an eye.

If he, for one minute, thought he had the ability to tell her what to do, he had another thought coming. If he was *that* attracted to her then he needed to put a cap on it. They were adults and would act accordingly. The mere thought that once alone they would tear each other's clothes off in some sort of heated lust was total rubbish. Although she was attracted to him, she knew how to handle herself. It *was* going to be hard to keep her hands to herself.

But no matter what, she would.

"You sure I'm not putting you out, Riley? I can certainly get a room at the hotel in town."

"I won't hear of it," Riley Westmoreland said, smiling. "Hell, you're practically family."

Rico threw his luggage on the bed, thinking he certainly hadn't felt like family earlier when he'd been alone with Megan. He still couldn't get over her wanting to go to Texas with him. Surely she had felt the sexual tension that seemed to surround them whenever they were within a few feet of each other.

"So how are things going with that investigation you're doing for Megan?" Riley asked, breaking into Rico's thoughts.

"Fine. In fact, I'm on my way to Texas to poke around a new lead."

Riley's brow lifted. "Really? Does Megan know yet?"

"Yes. I met with her at the hospital earlier today."

Riley chuckled. "I bet she was happy about that. We're all interested in uncovering the truth about Poppa Raphel, but I honestly think Megan is obsessed with it

and has been ever since Dillon and Pam shared those
journals with her. Now that Dillon has made Megan
the keeper of the journals she is determined to uncover
everything. She's convinced we have more relatives out
there somewhere."

Rico had read those journals and had found them
quite interesting. The journals, written by Raphel himself, had documented his early life after splitting from
his family.

"And it's dinner tonight over at the big house. Pam
called earlier to make sure I brought you. I hope you're
up for it. You know how testy pregnant women can get
at times."

Rico chuckled. Yes, he knew. In fact, he had noted
the number of pregnant women in the Westmoreland
family. Enough to look like there was some sort of epidemic. In addition to Pam, Derringer's wife, Lucia,
was expecting and so was Micah's wife, Kalina. There
were a number of Atlanta Westmorelands expecting
babies, as well.

Case in point, his own sisters. Jessica was pregnant
again, and Savannah had given birth to her second child
earlier that year. They were both happily married, and
he was happy for them. Even his mother had decided to
make another go of marriage, which had surprised him
after what she'd gone through with his father. But he
liked Brad Richman, and Rico knew Brad truly loved
his mother.

"Well, I'll let you unpack. We'll leave for Dillon's
place in about an hour. I hope you're hungry because
there will be plenty of food. The women are cooking,
and we just show up hungry and ready to eat," Riley
said, laughing.

A half hour later Rico had unpacked all the items

he needed. Everything else would remain in his luggage since he would be leaving for Texas the day after tomorrow. Sighing, he rubbed a hand down his face, noting his stubble-roughened jaw. Before he went out anywhere, he definitely needed to shave. And yes, he was hungry since he hadn't eaten since that morning, but dinner at Dillon's meant most of the Denver Westmorelands who were in town would be there. That included Megan. Damn. He wasn't all that sure he was ready to see her again. He was known as a cool and in-control kind of guy. But those elements of his personality took a flying leap around Megan Westmoreland.

Why did he like the way she said his name? To pronounce it was simple enough, but there was something about the way she said it, in a sultry tone that soothed and aroused.

Getting aroused was the last thing he needed to think about. It had been way too long since he'd had bedroom time with a woman. So he was in far worse shape than he'd realized. Seeing Megan today hadn't helped matters. The woman was way too beautiful for her own good.

Grabbing his shaving bag off the bed, Rico went into the guest bath that was conveniently connected to his room. Moments later, after lathering his face with shaving cream, he stared into the mirror as he slowly swiped a razor across his face. The familiar actions allowed his mind to wander, right back to Megan.

The first thing he'd noticed when he'd walked into her office was that she'd cut her hair. She still had a lot of curls, but instead of flowing to her shoulders, her hair crowned her face like a cap. He liked the style on her. It gave her a sexier look…not that she needed it.

He could just imagine being wheeled into surgery

only to discover she would be the doctor to administer the drug to knock you out. Counting backward while lying flat on your back and staring up into her face would guarantee plenty of hot dreams during whatever surgery you were having.

He jolted when he nicked himself. Damn. He needed to concentrate on shaving and rid his mind of Megan. At least he didn't have to worry about that foolishness of hers, about wanting to go with him to Texas. He felt certain, with the way her eyes had nearly popped out of the sockets and her jaw had dropped after what he'd said, that she had changed her mind.

He hadn't wanted to be so blatantly honest with her, but it couldn't be helped. Like he told her, he preferred working alone. The last time he had taken a woman with him on a case had almost cost him his life. He remembered it like it was yesterday. An FBI sting operation and his female partner had ended up being more hindrance than help. The woman blatantly refused to follow orders.

Granted, there was no real danger involved with Megan's case per se. In fact, the only danger he could think of was keeping his hands to himself where Megan was concerned. That was a risk he couldn't afford. And he had felt the need to be blunt and spell it out to her. Now that he had, he was convinced they had an understanding.

He would go to Texas, delve into whatever he could discover about Clarice Riggins and bring his report back to her. Megan was paying him a pretty hefty fee for his services, and he intended to deliver. But he would have to admit that her great-grandfather had covered his tracks well, which made Rico wonder what all the old man had gotten into during his younger days.

It didn't matter, because Rico intended to uncover it all. And like he'd told Megan, Clarice Riggins had given birth, but there was nothing to indicate that she and Raphel had married. It had been a stroke of luck that he'd found anything at all on Clarice, since there had been various spellings of the woman's name.

He was walking out of the bathroom when his cell phone rang, and he pulled it off the clip. He checked and saw it was a New York number. He had several associates there and couldn't help wondering which one was calling.

"This is Rico."

There was a slight pause and then… "Hello, son. This is your father."

Rico flinched, drew in a sharp breath and fought for control of his anger, which had come quick…as soon as he'd recognized the voice. "You must have the wrong number because I don't have a father."

Without giving the man a chance to say anything else, he clicked off the phone. As far as he was concerned, Jeff Claiborne could go to hell. Why on earth would the man be calling Rico after all this time? What had it been? Eighteen years? Rico had been happy with his father being out of sight and out of mind.

To be quite honest, he wished he could wash the man's memory away completely. He could never forget the lives that man had damaged by his selfishness. No, Jeff Claiborne had no reason to call him. No reason at all.

Two

Megan tried to downplay her nervousness as she continued to cut up the bell pepper and celery for the potato salad. According to Pam, Rico had been invited to dinner and would probably arrive any minute.

"Has Rico found anything out yet?"

Megan glanced over at her cousin-in-law. She liked Pam and thought she was perfect for Dillon. The two women were alone for now. Chloe and Bella had gone to check on the babies, and Lucia, who was in the dining room, was putting icing on the cake.

"Yes, there's a lead in Texas he'll follow up on when he leaves here," Megan said. She didn't want to mention anything about Clarice. The last thing she wanted to do was get anyone's hopes up.

"How exciting," Pam said as she fried the chicken, turning pieces over in the huge skillet every so often. "I'm sure you're happy about that."

Megan would be a lot happier if Rico would let her go to Texas with him, but, in a way, she had solved that problem and couldn't wait to see the expression on his face when he found out how. Chances were, he thought he'd had the last word.

She sighed, knowing if she lived to be a hundred years old she wouldn't be able to figure out men. Whenever they wanted a woman they assumed a woman would just naturally want them in return. How crazy was that bit of logic?

There was so much Megan didn't know when it came to men, although she had lived most of her life surrounded by them. Oh, she knew some things, but this man-woman stuff—when it came to wants and desires—just went over her head. Until she'd met Rico, there hadn't been a man who'd made her give him a second look. Of course, Idris Elba didn't count.

She lifted her gaze from the vegetables to look over at Pam. Megan knew Pam and Dillon had a pretty good marriage, a real close one. Pam, Chloe, Lucia and Bella were the older sisters she'd never had, and, at the moment, she needed some advice.

"Pam?"

"Hmm?"

"How would you react if a man told you he wanted you?"

Pam glanced her way and smiled. "It depends on who the man is. Had your brother told me that, I would have kicked my fiancé to the curb a lot sooner. The first thing I thought when I saw Dillon was that he was hot."

That was the same thing Megan had thought when she'd seen Rico. "So you would not have gotten upset had he said he wanted you?"

"Again, it depends on who the man is. If it's a man I

had the hots for, then no, I wouldn't have gotten upset. Why would I have? That would mean we were of the same accord and could move on to the next phase."

Megan raised a brow. "The next phase?"

"Yes, the I-want-to-get-to-know-you-better phase." Pam looked over at her. "So tell me. Was this a hypothetical question or is there a man out there who told you he wants you?"

Megan nervously nibbled on her bottom lip. She must have taken too long to answer because Pam grinned and said, "I guess I got my answer."

Pam took the last of the chicken out of the skillet, turned off the stove and joined Megan at the table. "Like I said, Megan, the question you should ask yourself is…if he's someone you want, too. Forget about what he wants for the moment. The question is what do *you* want?"

Megan sighed. Rico was definitely a looker, a man any woman would want. But what did she really know about him, other than that he was Jessica and Savannah's older brother, and they thought the world of him?

"He doesn't want to mix business with pleasure, not that I would have, mind you. Besides, I never told him that I wanted him."

"Most women don't tell a man. What they do is send out vibes. Men can pick up on vibes real quick, and depending on what those vibes are, a man might take them as a signal."

Megan looked perplexed. "I don't think I sent out anything."

Pam laughed. "I hate to say this, but Jillian can probably size a man up better than you can. Your brothers and cousins sheltered you too much from the harsh realities of life." Jillian was Pam's sister, who was a sophomore in college.

Megan shook her head. "It's not that they sheltered me, I just never met anyone I was interested in."

"Until now?"

Megan lifted her chin. "I'm really not interested in him, but I want us to work closer together, and he doesn't…because he wants me."

"Well, I'm sure there will be times at the hospital when the two of you will have no choice but to work together."

Pam thought the person they were discussing was another doctor. Megan wondered what Pam's reaction would be if she found out the person they were talking about was one of her dinner guests.

Megan heard loud male voices and recognized all of them. One stood out, the sound a deep, husky timbre she'd come to know.

Rico had arrived.

Rico paused in his conversation with Dillon and Ramsey when Megan walked into the room to place a huge bowl on the dining room table. She called out to him. "Hello, Rico."

"Megan."

If his gaze was full of male appreciation, it couldn't be helped. She had changed out of the scrubs he'd seen her in earlier and into a cute V-neck blue pullover sweater and a pair of hip-hugging jeans. She looked both comfortable and beautiful. She had spoken, which was a good indication that he hadn't offended her by what he'd told her. He was a firm believer that the truth never hurt, but he'd known more than one occasion when it had pissed people off.

"So, you're on your way to Texas, I hear." Dillon Westmoreland's question penetrated Rico's thoughts.

He looked at Dillon and saw the man's questioning gaze and knew he'd been caught ogling Megan. Rico's throat suddenly felt dry, and he took a sip of his wine before answering. "Yes. I might have a new lead. Don't want to say what it is just yet, until I'm certain it is one."

Dillon nodded. "I understand, trust me. When I took that time off to track down information on Raphel, it was like putting together pieces of a very complicated puzzle. But that woman," he said, inclining his head toward Pam when she entered the room, "made it all worthwhile."

Rico glanced over to where Pam was talking to Megan. He could see how Pam could have made Dillon feel that way. She was a beautiful woman. Rico had heard the story from his sisters, about how Dillon had met Pam while in Wyoming searching for leads on his great-grandfather's history. Pam had been engaged to marry a man who Dillon had exposed as nothing more than a lying, manipulating, arrogant SOB.

Rico couldn't help keeping his eye on Megan as her brother Ramsey and her cousins Dillon and Riley carried on conversations around him. Thoughts of her had haunted him ever since they'd met back in June. Even now, he lay awake with thoughts of her on his mind. How could one woman make such an impression on him, he would never know. But like he told her, he wanted her, so it was best that they keep their distance, considering his relationship with the Westmoreland family.

"So when are you leaving, Rico?"

He turned to meet Ramsey Westmoreland's inquisitive gaze. The man was sharp and, like Dillon, had probably caught Rico eyeing Megan. The hand holding Rico's wineglass tensed. He liked all the Westmorelands and appreciated how the guys included him in a number of their all-male get-togethers. The last thing he wanted was to lose their friendship because he couldn't keep his eyes off their sister and cousin.

"I'm leaving on Thursday. Why do you ask?"

Ramsey shrugged. "Just curious."

Rico couldn't shake the feeling that the man was more than just curious. He frowned and stared down at his drink. It was either that or risk the wrath of one of the Westmorelands if he continued to stare at Megan, who was busy setting the table.

Dillon spoke up and intruded into Rico's thoughts when he said, "Pam just gave me the nod that dinner is ready."

Everyone moved in the direction of the dining room. Rico turned to follow the others, but Ramsey touched his arm. "Wait for a minute."

Rico nodded. He wondered why Ramsey had detained him. Had Megan gone running to her brother and reported what Rico had said to her earlier? Or was Ramsey about to call him out on the carpet for the interest in Megan that he couldn't hide? In either of those scenarios, how could he explain his intense desire for Megan when he didn't understand it himself? He'd wanted women before, but never with this intensity.

When the two of them were left alone, Ramsey turned to him and Rico braced himself for whatever the man had to say. Rico was older brother to two sisters of his own so he knew how protective brothers could be. He hadn't liked either Chase or Durango in the beginning only because he'd known something was going on between them and his sisters.

Ramsey was silent for a moment, doing nothing more than slowly sipping his wine, so Rico decided to speak up. "Was there something you wanted to discuss with me, Ramsey?" There were a couple of years' difference in their ages, but at the moment Rico felt like it was a hell of a lot more than that.

"Yes," Ramsey replied. "It's about Megan."

Rico met Ramsey's gaze. "What about her?"

"Just a warning."

Rico tensed. "I think I know what you're going to say."

Ramsey shook his head, chuckling. "No. I don't think that you do."

Rico was confused at Ramsey's amusement. Hell, maybe he didn't know after all. "Then how about telling me. What's the warning regarding Megan?"

Ramsey took another sip of his drink and said, "She's strong-willed. She has self-control of steel and when she sets her mind to do something, she does it, often without thinking it through. And…if you tell her no, you might as well have said yes."

Rico was silent for a moment and then asked, "Is there a reason you're telling me this?"

Ramsey's mouth curved into a smile. "Yes, and you'll find out that reason soon enough. Now come on, they won't start dinner without us."

Megan tried drowning out all the conversation going on around her. As usual, whenever the Westmorelands got together, they had a lot to talk about.

She was grateful Pam hadn't figured out the identity of the man they'd been discussing and seated them beside each other. Instead, Rico was sitting at the other end of the table, across from Ramsey and next to Riley.

If she had to look at him, it would be quite obvious she was doing so.

Riley said something and everyone chuckled. That gave her an excuse to look down the table. Rico was leaning back against the chair and holding a half-filled glass of wine in his hand, smiling at whatever the joke was about. Why did he have to look so darn irresistible when he smiled?

He must have felt her staring because he shifted his gaze to meet hers. For a moment she forgot to breathe. The intensity of his penetrating stare almost made her lips tremble. Something gripped her stomach in a tight squeeze and sent stirrings all through her nerve endings.

At that moment, one thought resonated through her mind. The same one Pam had reiterated earlier. *It doesn't matter if he wants you. The main question is whether or not you want him.*

Megan immediately broke eye contact and breathed in slowly, taking a sip of her wine. She fought to get her mind back on track and regain the senses she'd almost lost just now. She could control this. She had to. Desire and lust were things she didn't have time for. The only reason she wanted to go to Texas with Rico was to be there when he discovered the truth about Raphel.

Thinking it was time to make her announcement, she picked up her spoon and tapped it lightly against her glass, but loud enough to get everyone's attention. When all eyes swung her way she smiled and said, "I have an announcement to make. Most of you know I rarely take vacation time, but today I asked for an entire month off, starting tomorrow."

Surprised gazes stared back at her...except one. She

saw a look of suspicion in Rico's eyes and noted the way his jaw tightened.

"What's wrong? You're missing Bailey already and plan to follow her to North Carolina?" her cousin Stern asked, grinning.

Megan returned his grin and shook her head. "Although I miss Bailey, I'm not going to North Carolina."

"Let me guess. You're either going to visit Gemma in Australia or Delaney in Tehran," Chloe said, smiling.

Again Megan shook her head. "Those are on my to-do list for later, but not now," she said.

When others joined in, trying to guess where she was headed, she held up her hand. "Please, it's not that big of a deal."

"It's a big deal if you're taking time off. You like working."

"I don't like working, but I like the job I do. There is a difference. And to appease everyone's curiosity, I talked to Clint and Alyssa today, and I'm visiting them in Texas for a while."

"Texas?"

She glanced down the table at Riley, which allowed her to look at Rico again, as well. He was staring at her, and it didn't take a rocket scientist to see he wasn't pleased with her announcement. Too bad, too glad. She couldn't force him to take her to Texas, but she could certainly go there on her own. "Yes, Riley, I'm going to Texas."

"When are you leaving?" her brother Zane asked. "I need to, ah, get that box from you before you leave."

She nodded, seeing the tense expression in Zane's features. She wondered about the reason for it. She was very much aware that he had a lock box in her hall closet. Although she'd been tempted, she'd never satisfied her curiosity by toying with the lock and looking inside. "That will be fine, Zane. I'm not leaving until Friday."

She took another quick glance at Rico before resuming dinner. He hadn't said anything, and it was just as well. There really wasn't anything he could say. Although they would end up in the same state and within mere miles from each other, they would not be together.

Since he didn't want her to accompany him, she would do a little investigating on her own.

Three

The next morning Rico was still furious.

Now he knew what Ramsey's warning had been about. The little minx was going to Texas, pretty damn close to where he would be. He would have confronted her last night, but he'd been too upset to do so. Now here he was—at breakfast time—and instead of joining Zane, Riley, Canyon and Stern at one of the local cafés that boasted hotcakes to die for, he was parked outside Megan's home so he could try and talk some sense into her.

Did she not know what red-hot desire was about? Did she not understand how it was when a man really wanted a woman to the point where self-control took a backseat to longing and urges? Did she not comprehend there was temptation even when she tried acting cool and indifferent?

Just being around her last night had been hard

enough, and now she was placing herself in a position where they would be around each other in Texas without any family members as buffers. Oh, he knew the story she was telling her family, that she would be visiting Clint in Austin. Chances were, she would—for a minute. He was friends with Clint and Alyssa and had planned to visit them as well, during the same time she planned to be there. Since Forbes wasn't that far from Austin, Clint had offered Rico the use of one of their cabins on the Golden Glade Ranch as his headquarters, if needed.

But now Megan had interfered with his plans. She couldn't convince Rico that she didn't have ulterior motives and that she didn't intend to show up in Forbes. She intended to do some snooping, with or without him. So what the hell was she paying him for if she was going to do things her way? He got out of the car and glanced around, seeing her SUV parked at the side of her house. She had a real nice spread, and she'd kept most of it in its natural state. In the background, you could see rolling hills and meadows, mountains and the Whisper Creek Canyon. It was a beautiful view. And there was a lake named after her grandmother Gemma. Gemma Lake was huge and, according to Riley, the fish were biting all the time. If Megan hadn't been throwing him for a loop, Rico would have loved to find a fishing pole while he was here to see if the man's claim was true.

Megan's home was smaller than those owned by her brothers and male cousins. Their homes were two or three stories, but hers was a single story, modest in size, but eye-catching just the same. It reminded him of a vacation cabin with its cedar frame, wraparound porch and oversize windows. It had been built in the perfect location to take advantage of both lake and canyon.

He'd heard the story of how the main house and the three hundred acres on which it sat had been willed to Dillon, since he was the oldest cousin. The remaining Denver Westmorelands got a hundred acres each once they reached their twenty-fifth birthdays. They had come up with pet names for their particular spreads. There was Ramsey's Web, Derringer's Dungeon, Zane's Hideout and Gemma's Gem. Now, he was here at Megan's Meadows.

According to Riley, Megan's property was prime land, perfect for grazing. She had agreed to let a portion of her land be used by Ramsey for the raising of his sheep, and the other by Zane and Derringer for their horse training business.

If Riley suspected anything because of all the questions Rico had asked last night about Megan, he didn't let on. And it could have been that the man was too preoccupied to notice, since Riley had his little black book in front of him, checking off the numbers of women he intended to call.

It was early, and Rico wondered if Megan was up yet. He would find out soon enough. Regardless, he intended to have his say. She could pretend she hadn't recognized the strong attraction between them, that sexual chemistry that kept him awake at night, but he wasn't buying it. However, just in case she didn't have a clue, he intended to tell her. Again. There was no need for her to go to Texas, and to pretend she was going just to visit relatives was a crock.

The weather was cold. Tightening his leather jacket around him, he moved quickly, walking up onto the porch. Knocking on the door loudly, he waited a minute and then knocked again. When there was no answer, he was about to turn around, thinking that perhaps she'd gone up to the main house for breakfast, when suddenly the door was snatched open. His jaw almost dropped. The only thing he could say when he saw her, standing there wearing the cutest baby-doll gown, was *wow*.

Megan stared at Rico, surprised to see him. "What are you doing here?"

He leaned in the doorway. "I came to talk to you. And what are you doing coming to the door without first asking who it is?"

She rolled her eyes. "I thought you were one of my brothers. Usually they are the only ones who drop by without notice."

"Is that why you came to the door dressed like that?"

"Yes, what do you want to talk to me about? You're letting cold air in."

"Your trip to Texas."

Megan stared at him, her lips tight. "Fine," she said, taking a step back. "Come in and excuse me while I grab my robe."

He watched her walk away, thinking the woman looked pretty damn good in a nightgown. Her shapely backside filled it out quite nicely and showed what a gorgeous pair of legs she had.

Thinking that the last thing he needed to be thinking about was her legs, he removed his jacket and placed it on the coatrack by the door before moving into the living room. He glanced around. Her house was nice and cozy. Rustic. Quaint. The interior walls, as well as the ceiling and floors, were cedar like the outside. The furniture was nice, appropriate for the setting and comfortable-looking. From where he stood, he could see an eat-in kitchen surrounded by floor-to-ceiling windows where you could dine and enjoy a view of the mountains and lake. He could even see the pier at her brother Micah's place that led to the lake and where the sailboat docked.

"Before we start talking about anything, I need my coffee."

Rico turned when she came back into the room, moving past him and heading toward the kitchen. He nodded, understanding. For him, it was basically the same, which was why he had drunk two cups already. "Fine. Take your time," he said. "I'm not going anywhere because I know what you're doing."

She didn't respond until she had the coffeemaker going. Then she turned and leaned back against a counter to ask, "And just what am I doing?"

"You're going to Texas for a reason."

"Yes, and I explained why. I need a break from work."

"Why Texas?"

She lifted her chin. "Why not Texas? It's a great state, and I haven't been there in a while. I missed that ball Clint, Cole and Casey do every year for their uncle. It will be good to see them, especially since Alyssa is expecting again."

"But that's not why you're going to Texas and you know it, Megan. Can you look me in the eyes and say you don't plan to set one foot in Forbes?"

She tilted her head to look at him. "No. I can't say that because I do."

"Why?"

Megan wondered how she could get him to understand. "Why not? These are my relatives."

"You are paying me to handle this investigation," he countered.

She tried not to notice how he filled the entrance to her kitchen. It suddenly looked small, as if there was barely any space. "Yes, and I asked to go to Forbes with you. It's important for me to be there when you find out if I have more relatives, but you have this stupid rule about working alone."

"Dammit, Megan, when you hired me you never told me you would get involved."

She crossed her arms over her chest. "I hadn't planned on getting involved. However, knowing I might have more kin out there changes everything. Why can't you understand that?"

Rico ran a frustrated hand down his face. In a way, he did. He would never forget that summer day when his mother had brought a fifteen-year-old girl into their home and introduced her as Jessica—their sister. Savannah had been sixteen, and he had been nineteen, a sophomore in college. It hadn't mattered to him that he hadn't known about Jessica before that time. Just the announcement that he had another sister had kicked his brotherly instincts into gear.

"I do understand, Megan," he said in a calm voice. "But still, there are things that I need to handle. Things I need to check out before anyone else can become involved."

She lifted a brow. "Things like what?"

Rico drew in a deep breath. Maybe he should have leveled with her yesterday, but there were things that had come up in his report on Raphel that he needed to confirm were fact or fiction. So far, everything negative about Raphel had turned out not to be true in Dillon's investigation. Rico wanted his final report to be as factual as possible, and he needed to do more research of the town's records.

She poured a cup of coffee for herself and one for him, as well. "What's wrong, Rico? Is there something you're not telling me?"

He saw the worry in her eyes as he accepted his coffee. "Look, this is my investigation. I told you that I was able to track down information on Clarice and the fact that she might have given birth to a child. That's all I know for now, Megan. Anything else is hearsay."

"Hearsay like what?"

"I'd rather not say."

After taking a sip of coffee, she said, "You're being evasive.

He narrowed his gaze. "I'm being thorough. If you want to go to Texas to visit Clint and Alyssa, then fine. But what I *don't* need is you turning up where you don't need to be."

"Where I don't need to be?" she growled.

"Yes. I have a job to do, and I won't be able to do it with you close by. I won't be able to concentrate."

"Men!" Megan said, stiffening her spine. "Do you all think it's all about you? I have brothers and male cousins, plenty of them. I know how you operate. You want one woman one day and another woman the next. Get over it already. Please."

Rico just stared at her. "And you think it's that simple?"

"*Yesss.* I'm Zane and Derringer's sister, Riley, Canyon and Stern's cousin. I see them. I watch them. I know their M.O. Derringer has been taken out of the mix by marrying Lucia, thank goodness. But the rest of them, and now the twins…oh, my God…are following in their footsteps.

"You see. You want. You do. But not me. *You,* Rico Claiborne, assume just because you want me that you're going to get me. What was your warning? If we go somewhere together alone, that you're going to *have* me. Who are you supposed to be? Don't I have a say-so in this matter? What if I told you that I *don't* want you?"

Rico just stared at her. "Then I would say you're lying to yourself. You want me. You might not realize it, but you want me. I see it every time you look at me. Damn, Megan, admit there's a strong attraction between us."

She rolled her eyes. "Okay, I find you attractive. But I find a lot of men attractive. No big deal."

"And are you sending out the same vibes to them that you're sending to me?" he asked in a deep, husky voice.

Megan recalled that Pam had said something about vibes. Was she sending them out to him without realizing she was doing so? No, she couldn't be. Because right now she wasn't feeling desire for him, she was feeling anger at him for standing there and making such an outlandish claim.

But still, she would have to admit that her heart was pounding furiously in her chest, and parts of her were quivering inside. So, could he be right about those vibes? Naw, she refused to believe it. Like she'd told him, she'd seen men in operation. Zane probably had a long list of women he wanted who he imagined were sending out vibes.

From the first, Rico had come across as a man who knew how to control any given situation, which was why she figured he was the perfect person for the job she'd hired him to do. So what was his problem now?

If he did want her, then surely the man could control his urges.

"Look, I assure you, I can handle myself, and I can handle you, Rico," she said, "All of my senses are intact, and you can be certain lust won't make me lose control. And nothing you or any man can say or do will place me in a position where I will lose my self-control." The men who thought so didn't call her "Iceberg Megan" for nothing.

"You don't think so?" Rico challenged her. "You aren't made of stone. You have feelings. I can tell that you're a very passionate woman, so consider your words carefully."

She chuckled as if what he'd said was a joke. "Passionate? Me?"

"Yes, you. When I first looked at you at the wedding reception and our gazes connected, the air between us was bristling with so much sexual energy I'm sure others felt it," he said silkily. "Are you going to stand there and claim you didn't feel it?"

Megan gazed down into her coffee and erased her smile. Oh, she remembered that day. Yes, she'd felt it. It had been like a surge of sexual, electrical currents that had consumed the space between them. It had happened again, too, every time she saw him looking at her. Until now, she'd assumed she had imagined it, but his words confirmed he had felt the connection, as well.

After that night at the wedding, she'd gone to bed thinking about him and had thought of him several nights after that. What she'd felt had bothered her, and she had talked to Gemma about it. Some of the things her married sister had shared with her she hadn't wanted to hear, mainly because Megan was a firm believer in self-control. Everybody had it, and everybody could manage it. Regardless of how attracted she was to Rico, she had self-control down pat. Hers was unshakable.

She'd had to learn self-control from the day she was told she would never see her parents again. She would never forget how Dillon and Ramsey had sat her down at the age of twelve and told her that not only her parents, but also her aunt and uncle, whom she'd adored, had been killed in a plane crash.

Dillon and Ramsey had assured her that they would keep the family together and take care of everyone, although the youngest—Bane and Bailey—were both under nine at the time. On that day, Ramsey had asked her to stay strong and in control. As the oldest girl in the Denver Westmoreland family, they had depended on her to help Gemma and Bailey through their grief. That didn't mean she'd needed to put her own grief aside, but it had meant that in spite of her grief, she'd had to be strong for the others. And she had. When the younger ones would come to her crying, she was the one who would comfort them, regardless of the circumstances or her emotions.

The ability to become emotionally detached, to stay in control, was how she'd known being an anesthesiologist was her calling. She went into surgery knowing some patients wouldn't make it through. Although she assured the patient of her skill in putting them to sleep, she never promised they would pull through. That decision was out of her hands. Some of the surgeons had lost patients and, in a way, she felt she'd lost them, as well. But no matter what, she remained in control.

Drawing in a deep breath, she eyed Rico. "You might have a problem with control, but I don't. I admit I find you desirable, but I can regulate my emotions. I can turn them on and off when I need to, Rico. Don't worry that I'll lose control one day and jump your bones, because it won't happen. There's not that much desire in the world."

Rico shook his head. "You honestly believe that, don't you?"

She placed her coffee cup on the counter. "Honestly believe what?"

"That you can control a desire as intense as ours."

"Yes, why wouldn't I?"

"I agree that certain desires can be controlled, Megan. But I'm trying to tell you, what you refuse to acknowledge or accept—desire as intense as ours can't always be controlled. What we have isn't normal."

She bunched her forehead. "Not normal? That's preposterous."

Rico knew then that she really didn't have a clue. This was no act. He could stand here until he was blue in the face and she still wouldn't understand. "What I'm trying to say, Megan," he said slowly, trying not to let frustration get the best of him, "is that I feel a degree of desire for you that I've never felt for any woman before."

She crossed her arms over her chest and glared at him. "Should I get excited or feel flattered about it?"

He gritted his teeth. "Look, Megan…"

"No, *you* look, Rico," she said, crossing the room to stand in front of him. "I don't know what to tell you. Honestly, I don't. I admitted that I'm attracted to you, as well. Okay, I'll admit it again. But on that same note, I'm also telling you I won't lose control over it. For crying out loud, there're more important things in life than sexual attraction, desire and passion. It's not about all of that."

"Isn't it?" He paused a moment, trying to keep his vexation in check. And it wasn't helping matters that she was there, standing right in front of him, with a stubborn expression on her face and looking as beautiful as any woman could. And he picked up her scent, which made him fight to keep a grip on his lust. The woman was driving him mad in so many ways.

"Let me ask you something, Megan," he said in a voice he was fighting to keep calm. "When was the last time you were with a man you desired?"

Rico's question surprised Megan, and she didn't say anything. Hell, she'd never been with a man she truly desired because she'd never been with a man period. She had dated guys in high school, college, and even doctors at the hospital. Unfortunately, they'd all had one thing in common. They had reminded her too much of her player-card-toting brothers and cousins, even hitting on her using some of the same lines she'd heard her family use. And a few bold ones had even had the nerve to issue ultimatums. She had retaliated by dropping those men like hot potatoes, just to show she really didn't give a royal damn. They said she was cold and couldn't be thawed and that's when they'd started calling her Iceberg Megan. Didn't bother her any because none of those men had gotten beyond the first boring kiss. She was who she was and no man—coming or going—would change it.

"I'm waiting on an answer," Rico said, interrupting her thoughts.

She gazed up at him and frowned. "Wait on. I don't intend to give you an answer because it's none of your business."

He nodded. "All right. You claim you can control the passion between us, right?"

"Yes."

"Then I want to see how you control this."

The next thing Megan knew, Rico had reached out, pulled her into his embrace and swooped his mouth down onto hers.

Desire that had been lingering on the edges was now producing talons that were digging deep into Megan's skin and sending heated lust all through her veins—and making her act totally out of control. He parted her lips with his tongue and instead of immediately going after her tongue, he rolled the tip around, as if on a tasting expedition. Then he gradually tasted more of it until he had captured it all. And when she became greedy, he pulled back and gave her just the tip again. Then they played the tongue game over and over again.

She felt something stir within her that had never stirred before while kissing a man. But then no man had ever kissed her like this. Or played mouth games with her this way.

He was electrifying her cells, muddling her brain as even more desire skittered up her spine. She tried steadying her emotions, regaining control when she felt heat flooding between her thighs, but she couldn't help but release a staggering moan.

Instead of unlocking their mouths, he intensified the kiss, as his tongue, holding hers in a dominant grip, began exploring every part of her mouth with strokes so sensual her stomach began doing somersaults. She felt her senses tossed in a number of wild spins, and surprised herself when she wrapped her arms around his neck and began running her fingers through the softness of his hair, absently curling a strand around her finger.

She could taste the hunger in his kiss, the passion and the desire. Her emotions were smoldering, and blocking every single thought from her already chaotic mind. The man was lapping up her mouth, and each stroke was getting hotter and hotter, filling her with emotions she had pushed aside for years. Was he ever going to let go of her mouth? Apparently no time soon.

This kiss was making her want to do things she'd never done before. Touch a man, run her hands all over him, check out that huge erection pressing against her belly.

She felt his hands rest on her backside, urging her closer to his front. And she shifted her hips to accommodate what he wanted. She felt the nipples of her breasts harden and knew her robe was no barrier against the heat coming from his body.

No telling how long they would have stood in the middle of her kitchen engaged in one hell of a feverish kiss if his cell phone hadn't gone off. They broke apart, and she drew in a much needed breath and watched him get his phone out of the back pocket of his jeans.

She took note of the angry look on his face while he talked and heard him say to the caller, "I don't want you calling me." He then clicked off the line without giving the person a chance to respond.

She tensed at the thought that the person he'd just given the brush-off was a woman. Megan lifted her chin. "Maybe you should have taken that call."

He glanced over at her while stuffing his phone back into the pocket of his jeans. She watched as his hazel eyes became a frosty green. "I will never take *that* call."

She released a slow, steady breath, feeling his anger as if it were a personal thing. She was glad it wasn't directed at her. She wondered what the woman had done to deserve such animosity from him. At the moment, Megan didn't care because she had her own problems. Rico Claiborne had made her lose control. He had kissed her, and she had kissed him back.

And rather enjoyed it.

Dread had her belly quaking and her throat tightening when she realized she wasn't an iceberg after all. Rico had effectively thawed her.

She drew in a deep breath, furious with herself for letting things get out of hand when she'd boasted and bragged about the control she had. All it had taken was one blazing kiss to make a liar out of her. It was a fluke, it had to be. He had caught her off guard. She didn't enjoy kissing him as much as she wanted to think she did.

Then why was she licking her lips and liking the taste he'd left behind? She glanced over and saw he'd been watching her and was following the movement of her tongue. Her fingers knotted into a fist at her side, and she narrowed her gaze. "I think you need to leave."

"No problem, now that I've proven my point. You're as passionate as you are beautiful, Megan. Nothing's changed. I still want you, and now that I've gotten a taste, I want you even more. So take my warning, don't come to Texas."

A part of Megan knew that if she was smart, she would take his warning. But the stubborn part of her refused to do so. "I'm going to Texas, Rico."

He didn't say anything for a long moment, just stood there and held her gaze. Finally, he said, "Then I guess I'll be seeing you at some point while you're there. Don't say I didn't warn you."

Rico strode away and, before opening the door to leave, he grabbed his jacket off the coatrack. He turned, smiled at her, winked and then opened the door and walked out.

Megan took a deep breath to calm her racing heart. She had a feeling that her life, as she'd always known it, would never, ever be the same. Heaven help her, she had tasted passion and already she was craving more.

Four

Upon arriving at Megan's place early Friday morning, Ramsey glanced down at the two overpacked traveling bags that sat in the middle of her living room. "Hey, you're planning on coming back, aren't you?" he asked, chuckling.

Megan smiled and tapped a finger to her chin. "Umm, I guess I will eventually. And those bags aren't *that* bad."

"They aren't? I bet I'll strain my back carrying them out to the truck. And how much you want to bet they're both overweight and you'll pay plenty when you check them in at the airport."

"Probably, but that's fine. A lot of it is baby stuff I bought for Alyssa. She's having a girl and you know how I like buying all that frilly stuff." He would know since his two-year-old daughter, Susan, had been the first female born to the Denver Westmorelands since

Bailey. Megan simply adored her niece and would miss her while away in Texas.

She looked up at Ramsey, her oldest brother, the one she most admired along with her cousin Dillon. "Ram?"

He looked over at her after taking a sip of the coffee she'd handed him as soon he had walked through the door. "Yes?"

"I was a good kid while growing up, wasn't I? I didn't give you and Dillon any trouble, right?"

He grinned, reached out and pulled one of her curls. "No, sport, you didn't give us any trouble. You were easier to handle than Bailey, the twins and Bane. But everyone was easier than those four."

He paused a moment and added, "And unlike a lot of men with sisters, I never once had to worry about guys getting their way with the three of you. You, Gemma and Bail did a good job of keeping the men in line yourselves. If a guy became a nuisance, you three would make them haul ass the other way. Dillon and I got a chuckle out of it, each and every time. Especially you. I think you enjoyed giving the guys a hard time."

She playfully jabbed him in the ribs. "I did not."

He laughed. "Could have fooled us." He grabbed her close for a brotherly hug. "At one time we thought you were sweet on Charlie Bristol when you were a senior in high school. We knew for a fact he was sweet on you. But according to Riley, he was too scared to ask you out."

Megan smiled over at him as she led him to the kitchen. She remembered Charlie Bristol. He used to spend the summers with one of his aunts who lived nearby. "He was nice, and cute."

"But you wouldn't give him the time of day," he said, sitting down at the table.

Ramsey was right, she hadn't. She recalled having a crush on Charlie for a quick second but she'd been too busy helping out with Gemma and Bailey to think about boys.

"I'm going to miss you, sport," Ramsey said, breaking into her thoughts.

Megan smiled over at him as she joined him at the table. "And I'm going to miss you, as well. Other than being with Gemma during the time she was giving birth to CJ, and visiting Delaney those two weeks in Tehran, this is the first real vacation I've taken, and the longest. I'll be away from the hospital for a full month."

"How will they make it without you? Ramsey teased.

"I'm sure they'll find a way." Even while attending college, she had stayed pretty close to home, not wanting to go too far away. For some reason, she'd felt she was needed. But then, she'd also felt helpless during Bailey's years of defiance. She had tried talking to her baby sister, but it hadn't done any good. She'd known that Bailey's, the twins' and Bane's acts of rebellion were their way of handling the grief of losing their parents. But still, at the time, she'd wished she could do more.

"Ram, can I ask you something?"

He chuckled. "Another question?" He faked a look of pain before saying, "Okay, I guess one more wouldn't hurt."

"Do you think having control of your emotions is a bad thing?" She swallowed tightly as she waited for his answer.

He smiled at her. "Having too much self-control isn't healthy, and it can lead to stress. Everyone needs to know how to let loose, release steam and let their hair down every once in a while."

Megan nodded. Releasing steam wasn't what she was dealing with. Letting go of a buildup of sexual energy was the problem. And that kiss the other day hadn't helped matters any.

She hadn't seen Rico since then, and she knew he'd already left for Texas. She'd been able to get that much out of Riley when he'd dropped by yesterday. "So it's okay to…"

"Get a little wild every once in a while?" He chuckled. "Yes, I think it is, as long as you're not hurting anyone."

He paused a second and then asked, "You're planning to enjoy yourself while you're in Texas, right?"

"Yes. But as you know, it won't be all fun, Ram." Ramsey and Dillon were the only ones she'd told the real reason why she was going to Texas. They also knew she had asked Rico to take her with him, and he'd refused. Of course, she hadn't told them what he'd told her as the reason behind his refusal. She'd only told them Rico claimed he preferred working alone and didn't need her help in the investigation. Neither Dillon nor Ramsey had given their opinions about anything, because she hadn't asked for them. The "don't ask—don't tell" rule was one Dillon and Ramsey implemented for the Westmorelands who were independent adults.

"You can do me a favor, though, sport," he said in a serious tone.

She lifted an eyebrow. "What?"

"Don't be too hard on Rico for not wanting to take you along. You're paying him to do a job, and he wants to do it."

Megan rolled her eyes. "And he will. But I want to be there. I could help."

"Evidently he doesn't want your help."

Yes, but he does want something else, Megan thought. She could just imagine what her brother would think if he knew the real reason Rico didn't want her in Texas. But then, Ramsey was so laid-back it probably wouldn't faze him. He'd known for years how Callum had felt about Gemma. But he'd also known his sisters could handle their business without any interference from their big brother unless it became absolutely necessary.

"But what if there are other Westmorelands somewhere?" she implored. "I told you what Rico said about Clarice having a baby."

"Then Rico will find out information and give it to you to bring to us, Megan. Let him do his job. And another thing."

"Yes?"

"Rico is a good guy. I like him. So do the rest of the Westmorelands. I judge a man by a lot of things and one is how he treats his family. He evidently is doing something right because Jessica and Savannah think the world of their brother."

Megan leaned back in her chair and frowned. "Is there a reason you're telling me that?"

Ramsey was silent for a moment as he stared at her. Then a slow smile touched his lips. "I'll let you figure that one out, Megan."

She nodded and returned his smile. "Fair enough. And about that self-control we were discussing earlier?"

"Yes, what about it?" he asked.

"It *is* essential at times," she said.

"I agree, it is. At times."

"But I'm finding out I might not have as much as I thought. That's not a bad thing, right, Ram?"

Ramsey chuckled. "No, sport, it's just a part of being human."

Rico had just finished eating his dinner at one of the restaurants in Forbes when his cell phone vibrated. Standing, he pulled it out of his back pocket. "This is Rico."

"Our father called me."

Rico tensed when he heard Savannah's voice. He sat back down and leaned back in his chair. "He called me as well, but I didn't give him a chance to say anything," he said, trying to keep his anger in check.

"Same here. I wonder what he wants, and I hope he doesn't try contacting Jessica. How long has it been now? Close to eighteen years?"

"Just about. I couldn't reach Jessica today, but I did talk to Chase. He said Jess hadn't mentioned anything about getting a call from Jeff Claiborne, and I think if she had, she would have told him," said Rico.

"Well, I don't want him upsetting her. She's pregnant."

"And you have a lot on your hands with a new baby," he reminded her.

"Yes, but I can handle the likes of Jeff regardless. But, I'm not sure Jessica can, though. It wasn't our mother who committed suicide because of him."

"I agree."

"Where are you?" Savannah asked him.

"Forbes, Texas. Nice town."

"Are you on a work assignment?"

"Yes, for Megan," he replied, taking a sip of his beer.

"Is she there with you?"

Rico's eyebrows shot up. "No. Should she be?"

"Just asking. Well, I'll be talking with—"

"Savannah?" he said in that particular tone when he knew she was up to something. "Why would you think Megan was here with me? I don't work that way."

"Yes, but I know the two of you are attracted to each other."

He took another sip of his beer. "Are we?"

"Yes. I noticed at Micah's wedding. I think everyone did."

"Did they?"

"Yes, Rico, and you're being evasive."

He laughed. "And you're being nosy. Where's Durango?" he asked, changing the subject.

"Outside giving Sarah her riding lessons."

"Tell him I said hello and give my niece a hug."

"I will...and Rico?"

"Yes?"

"I like Megan. Jess does, too."

Rico didn't say anything for a long moment. He took another sip of his beer as he remembered the kiss they'd shared a couple of days ago. "Good to hear because I like her, too. Now, goodbye."

He clicked off the phone before his sister could grill him. Glancing around the restaurant, he saw it had gotten crowded. The hotel had recommended this place, and he was glad they had. They had served good Southern food, the tastiest. But nothing he ate, no matter how spicy, could eradicate Megan's taste from his tongue. And personally, he had no problem with that because what he'd said to Savannah was true. He liked Megan. A capricious smile touched his lips. Probably, too damn much.

He was about to signal the waitress for his check

when his phone rang. He hoped it wasn't Savannah calling back being nosy. He sighed in relief when he saw it was Martin Felder, a friend who'd once worked with the FBI years ago but was now doing freelance detective work. He was an ace when it came to internet research. "Sorry, I meant to call you earlier, Rico, but I needed to sing Anna to sleep."

Rico nodded, understanding. Martin had become a single father last year when his wife, Marcia, had died from pancreatic cancer. He had pretty much taken early retirement from the Bureau to work from home. He had been the one to discover information about Clarice's pregnancy.

"No problem, and I can't tell you enough about what a great job you're doing with Anna."

"Thanks, Rico. I needed to hear that. She celebrated her third birthday last week, and I wished Marcia could have been here to see what a beautiful little girl we made together. She looks more and more like her mom every day."

Martin paused a minute and then said, "I was on the internet earlier today and picked up this story of a woman celebrating her one-hundredth birthday in Forbes. They were saying how sharp her memory was for someone her age."

"What's her name?" Rico asked, sitting up straight in his chair.

"Fanny Banks. She's someone you might want to talk to while in town to see if she remembers anything about Clarice Riggins. I'll send the info over to you."

"That's a good idea. Thanks." Rico hung up the phone and signaled for the waitress.

A few moments later, back in his rental car, he was reviewing the information Martin had sent to his iPhone. The woman's family was giving her a birthday party tomorrow so the earliest he would be able to talk to her would be Saturday.

His thoughts shifted to Megan and the look in her eyes when she'd tried explaining why it was so important for her to be there when he found out information on Raphel. Maybe he *was* being hard-nosed about not letting her help him. And he had given her fair warning about how much he wanted her. They'd kissed, and if she hadn't realized the intensity of their attraction before, that kiss should have cinched it and definitely opened her eyes.

It had definitely opened his, but that's not all it had done. If he'd thought he wanted her before then he was doubly certain of it now. He hadn't slept worth a damn since that kiss and sometimes he could swear her scent was in the air even when she wasn't around. He had this intense physical desire for her that he just couldn't kick. Now he had begun to crave her and that wasn't good. But it was something he just couldn't help. The woman was a full-blown addiction to his libido.

He put his phone away, thinking Megan should have arrived at Clint's place by now. It was too late to make a trip to Austin tonight, but he'd head that way early tomorrow…unless he could talk himself out of it overnight.

And he doubted that would happen.

Five

"I can't eat a single thing more," Megan said, as she looked at all the food Alyssa had placed on the table for breakfast. It wouldn't be so bad if she hadn't arrived yesterday at dinnertime to a whopping spread by Chester, Clint's cook, housekeeper and all-around ranch hand.

Megan had met Chester the last time she'd been here, and every meal she'd eaten was to die for. But like she'd said, she couldn't eat a single thing more and would need to do some physical activities to burn off the calories.

Clint chuckled as helped his wife up from the table. Alyssa said the doctor claimed she wasn't having twins but Megan wasn't too sure.

"Is there anything you need me to do?" she asked Alyssa when Clint had gotten her settled in her favorite recliner in the living room.

Alyssa waved off Megan's offer. "I'm fine. Clint is doing great with Cain," she said of her three-year-old son, who was the spitting image of his father. "And Aunt Claudine will arrive this weekend."

"How long do you think your aunt will visit this time?" Megan asked as she took the love seat across from Alyssa.

"If I have anything to do with it, she won't be leaving," Chester hollered out as he cleared off the kitchen table.

Megan glanced over at Clint, and Alyssa only laughed. Then Clint said, "Chester is sweet on Aunt Claudine, but hasn't convinced her to stay here and not return to Waco."

"But I think he might have worn her down," Alyssa said, whispering so Chester wouldn't hear. "She mentioned she's decided to put her house up for sale. She told me not to tell Chester because she wants to surprise him."

Megan couldn't help but smile. She thought Chester and Alyssa's aunt Claudine, both in their sixties, would make a nice couple. She bet it was simply wonderful finding love at that age. It would be grand to do so at any age…if you were looking for it or interested in getting it. She wasn't.

"If it's okay, I'd like to go riding around the Golden Glade, especially the south ridge. I love it there."

Clint smiled. "Most people do." He looked lovingly at Alyssa. "We've discovered it's one of our most favorite places on the ranch."

Megan watched as Alyssa exchanged another loving look with Clint. She knew the two were sharing a private moment that involved the south ridge in some way. They made a beautiful couple, she thought. Like all the other Westmoreland males, Clint was too hand-some for his own good, and Alyssa, who was even more beautiful while pregnant, was his perfect mate.

Seeing the love radiating between the couple—the same she'd witnessed between her cousins and their wives, as well as between her brothers and their wives—made a warm feeling flow through Megan. It was one she'd never felt before. She drew in a deep breath, thinking that feeling such a thing was outright foolish, but she couldn't deny what she'd felt just now.

As if remembering Megan was in the room, Clint turned to her, smiled and said, "Just let Marty know that you want to go riding, and he'll have one of the men prepare a horse for you."

"Thanks." Megan decided it was best to give Clint and Alyssa some alone time. Cain was taking a nap, and Megan could make herself scarce real fast. "I'll change into something comfortable for riding."

After saying she would see them later, she quickly headed toward the guest room.

One part of Rico's mind was putting up one hell of an argument as to why he shouldn't be driving to Austin for Megan. Too bad the other part refused to listen. Right now, the only thing that particular part of his brain understood was his erection throbbing some-thing fierce behind the zipper of his pants. Okay, he knew it shouldn't be just a sexual thing. He shouldn't be allowing all this lust to be eating away at him, prac-tically nipping at his balls, but hell, he couldn't help it. He wanted her. Plain and simple.

Although there was really nothing plain and simple about it, anticipation made him drive faster than he should. *Slow down, Claiborne. Are you willing to get a speeding ticket just because you want to see her again?*

Yes.

He drew in a sharp breath, not understanding it. So he continued driving and when he finally saw Austin's city-limits marker, he felt a strong dose of adrenaline rush through his veins. It didn't matter that he still had a good twenty minutes to go before reaching the Golden Glade Ranch. Nor did it matter that Megan would be surprised to see him, and even more surprised that he would be taking her back with him to Forbes to be there when he talked to Fanny Banks.

But he would explain that taking her to meet Fanny would be all he'd let her do. He would return Megan to the Golden Glade while he finished up with the investigation. Nothing had changed on that front. Like he'd told her, he preferred working alone.

He checked the clock on the car's dashboard. Breakfast would be over by the time he reached the ranch. Alyssa might be resting, and if Clint wasn't around then he was probably out riding the range.

Rico glanced up at the sky. Clear, blue, and the sun was shining. It was a beautiful day in late September, and he planned to enjoy it. He pressed down on the accelerator. Although he probably didn't need to be in a hurry, he was in one anyway.

A short while later he released a sigh of anticipation when he saw the marker to the Golden Glade Ranch. Smiling, he made a turn down the long, winding driveway toward the huge ranch house.

Megan was convinced that the south-ridge pasture of the Golden Glade was the most beautiful land she'd ever seen. The Westmorelands owned beautiful property back in Denver, but this here was just too magnificent for words.

She dismounted her horse and, after tying him to a hitching post, she gazed down in the valley where it seemed as though thousands upon thousands of wild horses were running free.

The triplets, Clint, Cole and Casey, had lived on this land with their Uncle Sid while growing up. Sid Roberts had been a legend in his day. First as a rodeo star and then later as a renowned horse trainer. Megan even remembered studying about him in school. In their uncle's memory, the triplets had dedicated over three thousand acres of this land along the south ridge as a reserve. Hundreds of wild horses were saved from slaughter by being shipped here from Nevada. Some were left to roam free for the rest of their days, and others were shipped either to Montana, where Casey had followed in her uncle's footsteps as a horse trainer, or to Denver, where some of her cousins and brothers were partners in the operation.

Megan could recall when Zane, Derringer and Jason had decided to join the partnership that included Clint, their cousin Durango, Casey and her husband, McKinnon. All of the Westmorelands involved in the partnership loved horses and were experts in handling them.

Megan glanced across the way and saw a cabin nestled among the trees. She knew it hadn't been here the last time she'd visited. She smiled, thinking it was probably a lovers' hideaway for Clint and Alyssa and was probably the reason for the secretive smile they'd shared this morning.

Going back to the horse, she unhooked a blanket she'd brought and the backpack that contained a book to read and a Ziploc bag filled with the fruit Chester had packed. It didn't take long to find the perfect spot to spread the blanket on the ground and stretch out. She looked up at the sky, thinking it was a gorgeous day and it was nice to be out in it. She enjoyed her job at the hospital, but there was nothing like being out under the wide-open sky.

She had finished one chapter of the suspense thriller that her cousin Stone Westmoreland, aka Rock Mason, had written. She was so engrossed in the book that it was a while before she heard the sound of another horse approaching. Thinking it was probably Clint or one of the ranch hands coming to check on her, to make sure she was okay, she'd gotten to her feet by the time a horse and rider came around the bend.

Suddenly she felt it—heat sizzling down her spine, fire stirring in her stomach. Her heart began thumping hard in her chest. She'd known that she would eventually run in to Rico, but she'd thought it would be when she made an appearance in Forbes. He had been so adamant about her not coming to Texas with him that she'd figured she would have to be the one to seek him out and not the other way around.

Her breasts began tingling, and she could feel her nipples harden against her cotton shirt when he brought his horse to a stop beside hers. Nothing, she thought, was more of a turn-on than seeing a man, especially this particular man, dismount from his horse…with such masculine ease and virile precision, and she wondered if he slid between a woman's legs the same way.

She could feel her cheeks redden with such brazen thoughts, and her throat tightened when he began walking toward her. Since it seemed he didn't have anything to say, she figured she would acknowledge his presence. "Rico."

He tilted his hat to her. She thought he looked good in his jeans, chambray shirt and the Stetson. "Megan."

She drew in a deep breath as he moved toward her. His advance was just as lethal, just as stealthy, as a hunter who'd cornered his prey. "Do you know why I'm here?" he asked her in a deep, husky voice.

Megan she shook her head. "No. You said you wanted to work alone."

He smiled, and she could tell it didn't quite reach his eyes. "But you're here, which means you didn't intend on letting me do that."

She lifted her chin. "Just pretend I'm not here, and when you see me in Forbes, you can pretend I'm not there."

"Not possible," he said throatily, coming to a stop in front of her. Up close, she could see smoldering desire in the depths of his eyes. That should have jarred some sense into her, but it didn't. Instead it had just the opposite effect.

Megan tilted her head back to look up at him and what she saw almost took her breath away again—hazel eyes that were roaming all over her, as if they were savoring her. There was no way she could miss the hunger that flared in their depths, making her breath come out in quick gulps.

"I think I need to get back to the ranch," she said.

A sexy smile touched his lips. "What's the rush?"

There was so much heat staring at her that she knew any minute she was bound to go up in flames. "I asked why you're here, Rico."

Instead of answering, he reached out and gently cradled her face between his hands and brought his mouth so close to hers that she couldn't keep her lips from quivering. "My answer is simple, Megan. I came for you."

He paused a moment and then added, "I haven't been able to forget that kiss and how our tongues tangled while I became enmeshed in your taste. Nothing has changed other than I think you've become an addiction, and I want you more than before."

And then he lowered his mouth to hers.

He knew the instant she began to lose control because she started kissing him back with a degree of hunger and intimacy that astounded him.

He wrapped his arms around her waist while they stood there, letting their tongues tangle in a way that was sending all kinds of sensual pulses through his veins. This is what had kept him up nights, had made him drive almost like a madman through several cities to get here. He had known this would be what awaited him. Never had a single kiss ignited so much sexual pressure within him, made him feel as if he was ready to explode at any moment.

She shifted her body closer, settling as intimately as a woman still wearing clothes could get, at the juncture of his legs. The moment she felt his hard erection pressing against her, she shifted her stance to cradle his engorged shaft between her thighs.

If he didn't slow her down, he would be hauling her off to that blanket she'd spread on the ground. Thoughts of making love to her here, in such a beautiful spot and under such a stunning blue sky, were going through his mind. But he knew she wasn't ready for that. She especially wasn't ready to take it to the level he wanted to take it.

His thoughts were interrupted when he felt her hand touch the sides of his belt, trying to ease his shirt out of his pants. She wanted to touch some skin, and he had no problems letting her do so. He shifted again, a deliberate move on his part to give her better access to what she wanted, although what she wanted to do was way too dangerous to his peace of mind. It wouldn't take much to push him over the edge.

When he felt her tugging at his shirt, pulling it out of his jeans, he deepened the kiss, plunging his tongue farther into her mouth and then flicking it around with masterful strokes. He wasn't a man who took advantage of women, but then he was never one who took them too seriously, either, even while maintaining a level of respect for any female he was involved with.

But with Megan that respect went up more than a notch. She was a Westmoreland. So were his sisters. That was definitely a game changer. Although he wanted Megan and intended to have her, he needed to be careful how he handled her. He had to do things decently and in the right order. As much as he could.

But doing anything decently and in the right order was not on his mind as he continued to kiss her, as his tongue explored inside her mouth with a hunger that had his erection throbbing.

And when she inched her hand beneath his shirt to touch his skin, he snatched his mouth from hers to draw in a deep breath. He held her gaze, staring down at her as the silence between them extended. Her touch had nearly scorched him it had been so hot. He hadn't been prepared for it. Nor had he expected such a reaction to it.

He might have reeled in his senses and moved away from her if she hadn't swiped her tongue across her lips. That movement was his downfall, and he felt fire roaring through his veins. He leaned in closer and began licking her mouth from corner to corner. And when she let out a breathless moan, he slid his tongue back inside to savor her some more.

Their tongues tangled and dueled and he held on to her, needing the taste as intense desire tore through him. He knew he had to end the kiss or it could go on forever. And when her hips began moving against him, rotating against his huge arousal, he knew where things might lead if he didn't end the kiss here and now.

He slowly pulled back and let out a breath as his gaze seized her moistened lips. He watched the eyes staring back at him darken to a degree that would have grown hair on his chest, if he didn't have any already.

"Rico?"

Heat was still simmering in his veins, and it didn't help him calm down when she said his name like that. "Yes?"

"You did it again."

He lifted a brow. "What did I do?"

"You kissed me."

He couldn't help but smile. "Yes, and you kissed me back."

She nodded and didn't deny it. "We're going to have to come to some kind of understanding. About what we can or cannot do when we're alone."

His smile deepened. *That would be interesting.* "Okay, you make out that list, and we can discuss it."

She tilted her head back to look at him. "I'm serious."

"So am I, and make sure it's a pretty detailed list because if something's not on there, I'll be tempted to try it."

When she didn't say anything, he chuckled and told

her she was being too serious. "You'll feel better after getting dinner. You missed lunch."

She shook her head as he led her over to the horses. "I wasn't hungry."

He licked his mouth, smiled and said, "Mmm, baby, you could have fooled me."

Six

Once they had gotten back to the ranch and dismounted, Rico told the ranch hand who'd come to handle the horses not to bother, that he would take care of them.

"You're from Philadelphia, but you act as if you've been around horses all your life," she said, watching him remove the saddles from the animals' back.

He smiled over at her across the back of the horse she'd been riding. "In a way, I have. My maternal grandparents own horses, and they made sure Savannah and I took riding lessons and that we knew how to care for one."

She nodded. "What about Jessica?"

He didn't say anything for a minute and then said, "Jessica, Savannah and I share the same father. We didn't know about Jess until I was in college."

"Oh." Megan didn't know the full story, but it was

obvious from Rico and Savannah's interracial features that the three siblings shared the same father and not the same mother. She had met Rico and Savannah's mother at one of Jessica's baby showers and thought she was beautiful as well as kind. But then Megan had seen the interaction between the three siblings and could tell their relationship was a close one.

"You, Jessica and Savannah are close, I can tell. It's also obvious the three of you get along well."

He smiled. "Yes, we do, especially since I'm no longer trying to boss them around. Now I gladly leave them in the hands of Chase and Durango and have to admit your cousins seem to be doing a good job of keeping my sisters happy."

Megan would have to agree. But then she would say that all the Westmorelands had selected mates that complemented them, and they all seemed so happy together, so well connected. Even Gemma and Callum. She had visited her sister around the time Gemma's baby was due to be born and Megan had easily felt the love radiating between Gemma and her husband. And Megan knew Callum Junior, or CJ as everyone called him, was an extension of that love.

"We'll be leaving first thing in the morning, Megan."

She glanced back over at Rico, remembering what he'd said when he'd first arrived. He had come for her. "And just where are we supposed to be going?"

She couldn't help noticing how a beam of light that was shining in through the open barn door was hitting him at an angle that seemed to highlight his entire body. And as weird as it sounded, it seemed like there was a halo over his head. She knew it was a figment of her imagination because the man was no angel.

"I'm taking you back to Forbes with me," he said,

leading both horses to their stalls. "You did say you wanted to be included when I uncover information about Clarice."

She felt a sudden tingling of excitement in her stomach. Her face lit up. "Yes," she said, following him. "You found out something?"

"Nothing more than what I told you before. However, my man who's doing internet research came across a recent news article. There's a woman living in Forbes who'll be celebrating her one-hundredth birthday today. And she's lived in the same house for more than seventy of those years. Her address just happens to be within ten miles of the last known address we have for Clarice. We're hoping she might remember her."

Megan nodded. "But the key word is *remember*. How well do you think a one-hundred-year-old person will be able to remember?"

Rico smiled. "According to the article, she credits home remedies for her good health. I understand she still has a sharp memory."

"Then I can't wait for us to talk to her."

Rico closed the gate behind the horses and turned to face her. "Although I'm taking you along, Megan, I'm still the one handling this investigation."

"Of course," she said, looking away, trying her best not to get rattled by his insistence on being in charge. But upon remembering what Ramsey had said about letting Rico do his job without any interference from her, she decided not to make a big deal of it. The important thing was that Rico was including her.

He began walking toward the ranch house, and she fell in step beside him. "What made you change your mind about including me?" she asked as she tilted her head up.

He looked over at her. "You would have shown up in Forbes eventually, and I decided I'm going to like having you around."

Megan stopped walking and frowned up at him. "It's not going to be that kind of party, Rico."

She watched how his lips curved in a smile so sensuous that she had to remind herself to breathe. Her gaze was drawn to the muscular expanse of his chest and how the shirt looked covering it. She bet he would look even better shirtless.

Her frown deepened. She should not be thinking about Rico without a shirt. It was bad enough that she had shared two heated kisses with him.

"What kind of party do you think I'm having, Megan?"

She crossed her arms over her chest. "I don't know, you tell me."

He chuckled. "That's easy because I'm not having a party. You'll get your own hotel room, and I'll have mine. I said I wanted you. I also said eventually I'd have you if you came with me. But I'll let you decide when."

"It won't happen. Just because we shared two enjoyable kisses and—"

"So you did enjoy them, huh?"

She wished she could swipe that smirk off his face. She shrugged. "They were okay."

He threw his head back and laughed. "Just okay? Then I guess I better improve my technique the next time."

She nibbled on her bottom lip, thinking if he got any better she would be in big trouble.

"Don't do that."

She raised a brow. "Don't do what?"

"Nibble on your lip that way. Or else I'm tempted to improve my technique right here and now."

Megan swallowed, and as she stood there and stared up at him, she was reminded of how his kisses could send electrical currents racing through her with just a flick of his tongue.

"I like it when you do that."

"Do what?"

"Blush. I guess guys didn't ever talk to you that way, telling you what they wanted to do to you."

She figured she might as well be honest with him. "No."

"Then may I make a suggestion, Megan?"

She liked hearing the sound of her name from his lips. "What?"

"Get used to it."

Rico sat on a bar stool in the kitchen while talking to Clint. However, he was keeping Megan in his peripheral vision. When they'd gotten back to the house, Clint had been eager to show Rico a beauty of a new stallion he was about to send to his sister Casey to train, and Alyssa wanted to show Megan how she'd finished decorating the baby's room that morning.

Cain was awake, and, like most three-year-olds, he wanted to be the life of the party and hold everyone's attention. He was doing so without any problems. He spoke well for a child his age and was already riding a horse like a pro.

Rico had admired the time Clint had spent with his son and could see the bond between them. He thought about all the times he had wished his father could have been home more and hadn't been. Luckily, his grandfather had been there to fill the void when his father had been living a double life.

Megan had gone upstairs to take a nap, and by the time he'd seen her again it had been time for dinner. She had showered and changed, and the moment she had come down the stairs it had taken everything he had to keep from staring at her. She was dressed in a printed flowing skirt and a blouse that showed what a nice pair of shoulders she had. He thought she looked refreshed and simply breathtaking. And his reaction upon seeing her reminded him of how it had been the first time he'd seen her, that day three months ago.

"Rico?" Clint said, snapping his fingers in front of his face.

Rico blinked. "Sorry. My mind wandered there for a minute."

"Evidently," Clint said, grinning. "How about if we go outside where we can talk without your mind wandering so much?"

Rico chuckled, knowing Clint knew full well where his concentration had been. "Fine," he said, grabbing his beer off the counter.

Moments later, while sitting in rocking chairs on the wraparound porch, Clint had brought Rico up to date on the horse breeding and training business. Several of the horses would be running in the Kentucky Derby and Preakness in the coming year.

"So how are things going with the investigation?" Clint asked when there was a lull in conversation. "Megan mentioned to Alyssa something about an old lady in Forbes who might have known Clarice."

"Yes, I'm making plans to interview her in a few days, and Megan wants to be there when I do." Rico spent the next few minutes telling Clint what the news article had said about the woman.

"Well, I hope things work out," Clint said. "I know how it is when you discover you have family you never knew about, and I guess Megan is feeling the same way. If it hadn't been for my mother's deathbed confession, Cole, Casey and I would not have known that our father was alive. Even now, I regret the years I missed by not knowing."

Clint stood and stretched. "Well, I'm off to bed now. Will you and Megan at least stay for breakfast before taking off tomorrow?"

Rico stood, as well. "Yes. Nothing like getting on the road with a full stomach, and I'm sure Chester is going to make certain we have that."

Clint chuckled. "Yes, I'm certain, as well. Good night."

By the time they went back into the house, it was quiet and dark, which meant Alyssa and Megan had gone to bed. Rico hadn't been aware that he and Clint had talked for so long. It was close to midnight.

Clint's ranch house was huge. What Rico liked most about it was that it had four wings jutting off from the living room—north, south, east and west. He noted that he and Megan had been given their own private wing—the west wing—and he couldn't help wondering if that had been intentional.

He slowed his pace when he walked past the guest room Megan was using. The door was closed but he could see light filtering out from the bottom, which meant she was still up. He stopped and started to knock and then decided against it. It was late, and he had no reason to want to seek her out at this hour.

"Of course I can think of several reasons," he muttered, smiling as he entered the guest room he was using. He wasn't feeling tired or sleepy so he decided to work awhile on his laptop.

Rico wasn't sure how long he had been sitting at the desk, going through several online sites, piecing together more information about Fanny Banks, when he heard the opening and closing of the door across the hall, in the room Megan was using. He figured she had gotten up to get a cup of milk or tea. But when moments passed and he didn't hear her return to her room, he decided to find out where she'd gone and what she was doing.

Deciding not to turn on any lights, he walked down the hall in darkness. When he reached the living room, he glanced around before heading for the kitchen. There, he found her standing in the dark and looking out the window. From the moonlight coming in through the glass, he could tell she was wearing a bathrobe.

Deciding he didn't want to startle her, he made his presence known. "Couldn't you sleep?"

She swung around. "What are you doing up?"

He leaned in the doorway with his shoulder propped against a wall. "I was basically asking you the same thing."

She paused a moment and didn't say anything and then said, "I tried sleeping but couldn't. I kept thinking about my dad."

His brows furrowed. "Your dad?"

"Yes. This Saturday would have been his birthday. And I'm proud to say I was a daddy's girl," she said, smiling.

"Were you?"

She grinned. "Yes. Big-time. I remember our last conversation. It was right before he and Mom got ready to leave for the airport. As usual, the plan was for Mrs. Jones to stay at the house and keep us until my parents returned. He asked that I make sure to help take care of Gemma, Bailey and the twins. Ramsey was away at college, Zane was about to leave for college and Derringer was in high school. I was twelve."

She moved away from the window to sit at the table. "The only thing was, they never returned, and I didn't do a good job of taking care of Bailey and the twins. Gemma was no problem."

Rico nodded. Since getting to know the Denver Westmorelands, he had heard the stories about what bad-asses Bailey, the twins and Bane were. And each time he heard those stories, his respect and admiration for Dillon and Ramsey went up a notch. He knew it could not have been easy to keep the family together the way they had. "I hope you're not blaming yourself for all that stupid stuff they did back then."

She shook her head. "No, but a part of me wishes I could have done more to help Ramsey with the younger ones."

Rico moved to join her at the table, figuring the best thing to do was to keep the conversation going. Otherwise, he would be tempted to pull her out of that chair and kiss her again. Electricity had begun popping the moment their gazes had connected. "You were only twelve, and you did what you could, I'm sure," he said, responding to what she'd said. "Everybody did. But people grieve in different ways. I couldn't imagine losing a parent that young."

"It wasn't easy."

"I bet, and then to lose an aunt and uncle at the same time. I have to admire all of you for being strong during that time, considering what all of you were going through."

"Yes, but think of how much easier it would have been had we known the Atlanta, Montana and Texas Westmorelands back then. There would have been others, and Dillon and Ramsey wouldn't have had to do it alone. Oh, they would have still fought to keep us together, but they would have had some kind of support system. You know what they say…it takes a village to raise a child."

Yes, he'd heard that.

"That's one of the reasons family is important to me, Rico. You never know when you will need the closeness and support a family gives to each other." Silence lingered between them for a minute and then she asked, "What about you? Were you close to your parents…your father…while growing up?"

He didn't say anything for a while. Instead, he got up and walked over to the refrigerator. To answer her question, he needed a beer. He opened the refrigerator and glanced over his shoulder. "I'm having a beer. Want one?"

"No, but I'll take a soda."

He nodded and grabbed a soda and a beer out of the refrigerator and then closed the door. Returning to the table, he turned the chair around and straddled it. "Yes. Although my father traveled a lot as a salesman, we were close, and I thought the world of him."

He popped the top on his beer, took a huge swig and then added, "But that was before I found out what a two-bit, lying con artist he was. He was married to my mother, who was living in Philly, while he was involved with another woman out in California, stringing both of them along and lying through his teeth. Making promises he knew he couldn't keep."

Rico took another swig of his beer. "Jessica's grandfather found out Jeff Claiborne was an imposter and told Jessica's mother and my mother. Hurt and humiliated that she'd given fifteen years to a man who'd lied to her, Jessica's mother committed suicide. My mother filed for a divorce. I was in my first year of college. He came to see me, tried to make me think it was all Mom's fault and said, as males, he and I needed to stick together, and that Mom wouldn't divorce him if I put in a good word for him."

Rico stared into his beer bottle, remembering that time, but more importantly, remembering that day. He glanced back at her. "That day he stopped being my hero and the man I admired most. It was bad enough that he'd done wrong and wouldn't admit to it, but to involve me and try to pit me against Mom was unacceptable."

Rico took another swig of his beer. A long one this time. He rarely talked about that time in his life. Most people who knew his family knew the story, and chances were that Megan knew it already since she was friends with both of his sisters.

She reached out and took his hand in hers, and he felt a deep stirring in his groin as they stared at each other, while the air surrounding them became charged with a sexual current that sent sparks of desire through his body. He knew she felt it, as well.

"I know that must have been a bad time for you, but that just goes to show how a bad situation can turn into a good one. That's what happened for you, Savannah and Jessica once the three of you found out about each other, right?"

Yes, that part of the situation had turned out well, because he couldn't imagine not having Jessica and Savannah in his life. But still, whenever he thought of how Jessica had lost her mother, he would get angry all over again. Yet he said, "Yes, you're right."

She smiled and released his hand. "I've been known to be right a few times."

For some reason, he felt at ease with her, more at ease than he'd felt with any other woman. Why they were sitting here in the dark he wasn't sure. In addition to the sexual current in the room, there was also a degree of intimacy to this conversation that was ramping up his libido, reminding him of how long it had been since he'd slept with a woman. And when she had reached out and touched his hand that hadn't helped matters.

He studied her while she sipped on her soda. Even with the sliver of light shining through the window from the outside, he could see the smooth skin of her face, a beautiful shade of mocha.

She glanced over at him, caught him staring, and he felt thrumming need escalate all through him. He'd kissed her twice now and could kiss her a dozen more times and be just as satisfied. But at some point he would want more. He intended to get more. She had been warned, and she hadn't heeded his warning. The attraction between them was too great.

He wouldn't make love to her here. But they would make love, that was a given.

However, he *would* take another kiss. One that would let her know what was to come.

She stood. "I think I'll go back to bed and try to sleep. You did say we were leaving early, right?" she asked, walking over to the garbage with her soda can.

"Yes, right after breakfast." He didn't say anything but his gaze couldn't help latching on to her backside. Even with her bathrobe on, he could tell her behind was a shapely one. He'd admired it in jeans earlier that day.

On impulse, he asked, "Do you want to go for a ride?"

She turned around. "A ride?"

"Yes. It's a beautiful night outside."

A frown tugged at her brow. "A ride where?"

"The south ridge. There's a full moon, and the last time I went there at night with Clint while rounding up horses under a full moon, the view of the canyon was breathtaking."

"And you want us to saddle horses and—"

"No," he chuckled. "We'll take my truck."

She stared at him like he couldn't be thinking clearly. "Do you know what time it is?"

He nodded slowly as he held her gaze. "Yes, a time when everyone else is sleeping, and we're probably the only two people still awake."

She tilted her head and her gaze narrowed. "Why do you want me to take a ride with you at this hour, Rico?"

He decided to be honest. "Because I want to take you someplace where I can kiss you all over."

Seven

The lower part of Megan's stomach quivered, and she released a slow breath. What he was asking her, and pretty darn blatantly, was to go riding with him to the south ridge where they could park and make out. They were too old for that sort of thing, weren't they? Evidently he didn't think so, and he was a lot older than she was.

And what had he said about kissing her all over? Did he truly know what he was asking of her? She needed to be sure. "Do you know what you're asking me when you ask me to go riding with you?"

A smile that was so sexy it could be patented touched his lips. "Yeah."

Well, she had gotten her answer. He had kissed her twice, and now wanted to move to the next level. What had she really expected from a man who'd told her he wanted her and intended to have her? In that case, she had news for him: two kisses didn't mean a thing. She had let her guard down and released a little of her emotional control, but that didn't mean she would release any more. Whenever he kissed her, she couldn't think straight, and she considered doing things that weren't like her.

She stood there and watched his hazel eyes travel all over her, roaming up and down. When his gaze moved upward and snagged hers, the very air between them crackled with an electrical charge that had certain parts of her tingling.

"Are you afraid of me, Megan?" he asked softly.

Their gazes held for one searing moment. No, she wasn't afraid of him per se, but she was afraid of the things he had the ability to make her feel, afraid of the desires he could stir in her, afraid of how she could lose control around him. How could she make him understand that being in control was a part of her that she wasn't ready to let go of yet?

She shook her head. "No, I'm not afraid of you, Rico. But you say things and do things I'm not used to. You once insinuated that my brothers and cousins might have sheltered me from the realities of life, and I didn't agree with you. I still don't, but I will say that I, of my own choosing, decided not to take part in a lot of things other girls were probably into. I like being my own person and not following the crowd."

He nodded, and she could tell he was trying to follow her so she wasn't surprised when he asked, "And?"

"And I've never gone parking with a guy before." There, she'd said it. Now he knew what he was up against. But when she saw the unmistakable look of deep hunger in his eyes, her heart began pounding, fast and furious.

Then he asked, "Are you saying no guy has ever taken you to lover's lane?"

Why did his question have to sound so seductive, and why did she feel like her nerve endings were being scorched? "Yes, that's what I'm saying, and it was my decision and not theirs."

He smiled. "I can believe that."

"I saw it as a waste of time." She broke eye contact with him to look at his feet. They were bare. She'd seen men's feet before, plenty of times. With as many cousins and brothers as she had she couldn't miss seeing them. But Rico's were different. They were beautiful but manly.

"Did you?"

She glanced back up at him. "Yes, it was a waste of time because I wasn't into that sort of thing."

"You weren't?"

She shook her head. "No. I'm too in control of my emotions."

"Yet you let go a little when we kissed," he reminded her.

And she wished she hadn't. "Yes, but I can't do that too often."

He got up from the table, and she swallowed deeply while watching him cross the floor and walk over to her on those beautiful but manly bare feet. He came to a stop in front of her, reached out and took her hand. She immediately felt that same sexual charge she'd felt when she'd taken his hand earlier.

"Yet you did let go with me."

Yes, and that's what worried her. Why with him and only him? Why not with Dr. Thad Miller, Dr. Otis Wells or any of the other doctors who'd been trying

for years to engage her in serious—or not so serious—
affairs?

"Megan?"

"Yes?"

"Would you believe me if I were to say I would never
intentionally hurt you?"

"Yes." She could believe that.

"And would it help matters if I let you set the pace?"
he asked huskily in a voice that stirred things inside
of her.

"What do you mean?"

"You stay in control, and I'll only do what you allow
me to do and nothing more."

She suddenly felt a bit disoriented. What he evidently didn't quite yet understand was that he was a
threat to her self-imposed control. But then, hadn't
Ramsey said that she should let loose, be wild, release
steam and let her hair down every once in a while? But
did that necessarily mean being reckless?

"Megan?"

She stared up at him, studying his well-defined features. Handsome, masculine. Refined. Strong. Controlled. But was he really controlled? His features were
solid, unmovable. The idea that perhaps he shared
something in common with her was a lot to think about.
In the meantime...

Taking a ride with him couldn't hurt anything. She
couldn't sleep, and perhaps getting out and letting the
wind hit her face would do her some good. He did say
he would let her be in control, and she believed him. Although he had a tendency to speak his mind, he didn't
come across as the type of man who would force himself on any woman. Besides, he knew her brothers and
cousins, and was friends with them. His sisters were

married to Westmorelands, and he wouldn't dare do anything to jeopardize those relationships.

"Okay, I'll go riding with you, Rico. Give me a minute to change clothes."

Rico smiled the moment he and Megan stepped outside. He hadn't lied. It was a beautiful night. He'd always said if he ever relocated from Philadelphia, he would consider moving to Texas. It wasn't too hot and it wasn't too cold, most of the time. He had fallen in love with the Lone Star state that first time he'd gone hunting and fishing with his grandfather. His grandparents had never approved of his mother's marriage, but that hadn't stopped them from forging a relationship with their grandchildren.

"There's a full moon tonight," Megan said when he opened the SUV's door for her.

"Yes, and you know what they say about a full moon, don't you?"

She rolled her eyes. "If you're trying to scare me, please don't. I've been known to watch scary movies and then be too afraid to stay at my own place. I've crashed over at Ramsey's or Dillon's at times because I was afraid to go home."

He wanted to tell her that if she got scared tonight, she could knock on his bedroom door and join him there at any time, but he bit back the words. "Well, then I won't scare you," he said, grinning as he leaned over to buckle her seat belt. She had changed into a pretty dress that buttoned up the front. There were a lot of buttons, and his fingers itched to tackle every last one of them.

And he thought she smelled good. Something sweet and sensual with an allure that had him wanting to do more than buckle her seat belt. He pulled back. "Is that too tight?"

"No, it's fine."

He heard the throatiness in her voice and wondered if she was trying to downplay the very thing he was trying to highlight. "All right." He closed the door and then moved around the front of the truck to get in the driver's side.

"If it wasn't for that full moon it would be pitch-black out here."

He smiled. "Yes, you won't be able to see much, but what I'm going to show you is beautiful. That's why Clint had that cabin built near there. It's a stunning view of the canyon at night, and whenever there's a full moon the glow reflects off certain boulders, which makes the canyon appear to light up."

"I can't wait to see it."

And I can't wait to taste you again, he thought, as he kept his hand firmly on the steering wheel or else he'd be tempted to reach across, lift the hem of her dress and stroke her thigh. When it came to women, his manners were usually impeccable. However, around Megan he was tempted to touch, feel and savor.

He glanced over at her when he steered the truck around a bend. She was gnawing on her bottom lip, which meant she was nervous. This was a good time to get her talking, about anything. So he decided to let the conversation be about work. Hers.

"So you think they can do without you for thirty days?"

She glanced over at him and smiled. "That's the same thing Ramsey asked. No one is irreplaceable, you know."

"What about all those doctors who're pining for you?"

She rolled her eyes. "Evidently you didn't believe me when I said I don't date much. Maybe I shouldn't tell you this, but they call me Iceberg Megan behind my back."

He jerked his eyes from the road to glance over at her. "Really?"

"Yes."

"Does it bother you?"

"Not really. They prefer a willing woman in their beds, and I'm not willing and their beds are the last places I'd want to be. I don't hesitate to let them know it."

"Ouch."

"Whatever," she said, waving her hand in the air. "I don't intend to get in any man's bed anytime soon."

He wondered if she was issuing a warning, and he decided to stay away from that topic. "Why did you decide to become an anesthesiologist?"

She leaned back in the seat, getting comfortable. He liked that. "When I got my tonsils out, this man came around to talk to me, saying he would be the one putting me to sleep. He told me all about the wonderful dreams I would have."

"And did you?"

She looked confused. "Did I what?"

"Have wonderful dreams?"

"Yes, if you consider dreaming about a promised trip to Disney World a wonderful dream."

He started to chuckle and then he felt the rumble in his stomach when he laughed. She was priceless. Wonderful company. Fun to have around. "Did you get that trip to Disney World?"

"Yes!" she said with excitement in her voice. "It was the best ever, and the first of many trips our family took together. There was the time…"

He continued driving, paying attention to both the rugged roads and to her. He liked the sound of her voice, and he noticed that more than anything else, she liked talking about her family. She had adored her parents, her uncle and aunt. And she thought the world of her brothers, cousins and sisters. There were already a lot of Westmorelands. Yet she was hoping there were still more.

His mother had been an only child, and he hadn't known anything about his father's family. Jeff Claiborne had claimed he didn't have any. Now Rico wondered if that had been a lie like everything else.

She gasped. He glanced over at her and followed her gaze through the windshield to look up at the sky. He brought the truck to a stop. "What?"

"A shooting star. I saw it."

"Did you?"

She nodded and continued to stare up at the sky. "Yes."

He shifted his gaze to stare back at her. "Hurry and make a wish."

She closed her eyes. A few minutes later she re-opened them and smiled over at him. "Done."

He turned the key in the ignition to start the truck back up. "I'm glad."

"Thanks for taking the time to let me do that. Most men would have thought it was silly and not even suggested a wish."

He grinned. "I'm not like most men."

"I'm beginning to see that, Mr. Claiborne."

He smiled as he kept driving, deciding not to tell her that if the truth be known, she hadn't seen anything yet.

Eight

"I think this is a good spot," Rico said, bringing the car to a stop.

Megan glanced around, not sure just what it was a good spot for, but decided not to ask. She looked over at him and watched as he unbuckled his seat belt and eased his seat back to accommodate his long legs. She decided to do the same—not that her legs were as long as his, mind you. He was probably six foot four to her five foot five.

When she felt his gaze on her, she suddenly felt heated. She rolled down her window and breathed in the deep scent of bluebonnets, poppies and, of all things, wild pumpkin. But there was another scent she couldn't ignore. The scent of man. Namely, the man sitting in the truck with her.

"Lean toward the dash and look out of the windshield."

Slowly, she shifted in her seat and did as he instructed. She leaned forward and looked down and what she saw almost took her breath away. The canyon appeared lit, and she could still see horses moving around. Herds of them. Beautiful stallions with their bands of mares. Since she and Rico were high up and had the help of moonlight, she saw a portion of the lake.

"So what do you think of this place, Megan?"

She glanced over at him. "It's beautiful. Quiet." *And secluded,* she thought, realizing just how alone they were.

"It didn't take you long to change clothes," he said.

She chuckled. "A habit you inherit when you have impatient brothers. Zane drove me, Gemma and Bailey to school every day when he was around. And when he wasn't, the duty fell on Derringer."

Rico seemed to be listening so she kept on talking, telling him bits and pieces about her family, fun times she'd encountered while growing up. She knew they were killing time and figured he was trying to make sure she was comfortable and not nervous with him. He wanted her to be at ease. For what, she wasn't sure, although he'd told her what he wanted to do and she'd come anyway. They had kissed twice so she knew what to expect, but he'd also said he would let her stay in control of the situation.

"You're hot?"

She figured he was asking because she'd rolled down the window. "I was, but the air is cooler outside than I thought," she said, rolling it back up. She took a deep, steadying breath and leaned forward again, trying to downplay the sexual energy seeping through her bones. He hadn't said much. He'd mainly let her talk and listened to what she'd said. But as she stared down at the canyon again she felt his presence in an intense way.

"Megan?"

Her pulse jumped when he said her name. With a deliberate slowness, she glanced over at him. "Yes?"

"I want you over here, closer to me."

She swallowed and then took note that she was sort of hugging the door. The truck had bench seats, and there was a lot of unused space separating them. Another body could sit between them comfortably. "I thought you'd want your space."

"I don't. What I want is you."

It was what he said as well as how he'd said it that sent all kinds of sensations oozing through her. His voice had a deep, drugging timbre that made her feel as if her skin were being caressed.

Without saying anything, she slid across the seat toward him, and he curved his arms across the back of the seat. "A little closer won't hurt," he said huskily.

She glanced up at him. "If I get any closer, I'll end up in your lap."

"That's the idea."

Megan's brows furrowed. He wanted her in his lap? He had to be joking, right? She studied his gaze and saw he was dead serious. Her stomach quivered as they stared at each other. The intensity in the hazel eyes that held her within their scope flooded her with all kinds of feelings, and she was breathless again.

"Do you recall the first time we kissed, Megan?"

She nodded. "Yes." How on earth could she forget it?

"Afterward, I lay awake at night remembering how it had been."

She was surprised a man would do that. She thought

since kisses came by the dozen, they didn't remember one from the next. "You did?"

"Yes. You tasted good."

She swallowed and felt her bottom lips began to tremble. "Did I?"

He reached out and traced a fingertip across her trembling lips. "Yes. And do you know what else I remembered?"

"No, what?"

"How your body felt pressed against mine, even with clothes on. And of course that made me think of you without any clothes on."

Desire filtered through her body. If he was saying these things to weaken her, break down her defenses, corrode her self-control, it was working. "Do you say this to all the girls?" she asked—a part of her wanted to know. Needed to know.

He frowned. "No. And in a way, that's what bothers me."

She knew she shouldn't ask but couldn't stop herself from doing so. "Bothers you how?"

He hesitated for a moment, broke eye contact with her to look straight ahead, out the window. Slowly, methodically, he returned his gaze back to her. "I usually don't let women get next to me. But for some reason I'm allowing you to be the exception."

He didn't sound too happy about it, either, she concluded. But then, wasn't she doing the same thing? She had let him kiss her twice, where most men hadn't made it as far as the first. And then she was here at two in the morning, sitting in a parked truck with him in Texas. If that wasn't wild, she didn't know what was.

"You have such warm lips."

He could say some of the most overwhelming

words…or maybe to her they were overwhelming because no other man had said them to her before. "Thanks."

"You don't have to thank me for compliments. Everything I say is true. I will never lie to you, Megan."

For some reason, she believed him. But if she wasn't supposed to thank him, what was she supposed to say? She tilted her head back to look at him and wished she hadn't. The intense look in his gaze had deepened, and she felt a stirring inside of her, making her want things she'd never had before.

He must have seen something in her eyes, because he whispered, "Come here." And then he lifted her into his arms, twisted his body to stretch his legs out on the seat and sat her in his lap. Immediately, she felt the thick, hard erection outlined against his zipper and pressed into her backside. That set off a barrage of sensations escalating through her, but nothing was as intense as the sensual strokes she felt at the juncture of her thighs.

And then, before she could take her next breath, he leaned down and captured her lips in his.

Rico wasn't sure just what there was about Megan that made him want to do this over and over again— mate his mouth with hers in a way that was sending him over the edge, creating more memories that would keep him awake at night. All he knew was that he needed to taste her again like he needed to breathe.

In the most primal way, blood was surging through his veins and desire was slamming through him, scorching his senses and filling him with needs that only she could satisfy. He couldn't help but feel his erection pressing against her and wishing he could be skin-to-skin with her, but he knew this wasn't the time or the place. But kissing her here, now, was essential.

His tongue continued to explore her mouth with an intensity that had her trembling in his arms. But he wouldn't let up. It couldn't be helped. There was something between them that he couldn't explain. It was wild and, for him, unprecedented. First there had been that instant attraction, then the crackling of sexual chemistry. Then, later, after their first kiss, that greedy addiction that had him in a parked truck, kissing her senseless at two in the morning.

He slowly released her mouth to stare down at her and saw the glazed look in her eyes. Then he slowly began unbuttoning her shirt dress. The first sign of her bra had him drawing in a deep breath of air—which only pulled her scent into his nostrils, a sensuous blend of jasmine and lavender.

Her bra had a front clasp and as soon as his fingers released it, her breasts sprang free. Seeing them made him throb. As he stared down at them, he saw the nipples harden before his eyes, making hunger take over his senses. Releasing a guttural moan, he leaned down and swooped a nipple between his lips and began sucking on it. Earnestly.

Megan gasped at the contact of his wet mouth on her breast, but then, when the sucking motion of his mouth made her sex clench, she threw her head back and moaned. His tongue was doing the same things to her breasts that it had done inside her mouth, and she wasn't sure she could take it. The strokes were so keen and strong, she could actually feel them between her legs.

She reached out and grabbed at his shoulder and when she couldn't get a firm grip there, she went for his hair, wrapping some of the silky strands around her finger as his mouth continued to work her breasts, sending exquisite sensations ramming through her.

But what really pushed her over the edge was when his hand slid underneath her dress to touch her thigh. No man had ever placed his hand underneath her dress. Such a thing could get one killed. If not by her, then surely by her brothers. But her brothers weren't here. She was a grown woman.

And when Rico slid his hands higher, touching her in places she'd never been touched, his fingertips making their way to her center, she shamelessly lifted her hips and shifted her legs wider to give him better access. Where was her self-control? It had taken a freaking hike the moment he had touched his mouth to hers.

Then he was kissing her mouth again, but she was fully aware of his hand easing up her thigh, easing inside the crotch of her panties to touch her.

She almost shot out of his lap at the contact, but he held her tight and continued kissing her as his fingers stroked her, inching toward her pulsating core.

He broke off the kiss and whispered, "You feel good here. Hot. Wet. I like my fingers here, touching you this way."

She bit down on her lips to keep from saying that she liked his fingers touching her that way, as well. Whether intentional or not, he was tormenting her, driving her over the edge with every stroke. She was feeling light-headed, sensually intoxicated. He was inciting her to lose control, and she couldn't resist. The really sad thing was that a part of her didn't want to resist.

"And do you know what's better than touching you here?" he asked.

She couldn't imagine. Already she had been reduced to a trembling mess as he continued to stroke her. She gripped his hair tighter and hoped she wasn't causing him any pain. "No, I can't imagine," she whispered, struggling to get the words out. Forcing anything from her lungs was complicated at the moment.

"Then let me show you, baby."

Her mind had been so focused on his term of endearment that she hadn't realized he had quickly shifted their bodies so her head was away from him, closer to the passenger door. The next thing she knew he had pushed the rest of her dress aside, eased off her panties and lifted her hips to place her thighs over his shoulders.

He met her gaze once, but it was enough for her to see the smoldering heat in his eyes just seconds before he lowered his head between her legs. Shock made her realize what he was about to do, and she called out his name. "Rico!"

But the sound was lost and became irrelevant the moment his mouth touched her core and his tongue slid between the folds. And when he began stroking her, tasting her, she couldn't help but cry out his name again. "Rico."

He didn't let up as firm hands held her hips steady and a determined mouth licked her like she was a meal he just had to have. She continued to moan as blood gushed through her veins. His mouth was devouring her, driving her over the edge, kicking what self-control remained right out the window. The raw hunger he was exhibiting was sending her senses scurrying in all directions. She closed her eyes as moan after moan after moan tore from her lips. The feelings were intense. Their magnitude was resplendent and stunning. Pleasure coiled within her then slowly spread open as desire sharpened its claws on her. Making her feel things she had never felt before. Sensations she hadn't known were possible. And the feel of his stubble-roughened jaw on her skin wasn't helping her regain control.

"Rico," she whispered. "I—I need…" She couldn't finish her thought because she didn't have a clue what she needed. She'd never been with a man like this before, and neither had Gemma before Callum. All her sister had told Megan was that it was something well worth the wait. But if this was the prologue, the wait just might kill her.

And then he did something, she wasn't sure what, with his tongue. Some kind of wiggly formation followed by a fierce jab that allowed his mouth to actually lock down on her.

Sensations blasted through her, and she flung back her head and let out a high-pitched scream. But he wouldn't let go. He continued to taste and savor her as if she was not only his flavor of the day, but also his flavor of all time. She pushed the foolish thought from her mind as she continued to be bombarded with feelings that were ripping her apart.

She gasped for breath before screaming again when her entire body spiraled into another orgasm. She whimpered through it and held tight to his hair as she clutched his shoulders. He kept his mouth locked on her until the very last moan had flowed from her lips. She collapsed back on the car seat, feeling totally drained.

Only then did he pull back, adjusting their bodies to bring her up to him. He tightened his hold when she collapsed weakly against his chest. Then he lowered his head and kissed her, their lips locked together intensely. At that moment, she was craving this contact, this closeness, this very intimate connection. Moments later, when he released her mouth, he pulled her closer to him, tucking her head beneath his jaw, and whispered, "This is only the beginning, baby. Only the beginning."

Nine

The next morning, Rico and Megan left the Golden Glade Ranch after breakfast to head out to Forbes. He had been driving now for a little more than a half hour and his GPS indicated they had less than a hundred miles to go. He glanced up at the skies, saw the gray clouds and was certain it would rain before they reached their destination.

Rico then glanced over at Megan and saw she was still sleeping soundly and had been since he'd hit the interstate. Good. He had a feeling she hadn't gotten much sleep last night.

She had pretty much remained quiet on the drive back to the ranch from the south ridge, and once there, she quickly said good-night and rushed off to her room, closing the door behind her. And then this morning at breakfast, she hadn't been very talkative. Several times he had caught her barely able to keep her eyes open.

If Clint and Alyssa had found her drowsiness strange, neither had commented on it.

Rico remembered every single thing about last night, and, if truth be told, he hadn't thought of much of anything else since. Megan Westmoreland had more passion in her little finger than most women had in their entire bodies. And just the thought that no other man had tempted her to release all that passion was simply mind-boggling to him.

Ramsey had warned him that she was strong-willed. However, even the most strong-willed person couldn't fight a well-orchestrated seduction. But then, being overcome with passion wasn't a surrender. He saw it as her acceptance that nothing was wrong with enjoying her healthy sexuality.

I like being my own person and not following the crowd. Those were the words she had spoken last night. He remembered them and had both admired and respected her for taking that stance. His sisters had basically been the same and had handled their own business. Even when Savannah had gotten pregnant by Durango, she had been prepared to go at it alone had he not wanted to claim the child as his. And knowing his sister, marriage had not been on her mind when she'd gone out to Montana to tell Durango he was going to be a father. Thanks to Jeff Claiborne, a bad taste had been left in Savannah's mouth where marriage was concerned. That same bad taste had been left in Rico's, as well.

But Savannah had married Durango and was happy and so were Jess and Chase. Rico was happy for them, and with them married off, he had turned his time and attention to other things. His investigation business mainly. And now, he thought, glancing over at Megan

again, to her. She was the first woman in years who
had garnered any real attention from him.

What he'd told her last night was true. What they'd
started was just the beginning. She hadn't responded
to what he'd said one way or the other, but he hadn't
really expected her to. He had been tempted to ask if
she'd wanted to talk about last night but she had dozed
off before he could do so.

But before he had a conversation with her about
anything, it would be wise to have one with himself.
When it came to her, he was still in a quandary as to
why he was as attracted to her as he was. What was
there about her that he wanted to claim?

He would let her sleep, and when she woke up, they
would talk.

The sound of rain and thunder woke Megan. She
first glanced out the windshield and saw how hard it
was raining, before looking over at Rico as he maneu-
vered the truck through the downpour. His concentration was on his driving, and she decided to allow her
concentration to be on him.

Her gaze moved to the hands that gripped the steering wheel. They were big and strong. Masculine hands.
Even down to his fingertips. They were hands that had
touched her in places no other man would have dared.
But he had. And what had happened as a result still
had certain parts of her body tingling.

She started to shift in her seat but then decided to
stay put. She wasn't ready for him to know she was
awake. She needed time to think. To ponder. To pull
herself together. She was still a little rattled from last
night when she had literally come unglued. Ramsey
had said that everyone needed to let loose and let her

hair down every once in a while, and she had definitely taken her brother's suggestion.

She didn't have any regrets, as much as she wished she did. The experience had been simply amazing. With Rico's hands, mouth and tongue, she had felt things she had never felt before. He had deliberately pushed her over the edge, given her pleasure in a way she'd never received it before and wouldn't again.

This is only the beginning.

He had said that. She remembered his words clearly. She hadn't quite recovered from the barrage of pleasurable sensations that had overtaken her, not once but twice, when he had whispered that very statement to her. Even now she couldn't believe she had let him do all those things to her, touch her all over, touch her in all those places.

He'd said he would let her stay in control, but she had forgotten all about control from the first moment he had kissed her. Instead, her thoughts had been on something else altogether. Like taking every single thing he was giving, with a greed and a hunger that astounded her.

"You're awake."

She blinked and moved her gaze from his hands to his face. He'd shaven, but she could clearly remember the feel of his unshaven jaw between her legs. She felt a tingling sensation in that very spot. Maybe, on second thought, she should forget it.

She pulled up in her seat and stared straight ahead. "Yes, I'm awake."

Before she realized what he was doing, he had pulled the car over to the shoulder of the road, unleashed his seat belt and leaned over. His mouth took hers in a deep, languid and provocative kiss that whooshed the very air from her lungs. It was way too passionate and too roastingly raw to be a morning kiss, one taken on the side of the road amidst rush-hour traffic. But he was doing so, boldly, and with a deliberate ease that stirred everything within her. She was reminded of last night and how easily she had succumbed to the passion he'd stirred, the lust he had provoked.

He released her mouth, but not before one final swipe of his tongue from corner to corner. Her nipples hardened in response and pressed tightly against her blouse. Her mouth suddenly felt hot. Taken. Devoured.

"Hello, Megan," he said, against her lips.

"Hello." If this was how he would wake her up after a nap, then she would be tempted to doze off on him anytime.

"Did you get a good nap?"

"Yes, if you want to call it that."

He chuckled and straightened in his seat and resnapped his seat belt. "I would. You've been sleeping for over an hour."

She glanced back at him. "An hour?"

"Yes, I stopped for gas, and you slept through it."

She stretched her shoulders. "I was tired."

"I understand."

Yes, he would, she thought, refusing to look over at him as he moved back into traffic. She licked her lips and could still taste him there. Her senses felt short-circuited. Overwhelmed. She had been forewarned, but she hadn't taken heed.

"You feel like talking?"

Suddenly her senses were on full alert. She did look at him then. "What about?"

"Last night."

She didn't say anything. Was that the protocol with a man and a woman? To use the morning after to discuss the night before? She didn't know. "Is that how things are done?"

He lifted a brow. "What things?"

"The morning-after party where you rehash things. Say what you regret, what you wished never happened, and make promises it won't happen again."

She saw the crinkling of a smile touch the corners of his lips. "Not on my watch. Besides, I told you it will happen again. Last night was just the beginning."

"And do I have a say in the matter?"

"Yes." He glanced over at her. "All you have to say is that you don't want my hands on you, and I'll keep them to myself. I've never forced myself on any woman, Megan."

She could believe that. In fact, she could very well imagine women forcing themselves on him. She began nibbling at her bottom lip. She wished it could be that simple, just tell him to keep his hands to himself, but the truth of the matter was...she liked his hands on her. And she had thoroughly enjoyed his mouth and tongue on her, as well. Maybe a little too much.

Looking over at him, she said. "And if I *don't* tell you to keep your hands to yourself?"

"Then the outcome is inevitable," he said quietly, with a calmness that stirred her insides. She knew he meant it. From the beginning, he had given her fair warning. "Okay, let's talk," she said softly.

He pulled to the side of the road again, which had her wondering if they would ever reach their destination. He unfastened his seat belt and turned to her. "It's like this, Megan. I want you. I've made no secret of that. The degree of my attraction to you is one that I can't figure out. Not that I find the thought annoying, just confusing, because I've never been attracted to a woman to this magnitude before."

Welcome to the club, she thought. She hadn't ever been this attracted to a man before, either.

"This should be a business trip, one to find the answers about your family's history. Now that you're here, it has turned into more."

She lifted a brow. "What has it turned into now?"

"A fact-finding mission regarding us. Maybe constantly being around you will help me understand why you've gotten so deeply under my skin."

Megan's heart beat wildly in her chest. He wanted to explore the reason why they were so intensely attracted to each other? Did there need to be any other reason than that he was man and she was woman? With his looks, any woman in her right mind would be attracted to him, no matter the age. He had certainly done a number on Grace, without even trying. But Megan had been around good-looking men before and hadn't reacted the way she had with him.

"I won't crowd you, and when we get to Forbes you will have your own hotel room if you want."

He paused a moment and then added, "I'm not going to assume anything in this relationship, Megan. But you best believe I plan to seduce the hell out of you. I'm not like those other guys who never made it to first base. I plan on getting in the game and hitting a home run."

You are definitely in the game already, Rico Claiborne. She broke eye contact with him to gaze out the window. If nothing else, last night should have solidified the knowledge that her resistance was at an all-time low around him. Her self-control had taken a direct hit, and since he was on a fact-finding mission, maybe she needed to be on one, as well. Why was she willing to let him go further than any man had before?

"If you think I'm going to sit here and say I regret anything about last night, then you don't have anything to worry about, Rico."

He lifted a brow. "I don't?"

"No."

She wouldn't tell him that he had opened her eyes about a few things. That didn't mean she regretted not engaging in any sort of sexual activity before, because she didn't. What it meant was that there was a reason Rico was the man who'd given her her first orgasm. She just didn't know what that reason was yet, which was why she wanted to find out. She needed to know why he and he alone had been able to make her act in a way no other man before him had been capable of making her act.

"So we have an understanding?" he asked.

"Sort of."

He raised a brow. "Sort of?" He started the ignition and rejoined traffic again. It had stopped raining, and the sun was peeking out from beneath the clouds.

"Yes, there's still a lot about you that I don't know."

He nodded. "Okay, then ask away. Anything you want."

"Anything?"

A corner of his mouth eased into a smile. "Yes, anything, as long I don't think it's private and privileged information."

"That's fair." She considered the best way to ask her first question, then decided to just come out with it. "Have you ever been in love?"

He chuckled softly. "Not since Mrs. Tolbert."

"Mrs. Tolbert?"

"Yes, my third-grade teacher."

"You've got to be kidding me."

He glanced over at her and laughed at her surprised expression. "Kidding you about what? Being in love with Mrs. Tolbert or that she was my third-grade teacher?"

"Neither. You want me to believe that other than Mrs. Tolbert, no other woman has interested you?"

"I didn't say that. I'm a man, so women interest me. You asked if I've ever been in love, and I told you yes, with Mrs. Tolbert. Why are you questioning my answer?"

"No reason. So you're like Zane and Riley," she said.

"Maybe you need to explain that."

"Zane and Riley like women. Both claim they have never been in love and neither wants their names associated with the word."

"Then I'm not like Zane and Riley in that respect. Like I said, women interest me. I am a man with certain needs on occasion. However, falling in love doesn't scare me and it's not out of the realm of possibility. But I haven't been in a serious relationship since college."

She was tempted to ask him about that phone call he'd refused to take at her place the other day. Apparently, some woman was serious even if he wasn't. "But you have been in a serious relationship before?"

"Yes."

Her brow arched. "But you weren't in love?"

"No."

"Then why were you in the relationship?"

He didn't say anything for a minute. "My maternal grandparents are from old money and thought that as their grandson the woman I marry should be connected to old money, as well. They introduced me to Roselyn.

We dated during my first year of college. She was nice, at least I thought she was, until she tried making me choose between her and Jessica."

Megan's eyes widened. "Your sister?"

"Yes. Roselyn said she could accept me as being interracial since it wasn't quite as obvious, but there was no way she could accept Jessica as my sister."

Megan felt her anger boiling. "Boy, she had some nerve."

"Yes, she did. I had just met Jessica for the first time a month before and she felt that since Jessica and I didn't have a bond yet, she could make such an ultimatum. But she failed to realize something."

"What?"

"Jessica was my sister, whether Roselyn liked it or not, and I was not going to turn my back on Jessica or deny her just because Roselyn had a problem with it. So I broke things off."

Good for you, Megan thought. "How did your grandparents feel about you ending things?"

"They weren't happy about it, at least until I told them why. They weren't willing to make the same mistake twice. They were pretty damn vocal against my mother marrying my father, and they almost lost her when Mom stopped speaking to them for nearly two years. There was no way they would risk losing me with that same foolishness."

"You're close to your grandparents?"

"Yes, very close."

"And your father? I take it the two of you are no longer close."

She saw how his jaw tightened and knew the answer before he spoke a single word. "That's right. What he did was unforgivable, and neither Jess, Savannah or I have seen him in almost eighteen years."

"That's sad."

"Yes, it is," he said quietly.

Megan wondered if the separation had been his father's decision or his but decided not to pry. However, there was another question—a very pressing one—that she needed answered right away. "Uh, do you plan to stop again anytime soon?" She recalled he'd said he had stopped for gas while she was asleep. Now she was awake, and she had needs to take care of.

He chuckled. "You have to go to the little girl's room, do you?"

She grinned. "Yes, you can say that."

"No problem, I'll get off at the next exit."

"Thanks."

He smiled over at her, and she immediately felt her pulse thud and the area between her thighs clench. The man was too irresistible, too darn sexy, for his own good. Maybe she should have taken heed of his warning and not come to Texas. She had a feeling things were going to get pretty darn wild now that they were alone together. Real wild.

Ten

Rico stopped in front of Megan and handed her the key. "This is for your room. Mine is right next door if you need me for anything. No matter how late it is, just knock on the connecting door. Anytime you want."

She grinned at his not-so-subtle, seductive-as-sin hint as she took the key from him. "Thanks, I'll keep that in mind."

She glanced around. Forbes, Texas, wasn't what she'd imagined. It was really a nice place. Upon arriving to town, Rico had taken her to one of the restaurants for lunch. It was owned by a Mexican family. In fact, most of the townspeople were Mexican, descended from the settlers who had founded the town back in the early 1800s. She had been tempted to throw Raphel's name out there to see if any of them had ever heard of him but had decided not to. She had promised Rico she would let him handle the investigation, and she intended to keep her word.

"You can rest up while I make a few calls. I want to contact Fanny Banks's family to see if we can visit in a day or so."

"That would be nice," she said as they stepped on the elevator together. The lady at the front desk had told them the original interior of the hotel had caught fire ten years ago and had been rebuilt, which was why everything inside was pretty modern, including the elevator. From the outside, it looked like a historical hotel.

They were the only ones on the elevator, and Rico stood against the panel wall and stared over at her. "Hey, come over here for a minute."

She swallowed, and her nipples pressed hard against her shirt. "Why?"

"Come over here and find out."

He looked good standing over there, and the slow, lazy smile curving his mouth had her feeling hot all over. "Come here, Megan. I promise I won't bite."

She wasn't worried about him taking a bite out of her, but there were other things he could do that were just as lethal and they both knew it. She decided two could play his game. "No, you come over here."

"No problem."

When he made a move toward her, she retreated and stopped when her back touched the wall. "I was just kidding."

"But I kid you not," he said, reaching her and caging her with hands braced against the wall on either side of her. "Open up for me."

"B-but, what if this elevator stops to let more people on? We'll be on our floor any minute."

He reached out and pushed the elevator stop button. "Now we won't." Then he leaned in and plied her mouth with a deep and possessively passionate kiss.

She did as he'd asked. She opened up for him, letting him slide his tongue inside her mouth. He settled the middle of himself against her, in a way that let her feel his solid erection right in the juncture of her thighs. The sensations that swamped her were unreal, and she returned his kiss with just as much hunger as he was showing.

Then, just as quickly as he'd begun, he pulled his mouth away. Drawing in a deep breath, she angled her head back to gaze up at him. "What was that for?"

"No reason other than I want you."

"You told me. Several times," she murmured, trying to get her heart to stop racing and her body to cease tingling. She glanced up at him—the elevator wasn't that big and he was filling it, looking tall, dark and handsome as ever. He was looking her up and down, letting his gaze stroke over her as if it wouldn't take much to strip her naked then and there.

"And I intend to tell you several more times. I plan to keep reminding you every chance I get."

"Why?" Was it some power game he wanted to play? She was certain he had figured out that her experience with men was limited. She had all but told him it was, so what was he trying to prove? Was this just one of the ways he intended to carry out his fact-finding mission? If that was the case, then she might have to come up with a few techniques of her own.

He pushed the button to restart the elevator, and she couldn't help wondering just where her self-control was when she needed it.

* * *

Rico entered his hotel room alone and tossed his keys on the desk. Never before had he mixed business with pleasure, but he was doing so now without much thought. He shook his head. No, that wasn't true, because he was giving it a lot of thought. And still none of it made much sense.

He was about to pull off his jacket when his phone rang. He pulled his cell out of his jeans pocket and frowned when he recognized the number. Jeff Claiborne. Couldn't the man understand plain English? He started to let the call go to voice mail but impulsively decided not to.

Rico clicked on the phone. "What part of *do not call me back* did you not understand?"

"I need your help, Ricardo."

Rico gritted his teeth. "My help? The last thing you'll get from me is my help."

"But if I don't get it, I could die. They've threatened to kill me."

Rico heard the desperation in his father's voice. "Who are they?"

"A guy I owe a gambling debt. Morris Cotton."

Rico released an expletive. His grandfather had told Rico a few years ago that he'd heard Jeff Claiborne was into some pretty shady stuff. "Sounds like you have a problem. And I give a damn, why? And please don't say because you're my father."

There was a pause. "Because I'm a human being who needs help."

Rico tilted his head back and stared up at the ceiling. "You say you're in trouble? Your life is threatened?"

"Yes."

"Then go to the police."

"Don't you understand? I can't go to the police. They will kill me unless…"

"Unless what?"

"I come up with one hundred thousand dollars."

Rico's blood boiled with rage. "And you thought you could call the son and daughter you hadn't talked to in close to eighteen years to bail you out? Trust me, there's no love lost here."

"You can't say I wasn't a good father!"

"You honestly think that I can't? You were an imposter, living two lives, and in the end an innocent woman took her life because of you."

"I didn't force her to take those pills."

Rico couldn't believe that even after all this time his father was still making excuses and refusing to take ownership of his actions. "Let me say this once again. You won't get a penny out of me, Jessica or Savannah. We don't owe you a penny. You need money, work for it."

"Work? How am I supposed to work for that much money?"

"You used to be a salesman, so I'm sure you'll think of something."

"I'll call your mother. I heard she remarried, and the man is loaded. Maybe she—"

"I wouldn't advise you to do that," Rico interrupted to warn him. "She's not the woman you made a fool of years ago."

"She was my only wife."

"Yes, but what about Jessica's mother and the lies you told to her? What about how she ended her life because of you?"

There was a pause and then… "I loved them both."

Not for the first time, Rico thought his father was

truly pitiful. "No, you were greedy as hell and used them both. They were good women, and they suffered because of you."

There was another pause. "Think about helping me, Ricardo."

"There's nothing to think about. Don't call me back." Rico clicked off the phone and released a deep breath. He then called a friend who happened to be a high-ranking detective in the NYPD.

"Stuart Dunn."

"Stuart, this is Rico. I want you to check out something for me."

A short while later Rico had showered and re-dressed, putting on khakis instead of jeans and a Western-style shirt he had picked up during his first day in Forbes. He knew one surefire way to get information from shop owners was to be a buying customer. Most of the people he'd talked to in town had been too young to remember Clarice. But he had gone over to the *Forbes Daily Times* to do a little research, since the town hadn't yet digitally archived their oldest records.

Unfortunately, the day he'd gone to the paper's office, he'd been told he would have to get the permission of the paper's owner before he could view any documents from the year he wanted. He'd found that odd, but hadn't put up an argument. His mind had been too centered on heading to Austin to get Megan.

Now that he had her—and right next door—he could think of a number of things he wanted to do with her, and, as far as he was concerned, every one of them was fair game. But would acting on those things be a smart move? After all, she was cousin-in-law to his sisters. But he *had* warned her, not once but several times. However, just to clear his mind of any guilt, he would try rattling her to the point where she might decide to leave. He would give her one last chance.

And if that didn't work, he would have no regrets, no guilty conscience and no being a nice, keep-your-hands-to-yourself kind of guy. He would look forward to putting his hands—his mouth, tongue, whatever he desired—all over her. And he desired plenty. He would mix work with pleasure in a way it had never been done before.

Suddenly, his nostrils flared as he picked up her scent. Seconds later, there was a knock at his hotel room door. Amazing that he had actually smelled her through that hard oak. He'd discovered that Megan had an incredible scent that was exclusively hers.

He crossed the room and opened the door. There she was, looking so beautiful he felt the reaction in his groin. She had showered and changed clothes, as well. Now she was wearing a pair of jeans and a pullover sweater. She looked spectacular.

"I'm ready to go snooping."

He lifted a brow. "Snooping?"

"Yes, I'm anxious to find out about Raphel, and you mentioned you were going back to the town's newspaper office."

Yes, he had said that in way of conversation during their drive. He figured they had needed to switch their topic back to business or else he would have been tempted to pull to the side of the road and tear away at her mouth again.

"I'm ready," he said, stepping out into the hall and closing his hotel room door behind him. "I thought you would be taking a nap while I checked out things myself."

"I'm too excited to rest. Besides, I slept a lot in the car. Now I'm raring to go."

He saw she was. Her eyes were bright, and he could see excitement written all over her face. "Just keep in mind that this is my investigation. If I come across something I think is of interest I might mention it or I might not."

She frowned up at him as they made their way toward the elevator. "Why wouldn't you share anything you find with me?"

Yes, why wouldn't he? There was still that article Martin Felder had come across. Rico had been barely able to read it from the scan Martin had found on the internet, but what he'd read had made Rico come to Forbes himself to check out things.

"That's just the way I work, Megan. Take it or leave it. I don't have to explain the way I operate to you as long as the results are what you paid me to get."

"I know, but—"

"No buts." He stopped walking, causing her to stop, as well. He placed a stern look on his face. "We either do things my way or you can stay here until I get back." He could tell by the fire that lit her eyes at that moment that he'd succeeded in rattling her.

She crossed her arms over her chest and tilted her head back to glare up at him. "Fine, but your final report better be good."

He bent slowly and brushed a kiss across her lips. "Haven't you figured out yet that everything about me is good?" he whispered huskily.

"Arrogant ass."

He chuckled as he continued brushing kisses across her lips. "Hmm, I like it when you have a foul mouth."

She angrily pushed him away. "I think I'll take the stairs."

He smiled. "And I think I'll take you. Later."

She stormed off toward the door that led to the stairwell. He stared after her. "You're really going to take the stairs?"

"Watch me." She threw the words over her shoulder.

"I am watching you, and I'm rather enjoying the sight of that cute backside of yours right now."

She turned and stalked back over to him. The indignant look on her face indicated he might have pushed her too far. She came to a stop right in front of him and placed her hands on her hips. "You think you're the only one who can do this?"

He intentionally looked innocent. "Do what?"

"Annoy the hell out of someone. Trust me, Rico. You don't want to be around me when I am truly annoyed."

He had a feeling that he really wouldn't. "Why are you getting annoyed about anything? I meant what I said about making love to you later."

She looked up at the ceiling and slowly counted to ten before returning her gaze back to him. "And you think that decision is all yours to make?"

"No, it will be ours. By the time I finish with you, you'll want it as much as I do. I guarantee it."

She shook her head, held up her hand and looked as if she was about to say something that would probably blister his ears. But she seemed to think better of wasting her time doing so, because she tightened her lips together and slowly backed up as if she was trying to retain her control. "I'll meet you downstairs." She'd all but snarled out the words.

He watched her leave, taking the stairs.

Rico rubbed his hand over his jaw. Megan had had

a particular look in her eyes that set him on edge. She had every reason to be ticked off with him since he had intentionally pushed her buttons. And now he had a feeling she would make him pay.

The nerve of the man, Megan thought as she took the stairs down to the lobby. When she had decided to take this route she had forgotten that they were on the eighth floor. If she needed to blow off steam, this was certainly one way to do it.

Rico had deliberately been a jerk, and he had never acted that way before. If she didn't know better she would think it had been intentional. Her eyes narrowed suspiciously, and she suddenly slowed her pace. Had it been intentional? Did he assume that if he was rude to her she would pack up and go running back to Denver?

Well, if that's what he thought, she had news for him. It wouldn't happen. Now that she was here in Forbes, she intended to stay, and he would find out that two could play his game.

Not surprisingly, he was waiting for her in the lobby when she finally made it down. Deciding to have it out with him, here and now, she walked over and stared up at him. "I'm ready to take you on, Rico Claiborne."

He smiled. "Think you can?"

"I'm going to try." She continued to hold his gaze, refusing to back down. She felt the hot, explosive chemistry igniting between them and knew he felt it, too.

"I don't think you know what you're asking for, Megan."

Oh, she knew, and if the other night was a sample, she was ready to let loose and let her hair down again. "Trust me, I know."

His smile was replaced with a frown. "Fine. Let's go."

They were on their way out the revolving doors when his cell phone rang. They stopped and he checked his caller ID, hoping it wasn't Jeff Claiborne again, and answered it quickly when he saw it was Fanny Banks's granddaughter returning his call. Moments later, after ending the call, he said to Megan, "Change in plans. We'll go to the newspaper office later. That was Dorothy Banks, and her grandmother can see us now."

Eleven

"Yes, may I help you?"

"Yes, I'm Rico Claiborne and this is Megan Westmoreland. You were expecting us."

The woman, who appeared to be in her early fifties, smiled. "Yes, I'm Dorothy Banks, the one you spoke to on the phone. Please come in."

Rico stepped aside to let Megan enter before him and followed her over the threshold, admiring the huge home. "Nice place you have here."

If the house wasn't a historical landmark of some sort then it should be. He figured it had to have been built in the early 1900s. The huge two-story Victorian sat on what appeared to be ten acres of land. The structure of the house included two huge columns, a wraparound porch with spindles, and leaded glass windows. More windows than he thought it needed, but if you were a person who liked seeing what was happening outside, then it would definitely work. The inside was just as impressive. The house seemed to have retained the original hardwood floors and inside walls. The furniture seemed to have been selected to complement the original era of the house. Because of all the windows, the room had a lot of light from the afternoon sunshine.

"You mentioned something about Ms. Westmoreland being a descendant of Raphel Westmoreland?" the woman asked.

"Yes. I'm helping her trace her family roots, and in our research, the name Clarice Riggins came up. The research indicated she was a close friend of Raphel. Since Ms. Banks was living in the area at the time, around the early nineteen hundreds, we thought that maybe we could question her to see if she recalls anyone by that name."

Dorothy smiled. "Well, I can tell you that, and the answer is yes. Clarice Riggins and my grandmother were childhood friends. Although Clarice died way before I was born, I remember Gramma Fanny speaking of her from time to time when she would share fond memories with us."

Megan had reached out and touched his hand. Rico could tell she had gotten excited at the thought that the Bankses knew something about Clarice.

"But my grandmother is the one you should talk to," Dorothy added.

"We would love to," Megan said excitedly. "Are you sure we won't be disturbing her?

The woman stood and waved her hand. "I'm positive. My grandmother likes talking about the past." She chuckled. "I've heard most of it more times than I can count. I think she would really appreciate a new set of ears. Excuse me while I go get her. She's sitting

on the back porch. The highlight of her day is watching the sun go down."

"And you're sure we won't be disrupting her day?"
Megan asked.

"I'm positive. Although I've heard the name Clarice,
I don't recall hearing the name of Raphel Westmoreland
before. Gramma Fanny will have to tell you if she has."

Megan turned enthusiastic eyes to Rico. "We might
be finding out something at last."

"Possibly. But don't get your hopes up, okay?"

"Okay." She glanced around. "This is a nice place.
Big and spacious. I bet it's the family home and has
been around since the early nineteen hundreds."

"Those were my thoughts."

"It reminds me of our family home and—"

Megan stopped talking when Dorothy returned,
walking with an older woman using a cane. Both
Megan and Rico stood. Fanny Banks was old, but she
didn't look a year past eighty. To think the woman
had just celebrated her one-hundredth birthday was
amazing.

Introductions were made. Megan thought she might
have been mistaken, but she swore she'd seen a hint of
distress in Fanny's gaze. Why? In an attempt to assure
the woman, Megan took her hand and gently tightened
her hold and said, "It's an honor to meet you. Happy
belated birthday. I can't believe you're a hundred. You
are beautiful, Mrs. Banks."

Happiness beamed in Fanny Banks's eyes. "Thank
you. I understand you have questions for me. And call
me Ms. Fanny. Mrs. Banks makes me feel old."

"All right," Megan said, laughing at the teasing. She
looked over at Rico and knew he would do a better job
of explaining things than she would. The last thing she

wanted was for him to think she was trying to take over his job.

They continued to stand until Dorothy got Ms. Fanny settled into an old rocking chair. Understandably, she moved at a slow pace.

"Okay, now what do you want to ask me about Clarice?" Ms. Fanny asked in a quiet tone.

"The person we really want information about is Raphel Westmoreland, who we believe was an acquaintance of Clarice's."

Megan saw that sudden flash of distress again, which let her know she hadn't imagined it earlier. Ms. Fanny nodded slowly as she looked over at Megan. "And Raphel Westmoreland was your grandfather?"

Megan shook her head. "No, he was my great-grandfather, and a few years ago we discovered he had a twin brother we hadn't known anything about."

She then told Ms. Fanny about the Denver Westmorelands and how they had lost Raphel's only two grandsons and their wives in a plane crash, leaving fifteen of them without parents. She then told Fanny how, a few years ago, they discovered Raphel had a twin named Reginald, and how they had begun a quest to determine if there were more Westmorelands they didn't know about, which had brought them here.

Ms. Fanny looked down at her feeble hands as if studying them…or trying to make up her mind about something. She then lifted her gaze and zeroed in on Megan with her old eyes. She then said, "I'm so sorry to find out about your loss. That must have been a difficult time for everyone."

She then looked down at her hands again. Moments later, she looked up and glanced back and forth between Rico and Megan. "The two of you are forcing me to break a promise I made several years ago, but I think you deserve to know the truth."

Nervous tension flowed through Megan. She glanced over at Rico, who gazed back at her before he turned his attention back to Ms. Fanny and asked, "And what truth is that?"

The woman looked over at her granddaughter, who only nodded for her to continue. She then looked at Megan. "The man your family knew as Raphel Westmoreland was an imposter. The real Raphel Westmoreland died in a fire."

Megan gasped. "No." And then she turned and collapsed in Rico's arms.

"Megan," Rico whispered softly as he stroked the side of her face with his fingertips. She'd fainted, and poor Ms. Fanny had become nervous that she'd done the wrong thing, while her granddaughter had rushed off to get a warm facecloth, which he was using to try to bring Megan back around.

He watched as she slowly opened her eyes and looked at him. He recognized what he saw in her gaze. A mixture of fear and confusion. "She's wrong, Rico. She has to be. There's no way my great-grandfather was not who he said he was."

Rico was tempted to ask why was she so certain but didn't want to upset her any more than she already was. "Then come on, sit up so we can listen to her tell the rest of it and see, shall we?"

Megan nodded and pulled herself up to find she was still on the sofa. There was no doubt in her mind that both Ms. Fanny and Dorothy had heard what she'd just said. Manners prompted her to apologize. "I'm sorry, but what you said, Ms. Fanny, is overwhelming. My great-grandfather died before I was born so I never knew him, but all those who knew him said he was a good and honest person."

Ms. Fanny nodded. "I didn't say that he wasn't, dear. What I said is that he wasn't the real Raphel."

Tightening his hand on Megan's, Rico asked, "If he wasn't Raphel, then who was he?"

Ms. Fanny met Rico's gaze. "An ex-convict by the name of Stephen Mitchelson."

"An ex-convict!" Megan exclaimed, louder than she'd intended to.

"Yes."

Megan was confused. "B-but how? Why?"

It took Ms. Fanny a while before she answered then she said, "It's a long story."

"We have time to listen," Rico said, glancing over at Megan. He was beginning to worry about her. Finding out upsetting news like this was one of the reasons he hadn't wanted her here, yet he had gone and brought her anyway.

"According to Clarice, she met Raphel when she was visiting an aunt in Wyoming. He was a drifter moving from place to place. She told him about her home here and told him if he ever needed steady work to come here and her father would hire him to work on their ranch."

She paused a moment and then said, "While in Wyoming, she met another drifter who was an ex-con by the name of Stephen Mitchelson. She and Stephen became involved, and she became pregnant. But she knew her family would never accept him, and she thought she would never see him again."

Ms. Fanny took a sip of water from the glass her granddaughter handed her. "Only the man who showed

up later, here in Texas, wasn't Raphel but Stephen. He
told her Raphel had died in a fire. To get a fresh start,
he was going to take Raphel's identity and start a new
life elsewhere. And she let him go, without even telling him she was pregnant with his child. She loved him
that much. She wanted to give him a new beginning."

Ms. Fanny was quiet for a moment. "I was there the
day she made that decision. I was there when he drove
away and never looked back. I was also there when she
gave birth to their child. Alone."

The room was silent and then Megan spoke softly.
"What happened to her and the baby?"

"She left here by train to go stay with extended family in Virginia. Her father couldn't accept she had a
baby out of wedlock. But she never made it to her destination. The train she was riding on derailed, killing
her and the baby."

"My God," Megan said, covering her hands with her
face. "How awful," she said. A woman who had given
up so much had suffered such a tragic ending.

She drew in a deep breath and wondered how on
earth she was going to return home to Denver and tell
her family that they weren't Westmorelands after all.

Several hours later, back in his hotel room, Rico sat
on the love seat and watched as Megan paced the floor.
After leaving the Bankses' house, they had gone to
the local newspaper office, and the newspaper articles
they'd read hadn't helped matters, nor had their visit to
the courthouse. The newspapers had verified the train
wreck and that Clarice and her child had been killed.
There was also a mention of the fire in Wyoming and
that several men had been burned beyond recognition.

There were a lot of unanswered questions zigzagging through Rico's mind but he pushed them aside to concentrate on Megan. At the moment, she was his main concern. He leaned forward and rested his arms on his thighs. "If you're trying to walk a hole in the floor, you're doing a good job of it."

She stopped, and when he saw the sheen of tears in her eyes, he was out of his seat in a flash. He was unsure of what he would say, but he knew he had to say something. "Hey, none of that," he whispered quietly, pulling her into his arms. "We're going to figure this out, Megan."

She shook her head and pushed away from him. "This is all my fault. In my eagerness to find out everything about Raphel, I may have caused the family more harm than good. You heard Fanny Banks. The man everyone thought was Raphel was some ex-convict named Stephen Mitchelson. What am I going home to say? We're not really Westmorelands, we're Mitchelsons?"

He could tell by the sound of her voice she was really torn up over what Fanny Banks had said. "But there might be more to what she said, Megan."

"But Fanny Banks was there, Rico," she countered. "I always said there was a lot about my great-grandfather that we didn't know. He went to his grave without telling anyone anything about having a twin brother or if he had family somewhere. Now I know why. He probably didn't know any of Raphel's history. He could never claim anyone. I don't know how the fourth woman named Isabelle fits in, but I do know Raphel—Stephen—finally settled down with my great-grandmother Gemma. From the diary she left behind, the one that Dillon let me read, I know they had a good marriage, and she always said he was a kind-hearted man. He certainly didn't sound like the kind who would have been an ex-con. The only thing I ever heard about Raphel was that he was a kind, loving and honorable man."

"That still might be the case, Megan."

As if she hadn't heard him, she said, "I have to face the possibility that the man my father and uncle idolized, the man they thought was the best grandfather in the entire world, was nothing but a convict who wasn't Raphel Westmoreland and—"

"Shh, Megan," he whispered, breaking in and pulling her closer into his arms. "Until we find out everything, I don't want you getting upset or thinking the worst. We'll go to the courthouse tomorrow and dig around some more."

Sighing deeply, she pulled away from him, swiped at more tears and tilted her head back to look up at him. "I need to be alone for a while so I'm going to my room. Thanks for the shoulder to cry on."

Rico shoved his hands into the pockets of his khakis. "What about dinner?"

"I'm not hungry. I'll order room service later."

"You sure?"

She shrugged. "Right now, Rico, I'm not sure about anything. That's why I need to take a shower and relax."

He nodded. "Are you going to call Dillon or Ramsey and tell them the latest developments?"

She shook her head. "Not yet. It's something I wouldn't be able to tell them over the phone anyway." She headed for the door. "Good night. I'll see you in the morning."

"Try to get some sleep," he called out to her. She nodded but kept walking and didn't look back. She opened the connecting door and then closed it behind her.

Rico rubbed his hand down his face, feeling frustration and anger all rolled into one. He glanced at his watch and pulled his cell phone out of his back pocket. A few moments later a voice came on the line. "Hello."

"This is Rico. A few things came up that I want you to check out." He spent the next twenty minutes bringing Martin up to date on what they'd found out from Fanny Banks.

"And you're actually questioning the honesty of a one-hundred-year-old woman?"

"Yes."

Martin moaned. "Ah, man, she's one hundred."

"I know."

"All right. In that case, I'll get on it right away. If the man was an imposter then I'll find out," Martin said. "But we are looking back during a time when people took on new identities all the time."

That's the last thing Rico wanted to hear.

After hanging up the phone he stared across the room at the door separating him from Megan. Deciding to do something with his time, before he opened the connecting door, he grabbed his jacket and left to get something to eat.

An hour later, Megan had showered, slipped into a pair of pajamas and was lounging across her bed when she heard the sound of Rico returning next door. When she'd knocked on the connecting door earlier and hadn't gotten a response, she figured he had gone to get something to eat. She had ordered room service and had wanted to know if he wanted to share since the hotel had brought her plenty.

Now she felt fed and relaxed and more in control of her emotions. And what she appreciated more than anything was that when she had needed him the most,

Rico had been there. Even while in the basement of
the newspaper office, going through microfilm of old
newspapers and toiling over all those books to locate
the information they wanted, he had been there, ready
to give her a shoulder to cry on if she needed one. And
when she had needed one, after everything had gotten
too emotional for her, she'd taken him up on his offer.

He had been in his room for no more than ten minutes when she heard a soft knock on the connecting
door. "Come in."

He slowly opened the door, and when he appeared
in her room the force of his presence was so powerful
she had to snatch her gaze away from his and train it
back on the television screen.

"I was letting you know I had returned," he said.

"I heard you moving around," she said, her fingers
tightening around the remote.

"You've had dinner?" he asked her.

From out of the corner of her eye, she could see him
leaning in the doorway, nearly filling it completely.
"Yes, and it was good."

"What did you have?"

"A grilled chicken salad. It was huge." *Just like you,*
she thought and immediately felt the blush spread into
her features.

"Why are you blushing?"

Did the man not miss anything? "No reason."

"Then why aren't you looking at me?"

Yes, why wasn't she looking at him? Forcing herself
to look away from the television, she slid her eyes over
to his and immediately their gazes clung. That was the
moment she knew why it had been so easy to let her
guard down around him, why it had been so effortless
to lose her control and why, even now, she was filled

with a deep longing and the kind of desire a woman had for the man she loved.

She had fallen in love with Rico.

A part of her trembled inside with that admission. She hadn't known something like this could happen this way, so quickly, completely and deeply. He had gotten to her in ways no other man had. Around him she had let go of her control and had been willing to let emotions flow. Her love hadn't allowed her to hold anything back. And when she had needed his strength, he'd given it. Unselfishly. He had an honorable and loyal spirit that had touched her in ways she'd never been touched before. Yes, she loved him, with every part of her being.

She sucked in a deep breath because she also knew that what she saw in his eyes was nothing more than pent-up sexual energy that needed to be released. And as she continued to watch him, his lips curved into a smile.

Now it was her time to ask all the questions. "Why are you smiling?"

"I don't think you want to know," he said, doing away with his Eastern accent and replacing it with a deep Texas drawl.

"Trust me, I do." Tonight she needed to think about something other than her grandfather's guilt or innocence, something other than how, in trying to find out about him, she might have exposed her family to the risk of losing everything.

"Since you really want to know," he said, straightening his stance and slowly coming toward her. "I was thinking of all the things I'd just love to do to you."

His words made her nipples harden into peaks, and

she felt them press hard against her pajama top. "Why just think about it, Rico?"

He stopped at the edge of the bed. "Don't tempt me, Megan."

She tilted her head to gaze up at him. "And don't tempt me, Rico."

"What do you know about temptation?"

She became caught up by the deep, sensuous look in his eyes. In one instant, she felt the need to look away, and then, in another instant, she felt the need to be the object of his stare. She decided to answer him the best way she knew how. "I know it's something I've just recently been introduced to," she said, remembering the first time she'd felt this powerful attraction, at Micah's wedding.

"And I know just how strong it was the first time I saw you. Something new for me. Then I remember our first kiss, and how the temptation to explore more was the reason I hadn't wanted it to end," she whispered softly.

"But I really discovered what temptation was the night you used your mouth on me," she said, not believing they were having this sort of conversation or that she was actually saying these things. "I've never known that kind of pleasure before, or the kind of satisfaction I experienced when you were finished, and it tempted me to do some things to you, to touch you and taste you."

She saw the darkening of his eyes, and the very air became heated, sensuously so. He reached out, extending his hand to hers, and she took it. He gently pulled her up off the bed. The feel of the hard, masculine body pressed against hers, especially the outline of his arousal through his khakis, made her shiver with desire. When his hand began roaming all over her, she drew in a deep breath.

"I want to make love to you, Megan," he said, lowering his head to whisper in her ear. "I've never wanted a woman as much as I want you."

For some reason she believed him. Maybe it was because she wanted to believe. Or it could be that she wanted the feeling of being in his arms. The feeling of him inside her while making love. She wanted to be the woman who could satisfy him as much as he could satisfy her.

He tilted her chin up so their gazes could meet again. She was getting caught up in every sexy thing about him, even his chin, which looked like it needed a shave, and his hair, which seemed to have grown an inch and touched his shoulders. And then he leaned down and captured her mouth in one long, drugging kiss. Pleasure shot to all parts of her body, and her nerve endings were bombarded with all sorts of sensations while he feasted on her mouth like it was the last morsel he would ever taste.

At that moment, she knew what she wanted. She wanted to lose control in a way she'd never lost it before. She wanted to get downright wild with it.

She pulled back from the kiss and immediately went for his shirt, nearly tearing off the buttons in her haste. "Easy, baby. What are you doing?"

"I need to touch you," she said softly.

"Then here, let me help," he said, easing his shirt from his shoulders. A breathless moan slipped from her throat. The man was so perfectly made she could feel her womb convulsing, clinching with a need she was beginning to understand.

Her hand went to his belt buckle and within seconds

she had slid it out of the loops to toss it on the floor. On instinct, she practically licked her lips as she eased down his zipper. Never had she been this bold with a man, never this brazen. But something was driving her to touch him, to taste him, the same way he had done to her last night.

All she could register in her mind was that this scenario was one she had played out several times in her dreams. The only thing was, all the other times she would wake up. But this was reality at its best.

"Let me help you with this, as well," he whispered.

And then she watched as he eased his jeans and briefs down his legs and revealed an engorged erection. He was huge, and on instinct, her hand reached out and her fingers curled around the head. She heard how his breathing changed. How he was forcing air into his lungs.

When she began moving her fingers, getting to know this part of him, she felt rippling muscles on every inch of him. The thick length of his aroused shaft filled her hand and then some. This was definitely a fine work of art. Perfect in every way. Thick. Hard. With large veins running along the side.

"Do you have what you want?" he asked in a deep, husky tone.

"Almost." And that was the last word she spoke before easing down to her knees and taking him into her mouth.

A breathless groan escaped from between Rico's lips. He gripped the curls on Megan's head and threw his head back as her mouth did a number on him. He felt his muscles rippling as her tongue tortured him in ways he didn't know were possible. Her head, resting against his belly, shifted each time her mouth moved and sent pleasurable quivers all through him.

He felt his brain shutting down as she licked him from one end to the other, but before it did, he had to know something. "Who taught you this?"

The words were wrenched from his throat, and he had to breathe hard. She paused a moment to look up at him. "I'll tell you later."

She then returned to what she was doing, killing him softly and thoroughly. What was she trying to do? Lick him dry and swallow him whole? Damn, it felt like it. Every lick of her tongue was causing him to inhale, and every long powerful suck was forcing him to exhale. Over and over again. He felt on the edge of exploding, but forced himself not to. He wanted it to be just like in his dreams. He wanted to spill inside of her.

"Megan." He gently tugged on a section of her hair, while backing up to pull out of her mouth.

And before she could say anything, he had whipped her from her knees and placed her on the bed, while removing her pajama top and bottoms in the process. He wanted her, and he wanted her now.

Picking up his jeans off the floor, he retrieved a condom packet from his wallet and didn't waste any time while putting it on. He glanced at her, saw her watching and saw how her gaze roamed over his entire body. "Got another question for you, Megan, and you can't put off the answer until later. I need to know now."

She shifted her gaze from below his waist up to face. "All right. What's your question?"

"How is your energy level?"

She lifted a brow. "My energy level?"

"Yes."

"Why do you want to know?"

"Because," he said, slowly moving toward the bed. "I plan to make love to you all night."

Twelve

All night?

Before Megan had time to digest Rico's proclamation, he had crawled on the bed with her and proceeded to pull her into his arms and seize her mouth. They needed to talk. There were other things he needed to know besides her energy level; things she wanted to tell him. She wanted to share with him what was in her heart but considering what they were sharing was only temporary, it wouldn't be a good idea. The last thing she wanted was for him to feel guilty about not reciprocating her feelings. And then there was the issue of her virginity. He didn't have a clue right now, but pretty soon he would, she thought as he slid his tongue between her lips.

His skin, pressed next to hers, felt warm, intoxicating, and he was kissing her with a passion and greed that surpassed anything she'd ever known. There was no time for talking. Just time to absorb this, take it all in and enjoy. A shiver ran through her when he released her mouth and lowered his head to aim for her breasts, sucking a nipple.

He really thought they could survive an all-nighter? she asked herself. No way. And when he reached down to slide his fingers between her legs and stroked her there, she moaned out his name. "Rico."

He paid her no mind, but continued to let his mouth lick her hardened nipple, while his hand massaged her clit, arousing her to the point where jolts of pleasure were running through her body.

She knew from his earlier question that he assumed she was experienced with this sort of thing. Little did he know she was as green as a cucumber. Again she thought, he needed to be told, but not now. Instead, she reached out to grip his shoulders as his fingers circled inside of her, teasing her mercilessly and spreading her scent in the air.

Then he leaned up, leaving her breasts. Grabbing a lock of her hair with his free hand, he tugged, pulling her face to his and kissing her hard on the mouth, sending her passion skyrocketing while shock waves of pleasure rammed through her.

He pulled his mouth from hers and whispered against her moist lips. "You're ready for me now. You're so wet I can't wait any longer," he said, nibbling on her earlobe and running his tongue around the rim of her ear, so close that she could feel his hot breath.

He moved to slide between her legs and straddle her thighs, looked down at her and whispered, "I'm going to make it good for you, baby. The best you've ever had."

She opened her mouth to tell him not only would it

be the best, but that it would also be the first she ever had when his tongue again slid between her lips. That's when she felt him pressing hard against her, trying to make an entry into her.

"You're tight, baby. Relax," he whispered against her cheek as he reached down and grabbed his penis, guiding it into her. He let the head stroke back and forth along her folds. She started moaning and couldn't stop. "There, you're letting go. Now I can get inside you," he whispered huskily.

"It's not going to be easy," she whispered back.

He glanced down at her. "Why do you say that?" he asked as he continued to stroke her gently, sliding back and forth through her wetness.

Megan knew he deserved an answer. "I'm tight down there for a reason, Rico."

"What reason is that?"

"Because I've never made love with a man before."

His hand went still. "Are you saying—"

"Yes, that's what I'm saying. But I've never wanted any man before." *Never loved one before you,* she wanted to say, but didn't. "Don't let that stop you from making love to me tonight, Rico."

He leaned in and gently kissed her lips. "Nothing can stop me from making love to you, sweetheart. I couldn't stop making love to you tonight even if my life depended on it."

And then he was kissing her again, this time with a furor that had her trembling. Using his knees, he spread her legs wider, and she felt the soft fabric against her skin when he grabbed a pillow to ease under her backside. He pulled back from the kiss. "I wish I could tell you it's not going to hurt. But…"

"Don't worry about it. Just do it."

He looked down at her. "Just do it?"

"Yes, and please do it now. I can't wait any longer. I've waited twenty-seven years for this, Rico." *And for you.*

She looked dead center into his eyes. She felt the head of him right there at her mound. He reached out and gently stroked the side of her face and whispered, "I want to be looking at you when I go inside of you."

Their gazes locked. She felt the pressure of him entering her and then he grabbed her hips, whispered for her to hold on and pushed deeper with a powerful thrust.

"Rico!" she cried out, but he was there, lowering his head and taking her mouth while he pushed even farther inside her, not stopping until he was buried deep. And then, as if on instinct, her inner muscles began clenching him hard.

He threw his head back and released a guttural moan. "What are you doing to me?"

He would ask her that. "I don't know. It just feels right" was the only reply she could give him. In response, he kissed her again while his lower body began moving. Slowly at first, as if giving her body time to adjust. And then he changed the rhythm, while leaning down to suck on her tongue.

Megan thought she was going to go out of her mind. Never had she thought, assumed, believed—until now. He was moving at a vigorous pace, and she cried out, not in pain but in sensations so pleasurable they made her respond out loud.

Her insides quivered, and she went after his tongue with speed and hunger. She cried out, screamed, just like she'd done that night at the south ridge. That only made him thrust harder and penetrate deeper. Then they both ignited in one hell of an explosion that sent sparks flying all through her body, and especially to the area where their bodies were joined.

He shook, she shook and the bed shook almost off the hinges as he continued to pound into her…making her first time a time she would always remember. It seemed as if it took forever for them to come down off their orgasmic high. When they did, he shifted his weight off hers and pulled her to him.

"We'll rest up a bit," he said silkily. "How do you feel?"

She knew her eyes were filled with wonderment at what they'd done. "I feel good." And she meant it.

Her heart was beating fast, and her pulse was off the charts. She had totally and completely lost control. But all that was fine because she had gotten the one thing she'd wanted. A piece of Rico Claiborne.

Rico pulled her closer to him, tucked her body into the curve of his while he stroked a finger across her cheek. He'd only left the bed to dispose of the condom and get another. Now he was back and needed the feel of her in his arms. She had slept for a while, but now she was awake and he had questions.

"I think it's time to tell me how someone who can work their mouth on a man the way you do has managed to remain a virgin. I can think of one possibility, but I want to hear it from you."

She smiled up at him. "What? That I prefer oral sex to the real thing?" She shook her head. "That's not it, and just to set the record straight, I've never gone down on a man until you."

He leaned back and lifted a brow. "Are you saying that—"

"Yes. What I did to you tonight was another first for me."

He chuckled. "Hell, you could have fooled me."

Excitement danced in her eyes. "Really? I was that good?"

"Yeah," he said, running a finger across her cheek again. "Baby, you were that good. So, if I was your first, how did you know what to do?"

She snuggled closer to him. "I was snooping over at Zane's place one day, looking for a pair of shoes I figured I'd left there, and came across this box under his bed. I was curious enough to look inside and discovered a bunch of DVDs marked with Xs. So of course I had to see what was on them."

Rico chuckled again. "Is that the box he mentioned he would get from you after dinner the other night?"

She smiled. "No, that's another box altogether, a lock box. So he would know if I had tampered with it. Those videos were in a shoe box, and to this day I've never told Zane about it. I was only seventeen at the time, but I found watching them pretty darn fascinating. I was curious about how a woman could give a man pleasure that way, with her mouth."

"But not curious enough to try it on anyone until now?"

There was amusement in his voice, but to her it wasn't amusing, not even a little bit, because what he'd said was true. She hadn't had any desire to try it out on any other man but him. "Yes."

"I'm glad. I'm also surprised you've never been curious enough to sleep with anyone."

"I couldn't see myself sharing a bed with a man just for the sake of curiosity. Had I been in a serious relationship things might have been different, but most of my life has been filled with either going to school or working. I never had time for serious relationships. And the few times that a man wanted to make it serious, I just wasn't feeling it."

But she hadn't had a problem feeling him. She had wanted him. Had wanted to taste him the way he had tasted her. Had wanted to put her mouth on him the same way he'd put his on her. And she didn't regret doing so.

But nothing had prepared her for when he had shed his pants and briefs and shown his body to her. He was so magnificently made, with a masculine torso and rippling muscles. What had captured her attention more than anything else was the engorged erection he had revealed. Seeing it had aroused her senses and escalated her desires.

But for her, last night had been about more than just sex. She loved him. She wasn't certain just how she felt being in a one-sided love affair, but she wouldn't worry about it for now. She had let her hair down and was enjoying the situation tremendously. She had been in control of her emotions for so long, and she'd thought that was the best way to be, but now she was seeing a more positive side of being out of control. She knew what it felt like to be filled with a need that only one man could take care of. She knew how it felt to be wild.

And she wanted to experience more of it.

She pulled away from Rico and shifted her body to straddle his.

"Hey, what do you think you're doing?" he asked, trying to pull her back into his arms.

She shook her head. "Taking care of this," she whispered. "You said I can have control so I'm claiming ownership. You also told me you wanted me, and you told me what would happen if we were together. It did happen, and now I want to show you how much I want you."

"But you're sore."

She chuckled. "And I'll probably be sore for a long time. You aren't a small man, you know. But I can handle it, and I can handle you. I want to handle you, Rico, so let me."

He held her gaze, and the heat radiating between them filled the room with desire. His hands lifted and stroked her face, touched her lips that had covered his shaft, and she understood the degree of hunger reflected in his eyes. There was no fighting the intense passion they seemed to generate. No fighting it, and no excusing it.

"Then you are going to handle it, baby. You are the only woman who can," she heard him whisper.

Pleased by what he said, she lowered her head, and he snagged her mouth by nibbling at her lips, stroking them with his tongue. She gripped his shoulders, and his erection stood straight up, aimed right for her womanly core like it had a mind of its own and knew what it wanted.

The need to play around with his mouth drove her to allow his tongue inside her lips. And then she toyed with his tongue, sucked on it and explored every aspect of his mouth. The way his hand was digging into her scalp made her tongue lash out even more, and she felt him tremble beneath her. The thought that she could make him feel this way, give him this much pleasure, sent her blood rushing through her veins.

She eased the lower part of her body down but deliberately did it in a way that had his penis under her and not inside of her. Then she moved her thighs to grind herself against his pubic bone.

"Oh, hell." The words rushed from his lips, and she closed her eyes, liking the feel of giving him such an intimate massage. Moving back and forth, around in circular motions, christening his flesh with her feminine essence.

"I need you now, Megan. I can't take any more." His voice was filled with torment. Deciding to put him out of his misery, she leaned up and positioned her body so he could slide inside of her.

Megan shuddered when she felt the head of his shaft pierce through her wetness, pushing all the way until it could go no more. She held his gaze as she began to ride him. She'd always heard that she was good at riding a horse, and she figured riding a man couldn't be much different. So she rode him. Easing lower then easing back up, she repeated the steps until they became a sensual cycle. She heard his growl of pleasure, and the sound drove her to ride him hard.

Grabbing her hips, he lifted his own off the bed to push deeper inside of her. "Aw, hell, you feel so damn good, Megan." His shaft got even larger inside of her, burying deeper.

His words triggered a need within her, a need that was followed by satisfaction when her body exploded. She screamed and continued coming apart until she felt his body explode, as well. Pleasure was ripping through her, making it hard to breathe. He was rock-solid, engorged, even after releasing inside of her. He wouldn't go down. It was as if he wasn't through with her yet.

He shifted their bodies, pulling her beneath him with her back to him. "Let me get inside you this way, baby. I want to ride you from behind."

Pulling in as much energy as she could, she eased up on all fours, and no sooner had she done so than she felt the head of his erection slide into her. And then he began moving, slowly at first, taking long, leisurely strokes. Each one sent bristles of pleasure brushing over her. But then he increased the rhythm and made the strokes deeper, harder, a lot more provocative as he rode her from the back. She moved her hips against him, felt his stomach on the cheeks of her backside while his hand caressed her breasts.

She glanced over her shoulder, their gazes connected, and she saw the heated look in his eyes. It fueled even more desire within her, making her moan and groan his name aloud.

"Rico."

"That sounds good, baby. Now I want to hear you say 'Ricardo.'"

As spasms of pleasure ripped through her, she whispered in a low, sultry voice. "Ricardo."

Hearing her say his birth name made something savage inside of Rico snap. He grabbed her hips as unadulterated pleasure rammed through him, making him ride her harder, his testicles beating against her backside. The sound of flesh against flesh echoed loudly through the room and mingled with their moans and groans.

And then it happened. The moment he felt her inner muscles clamp down on him, felt her come all over him, he exploded. He wouldn't be surprised if the damn condom didn't break from the load. But, at that moment, the only thing he wanted to do was fill her with his essence. Only her. No other woman.

He continued to shudder, locked tight inside of her. He threw his head back and let out a fierce, primal growl. The same sound a male animal made when he found his true mate. As pleasure continued to rip through him, he knew, without a shadow of a doubt, that he had found his.

He lowered his head and slipped his tongue inside her mouth, needing the connection as waves of pleasure continued to pound into him. It seemed to take forever before the last spasm left his body. But he couldn't move. Didn't want to. He just wanted to lie there and stay intimately connected to her.

But he knew being on all fours probably wasn't a comfortable position for her, so he eased their bodies down in a way that spooned his body against hers but kept him locked inside of her. He needed this moment of just lying with her, being inside of her while holding her in his arms.

She was so damn perfect. What they'd just shared had been so out-of-this-world right. He felt fulfilled in a way he had never felt before, in a way he hadn't thought he was capable of feeling.

"Anything else you think I ought to know?" he asked, wrapping his arms around her, liking the feel of her snuggled tightly to him.

"There is this thing about you using a condom,"

"Mmm, what about it?"

"You can make it optional if you want. I take birth control injections, to stay regulated, so I'm good."

He had news for her. She was better than good. "Thanks for telling me."

"And I'm healthy so I'm safe that way, as well," she added.

"So am I," he assured her softly, gently rubbing her stomach, liking the knowledge that the next time they made love they could be skin-to-skin.

"Rico."

He looked down at her. She had tilted her head back
to see him.

"Yes?"

"I like letting go with you. I like getting wild."

He lowered his head to brush a kiss across her lips.
"And I like letting go and getting wild with you, too."

And he meant it in a way he wasn't ready to explain
quite yet. Right now, he wanted to do the job she had
hired him to do. He hadn't accepted everything Ms.
Fanny and her daughter had said, although the newspapers and those documents somewhat supported their
claims, especially the details of the fire and the train
wreck. There was still a gut feeling that just wouldn't
go away.

Something wasn't adding up, but he couldn't pin-
point what it was. He had been too concerned about
the impact of their words on Megan to take the time
to dissect everything. He hadn't been on top of his A-
game, which is one of the reasons he hadn't wanted her
here. He tended to focus more on her than on what he
was supposed to be doing.

But now, as he replayed everything that had trans-
pired over the past fourteen hours in his mind, a lot of
questions were beginning to form. In the morning, he
would talk to Megan over breakfast. Right now, he just
wanted to hold her in his arms for a while, catch a little
sleep and then make love to her again.

If he had thought he was addicted to her before, he
knew he was even more so now.

Thirteen

"I think Fanny Banks's story isn't true."

Megan peered across the breakfast table at Rico. It took a few seconds for his words to fully sink in. "You do?"

"Yes. Someone is trying to hide something."

Serious doubt appeared in her gaze. "I don't know, Rico. What could they be trying to hide? Besides, we saw the articles in the newspapers, which substantiated what she said."

"Did they?"

Megan placed her fork down and leaned back in her chair. "Look, I admit I was upset by what I learned, and I wish more than anything that Fanny Banks might have gotten her information wrong or that at one hundred years old she couldn't possible remember anything. But her memory is still sharp."

"Too sharp."

Megan leaned forward, wondering why he suddenly had a doubtful attitude. "Okay, why the change of heart? You seemed ready to accept what she said."

"Yes, I was too ready. I was too quick to believe it because, like you, I thought it made sense, especially after reading those newspaper articles. But last night while you slept, I lay there and put things together in my mind and there's one thing that you and I can't deny that we didn't give much thought to."

She lifted a brow. "And what is that?"

"It's no coincidence that the Westmorelands of Atlanta and the Denver Westmorelands favor. And I don't mean a little bit. If you put them in a room with a hundred other people and asked someone to pick out family members, I'd bet ninety-eight percent of all the Westmorelands in the room would get grouped together."

Megan opened her mouth to say something and then decided there was nothing she could say because he was right. The first time the two groups had gotten together, and Dare Westmoreland—one of the Atlanta Westmorelands who was a sheriff in the metro area—had walked into the room, every member of the Denver Westmorelands' jaws had dropped. He and Dillon favored so much it was uncanny.

"And that level of similarity in looks can only come from the same genes," Rico added. "If push comes to shove, I'll have DNA testing done."

She picked up her fork. "You still haven't given me a reason for Ms. Banks to make up such a story."

Rico tossed down his napkin. "I don't have a reason, Megan, just a gut feeling."

He reached across the table and took her hand in his. "I saw yesterday that what she said took a toll on you and that became my main concern. I got caught up in your hurt and pain. I felt it, and I didn't want that for you."

She understood what he meant. Last night, making love to him had been an eye opener. She had felt connected to him in a way she'd never been connected to a man. She was in tune to her emotions and a part of her felt in tune to his, as well. Their time together had been so special that even now the memories gave her pause. "If your theory is true, how do we prove it?" she asked him.

"We don't. We visit them again and ask questions we didn't ask yesterday when our minds were too numb to do so."

He gently tightened his hold on her hand. "I need you to trust me on this. Will you do that?"

She nodded. "Yes, I will trust you."

After making a call to the Banks ladies after breakfast, they discovered they would have to put their visit on hold for a while. Dorothy Banks's daughter advised them that her mother and great-grandmother weren't at home and had gone on a day trip to Brownwood and wouldn't be returning until that evening.

So Rico and Megan went back to their hotel. The moment they walked into the room he gently grabbed her wrist and tugged her to him. "You okay? How is the soreness?"

He found it odd to ask her that since he'd never asked a woman that question before. But then he couldn't recall ever being any woman's first.

She rested her palms on his chest and smiled up at him. "My body is fine. Remember, I do own a horse that I ride every day, and I think that might have helped some." She paused and then asked, "What about you?"

He raised a brow. "Me?"

"Yes," she said, smiling. "I rode you pretty darn hard."

Yes, she had. The memory of her doing so made his erection thicken against her. "Yes, but making love with you was amazing," he said, already feeling the air crackling with sexual energy. "Simply incredible. I enjoyed it tremendously."

Her smile widened, as if she was pleased. "Did you?"

"Yes. I can't really put it into words."

She leaned closer and ran the tip of her tongue alongside his lips. Tempting him. Seducing him, slowly and deliberately. "Then show me, Rico. Show me how much you enjoyed it. Let's get wild again."

He was already moving into action, tugging off his shirt and bending down to remove his shoes and socks. She wanted wild, he would give her wild. Texas wild. Following his lead, she began stripping off her clothes. He lowered his jeans and briefs while watching her ease her own jeans down her thighs. He discovered last night that she wore the cutest panties. Colorful. Sexy. No thongs or bikinis. They were hip-huggers, and she had the shapely hips for them. They looked great on her. Even better off her.

He stood there totally nude while she eased her panties down. She was about to toss them aside when he said, "Give them to me."

She lifted a brow as she tossed them over to him. He caught them with one hand and then raised them to his nose. He inhaled her womanly scent. His erection throbbed and his mouth watered, making him groan. He tossed her panties aside and looked at her, watching her nipples harden before his eyes.

He lowered his gaze to her sex. She kept things simple, natural. Some men liked bikini or Brazilian, but he preferred natural. She was beautiful there, her womanly core covered with dark curls.

His tongue felt thick in his mouth, and he knew where he wanted it to be. He moved across the room and dropped to his knees in front of her. Grabbing her thighs he rested his head against her stomach and inhaled before he began kissing around her belly button and along her inner and outer thighs. He tasted her skin, licking it all over and branding it as his. And then he came face-to-face with the core of her and saw her glistening folds. With the tip of his tongue, he began lapping her up.

She grabbed hold of his shoulders, dug her fingernails into the blades, but he didn't feel any pain. He felt only pleasure as he continued to feast on her. Savoring every inch of her.

"Rico."

He heard her whimper his name, but instead of letting up, he penetrated her with his tongue, tightened his hold on her hips and consumed her.

He liked having his tongue in her sex, tasting her honeyed juices, sucking her and pushing her into the kind of pleasure only he had ever given her. Only him.

"Rico!"

She called out his name a little more forcefully this time, and he knew why. She removed her hands from his shoulders to dig into his hair as she released another high-pitched scream that almost shook the room. If hotel security came to investigate, it would be all her fault.

Moments later, she finished off her orgasm with an intense moan and would have collapsed to the floor had he not been holding her thighs. He stood. "That was just an appetizer, baby. Now for the meal."

Picking her up in his arms he carried her to the bedroom, but instead of placing her on the bed, he grabbed one of the pillows and moved toward the huge chair. He sat and positioned her in his lap, facing him. Easing up he placed the pillows under his knees.

"Now, this is going to work nicely. You want wild, I'm about to give you wild," he whispered, adjusting her body so that she was straddling him with her legs raised all the way to his shoulders. He lifted her hips just enough so he could ease into her, liking the feel of being skin-to-skin with her. The wetness that welcomed him as he eased inside made him throb even more, and he knew he must be leaking already, mingling with her wetness.

"You feel so good," he said in a guttural tone. They were almost on eye level, and he saw the deep desire in the depths of her gaze. She moved, gyrating her hips in his lap. Her movement caused him to moan, and then he began moving, setting the rhythm, rocking in place, grasping her hips tightly to receive his upward thrusts. And she met his demands, tilting her hips and pushing forward to meet him.

He could feel heat building between them, sensations overtaking them so intensely that he rocked harder, faster. His thrusts were longer, deeper, even more intense as they worked the chair and each other.

He knew the moment she came. He felt it gush all around him, triggering his own orgasm. He shuddered uncontrollably, as his body did one hell of a blast inside of her. She stared into his face and the look in her eyes told him she had felt his hot release shooting inside of her. And he knew that was another new experience for her. The thought was arousing, and he could only groan raggedly. "Oh, baby, I love coming inside of you. It feels so good."

"You feel good," she countered. And then she was kissing him with a passion that was like nothing he'd ever experienced before. No woman had ever put this much into her kiss. It was raw, but there was something else, something he couldn't define at the moment. It was more than just tongues tangling and mating aggressively. There were emotions beneath their actions. He felt them in every part of his body.

He would have given it further thought if she hadn't moved her mouth away to scream out another orgasm. As she sobbed his name, he felt his body explode again, as well. He cried out her name over and over as he came, increasing the rocking of the chair until he was convinced it would collapse beneath them.

But it didn't. It held up. Probably better than they did, he thought, as they fought for air and the power to breathe again. Megan's head fell to his chest and he rubbed her back gently. Passion had his vision so blurred he could barely see. But he could feel, and what he was feeling went beyond satisfying his lust for her. It was much deeper than that. With her naked body connected so tightly to his, he knew why they had been so in tune with each other from the first. He understood why the attraction had been so powerful that he hadn't been able to sleep a single night since without dreaming of her.

He loved her.

There was no other way to explain what he was feeling, no other way to explain why spending the rest of his life without her was something he couldn't do. He pulled in a deep breath before kissing her shoulder blades. When he felt her shiver, his erection began hardening inside of her all over again.

She felt it and lifted her head to stare at him with languid eyes, raising both brows. "You're kidding, right? You've just got to be."

He smiled and combed his hands through the thick curls on her head. "You said you wanted wild," he murmured softly.

She smiled and wrapped her hands around his neck, touching her own legs, which were still on his shoulders. "I did say that, didn't I?" she purred, beginning to rotate her hips in his lap.

He eased out of the chair with their bodies still locked together. "Yes, and now I'm going to take you against the wall."

"Hey, you awake over there?" Rico asked when he came to a traffic light. He glanced across the truck seat at Megan. She lifted her head and sighed. Never had she felt so satiated in her life. For a minute, she'd thought he would have to carry her out of the hotel room and down to the truck.

They had made love a couple more times after the chair episode. First against the wall like he'd said, and then later, after their nap, they'd made out in the shower. Both times had indeed been wild, and such rewarding experiences. Now she was bone-tired. She knew she would have to perk up before they got to the Bankses' place.

"I'm awake, but barely."

"You wanted it wild," he reminded her.

She smiled drowsily. "Yes, and you definitely know how to deliver."

He chuckled. "Thanks. And that's Texas wild. Wait

until I make love to you in Denver and show you Colorado wild."

She wondered if he realized what he'd insinuated. It sounded pretty much like he had every intention of continuing their affair. And since he didn't live in Denver did that mean he planned to come visit her at some point for pleasure rather than business?

Before she could ask him about what he'd said, his cell phone rang. After he checked the ID, Megan heard him let out a low curse. "I thought I told you not to call me."

"You didn't say you would sic the cops on me," Jeffery Claiborne accused.

"I didn't sic the cops on you. I wanted to check out your story. I have, and you lied. You need money for other things, and I'm not buying." He then clicked off the phone.

Megan had listened to the conversation. That was the second time he'd received a similar phone call in her presence. The thought that he was still connected to some woman in some way, even if he didn't want to be bothered, annoyed her. She tried pushing it from her mind and discovered she couldn't. A believer in speaking her mind, she said, "Evidently someone didn't understand your rule about not getting serious."

He glanced over at her. His gaze penetrated hers. "What are you talking about?"

"That call. That's the second time she's called while I was with you."

"She?"

"Yes, I assume it's a female," she said, knowing she really didn't have any right to assume anything.

He said nothing for a minute and then. "No, that

wasn't a female. That was the man who used to be my
father."

She turned around in her seat. "Your father?" she
asked, confirming what he'd said.

"Yes. He's called several times trying to borrow
money from me. He's even called Savannah. Claims
his life is in jeopardy because he owes a gambling debt.
But I found out differently. Seems he has a drug problem, and he was fired from his last job a few months
ago because of it."

Now it was her time to pause. Then she said, "So
what are you going to do?"

He raised his brow and looked over at her. "What
am I going to do?"

"Yes."

"Nothing. That man hurt my mother and because of
him Jess lost hers."

Megan swallowed tightly, telling herself it wasn't
any of her business, but she couldn't help interfering.
"But he's your father, Rico."

"And a piss-poor one at that. I could never understand why he wasn't around for all the times that were
important to me while growing up. His excuse was always that as a traveling salesman he had to be away. It
never dawned on me, until later, that he really wasn't
contributing to the household since we were mostly
living off my mother's trust fund."

He stopped at another traffic light and said, "It was
only later that we found out why he spent so much time
in California. He was living another life with another
family. He's never apologized for the pain he caused all
of us, and he places the blame on everyone but himself.
So, as far as me doing anything for him, the answer is

I don't plan on doing a single thing, and I meant what I just told him. I don't want him to call me."

Megan bit down on her lips to keep from saying anything else. It seemed his mind was pretty made up.

"Megan?"

She glanced over at him. "Yes?"

"I know family means a lot to you, and, believe it or not, it means a lot to me, too. But some things you learn to do without…especially if they are no good. Jeff Claiborne is bad news."

"Sounds like he needs help, like drug rehab or something."

"Yes, but it won't be my money paying for it."

His statement sounded final, and Megan had a problem with it. It was just her luck to fall in love with a man who had serious issues with his father. What had the man done to make Rico feel this way? Should she ask him about it? She immediately decided not to. She had enough brothers and male cousins to know when to butt out of their business…until it was a safe time to bring it back up again. And she would.

Fourteen

"Mr. Claiborne, Ms. Westmoreland," Dorothy said, reluctantly opening the door to let them in. "My daughter told me you called. We've told you everything, and I'm not sure it will be good on my grandmother to have to talk about it again."

Rico stared at her. "Just the other day you were saying you thought it would be good for her to talk about it."

"Yes, but that was before I saw what discussing it did to her," she said "Please have a seat."

"Thanks," he said, and he and Megan sat down on the sofa. "If your grandmother isn't available then perhaps you won't mind answering a few questions for us."

"I really don't know anything other than what Gramma Fanny told me over the years," she said, taking the chair across from them. "But I'll try my best because my grandmother hasn't been herself since your visit. She had trouble sleeping last night and that's not like her. I guess breaking a vow to keep a promise is weighing heavily on her conscience."

For some reason Rico felt it went deeper than that. "Thanks for agreeing to talk to us." He and Megan had decided that he would be the one asking the questions. "Everybody says your grandmother's memory is sharp as a tack. Is there any reason she would intentionally get certain facts confused?"

The woman seemed taken back. "What are you trying to say, Mr. Claiborne?"

Rico sighed deeply. He hadn't told Megan everything yet, especially about the recent report he'd gotten from Martin while she'd been sleeping. "Stephen Mitchelson was not the one who survived that fire, and I'd like to know why your grandmother would want us to think that he was."

The woman look surprised. "I don't know, but you seem absolutely certain my grandmother was wrong."

He wasn't absolutely certain, but he was sure enough, thanks to the information Martin had dug up on Mitchelson, especially the man's prison photo, which looked nothing like the photographs of Raphel that the Westmorelands had hanging on their wall at the main house in Denver.

He knew Megan was just as surprised by his assertion as Ms. Banks's granddaughter. But there was that gut feeling that wouldn't go away. "It could be that Clarice lied to her about everything," he suggested, although he knew that probably wasn't the case.

"Possibly."

"But that isn't the case, and you know it, don't you, Mr. Claiborne?"

Rico turned when he heard Fanny Banks's frail voice. She was standing in the doorway with her cane.

"Gramma Fanny, I thought you were still sleeping," Dorothy said, rushing over to assist her grandmother.

"I heard the doorbell."

"Well, Mr. Claiborne and Ms. Westmoreland are back to ask you more questions. They think that perhaps you were confused about a few things," Dorothy said, leading her grandmother over to a chair.

"I wasn't confused," the older woman said, settling in her chair. "Just desperate, child."

Confusion settled on Dorothy's face. "I don't understand."

Fanny Banks didn't say anything for a minute. She then looked over at Rico and Megan. "I'm glad you came back. The other day, I thought it would be easier to tell another lie, but I'm tired of lying. I want to tell the truth…no matter who it hurts."

Rico nodded. "And what is the truth, Ms. Fanny?"

"That it was me and not Clarice who went to Wyoming that year and got pregnant. And Clarice, bless her soul, wanted to help me out of my predicament. She came up with this plan. Both she and I were single women, but she had a nice aunt in the East who wanted children, so we were going to pretend to go there for a visit for six months, and I would have the baby there and give my baby to her aunt and uncle. It was the perfect plan."

She paused for a minute. "But a few weeks before we were to leave, Raphel showed up to deliver the news that Stephen had died in a fire, and Raphel wanted me to have the belongings that Stephen left behind. While he was here, he saw Clarice. I could see that they were instantly attracted to each other."

Rico glanced over at Megan. They knew firsthand just how that instant-attraction stuff worked. "Please go on, Ms. Fanny."

"I panicked. I could see Clarice was starting something with Raphel, which could result in her changing our plans about going out East. Especially when Raphel was hired on by Clarice's father to do odds and ends around their place. And when she confided in me that she had fallen in love with Raphel, I knew I had to do something. So I told her that Raphel was really my Stephen, basically the same story I told the two of you. She believed it and was upset with me for not telling him about the baby and for allowing him to just walk away and start a new life elsewhere. She had no idea I'd lied. Not telling him what she knew, she convinced her father Raphel was not safe to have around their place. Her father fired him."

She paused and rubbed her feeble hands together nervously. "My selfishness cost my best friend her happiness with Raphel. He never understood why she began rebuffing his advances, or why she had him fired. The day we caught the train for Virginia is the day he left Forbes. Standing upstairs in my bedroom packing, we watched him get in his old truck and drive off. I denied my best friend the one happiness she could have had."

Rico drew in a deep breath when he saw the tears fall from the woman's eyes. "What about the baby? Did Clarice have a baby?"

Ms. Fanny nodded. "Yes. I didn't find out until we reached her aunt and uncle's place that Clarice had gotten pregnant."

Megan gasped. "From Raphel?"

"Yes. She thought she'd betrayed me and that we

were having babies from the same man. Even then I never told her the truth. She believed her parents would accept her child out of wedlock and intended to keep it. She had returned to Texas after giving birth only to find out differently. Her parents didn't accept her, and she was returning to Virginia to make a life for her and her baby when the train derailed."

"So it's true, both her and the baby died," Megan said sadly.

"No."

"No?" Rico, Megan and Dorothy asked simultaneously.

"Clarice didn't die immediately, and her son was able to survive with minor cuts and bruises."

"Son?" Megan whispered softly.

"Yes, she'd given birth to a son, a child Raphel never knew about...because of me. The baby survived because Clarice used her body as a shield during the accident."

Fanny didn't say anything for a minute. "We got to the hospital before she died, and she told us about a woman she'd met on the train, a woman who had lost her baby a year earlier...and now the woman had lost her husband in the train wreck. He was killed immediately, although the woman was able to walk away with only a few scratches."

Dorothy passed her grandmother a tissue so she could wipe away her tears. Through those tears, she added, "Clarice, my best friend, who was always willing to make sacrifices for others, who knew she would not live to see the next day, made yet another sacrifice by giving her child to that woman." Ms. Fanny's aged voice trembled as she fought back more tears. "Because she believed my lie, she wasn't certain she could leave her baby with me to raise because I would be constantly reminded of his father's betrayal. And her aunt couldn't afford to take on another child after she'd taken on mine. So Clarice made sure she found her baby a good home before she died."

Megan wiped tears away from her own eyes, looked over at Rico and said softly, "So there might be more Westmorelands out there somewhere after all."

Rico nodded and took her hand and entwined their fingers. "Yes, and if there are, I'm sure they will be found."

Rico glanced back at Fanny, who was crying profusely, and he knew the woman had carried the guilt of what she'd done for years. Now, maybe she would be able to move on with what life she had left.

Standing, Rico extended his hand to Megan. "We have our answers, now it's time for us to go."

Megan nodded and then hugged the older woman. "Thanks for telling us the truth. I think it's time for you to forgive yourself, and my prayer is that you will."

Rico knew then that he loved Megan as deeply as any man could love a woman. Even now, through her own pain, she was able to forgive the woman who had betrayed not only her great-grandfather, but also the woman who'd given birth to his child…a child he hadn't known about.

Taking Megan's hand in his, he bid both Banks women goodbye and together he and Megan walked out the door.

Rico pulled Megan into his arms the moment the hotel room door closed behind them, taking her mouth with a hunger and greed she felt in every portion of his body. The kiss was long, deep and possessive. In

response, she wrapped her arms around his neck and
returned the kiss with just as much vigor as he was putting into it. Never had she been kissed with so much
punch, so much vitality, want and need. She couldn't
do anything but melt in his arms.

"I want you, Megan." He pulled back from the kiss
to whisper across her lips, his hot breath making her
shudder with need.

"And I want you, too," she whispered back, then outlined his lips with the tip of her tongue. She saw the
flame that had ignited in his eyes, felt his hard erection
pressed against her and knew this man who had captured her heart would have her love forever.

Megan wanted to forget about Ms. Fanny's deceit,
her betrayal of Clarice, a woman who would have done
anything for her. She didn't want to think about the
child Clarice gave up before she died, the child her
great-grandfather had never known about. And she
didn't want to think of her great-grandfather and how
confused he must have been when the woman he had
fallen in love with—at first sight—had suddenly not
wanted anything to do with him.

She felt herself being lifted up in Rico's arms and
carried into the bedroom, where he placed her on the
bed. He leaned down and kissed her again, and she
couldn't help but moan deeply. When he released her
mouth, she whispered, "Let's get wild again."

They reached for each other at the same time, tearing at each other's clothes as desire, as keen as it could
get, rammed through her from every direction. They
kissed intermittently while undressing, and when all
their clothes lay scattered, Rico lifted her in his arms.
Instinctively, she wrapped her legs around him. The
thickness of him pressed against her, letting her know

he was willing, ready and able, and she was eager for the feel of him inside of her.

He leaned forward and took her mouth again. His tongue tasted her as if he intended to savor her until the end of time.

He continued to kiss her, to stimulate her to sensual madness as he walked with her over to the sofa. Once there, he broke off the kiss and stood her up on the sofa, facing him. Sliding his hands between her legs, he spread her thighs wide.

"You still want wild, I'm going to give you wild," he whispered against her lips. "Squat a little for me, baby. I want to make sure I can slide inside you just right."

She bent her knees as he reached out and grabbed her hips. His arousal was hard, firm and aimed right at her, as if it knew just where it should go. To prove that point, his erection unerringly slid between her wet folds.

"Mercy," he said. He inched closer, and their pelvises fused. He leaned forward, drew in a deep breath and touched his forehead to hers. "Don't move," he murmured huskily, holding her hips as he continued to ease inside of her, going deep, feeling how her inner muscles clenched him, trying to pull everything out of him. "I wish our bodies could stay locked together like this forever," he whispered.

She chuckled softly, feeling how deeply inside of her he was, how closely they were connected. "Don't know how housekeeping is going to handle it when they come in our room tomorrow to clean and find us in this position."

She felt his forehead move when he chuckled. His feet were planted firmly on the floor, and she was standing on the sofa. But their bodies were joined in a way that had tingling sensations moving all over her naked skin.

He then pulled his forehead back to look at her. "Ready?"

She nodded. "Yes, I'm ready."

"Okay, then let's rock."

With his hands holding her hips and her arms holding firm to his shoulders, they began moving, rocking their bodies together to a rhythm they both understood. Her nipples felt hard as they caressed his chest, and the way he was stroking her insides made her groan out loud.

"Feel that?" he asked, hitting her at an angle that touched her G-spot and caused all kinds of extraordinary sensations to rip through her. She released a shuddering moan.

"Yes, I feel it."

"Mmm, what about this?" he asked, tilting her hips a little to stroke her from another angle.

"Oh, yes." More sensations cascaded through her.

"And now what about this?" He tightened his hold on her hips, widened her legs even more and began thrusting hard within her. She watched his features and saw how they contorted with pleasure. His eyes glistened with a need and hunger that she intended to satisfy.

As he continued to rock into her, she continued to rock with him. He penetrated her with long, deep strokes. His mouth was busy at her breasts, sucking the nipples into his mouth, nipping them between his teeth. And then he did something below—she wasn't sure what—but he touched something inside of her that made her release a deep scream. He immediately silenced her by covering her mouth with his, still thrusting inside of her and gripping her hips tight. This was definitely wild.

She felt him. Hot molten liquid shot inside of her, and she let out another scream as she was thrown into another intense orgasm. She closed her eyes as the explosion took its toll.

"Wrap your legs around me now, baby."

She did so, and he began walking them toward the bed, where they collapsed together. He pulled her into his arms and gazed down at her. "I love you," he whispered softly.

She sucked in a deep breath and reached out to cup his jaw in her hand. "And I love you, too. I think I fell in love with you the moment you looked at me at the wedding reception."

He chuckled, pulling her closer. "Same here. Besides wanting you extremely badly, another reason I didn't want you to come to Texas with me was because I knew how much finding out about Clarice and Raphel meant to you. I didn't want to disappoint you."

"You could never disappoint me, but you will have to admit that we make a good team."

Rico leaned down and kissed her lips. "We most certainly do. I think it's time to take the Rico and Megan show on the road, don't you?"

She lifted a brow. "On the road?"

"Yes, make it permanent." When she still had a confused look on her face, he smiled and said, "You know. Marriage. That's what two people do when they discover they love each other, right?"

Joy spread through Megan, and she fought back her tears. "Yes."

"So is that a yes, that you will marry me?"

"Did you ask?"

He untangled their limbs to ease off the bed to get down on his knees. He reached out for her hand. "Megan Westmoreland, will you be my wife so I can have the right to love you forever?"

"Can we get wild anytime we want?"

"Yes, anytime we want."

"Then yes, Ricardo Claiborne, I will marry you."

"We can set a date later, but I intend to put an engagement ring on your finger before leaving Texas."

"Oh, Rico. I love you."

"And I love you, too. I'm not perfect, Megan, but I'll always try to be the man you need." He eased back in bed with a huge masculine smile on his face. "We're going to have a good life together. And one day I believe those other Westmorelands will be found. It's just so sad Fanny Banks has lived with that guilt for so many years."

"Yes, and she wasn't planning on telling us the truth until we confronted her again. Why was that?" Megan asked.

"Who knows? Maybe she was prepared to take her secret to the grave. I only regret Raphel never knew about his child. And there's still that fourth woman linked to his name. Isabelle Connors."

"Once I get back to Denver and tell the family everything, I'm sure someone will be interested in finding out about Isabelle as well as finding out what happened to Clarice and Raphel's child."

"You're anxious to find out as well, right?"

"Yes. But I've learned to let go. Finding out if there are any more Westmorelands is still important to me, but it isn't the most important thing in my life anymore. You are."

Megan sighed as she snuggled more deeply into Rico's arms. She had gotten the answers she sought, but there were more pieces to the puzzle that needed to be found. And eventually they would be. At the moment, she didn't have to be the one to find them. She felt cherished and loved.

But there were a couple of things she needed to discuss with Rico. "Rico?"

"Yes, baby?"

"Where will we live? Philly or Denver?"

He reached out and caressed the side of her face gently. "Wherever you want to live. My home, my life is with you. Modern technology makes it possible for me to work from practically anywhere."

She nodded, knowing her home and life was with him as well and she would go wherever he was. "And do you want children?"

He chuckled. "Most certainly. I intend to be a good father."

She smiled. "You'll be the best. There are good fathers and there are some who could do better…who should have done better. But they are fathers nonetheless."

She pulled back and looked up at him. "Like your father. At some point you're going to have to find it in your heart to forgive him, Rico."

"And why do you figure that?" She could tell from the tone of his voice and the expression on his face that he definitely didn't think so.

"Because," she said, leaning close and brushing a kiss across his lips. "Your father is the only grandfather our children will have."

"Not true. My mother has remarried, and he's a good man."

She could tell Rico wanted to be stubborn. "I'm

sure he is, so in that case our children will have two
grandfathers. And you know how important family is
to me, and to you, as well. No matter what, Jeff Claiborne deserves a second chance. Will you promise me
that you'll give him one?"

He held her gaze. "I'll think about it."

She knew when not to push. "Good. Because it
would make me very happy. And although I've never
met your dad, I believe he can't be all bad."

Rico lifted a brow. "How do you figure that?"

"Because you're from his seed, and you, Rico, are
all good. I am honored to be the woman you want as
your wife."

She could tell her words touched him, and he pulled
her back down to him and kissed her deeply, thoroughly
and passionately. "Megan Westmoreland Claiborne,"
Rico said huskily, finally releasing her lips. "I like the
sound of that."

She smiled up at him. "I like the sound of that, as
well."

Then she kissed him, deciding it was time to get
wild again.

Two weeks later, New York

Rico looked around at the less than desirable apartment complex, knowing the only reason he was here
was for closure. He might as well get it over with. The
door was opened on the third knock and there stood
the one man Rico had grown up loving and admiring—
until he'd learned the truth.

He saw his father study Rico's features until recognition set in. Rico was glad his father recognized him
because he wasn't sure if he would have recognized

his father if he'd passed the old man in the street. It was obvious that drugs and alcohol had taken their toll. Jeff looked ten years older than what Rico knew his age to be. And the man who'd always taken pride in how he looked and dressed appeared as if he was all but homeless.

"Ricardo. It's been a while."

Instead of answering, Rico walked past his father to stand in the middle of the small, cramped apartment. When his father closed the door behind him, Rico decided to get to the point of his visit.

He shoved his hands into his pockets and said, "I'm getting married in a few months to a wonderful woman who believes family is important. She also believes everyone should have the ability to forgive and give others a second chance."

Rico paused a moment and then added, "I talked to Jessica and Savannah and we're willing to do that…to help you. But you have to be willing to help yourself. Together, we're prepared to get you into rehab and pay all the expenses to get you straightened out. But that's as far as our help will go. You have to be willing to get off the drugs and the alcohol. Are you?"

Jeff Claiborne dropped down in a chair that looked like it had seen better days and held his head in his hands. "I know I made a mess of things with you, Jessica and Savannah. And I know how much I hurt your mom…and when I think of what I drove Janice to do…" He drew in a deep breath. "I know what I did, and I know you don't believe me, but I loved them both—in different ways. And I lost them both."

Rico really didn't want to hear all of that, at least not now. He believed a man could and should love only one woman, anything else was just being greedy and without morals. "Are you willing to get help?"

"Are the three of you able to forgive me?"

Rico didn't say anything for a long moment and then said, "I can't speak for Jessica and Savannah, but with me it'll take time."

Jeff nodded. "Is it time you're willing to put in?"

Rico thought long and hard about his father's question. "Only if you're willing to move forward and get yourself straightened out. Calling your children and begging for money to feed your drug habit is unacceptable. Just so you know, Jess and Savannah are married to good men. Chase and Durango are protective of their wives and won't hesitate to kick your ass—father or no father—if you attempt to hurt my sisters."

"I just want to be a part of their lives. I have grandkids I haven't seen," Jeff mumbled.

"And you won't be seeing them if you don't get yourself together. So back to my earlier question, are you willing to go to rehab to get straightened out?"

Jeff Claiborne stood slowly. "Yes, I'm willing."

Rico nodded as he recalled the man his father had been once and the pitiful man he had become. "I'll be back in two days. Be packed and ready to go."

"All right, son."

Rico tried not to cringe when his father referred to him as "son," but the bottom line, which Megan had refused to let him deny, was that he was Jeff Claiborne's son.

Then the old man did something Rico didn't expect. He held his hand out. "I hope you'll be able to forgive me one day, Ricardo."

Rico paused a moment and then he took his father's hand, inhaling deeply. "I hope so, too."

Epilogue

"Beautiful lady, may I have this dance?"

"Of course, handsome sir."

Rico led Megan out to the dance floor and pulled her into his arms. It was their engagement party, and she was filled with so much happiness being surrounded by family and friends. It seemed no one was surprised when they returned from Texas and announced they were engaged. Rico had taken her to a jeweler in Austin to pick out her engagement ring, a three-carat solitaire.

They had decided on a June wedding and were looking forward to the day they would become man and wife. This was the first of several engagement parties for them. Another was planned in Philly and would be given by Rico's grandparents. Megan had met them a few weeks ago, and they had welcomed her to the family. They thought it was time their only grandson decided to settle down.

He pulled her closer and dropped his arms past her waist as their bodies moved in sensual sync with the music. Rico leaned in and hummed the words to the song in her ear. There was no doubt in either of their minds that anyone seeing them could feel the heat between them…and the love.

Rico tightened his arms around her and gazed down at her. "Enjoying yourself?"

"Yes, what about you?"

He chuckled. "Yes." He glanced around. "There are a lot of people here tonight."

"And they are here to celebrate the beginning of our future." She looked over his shoulder and chuckled.

Rico lifted a brow. "What's so funny?"

"Riley. Earlier today, he and Canyon pulled straws to see who would be in charge of Blue Ridge Management's fortieth anniversary Christmas party this year, and I heard he got the short end and isn't happy about it. We have close to a thousand employees at the family's firm and making sure the holiday festivities are top-notch is important…and a lot of work. I guess he figures doing the project will somehow interfere with his playtime, if you know what I mean."

Rico laughed. "Yes, knowing Riley as I do, I have a good idea what you mean."

The music stopped, and Rico took her hand and led her out the French doors and onto the balcony. It was the first week in November, and it had already snowed twice. According to forecasters, it would be snowing again this weekend.

They had made Denver their primary home. However, they planned to make periodic trips to Philly to visit Rico's grandparents, mother and stepfather. They would make occasional trips to New York as well to check on Rico's father, who was still in rehab. Megan had met him and knew it would be a while before he recovered, but at least he was trying.

"You better have a good reason for bringing me out here," she said, shivering. "It's cold, and, as you can see, I'm not wearing much of anything."

He'd noticed. She had gorgeous legs and her dress showed them off. "I'll warm you."

He wrapped his arms around her, pulled her to him and kissed her deeply. He was right; he was warming her. Immediately, he had fired her blood. She melted a little with every stroke of his tongue, which stirred a hunger that could still astound her.

Rico slowly released her mouth and smiled down at her glistening lips. Megan was his key to happiness, and he intended to be hers. She was everything he could possibly want and then some. His goal in life was to make her happy. Always.

* * * * *

Don't miss Riley Westmoreland's story
ONE WINTER'S NIGHT
Available December 2012

Only from Harlequin Desire

REQUEST YOUR FREE BOOKS!

2 FREE NOVELS PLUS 2 FREE GIFTS!

Harlequin® *Desire*

ALWAYS POWERFUL, PASSIONATE AND PROVOCATIVE

YES! Please send me 2 FREE Harlequin Desire® novels and my 2 FREE gifts (gifts are worth about $10). After receiving them, if I don't wish to receive any more books, I can return the shipping statement marked "cancel." If I don't cancel, I will receive 6 brand-new novels every month and be billed just $4.30 per book in the U.S. or $4.99 per book in Canada. That's a saving of at least 14% off the cover price! It's quite a bargain! Shipping and handling is just 50¢ per book in the U.S. and 75¢ per book in Canada.* I understand that accepting the 2 free books and gifts places me under no obligation to buy anything. I can always return a shipment and cancel at any time. Even if I never buy another book, the two free books and gifts are mine to keep forever.

225/326 HDN FEF3

Name	(PLEASE PRINT)	
Address		Apt. #
City	State/Prov.	Zip/Postal Code

Signature (if under 18, a parent or guardian must sign)

Mail to the **Reader Service:**

IN U.S.A.: P.O. Box 1867, Buffalo, NY 14240-1867
IN CANADA: P.O. Box 609, Fort Erie, Ontario L2A 5X3

Not valid for current subscribers to Harlequin Desire books.

**Want to try two free books from another line?
Call 1-800-873-8635 or visit www.ReaderService.com.**

* Terms and prices subject to change without notice. Prices do not include applicable taxes. Sales tax applicable in N.Y. Canadian residents will be charged applicable taxes. Offer not valid in Quebec. This offer is limited to one order per household. All orders subject to credit approval. Credit or debit balances in a customer's account(s) may be offset by any other outstanding balance owed by or to the customer. Please allow 4 to 6 weeks for delivery. Offer available while quantities last.

Your Privacy—The Reader Service is committed to protecting your privacy. Our Privacy Policy is available online at www.ReaderService.com or upon request from the Reader Service.

We make a portion of our mailing list available to reputable third parties that offer products we believe may interest you. If you prefer that we not exchange your name with third parties, or if you wish to clarify or modify your communication preferences, please visit us at www.ReaderService.com/consumerschoice or write to us at Reader Service Preference Service, P.O. Box 9062, Buffalo, NY 14269. Include your complete name and address.

HDES11B

*Bestselling Harlequin® Blaze™ author Rhonda Nelson
is back with yet another irresistible Man out of Uniform.
Meet Jebb Willington—former ranger, current security
agent and all-around good guy. His assignment—to catch
a thief at an upscale retirement residence. The problem—
he's falling for sexy massage therapist Sophie O'Brien,
the woman he's trying to put behind bars....*

*Read on for a sneak peek at
THE PROFESSIONAL*

Available November 2012 only from Harlequin Blaze.

Oh, hell.

Former ranger Jeb Willingham didn't need extensive
army training to recognize the telltale sound that emerged
roughly ten feet behind him. He was Southern, after all,
and any born-and-bred Georgia boy worth his salt would
recognize the distinct metallic click of a 12-gauge shotgun.
And given the decided assuredness of the action, he knew
whoever had him in their sights was familiar with the gun
and, more important, knew how to use it.

"On your feet, hands where I can see them," she ordered.
He had to hand it to her. Sophie O'Brien was cool as a cucumber. Her voice was steady, not betraying the slightest bit
of fear. Which, irrationally, irritated him. He was a strange
man trespassing on her property—she ought to be afraid,
dammit. Why hadn't she stayed in the house and called 911
like a normal woman?

Oh, right, he thought sarcastically. Because she wasn't
a *normal* woman. She was kind and confident, fiendishly
clever and sexy as hell.

He wanted her.

And the hell of it? Aside from the conflict of interest and the tiny matter of *her name at the top of his suspect list?*

She didn't like him.

"Move," she said again, her voice firmer. "I'd rather not shoot you, but I will if you don't stand up and turn around."

Beautiful, Jeb thought, feeling extraordinarily stupid. He'd been an army ranger, one of the fiercest soldiers among Uncle Sam's finest…and he'd been bested by a massage therapist with an Annie Oakley complex.

With a sigh, he got up and flashed a grin at her. "Evening, Sophie. Your shrubs need mulching."

She gasped, betraying the first bit of surprise. It was ridiculous how much that pleased him. "You?" she breathed. "What the hell are you doing out here?"

He pasted a reassuring look on his face and gestured to the gun still aimed at his chest. "Would you mind lowering your weapon? It's a bit unnerving."

She brought the barrel down until it was aimed directly at his groin. "There," she said, a smirk in her voice. "Feel better?"

Has Jebb finally met his match? Find out in
THE PROFESSIONAL

Available November 2012
wherever Harlequin Blaze books are sold.

CHEKHOV

LADY WITH LAPDOG AND
OTHER STORIES

THE PENGUIN CLASSICS

FOUNDER EDITOR (1944–64): E. V. RIEU

Present Editors:
BETTY RADICE AND ROBERT BALDICK

ANTON PAVLOVICH CHEKHOV, the son of a former serf, was born in 1860 in Taganrog, a port on the sea of Azov. He received a classical education at the Taganrog Secondary School, then in 1879 he went to Moscow, where he entered the medical faculty of the university, graduating in 1884. During his university years he supported his family by contributing humorous stories and sketches to magazines. He published his first volume of stories, *Motley Stories*, in 1886 and a year later his second volume, *In the Twilight*, for which he was awarded the Pushkin prize by the Russian Academy. His most famous stories were written after his return from the convict island of Sakhalin, which he visited in 1890. For five years he lived on his small country estate near Moscow, but when his health began to fail he moved to the Crimea. After 1900, the rest of his life was spent at Yalta, where he met Tolstoy and Gorky. He wrote very few stories during the last years of his life, devoting most of his time to a thorough revision of his stories for a collected edition of his works, published in 1901, and to the writing of his great plays. In 1901 Chekhov married Olga Knipper, an actress of the Moscow Art Theatre. He died, of consumption, in 1904.

DAVID MAGARSHACK was born in Riga, Russia, and educated at a Russian secondary school. He came to England in 1920 and was naturalized in 1931. After graduating in English literature and language at University College, London, he worked in Fleet Street and published a number of novels. Since 1948 he has mainly been working on translations of the Russian classics. For the Penguin Classics he has also translated Dostoyevsky's *Crime and Punishment*, *The Idiot*, *The Devils*, and *The Brothers Karamazov*; *Dead Souls* by Gogol; and *Oblomov* by Goncharov. He has also written biographies of Chekhov, Dostoyevsky, Gogol, Pushkin, Turgenev and Stanislavsky, and he is the author of *Chekhov the Dramatist*, a critical study of Chekhov's plays, and a study of Stanislavsky's system of acting.

ANTON CHEKHOV

LADY WITH LAPDOG

AND OTHER STORIES

Translated with an Introduction
by David Magarshack

PENGUIN BOOKS

Penguin Books Ltd, Harmondsworth, Middlesex, England
Penguin Books Inc., 7110 Ambassador Road, Baltimore, Maryland 21207, U.S.A
Penguin Books Australia Ltd, Ringwood, Australia

—

This translation first published 1964
Reprinted 1967, 1969, 1970

—

Copyright © David Magarshack, 1964

—

Made and printed in Great Britain
by Hazell Watson & Viney Ltd
Aylesbury, Bucks
Printed in Linotype Estienne

Contents

Introduction

ANTON CHEKHOV, born at Taganrog, a port on the Sea of Azov, on 29 January 1860, began writing his short stories as a medical student in Moscow. His first story was published in a Petersburg humorous magazine in January 1880. The stories he published during the next three years in the Moscow and Petersburg humorous magazines all appeared under his pseudonym of Antosha Chekhonte. Already in those 'thoughtless and frivolous tales', as he subsequently described them, his characteristic quality of exposing the hidden motives of his characters and revealing the influence of their environment upon them was clearly discernible. His real chance as a writer came at the end of 1882, when he became a regular contributor to *Fragments*, a Petersburg weekly magazine of some literary standing, for which he wrote about 300 stories during the next three years. These stories, however, had to be very short, and it was not until Chekhov became a contributor to the big Petersburg dailies, the *Petersburg Gazette* and the *New Times*, that he was freed from the constraint of limiting his stories to a few hundred words. Gradually his stories began to appear in some of the most important monthly periodicals, and it was in these that the greatest stories of his mature period were published. The eleven stories in this volume were written between 1885 and 1899, that is during Chekhov's most productive period as a short story writer, and reading them one gets the impression of holding life itself, like a fluttering bird, in one's cupped hands.

Grief, the first story in this volume, was published in the *Petersburg Gazette* on 25 November 1885, still under Chekhov's pseudonym of Antosha Chekhonte. It immediately impressed the critics by its mixture of comedy and tragedy, a feature that was to become characteristic of Chekhov's art as a whole.

Agafya, one of the first stories to be signed by Chekhov's full

7

name, was published in the *New Times* on 15 March 1886, and so impressed the veteran novelist Dmitry Grigorovich, whose first stories, too, had dealt with the life of Russian peasants, that in an excited letter to Chekhov he hailed him as a writer of genius and warned him against frittering away his talent on writing trifles. Referring specifically to *Agafya*, Grigorovich declared that 'judging by the different qualities of your undoubted talent, your true feeling of inner analysis, your masterly descriptive passages, the way in which you give a complete picture of a cloud at sunset in a few words, etc., you are destined, I am quite sure, to become the author of many excellent and truly artistic works.' Grigorovich was even more outspoken two years later, when he again referred to *Agafya* in a letter to Chekhov: 'Only a true artist,' he wrote, 'could have written a story like *Agafya*. Its two characters are only lightly sketched and yet nothing more could have been added to make them more alive or get the figures and characters of each into sharper relief: not in a single word or movement does one feel that the story has been "made up" – everything in it is true, everything in it is just as it could have happened in real life. The same is true of the descriptive passages. ... Such a masterly way of conveying one's observations of life can be found only in Turgenev and Tolstoy.'

It was Grigorovich's letters that finally decided Chekhov to take his literary work more seriously, and subsequently to devote all his time to literature. The reference to Turgenev and Tolstoy, however, is much more pertinent than Grigorovich suspected, for both *Grief* and *Agafya* are largely derivative, *Agafya* in particular bearing a close resemblance to *Rendez-Vous*, one of Turgenev's last additions to his *Sportsman's Sketches*, though certainly treated in quite a different and much less sentimental way.

Misfortune, published in the *New Times* on 16 August 1886, is also largely derivative, showing quite clearly the influence of *Anna Karenina* (Chekhov was at the time quite obsessed with Tolstoy's great novel). But though derivative, these stories reveal an originality of mind and attitude that is largely due to the different social background in which these three great writers grew up, Turgenev and Tolstoy never really being able to shake off the influence of their aristocratic environment, while Chekhov, the son of a freed serf, was quite amazingly free from class consciousness as well as class prejudice.

It was three years later that Chekhov wrote *A Boring Story*, his first masterpiece, in which his great gifts as a creative artist and profound thinker found their fullest expression. Chekhov began writing *A Boring Story* in March 1889 and finished it at the end of September. 'Today,' he wrote to the poet Pleshcheyev on 3 September 1889, 'I have finished my story for the *Northern Herald*. ... I have never written anything like it before. The themes are quite new to me, and I am afraid that inexperience may have let me down badly.' On 14 September he informed the same correspondent that he had revised the story thoroughly. 'In my story,' he wrote, 'there are not two but fifteen different moods. Quite possibly you will think it is a lot of rubbish ... but I flatter myself with the hope that you will find two or three new characters in it who are of interest to every educated reader; you will also find two or three new situations in it. I further flatter myself with the hope that my rubbish will provoke a certain noisy reaction in the enemy camp, for in our age of telegraphs and telephones abuse is the sister of advertisement.' In a letter to another correspondent on 18 September, Chekhov wrote: 'This is not a story, it is a dissertation. It will be to the taste only of those who like heavy reading, and I should really have sent it to the *Artillery Journal*!' He sent off the story to the *Northern Herald*, a rather highbrow periodical, on 24 September. 'This letter,' he wrote to its literary editor, 'is being sent to the post together with the story, which I have given up trying to revise any more, saying to it: Get thee hence, accursed one, into the fire of boring criticism and the readers' indifference. I got tired of tinkering with it any longer. Its title is *A Boring Story (From an Old Man's Notebook)*. The most boring part of it, as you will see, consists of all sorts of arguments which, unfortunately, cannot be cut out, because my hero cannot do without them. These arguments are both fatal and necessary, like a heavy gun-carriage to a field-gun. They characterize the hero, his moods and his continuous shifting and shuffling.' Chekhov warned Alexey Suvorin, the editor of the *New Times*, with whom he was on very friendly terms at the time, not to try to identify the views of the hero of his story with his own views. 'If I present you with my professor's ideas,' he wrote, 'you must not look for Chekhov's ideas in them.'

The story, as Chekhov had expected, aroused a lively discussion in the literary journals, but little abuse. It was rightly considered the most important work Chekhov had so far produced. Six years later Chekhov used some of its themes in *The Seagull*.

The main theme of *The Grasshopper*, written in 1891 for the new periodical *North*, is the conflict between the 'two cultures' – science and art – and the misunderstandings that sometimes arise as a consequence in the private lives of people belonging to the two cultures. The story, published in January 1892 – 'a sentimental love story for family reading', as Chekhov described it, with his tongue in his cheek, to the editor of *North* – had a very unfortunate sequel, for it brought about a temporary rift between Chekhov and one of his most intimate friends, the landscape painter Isaac Levitan. It is in fact one of the very few stories which Chekhov drew direct from life, without bothering to camouflage it sufficiently. It is based on an incident in the lives of Levitan and Sophia Kuvshinnikov, the wife of a doctor. Sophia was taking painting lessons from Levitan, with whom she was having an affair, and with whom, like Olga and the painter Ryabovsky in the story, she had gone off on a Volga painting expedition. Chekhov was often present at Sophia's weekly parties, held at her flat under the watch-tower of a fire station, which – again like Olga in the story – Sophia had converted into a very arty-crafty place. Her parties were attended by artists, musicians and writers. Dr Kuvshinnikov, like Dr Dymov in the story, never put in an appearance at these parties, but at twelve o'clock he would open the dining-room door, holding a knife in one hand and a fork in the other, and solemnly announce that supper was served. Like Olga in the story, Sophia used to address her husband by his surname. Rushing up to him, she would exclaim: 'Kuvshinnikov, let me shake your honest hand!' And, addressing her friends, she would add: 'Look what an honest face he has!'

When the storm broke over his head after the publication of *The Grasshopper*, Chekhov is reported to have said: 'Why, my grasshopper is a pretty young girl, while Sophia Kuvshinnikov is neither so pretty nor so young.' It was certainly a lame excuse, but with the passage of time the incident has lost its significance. The story remains a brilliant work of art, in spite of Chekhov's perhaps too faithful reproduction of the artistic *avant-garde* circles of his day, which do not seem to have changed a great deal during the last seventy years.

Chekhov first entitled the story *Philistines*, then altered its title to *A Great Man* – which Kuvshinnikov, unlike Dymov, never was – but the new title did not satisfy him either. 'I really don't know what to do about the title of my story,' he wrote to the editor of *North* on 14 December 1891. 'I don't like *A Great Man*. Call it –' And he took for his title the first word in Krylov's fable *The Grasshopper and the Ant*, 'Poprygunya' – that is 'Jumpity-jump', the onomatopoeic adjectival noun Krylov used for the description of the grasshopper.

Ward 6 is the only major work Chekhov wrote in 1892 (he began writing it in March and finished it two months later). For some time Chekhov was a Tolstoyan, but he turned against Tolstoy's teachings at the end of 1890, after his return from Sakhalin, the Russian Devil's Island, where he had gone to study the conditions of life in the convict prisons and settlements. *Ward 6* is Chekhov's challenge to the main tenet of Tolstoy's faith – non-resistance to evil. The hero of the story, Dr Ragin, a non-resister to evil both by nature and conviction, is shown by Chekhov to be a perpetuator and in the end a victim of evil. But in spite of its main polemical theme, the story is a fully integrated work of art, none of its themes being arbitrarily imposed upon its characters, but rather flowing naturally out of them.

The story brought about Chekhov's return to the liberal camp, from which he had been alienated for a time because of his close friendship with the reactionary Suvorin. It was published in the leading liberal monthly *Russian Thought*, in which two years earlier Chekhov had been accused of being 'the high-priest of unprincipled writing', an accusation he indignantly repudiated, in a letter to its editor on 10 April 1890, as 'a libellous statement'. 'I never was,' he wrote, 'a writer without principles, or, which is the same thing, a scoundrel. I have written many stories and articles which I would gladly throw out as worthless, but I have never written a single line of which I should now be ashamed.'

A ruthlessly brilliant study of a type of predatory woman,

Ariadne was published in *Russian Thought* in December 1895. In Chekhov's notebooks the hero of *Ariadne* is described as 'an artist', but all that Chekhov preserved of his original character was his 'little round beard'. It is not without interest that Chekhov should have pleaded (through the mouth of the hero of his story) for co-education and equal rights for women as a remedy against the havoc wrought by the Ariadnes of this world. Chekhov himself visited Abbazia in the autumn of 1894 and, as can be gathered from his description of the place in *Ariadne*, he was not particularly impressed by that 'paradise on earth'.

The House with an Attic, originally entitled *My Fiancée*, was published in *Russian Thought* in April 1896. Chekhov spent the summer of 1891 on the estate of Bogimovo near the small town of Alexin and in *The House with an Attic* he described the empty mansion on that estate, with the vast drawing-room which he occupied and the wide sofa on which he slept. The avenue of fir trees, too, he found on a neighbouring estate.

In this seemingly sentimental story of a young girl's shattered love, Chekhov's main intention had been to carry on with his polemic against Tolstoy's beliefs as well as against the different palliatives with which the 'progressives' of that time sought to solve the most pressing political and economic problems. 'The people,' Chekhov makes the hero of his story declare, 'are entangled in a great chain, and you do not cut through that chain, but merely add more links to it.'

Ionych, published in 1898 in the September literary supplement of the popular weekly magazine *Neeva*, is one of the most perfect examples of Chekhov's genius for compressing a man's life within twenty odd pages. The title of the story – a familiar form of its hero's patronymic – shows the slightly contemptuous attitude of the townspeople towards the doctor for whose moral degeneration they were to a large extent responsible.

Chekhov's notebooks contain the following description of the main theme of the story:

The Philimonovs [changed to the Turkins in the story] are a talented family, so everyone says in the town. He is a civil servant, acts on the stage, does conjuring tricks, jokes ('Good morning, please'), she writes novels with a liberal flavour, talks in an affected manner: 'I'm in love with you – oh, what if my husband finds out!' She says this to everyone, in her husband's presence. The servant-boy in the entrance hall: 'Die, unhappy woman!' At first all this really strikes one as clever and amusing, in a dull and boring town. Three years later I went there for the third time, the servant-boy was already sprouting a moustache, and again: 'I'm in love with you – oh, what if my husband finds out!' And the same impersonation: 'Die, unhappy woman!' And when I left the Philimonovs, I could not help feeling that there were no more tedious and mediocre people in the whole world.

In another note Chekhov wrote:

Ionych. Got fat. When at the club in the evenings dines at the big table and when the conversation turns on the Turkins asks: 'What Turkins are you talking about? Those whose daughter plays the piano?' Has a large practice in town, but does not give up his country practice: greed has got the better of him.

According to Chekhov's sister, Chekhov gave a description of the Taganrog cemetery in *Ionych*.

The Darling, which Chekhov wrote in Yalta in the winter of 1898, was published on 3 January 1899, in the first number of the new periodical *Semya (Family)*.

The first outline of the subject matter of the story in Chekhov's notebooks already contains the characteristic traits of its silly but warmhearted heroine. 'She was the wife of an actor,' Chekhov wrote, 'she loved the theatre, seemed to have been completely absorbed in her husband's business, and everyone was surprised that it should have turned out to be so successful a marriage; but her husband died, she married a confectioner, and it seemed that she never liked anything so much as making jam and she despised the theatre, for she had become very religious in imitation of her second husband.'

The story, greatly altered in its final version, so delighted Tolstoy that he read it aloud to his friends on four consecutive nights, for curiously enough it seemed to him to confirm his own anti-feminist views. Tolstoy reprinted the story in 1906, two years after Chekhov's death, and in an afterword he wrote: 'Chekhov intended to curse, but the god of poetry commanded him to bless, and he unconsciously clothed this sweet creature in such exquisite radiance that she will always remain a model of what a woman should be in order to be happy herself.' *The Darling*, Tolstoy further argued, was so 'excellent' just because its effect was 'unintentional', for according to Tolstoy 'Chekhov wanted to cast the darling down, but instead he raised her up against his own will'. The length to which even a man of Tolstoy's attainments will go to find a justi-fication for his own preconceived ideas is truly remarkable.

Chekhov wrote *Lady with Lapdog* in Yalta between August and October 1899. It is a story of a great love arising out of a pick-up of a young married woman by a middle-aged roué. It was published in the December issue of *Russian Thought*, and (in a thoroughly revised version) in the complete edition of Chekhov's works three years later. Gorky wrote to Chekhov that after reading *Lady with Lapdog* everything he himself wrote seemed 'coarse and written not with a pen but with a log'. Gorky went on:

You are doing a great thing with your stories, arousing in people a feeling of disgust with their sleepy, half-dead existence. . . . Your stories are like ex-quisite cut-glass bottles with all the different scents of life in them, and, believe me, a sensitive nose will always find in them the delicate, pungent, and healthy scent of what is genuine and really valuable and necessary, which is to be found in every cut-glass bottle of yours.

D. M.

Grief

GRIGORY PETROV, a turner, who had long enjoyed a reputation as an excellent craftsman and at the same time as the most drunken ne'er-do-well in the whole Galchino district, was taking his wife to the rural district hospital. He had to drive about twenty miles, and yet the road was so terrible that not only a lie-abed like the turner Grigory but even the postman could not cope with it. A sharp cold wind blew straight in his face. The air was full of whirling clouds of snowflakes, and it was impossible to say whether the snow came from the sky or from the ground. Neither fields, telegraph poles, nor woods could be seen for the snow, and during a particularly strong gust of wind Grigory could not see even his shaft-bow. The feeble aged mare dragged herself along at a snail's pace. Her whole energy went into drawing her feet out of the deep snow and pulling forward with her head. The turner was in a hurry. He jumped up and down on his seat restlessly, now and again whipping the mare across her back.

'Don't cry, Matryona,' he muttered. 'Put up with it a little longer! We'll soon be at the hospital, and, God willing, you'll be all right in no time. Pavel Ivanych will give you some drops, or tell them to bleed you, or perhaps rub you down with some spirits, and I dare say it'll – it'll draw the pain from your side. He'll shout a bit, stamp his feet maybe, but he'll do his best for you, I'm sure he will. A nice gentleman he is, very obliging, bless him. Soon as we're there, he'll come running out of his room and start cursing. "What's all this?" he'll shout. "How did it happen? Why didn't you come earlier? Am I a dog, to be looking after you all day, damn you? Why didn't you come in the morning? Get out! I don't want to see you. Come tomorrow." But I'll say to him, "Your honour, sir. Pavel Ivanych, sir." . . . Keep going, can't you?' he shouted to the mare. 'Gee up, the devil take you!'

The turner Grigory kept whipping up his horse and went on muttering under his breath, without looking at his wife.

' "Your honour, sir. I'm telling you the truth, sir. God's my witness. Take my oath on the cross, I will. Left at the break of day, I did, sir. But how could I get here in time, sir, if God – the Holy Virgin – got angry and sent a blizzard like this? You can see for yourself, sir. Even a good horse wouldn't be able to make it, but that mare of mine – why, look at her, sir. It's not a horse – it's a disgrace!" Well, Pavel Ivanych frowns and then shouts: "I know you! You always find an excuse! Especially you, Grigory. I've known you for some time, haven't I? I expect you must have stopped at five pubs on the way." But I says to him: "Your honour, sir, what do you take me for? A heartless villain or a heathen? My old woman's giving up the ghost, she's dying, she is, and me run to pubs? Really, sir! May they all sink to the bottom of the sea, the pubs I mean, sir!" Then Pavel Ivanych will tell them to carry you to the hospital, and I'll bow down to him and say: "Pavel Ivanych, sir, we thank you humbly, sir. Forgive us, sir, fools and great sinners that we are. Don't be hard on us, ignorant peasants. You should have kicked us out, but instead you took the trouble to come out and get your feet covered with snow!" Well, Pavel Ivanych will look as if he was going to hit me, and say: "Instead of throwing yourself at my feet, you'd better stop swilling vodka and have pity on your old woman! You ought to be horsewhipped!" "Aye," I'll say, "quite right, sir. I ought to be whipped. May God strike me dead if I oughtn't to be whipped! But how can we help falling at your feet, sir, seeing as how you're our benefactor, our father, in a manner of speaking. Now, sir, I give you my word – God's my witness – spit in my eyes if I go back on it – as soon as my Matryona's well again, the moment she can stand on her feet again, I'll do everything you tell me! I'll do everything for your honour. A cigarette case, if you like, of Karelian birch. Croquet balls. Skittles. As good as any you can get from foreign parts. I'll do anything for you, sir. Anything you like, and I won't take a kopek from you. In Moscow they'd charge you four roubles for a cigarette case like that, but I won't charge you one kopek for it." The doctor will laugh and say: "All right, all right. Much obliged to you. Pity you're such a drunkard, though!" Well, old woman, you see I know how to talk to the gentry! There's not a gentleman in the world I couldn't talk to. Only God grant I don't lose the way. What a snowstorm! Can't see a thing for the snow!'

The turner went on muttering endlessly. He let his tongue run on mechanically, so as to stifle as much as possible the feeling of heaviness in his heart. There were many more words he could use, but there were even more thoughts and questions in his head. Grief had taken the turner unawares, like a bolt from the blue, and he was still unable to recover from the blow, he was still unable to come to his senses, to think clearly. He had till now lived a carefree life, in a kind of drunken stupor, knowing neither grief nor joy, and all of a sudden there was that terrible pain in his heart. The lighthearted tippler and idler found himself for no rhyme or reason in the position of a man who was busy and worried, a man in a hurry, struggling against nature herself.

Grigory remembered that his grief had started the night before. When he had come home in the evening, drunk as usual, and from old habit had begun to swear and brandish his fists, his wife had looked at her bully of a husband as she had never looked before. Usually the expression of her old eyes was martyred and meek, like that of a dog who is beaten a lot and given little to eat, but now she gazed sternly and fixedly at him, as saints do from icons, or dying people. It was this strange disturbing look in those eyes that had made him conscious of his feeling of grief. The bewildered turner had got a neighbour to lend him his horse, and he was now taking his wife to the hospital, in the hope that with his powders and ointments Pavel Ivanych would restore the old look in her eyes.

'Now, mind, Matryona,' he muttered, 'if Pavel Ivanych asks you if I beat you, say: "Never, sir!" And I promise not to beat you again. By the holy cross I won't! Besides, I've never beaten you from spite, have I now? I beat you because I felt like it, for no reason at all. I'm sorry for you — see? Another man wouldn't care a damn, but I'm taking you to the hospital. Doing my best. Lord, what a blizzard! Thy will be done, O Lord, only don't make me lose my way. Well, Matryona? Still got the pain in your side? Why don't you speak? I'm asking you: have you still got the pain in your side?'

It seemed strange to him that the snow did not melt on the old woman's face, strange that her face itself should have lengthened so oddly and become such a pale-greyish colour, the colour of grimy wax, and that it should look so stern, so grave.

'What a fool!' Grigory muttered. 'I ask you in good faith, before God, and you – well, I mean . . . Aye, you're a fool, that's what you are. I don't think I'll take you to Pavel Ivanych after all.'

The turner let fall the reins and sank into thought. He could not bring himself to look round at the old woman: he was terrified. But to ask her a question and not receive an answer was also terrifying. At last, to put an end to the suspense, he felt her cold hand without turning round to look at her. The raised hand fell back like a stone.

'Dead! Trouble! . . .'

And the turner wept. He was not so much sorry as vexed. His grief had only begun, and now it was all over. He had not really begun to live with his old woman, to open up his heart to her, to feel sorry for her, and now she was dead. He had lived forty years with her, but then those forty years had passed as though in a fog. What with drinking, fighting, and poverty he had not noticed how life had passed. And, as though to spite him, his old woman had died just when he was beginning to feel that he was sorry for her, that he could not live without her, that he had wronged her terribly.

'Why,' he recalled, 'she used to go begging. I sent her out to beg for bread myself, I did. Trouble! She should have lived another ten years, the silly woman, and now, I shouldn't wonder, she thinks I really am like that. Holy Mother, where am I going? It's burying she needs now, not medicines! Come on, turn round!'

Grigory turned back and whipped up his mare again. The road was getting worse and worse every hour. Now he could not see even the shaft-bow. Every now and then his sledge ran up against a young fir tree, some dark object scratched the turner's hand and flashed by his field of vision, and once more everything became a white whirling mass of snow.

'If only one could start life over again. . . .' thought Grigory.

Forty years ago, he remembered, Matryona had been young, beautiful, gay. She had come from a well-to-do family. They had married her to him because they had been impressed by the fact that he was a good craftsman. Everything pointed to a happy life, but the trouble was that, having flung himself dead drunk on the stove after the wedding, he had not seemed able to wake up properly. He could remember the wedding, but what happened after it he could not for the life of him remember, except perhaps that he had been drinking, lying about, and fighting. So forty years had been wasted.

The white clouds of snow began gradually to turn grey. Dusk was falling.

'Where am I going?' Grigory asked himself with a start. 'I have to make arrangements for her funeral, and I keep driving towards the hospital. I must be going mad.'

Grigory turned back again and once more he whipped up the horse. Mustering all her strength, the mare snorted and went off at a trot. The turner kept lashing across her back again and again. He could hear something banging away behind him and he knew without turning round that it was his dead wife's head banging against the side of the sledge. It was growing darker and darker, and the wind became colder and sharper. . . .

'Live my life all over again,' thought the turner. 'Get a new lathe and get new orders. I'd give the money to the old woman, I would!'

After a while he let go of the reins. He tried to find them, to pick them up, but he could not do so: his hands refused to move.

'Never mind,' he thought. 'The mare will go by herself. She knows the way. Better have a good sleep now. Just lie down till it's time for the funeral, the service.'

Grigory closed his eyes and dozed off. A little later he heard the horse stopping. He opened his eyes and saw something dark in front of him, something that looked like a cottage or a haystack.

He knew he ought to get out of the sledge, but his whole body felt so numb that he could not have stirred even if he were to freeze to death. And so he fell asleep peacefully.

He woke up in a large room with painted walls. Bright sunshine was streaming through the windows. Grigory could see people in the room, and his first impulse was to appear a staid, sensible man.

'Must order a funeral service for my wife,' he said. 'Tell the priest. . . .'

'All right, all right,' a voice interrupted him. 'Keep still there.'

'Why,' Grigory exclaimed in surprise, as he caught sight of the doctor, 'it's you, sir. Your honour, sir. My benefactor.'

He wanted to get up and go down on his knees to the doctor, but felt that his arms and legs refused to obey him.

'What's the matter with my legs, sir? My arms?'

'You can say good-bye to your arms and legs. You got them frozen. There, there. . . . What are you crying for? You've had your life, haven't you? You must be sixty if a day — isn't that enough for you?'

'What a thing to happen to a man, sir. What a grievous thing! I'm sorry, sir, but I wish I could live for another five or six years, sir. . . .'

'Whatever for?'

'Why, sir, the horse — the horse isn't mine. I've got to return it. And I've got to bury the old woman, too. And, sir, how quickly things happen in this world! Your honour, sir, Pavel Ivanych, a cigarette case of the best Karelian birch! Make you a croquet set, I will, sir. . . .'

The doctor waved his hand and went out of the ward. Good-bye to the turner!

Agafya

DURING my stay in the S— district, I often used to visit Savva Stukach, or simply Savka, at the Dubrovsk allotments. These allotments were my favourite spot for so-called 'general' fishing, when, on leaving home, you don't know on what day or at what hour you will be back, and you take all the fishing tackle you can lay your hands on, as well as enough food to last you for days. As a matter of fact, it was not so much the fishing that interested me as roaming carefree about the countryside, eating at any time I pleased, chatting to Savka, and having prolonged communion with the quiet summer nights. Savka was a fellow of about twenty-five; he was tall, handsome, and as strong as a horse. He had a reputation as a sensible and intelligent fellow, he knew how to read and write, he drank little, but as a workman this powerful young man was not worth a brass farthing. The great strength of his muscles, firm as ropes, was vitiated by persistent and invincible laziness. He lived, as did everyone else in the village, in his own cottage, had his own plot of land, but neither ploughed nor sowed nor engaged in any craft or trade. His old mother lived by begging, but he himself lived like a bird : he did not know in the morning what he was going to eat at noon. Not that he lacked will-power or energy, or that he was not sorry for his mother, but he simply felt no desire to work and was not conscious of any need for it. There was an air of serene, innate, almost artistic passion for living about his whole figure. He seemed to be without a care in the world, and took things as they came. When, however, Savka's young, healthy body was physiologically driven to do some muscular work, he engaged for a time in some freely undertaken but quite absurd occupation, such as turning some useless pegs or running races with the village women. His favourite position was that of concentrated immobility. He was able to stand in one place for hours without moving, his eyes fixed on one and the same point. He was precipitated into activity when the spirit moved him, and then too only if it was a matter of making a quick, abrupt movement, such as catching a dog by the tail, tearing a kerchief off a woman's head, or jumping across a wide crack in the ground. It goes without saying that, being too loath to budge, Savka had not a shirt to his back and lived worse than any tramp. In the course of time he owed a considerable sum of money for the rent of his plot of land and, since he was young and strong, the village council decided to make him repay his debt by doing a job usually offered to an old man, namely that of the watchman and scarecrow on the publicly owned allotments. Villagers kept pulling his leg about his premature old age, but it made no impression on him. The watchman's hut, situated in a quiet spot, was ideal for motionless contemplation and was just what he wanted.

I happened to be visiting Savka one beautiful evening in May. I remember lying on a torn threadbare rug near the hut, from which came a strong and fragrant smell of dried herbs. My hands under my head, I looked straight ahead of me. At my feet lay a wooden pitchfork, beyond it I could just make out as a black spot Savka's dog Kutka, and no more than five yards from me the ground fell abruptly away into the steep bank of a stream. All I could see were the tops of some willow bushes, which grew in a thick clump on this side of the stream, and the winding edge of the opposite bank, looking as if it were gnawed round by some animal. Far away, beyond the bank, on top of a hillock, the cottages of the village where Savka lived huddled together like a frightened covey of young partridges. Beyond the hill the sun was setting. All that was left of the sunset was a pale crimson shaft of light, and even that was beginning to be overspread with flecks of cloud, as burning coal might be with ashes.

To the right of the allotments, a spinney of alder trees was just visible as a black patch against the sky, the trees whispering softly and swaying with every gust of wind; to the left, the fields stretched as far as the eye could see. Far away, where the eye could no longer distinguish the fields from the sky, a light glimmered brightly. At a little distance from me Savka was sitting cross-legged Turkish fashion, his head drooping, and gazing pensively at Kutka. Our hooks, baited with small fishes, had been placed in the stream long ago, and there was nothing left for us to do but enjoy our rest, which Savka, who never got tired and always rested, liked so much. There was still a faint glimmer of the sunset left in the sky, but the summer night was already encompassing nature with its tender, sleep-inducing caress.

Everything sank into its first, deep sleep, and only some night-bird I did not recognize languidly gave voice to a long drawn-out articulated cry which sounded like: 'You seen Ni-ki-ta?' and at once replied: 'Seen! Seen! Seen!'

'Why doesn't the nightingale sing now?' I asked Savka.

Savka turned slowly towards me. His features were large, but they were clean, expressive, and soft as a woman's. Then he glanced with his gentle, pensive eyes at the spinney and the willow bushes, and, slowly pulling his pipe from his pocket, put it into his mouth and uttered the call of a hen nightingale. At once, as though in response to his piping, a corncrake gave its distinctive cry.

'There you have your nightingale,' Savka said with a contemptuous laugh. 'Jerk – jerk – jerk. Just as if it was jerking on a hook. And I expect he too thinks he can sing.'

'I like that bird,' I said. 'Do you know that when migrating corncrakes do not fly, but run along the ground? They only fly over rivers and seas. Otherwise, they travel on foot all the time.'

'Fancy that, the dirty dogs!' Savka muttered, throwing a respectful glance in the direction of the crying corncrake.

Knowing what a good listener Savka was, I told him everything I had gleaned from books about the habits of the corncrake, and from the corncrake I imperceptibly went over to the subject of bird migration. Savka listened attentively to me without blinking an eye, all the time smiling with pleasure.

'And which place do the birds like best?' he asked. 'Ours or the other one?'

'Ours, of course. The bird, you see, is born here and hatches out the chicks here, so that this is its native land. It only flies away because it doesn't want to freeze to death.'

'Interesting!' Savka drawled. 'Everything you learn is interesting. The bird, now. Or man. Or take this pebble, for instance. There's a lot of cleverness in everything. Now, if I'd known you'd

23

be coming, sir, I'd never have asked that woman to come. . . . She bothered me to come so much. One of 'em did, sir.'

'Don't worry,' I said, 'I won't be in your way. I could go and lie down in the spinney.'

'Good Lord, no, sir. She'd still be alive if she came tomorrow. Now, if only she'd be willing to sit here quiet like, sir, and listen to us talking! But she'd only be gawking like a fool. You can't talk sensibly when she's here.'

'Is it Darya you're expecting?' I asked, after a pause.

'No, sir. It's a new one. Very keen to come, she is, sir. I mean, Agafya, sir, the signalman's wife.'

Savka said it in his usual dispassionate and somewhat husky voice, as though he was talking about tobacco or porridge, but I started with surprise. I knew Agafya. She was quite a young peasant girl of about nineteen or twenty, who had married a railway signalman, a fine young fellow, only about a year before. She lived in the village, and her husband came home from the railway every night.

'You'll come to a bad end because of these affairs of yours with the village women,' I said with a sigh.

'I don't care,' Savka said. But after a moment's reflection he added: 'I've told them, sir, but they won't listen. They don't seem to care a hang, the silly fools.'

Neither of us spoke. In the meantime it was getting darker, and objects began losing their contours. The shaft of light beyond the hill had long disappeared, and the stars were becoming brighter and more luminous. The monotonous, melancholy churring of the crickets, the craking of the landrail, and the calls of the quail did not interfere with the stillness of the night but seemed to lend an even greater monotony to it. One got the impression that it was not the birds and insects whose restful sounds charmed the ear, but the stars that gazed down upon us from the sky.

Savka was the first to break the silence. He slowly turned his gaze from his black dog to me and said:

'I can see you are bored, sir. Let's have supper.'

And without waiting for my consent, he crawled on his stomach into the hut, fumbled about there, making the hut sway as though it were a leaf, then crawled back and placed before me my bottle of vodka and an earthenware bowl. In the bowl were hard-boiled eggs, flat rye cakes fried in lard, pieces of black bread, and a few more things. We each drank from a lopsided little glass and began eating. Coarse grey salt, dirty greasy cakes, rubbery hard-boiled eggs; yet how tasty it all was!

'You live like a tramp, but look at all these lovely things you've got,' I said, pointing to the bowl. 'Where do you get them all from?'

'The women bring it,' Savka growled.

'What do they bring it for?'

'Oh, I dunno. Take pity on me, I suppose.'

But it was not only the food. Savka's clothes too bore traces of women's 'pity'. That evening I noticed that he was wearing a new belt of worsted yarn and a bright crimson ribbon on which a little copper cross was suspended from his dirty neck. I knew of the fair sex's weakness for Savka, and knowing also how reluctant he was to talk about it, I did not question him any more. Besides, there was no time to carry on a conversation. Kutka, who had been hanging about near us waiting patiently for some scraps to be thrown to her, suddenly pricked up her ears and began to growl. A moment later we heard a distant intermittent splashing of water. 'Someone's wading across the ford,' said Savka. Three minutes later Kutka growled again and emitted a bark which sounded like a cough.

'Shut up!' her master shouted at her.

There was a hollow sound of timid footsteps in the dark, and from the spinney emerged the silhouette of a woman. I recognized her at once, in spite of the darkness – it was Agafya, the signalman's wife. She walked up to me hesitantly and stopped dead, panting. She was breathless not so much from walking as from fear and the unpleasant feeling experienced by most people at having to ford a stream at night. Catching sight of two men by the hut instead of one, she uttered a faint cry and recoiled a step.

'Oh, it's you!' said Savka, stuffing a flat cake into his mouth.

'Yes, it's me,' she murmured, letting fall a small bundle on to the ground. 'Yakov sends his regards and asked me to – er – give you this here . . .'

'What a story – Yakov!' Savka said, derisively. 'You needn't tell your lies here. The gentleman knows what you've come for. Sit down. Help yourself.'

Agafya cast a sidelong glance at me and sat down irresolutely.

'I was beginning to think you wasn't coming tonight,' said Savka after a long pause. 'What are you sitting there like that for? Come on, have a bite of something! Or would you like a drink of vodka?'

'Hark at him!' said Agafya. 'You'd think I was a drunkard.'

'You'd better have a drop all the same. It'll warm you, it will. Come on!'

Savka offered Agafya the lopsided glass. Agafya drank the vodka slowly, refused the offer of a flat cake, but just exhaled noisily.

'You've brought me something, I see,' Savka went on, untying the bundle and imparting a condescendingly jocular inflexion to his voice. 'A woman always brings you something. Can't do nothing without it. Oh, a few spuds and a pie. . . . They live well, they do,' he said with a sigh, turning to me. 'They're the only people in the whole village who have some spuds left over from the winter.'

It was too dark for me to see Agafya's face, but from the movement of her head and shoulders it seemed to me that she never took her eyes off Savka's face. Deciding that in the circumstances three was a crowd, I got up to go for a walk. But at that moment a nightingale in the spinney uttered two low contralto notes. Half a minute later it let out a succession of quick high notes, and, having tested its voice, burst into song. Savka leapt to his feet and began to listen.

'It's last night's,' he said. 'You wait!'

Then he darted off noiselessly to the spinney.

'What do you want that nightingale for?' I shouted after him. 'Wait!'

Savka waved his hand at me as if warning me against raising my voice and disappeared in the dark. When he wanted to, Savka could be an excellent hunter and fisherman, but there too his talents were wasted, just as his great strength was wasted. He was too lazy to follow the rules of the game, and his passion as a hunter was frittered away on mere tricks. So, for instance, he insisted on catching nightingales with his bare hands, or shooting pike with a shotgun, or standing for hours on the bank of a stream to catch a small fish on a large hook.

Left alone with me, Agafya cleared her throat and passed her hand a few times across her forehead. . . . She was beginning to feel a little tipsy.

'How are things with you, Agafya?' I asked after a long pause, when the silence was beginning to be a little embarrassing.

'Not so bad, thank you, sir. Please don't say a word to anyone, sir!' she added suddenly in a whisper.

'Don't worry, I won't,' I calmed her. 'But I must say, Agafya, you are taking a risk, aren't you? What if Yakov should find out?'

'He won't find out, sir.'

'But what if he should?'

'He won't, sir. I'll be home before him. He's in his signal box now. He won't be coming back till he's seen the goods train through, and I can hear the train coming from here.'

Agafya passed her hand across her forehead again and looked in the direction where Savka had gone. The nightingale was singing. Some nocturnal bird flew low over the ground and, noticing us, started, flapped its wings, and flew off towards the other side of the stream.

Soon the nightingale fell silent, but Savka was not coming back. Agafya got up, took a few unsteady steps, and sat down again.

'What's he thinking of?' she said, unable to restrain herself. 'The train isn't running tomorrow. I'll have to go back any minute now.'

'Savka!' I shouted. 'Savka!'

Not even an echo answered me. Agafya stirred uneasily and got up again.

'I must go now, sir,' she said in an agitated voice. 'The train will be here any minute now. I know when the trains are due.'

The poor girl was not mistaken. Within a quarter of an hour we heard the distant rumble of a train.

Agafya fixed her eyes on the spinney and began moving her hands impatiently.

'Well, where is he?' she said, laughing nervously. 'Where the devil can he have disappeared to? I'm going. I'm not going to wait another minute for him, sir.'

Meanwhile the noise of the train was getting more and more distinct. One could already distinguish the rumble of the wheels from the puffing of the engine. A moment later came the whistle, the train rushed with a hollow rumbling sound across the bridge, and – a minute later everything was still again.

'I'll wait another minute,' Agafya said with a sigh, sitting down determinedly. 'So be it. I'll wait.'

At last Savka appeared out of the darkness. He walked noiselessly on his bare feet on the freshly dug earth of the allotments, humming softly to himself.

'What horrible bad luck, sir!' he said, laughing gaily. 'As soon as I comes up to that bush, sir, and starts aiming with my hand, the perisher stops singing! The dirty dog! There I was, sir, waiting, waiting for him to start singing again, but I had to give it up in the end. . . .'

Savka sank clumsily on to the ground near Agafya and grabbed her round the waist with both hands to prevent himself from losing his balance.

'What are you looking so cross for?' he asked.

Soft-hearted and good-natured though he was, Savka despised women. He treated them with a singular lack of consideration, with an air of superiority, and even went so far as to laugh contemptuously at their falling in love with him. Who knows, perhaps this negligent and contemptuous treatment was one of the reasons why the village Dulcineas found him so extremely and irresistibly attractive. He was tall and handsome, and there was an expression of gentle tenderness in his eyes, even when he looked at the women he so despised, but this fascination could hardly be explained by these external qualities alone. Apart from his handsome looks and his peculiar manners, what influenced women was probably also Savka's pathetic role of a generally recognized failure and an unhappy exile from his own cottage and plot of land.

'Why don't you tell the gentleman what you came here for?' Savka went on, his arm still round Agafya's waist. 'Come on, tell him, married woman! Ha, ha! What do you think, Agafya? Shall we have another drop of vodka?'

I got up and, making my way between the ridges of earth, walked along the edge of the allotments. The dark beds looked like flattened graves. From them came the smell of dug-up earth and the tender humidity of the plants, which were beginning to be covered with dew. On the left a faint light could still be seen in the distance. It was twinkling genially and seemed to be smiling.

I heard a happy laugh. It was Agafya.

'And the train?' I thought. 'The train went past long ago.'

After a little while I went back to the hut. Savka was sitting motionless, his legs crossed Turkish fashion, humming quietly, almost inaudibly, a song which seemed to consist only of monosyllables. Agafya, intoxicated with the vodka, Savka's contemptuous caresses, and the closeness of the night, lay on the ground beside him, her face pressed to his knee. She was so absorbed in her sensations that she did not notice my arrival.

'Agafya,' I said, 'the train went long ago.'

'It's time you were going,' Savka said, understanding what I meant, and shook his head. 'What are you sprawling here for? Shameless hussy, you!'

Agafya gave a start and got up on one knee. She was suffering. For half a minute, as far as I could make out in the dark, her whole figure expressed struggle and hesitation. There was a moment when she seemed to come to, draw herself up, and be about to get up, but a kind of invincible and implacable force held her down, and she clung to Savka.

'To hell with him!' she cried with a wild deep-sounding laugh, and in that laugh there was reckless determination, weakness, and pain.

I walked slowly to the spinney and from there descended to the stream where we had placed our fishing tackle. The stream was asleep. A soft double-petalled flower on a tall stalk touched my cheeks tenderly, like a child who wants to let you know that it is not asleep. Having nothing to do I felt one line and pulled at it. It resisted feebly and then hung in the air – there was nothing on it. I could not see the opposite bank, or the village. In one cottage a light appeared for a few moments and then went out. I felt with my hands along the bank, found the hollow I had discovered during the day, and sat down in it as in an armchair. I sat there a long time. I saw the stars grow misty and lose their radiance, I felt a chill breeze pass over the earth like a light sigh, setting the awakening willow-leaves astir.

'Aga–a–fya!' I heard someone's hollow voice calling in the village. 'Agafya!'

It was Agafya's worried husband who had returned home and was looking for his wife all over the village. At the same time I could hear the sound of unrestrained laughter from the direction of the allotments. The signalman's wife had forgotten all about her husband, so intoxicated was she with her few hours of happiness which had to make up for the torment that was awaiting her next day.

When I woke up, Savka was sitting beside me and shaking me lightly by the shoulder. The stream, the spinney, the two banks, the green washed trees and fields – all were bathed in bright morning light. Through the thin tree-trunks the rays of the risen sun beat upon my back.

'So that's how you catch your fish, sir?' Savka said with an ironical smile. 'Get up, sir!'

I got up, stretched myself voluptuously, and my awakened breast eagerly began to inhale the moist fragrant air.

'Has Agafya gone?' I asked.

'There she is!' Savka said, pointing in the direction of the ford.

I looked up and saw Agafya. Lifting her dress, she was crossing the stream, dishevelled, with her kerchief slipped from her head. She could scarcely drag her feet.

'The cat knows whose meat she's eaten,' said Savka, screwing up his eyes as he looked at her. 'There she goes, sir, with her tail between her legs. Women, sir, are as lecherous as cats and as frightened as hares! Wouldn't go last night as you told her. Now she's going to get it good and proper, and I expect, sir, they'll give me a flogging too, in the district court, for meddling with married women. . . .'

Agafya got out on to the bank and walked across the fields towards the village. At first she walked bravely enough, but soon fear and agitation began to tell: she turned round, looking scared, and stopped to take breath.

'Aye, she has reason to be afraid, sir,' Savka declared with a mournful laugh, as he looked at the bright green strip of grass left by Agafya. 'She doesn't want to go! Her husband, I shouldn't be surprised, sir, has been waiting for her for hours. Can you see him, sir?'

Savka uttered the last words with a smile, but I felt my heart sinking. At the far end of the village stood Yakov, looking straight at his wife, who was returning to him. He did not stir. He was motionless as a post. What was he thinking, as he looked at her? What words had he prepared to greet her with? Agafya remained standing still for a short time, looked round again as though expecting help from us, and walked on. Never before have I seen anyone, drunk or sober, walking like that. Agafya seemed to be thrown into convulsions by her husband's looks. She was zig-zagging across the field, stopping dead, marking time, her legs giving way under her and her arms floundering about helplessly, or walking backwards. After walking a hundred paces, she looked back again and sat down on the ground.

'You'd better hide behind a bush,' I told Savka, 'or her husband will see you.'

'He knows who his Agafya's coming from as it is. Women don't go to the allotments at night to fetch a cabbage — everyone knows that, sir.'

I looked at Savka's face. It was pale and contorted with distaste and pity, as happens with people who watch animals being tortured.

'The cat laughs, the mouse weeps,' he said, with a sigh.

Agafya suddenly jumped up, tossed her head, and walked boldly towards her husband. She had obviously plucked up courage and made up her mind to face the music.

Misfortune

Sophia Petrovna, wife of the notary Lubyantsev, a beautiful young woman of about twenty-five, was walking slowly along a lane cut through a forest with her next-door neighbour, the lawyer Ilyin. It was past four o'clock in the afternoon. Fluffy white clouds gathered over the lane; here and there from beneath them peeped out bright blue patches of sky. The clouds were quite motionless, as though caught on the tops of the tall old fir trees. It was still and close.

In the distance the lane was cut across by a low railway embankment, on which a sentry was for some reason marching up and down. Just behind the embankment was a white church with six domes and a rusty roof.

'I didn't expect to meet you here,' said Mrs Lubyantsev, looking down and touching last year's leaves with the tip of her parasol. 'But now I'm glad I've met you. I must have a serious and final talk with you. Please, Mr Ilyin, if you really love and respect me, do stop pursuing me! You follow me about like a shadow, you always look at me in a way that isn't nice. You keep saying you love me, you write absurd letters, and . . . and I don't know how long you intend to go on like this. I mean, heaven only knows what the end of it will be!'

Ilyin was silent. Mrs Lubyantsev walked on a few steps, and went on.

'And this violent change has taken place in two or three weeks, after we'd known each other for five years. I'm surprised at you, sir!'

Mrs Lubyantsev threw a sidelong glance at her companion. He had screwed up his eyes and was staring intently at the fluffy clouds. The expression on his face was angry, sullen, and distracted, like that of a man who suffers but at the same time has to listen to a lot of nonsense.

'I'm surprised you can't see it yourself,' Mrs Lubyantsev went on, shrugging her shoulders. 'Don't you realize that the game you're playing isn't very nice? I'm a married woman and I love and respect my husband. I have a daughter. Doesn't that mean anything to you? Besides, as an old friend you know perfectly well my views on family life, on . . . on the family as the stable element of social life in general . . .'

Ilyin cleared his throat with annoyance and sighed.

'The family as the stable element,' he murmured. 'Good Lord!'

'Yes! I love my husband, I respect him. And anyway the peace of my family life is dear to me. I'd let myself be murdered rather than be the cause of Andrey's unhappiness or his daughter's. So for goodness sake leave me alone! Let's be dear good friends as before, and please give up these sighs and moans, which don't suit you. It's settled and done with once and for all. Not another word about it! Let's talk of something else.'

Mrs Lubyantsev cast another sidelong glance at Ilyin's face. Ilyin was staring at the sky. He was pale and was angrily biting his trembling lips. Mrs Lubyantsev could not understand why he was angry and what had made him so indignant, but his pallor moved her.

'Don't be angry,' she said affectionately. 'Let's be friends. Agreed? Here's my hand.'

Ilyin took her small plump hand in both his hands and raised it slowly to his lips.

'I'm not a schoolboy,' he muttered. 'I'm not in the least attracted by the idea of friendship with the woman I love.'

'Not another word. It's settled and done with. We've walked as far as the seat. Let's sit down.'

A sweet sensation of peace filled Mrs Lubyantsev's breast: the most difficult and delicate thing had been said, the painful question had been settled and done with. Now she could heave a sigh of relief and look Ilyin straight in the face. She looked at him, and a woman's egoistical feeling of superiority over the man who is in love with her excited her pleasantly. It flattered her that this huge strong man, with his manly angry face, with his big black beard, such an intelligent and highly educated man too, who was said to be very talented, should be sitting obediently beside her hanging his head. For two or three minutes neither of them spoke.

'Nothing has been settled and nothing is done with,' Ilyin began. 'You seem to be reciting copybook maxims to me. "I love and respect my husband. . . . The family as a stable element. . . ." I know all that myself, and I can tell you more. I admit quite honestly and sincerely that I consider my conduct criminal and immoral. Anything else? But why say what's already known? Fine words butter no parsnips, they say. You'd better tell me what I ought to do.'

'I've told you already. Go away!'

'I did go – you know that quite well. Five times I've gone and half-way there come back again! I can show you the through tickets. I've kept them all. I haven't the power to run away from you. I try hard. I try terribly hard, but what the hell is the use? I can't do anything if I haven't the stamina, if I'm weak and faint-hearted. I can't fight nature. Don't you understand? I can't! I run away from her, but she holds me back by my coat-tails. Vulgar odious weakness!'

Ilyin blushed, got up, and began striding up and down near the seat.

'It makes me wild!' he muttered, clenching his fists. 'I hate and despise myself! Good Lord, running after another man's wife like some debauched boy, writing idiotic letters, humiliating myself – horrible!'

Ilyin clutched his head, grunted, and sat down.

'And there's your insincerity, too!' he went on bitterly. 'If you are so opposed to my playing a not very nice game, then why have you come here? What brought you here? In my letters I only ask you for a categorical straightforward reply – yes or no. And instead of giving me a straightforward reply, you contrive to meet me every day "by accident", and regale me with quotations of copybook maxims!'

Mrs Lubyantsev flushed and got frightened. All at once she felt the sort of discomfiture decent women feel at suddenly being discovered naked.

'You seem to suspect me too of playing a game,' she murmured.

'I've always given you a straight answer and – and I ask you for one today too.'

'Oh, but does one *ask* for it in a situation like this? If you'd told me at once to go away I'd have been gone long ago! But you didn't say that to me, did you? You've never given me a straight answer. Strange indecision! The fact is, either you're playing with me, or –'

Ilyin did not finish and propped up his head on his fists. Mrs Lubyantsev tried to recall how she had behaved from first to last. She remembered that all the time she had been against Ilyin's attentions, not only in deed but even in her innermost thoughts. At the same time, though, she could not help feeling that there was a grain of truth in the lawyer's words. Not knowing what kind of truth it was, she could not find – hard as she tried – what to say to Ilyin in answer to his complaint. But as it was rather awkward to keep silent, she said, shrugging her shoulders:

'So it is I who am to blame, is it?'

'I don't blame you for your insincerity,' said Ilyin with a sigh. 'I'm sorry, it just slipped out. Your insincerity's quite natural. It's the sort of thing one expects. If people were all to come to an agreement and suddenly become sincere, everything would go to rack and ruin.'

Mrs Lubyantsev was not in a mood to engage in philosophical discussions, but she was glad of the chance of changing the subject.

'Why should it?' she asked.

'Because only savages and animals are sincere. Once civilization has introduced into life the need for such a luxury as woman's virtue, for instance, then sincerity's quite out of place.'

Ilyin poked his stick angrily into the sand. Mrs Lubyantsev listened to him without understanding much of what he was saying, but she liked his conversation. To begin with, she was pleased that a gifted man should speak about 'intellectual' things to an ordinary woman like her; then it gave her great pleasure to watch how this pale, animated, and still angry young face was working. She may not have understood much, but the sublime courage of modern man, who solves great problems and draws final conclusions without reflection or hesitation, was quite apparent to her.

She suddenly caught herself looking at him with admiration, and was frightened.

'I'm sorry,' she hastened to say, 'but I don't quite understand why you spoke of insincerity. Let me repeat my request: be a good kind friend and leave me in peace! I ask you sincerely.'

'All right, I'll try to fight it a little longer,' Ilyin said with a sigh. 'I'll do my best. Only I don't think anything will come of it. I'll either blow my brains out or — or start drinking in a most idiotic way. I'll have to pay for it whatever happens. Everything has its limit, a struggle with nature too. Tell me, how is one to fight against insanity? If you've been drinking, how are you to overcome your excitement? What can I do if your image has grown into my mind and stands constantly before my eyes, day and night, like that fir tree there? Come, tell me what great exploit I must accomplish to rid myself of this vile and unhappy state, when all my thoughts, desires and dreams do not belong to me but to some kind of demon who has got possession of me? I love you! I love you so much that I've gone off the rails, thrown up my work, given up my friends, forgotten my God. Never in my life have I been so much in love!'

Mrs Lubyantsev, who had not expected such a turn in the conversation, drew back from Ilyin and looked at his face in alarm. Tears started in his eyes, his lips trembled, and a sort of hungry, imploring expression spread over his face.

'I love you!' he murmured, bringing his eyes near her big, frightened eyes. 'You're so beautiful! I could sit here all my life, suffering and looking into your eyes. But — don't say anything, I beseech you!'

Mrs Lubyantsev, as though taken by surprise, began quickly, quickly to think of what to say to stop Ilyin. 'I shall go away,' she decided; but before she could make a move to get up, Ilyin was on his knees at her feet. . . . He embraced her knees, gazed into her face, and talked passionately, ardently, beautifully. Terrified and dazed, she did not hear his words; for some reason it was now, at this moment of peril, when her knees were pleasantly pressed together as in a warm bath, that she sought with a sort of wicked spite for some meaning in her sensations. She was angry with herself, because instead of protesting virtue all she was conscious of was weakness, indolence, and emptiness, like a drunken man who doesn't care a hang any more. Only deep, deep inside her something very remote taunted her malignantly: 'Why *don't* you go away? So that is how it is, is it?'

Trying to find some rational explanation in herself, she could not understand why she did not pull away the hand to which Ilyin stuck like a leech, nor what made her look so hurriedly to the right and left, at the same time as Ilyin, to make sure they were not observed. The clouds and the firs stood motionless and gazed at them sternly like old ushers who see some boy misbehaving but have been bribed not to report it to the school authorities. The sentry on the embankment stood still like a post and seemed to be looking at the seat.

'Let him stare,' thought Mrs Lubyantsev.

'But – but look here,' she said at last with despair in her voice, 'what will this lead to? What's going to happen afterwards?'

'I don't know, I don't know,' he whispered, brushing aside these unpleasant questions.

The hoarse, jarring whistle of a railway engine was heard in the distance. This irrelevant, cold sound of everyday, prosaic life made Mrs Lubyantsev start.

'I'm sorry, I must go now,' she said, getting up quickly. 'The train's coming. . . . Andrey's on it. He'll want his dinner.'

Mrs Lubyantsev turned her glowing face towards the embankment. First the engine crawled slowly past, then the carriages came into sight. It was not the train bringing the holiday-makers from their work in the town. It was a goods train. In a long row one after another, like the days of a man's life, the railway trucks moved slowly against the white background of the church, and there seemed to be no end to them.

But at last the train came to an end, and the last truck with the lighted lanterns disappeared into the green distance. Mrs Lubyantsev turned sharply and walked quickly back along the lane without looking at Ilyin. She was in full control of herself. Flushed with shame, offended not by Ilyin – no! – but by the cowardice, the shamelessness with which she, a respectable, virtuous woman, had allowed a stranger to embrace her knees, she was now thinking only of how to get back quickly to her country cottage and her family. The lawyer could hardly keep pace with her. Turning from the lane on to a path, she looked back at him so quickly that she caught sight only of the sand on his knees and she waved her hand for him to go.

Running back home, Mrs Lubyantsev stood still for five minutes in her room, her eyes wandering from the window to her writing desk and back again.

'You're vile!' she scolded herself. 'Vile!'

To punish herself, she went over every detail of her relationship with Ilyin, without concealing anything, and she remembered that though she had been against the lawyer's pursuit of her all this time, she had been *drawn* to go and have it out with him; moreover, when he was lying at her feet she had felt an extraordinary pleasure. She recalled everything without sparing herself, and now, choking with shame, she could have slapped her own face.

'Poor Andrey,' she thought, trying, as she remembered her husband, to impart the tenderest expression possible to her face. 'Varya, my poor little darling, doesn't know what a mother she has! Forgive me, my dears! I love you very – very much!'

And, wishing to prove to herself what an excellent wife and mother she was, to prove that corruption had not yet touched those 'stable foundations' of which she had spoken to Ilyin, she ran into the kitchen and began shouting at the cook for not having laid the table for her husband. She tried to imagine his tired and famished look, declared aloud how sorry she was for him, and laid the table for him herself, something she had never done before. Then she went to see her little daughter Varya, took her in her arms, and kissed her warmly; the girl seemed cold and heavy to her, but she would not admit it to herself, and she started telling her what a good, honest, and kind daddy she had.

But when her husband arrived soon after, she barely greeted him.

The onrush of illusory feelings had stopped, without proving anything but merely exasperating and enraging her by their falseness. She sat at the window, suffering and in a bad temper. Only when in trouble do people realize how difficult it is to master their own feelings and thoughts. Mrs Lubyantsev said afterwards that her mind was 'in a state of confusion which was as difficult to sort out as to count the number of flying sparrows quickly'. From the fact, for instance, that she was not pleased with her husband's arrival, and that she did not like the way he behaved at dinner, she suddenly concluded that she had begun to hate him.

Mr Lubyantsev, faint with hunger and fatigue, while waiting for the soup fell upon the sausage and ate it greedily, chewing loudly and moving his temples.

'Good gracious,' thought his wife, 'I love and respect him, but – why does he chew so disgustingly?'

Her thoughts were no less in disorder than her feelings. Mrs Lubyantsev, like everybody else who has had no experience of the struggle with unpleasant thoughts, tried her utmost not to think of her trouble, but the more zealously she tried the more vividly did she conjure up Ilyin in her imagination – the sand on his knees, the fluffy clouds, the train. . . .

'Why did I – fool that I am – go there today?' she tormented herself. 'Am I really the sort of person who can't answer for herself?'

There is no medicine for fear. Before Andrey Lubyantsev had finished his last course, she had already made up her mind to tell her husband everything and in this way escape from danger.

'I wonder if I could have a serious talk with you, Andrey,' she said after dinner, when her husband was taking off his coat and boots in order to lie down for a rest.

'What about?'

'Let's go away from here!'

'Oh? Where to? It's too early to go back to town.'

'No, I mean, take a trip, or something of the kind.'

'Take a trip . . .' the notary murmured, stretching himself. 'I dream of it myself. Only where can I get the money? And who'll look after the office?' And after a little reflection he added: 'I can see that you're bored. Why not go by yourself, if you want to?'

Mrs Lubyantsev agreed, but immediately realized that Ilyin would be only too glad of the chance and would travel in the same train with her, in the same compartment. . . . She pondered and looked at her husband, his hunger assuaged but still languid. For some reason her eyes lingered on his feet, very tiny feet, almost as small as a woman's, in striped socks; on the toes of the socks little threads were visible. . . .

Behind the drawn blind a bumble-bee was knocking against the window pane and buzzing. Mrs Lubyantsev looked at the little threads, listened to the bumble-bee, and tried to imagine what her trip would be like. Day and night Ilyin sits opposite, without taking his eyes off her, angry with himself for his weakness and pale with anguish. But as soon as it gets dark and the passengers fall asleep or go out to stretch their legs at a station, he seizes his chance, kneels before her, and clasps her legs, as he did by the seat. . . .

She gave a start, realizing that she was dreaming.

'Listen,' she said, 'I won't go by myself. You must come with me.'

'A fantastic dream, darling,' said Lubyantsev with a sigh. 'One must be sensible, and only wish for what is possible.'

'You'd come all right if you knew,' thought Mrs Lubyantsev.

Having decided to go away at all costs, she felt free from danger; her thoughts sorted themselves out gradually, she cheered up and even allowed herself to make plans. Whatever she might think or dream about, she was going anyway. While her husband was having his forty winks, it was gradually growing dark. She sat in the drawing-room, playing the piano. The evening animation outside the windows, the sound of music, but above all the thought that she was a clever girl to have solved her difficult problem, finally restored her good humour. Other women, her calm conscience told her, would certainly not have been able to resist had they found themselves in a situation like hers: they would have lost their heads completely, while she had nearly died of shame, she had suffered, but now she was running away from the danger, which perhaps had never even existed. She was so touched by her virtue and resolution that she even glanced at herself in the glass three times.

When it was dark, visitors came. The men sat down to cards in the dining-room, and the women sat in the drawing-room and on the terrace. Ilyin was late coming. He looked melancholy and gloomy, and seemed to be ill. He sat down in a corner of the sofa and did not get up the whole evening. Usually cheerful and talkative, he hardly even opened his mouth this time, frowning and rubbing his eyes. When he had to answer a question somebody asked him, he forced himself to smile, but only with his upper lip, and he answered abruptly and peevishly. He made about half a dozen jokes, but his jokes were harsh and insolent. Mrs Lubyantsev thought that he was on the brink of hysteria. Only now, sitting at the piano, she realized quite clearly for the first time that the unhappy man was in no laughing mood, that he was sick at heart and in a state of utter despair. Because of her he was ruining the best days of his career and his youth, wasting his last few pennies on his summer cottage, had left his mother and sisters to fend for themselves, but above all was on the point of breaking down in the unequal struggle with himself. Out of a simple ordinary feeling of humanity he ought to be taken seriously. . . .

She realized it all very clearly, so clearly that her heart failed her. And if she had gone up to Ilyin at that moment and said to him 'No!', there would have been such strength in her voice that it would have been hard to disobey. But she did not go up to him and she did not say it. She did not even think of doing so. The pettiness and egoism of youth seemed never to have revealed themselves in her as strongly as on that evening. She knew perfectly well that Ilyin was unhappy, and that he sat on the sofa as if on hot coals; her heart bled for him. But at the same time the presence of the man who was in love with her filled her with a triumphant sense of her own power. She was aware of her youth, her beauty, her inaccessibility, and – since she had decided to go away – she had her fling that evening. She flirted, she laughed continuously, she sang with special feeling and as one inspired. Everything filled her with merriment, everything seemed funny to her. She was amused at the recollection of the incident at the seat in the forest clearing, of the sentry who had been looking on. She found her guests funny, as well as Ilyin's insolent jokes and the pin in his tie she had never seen before. The pin was in the shape of a little red snake with diamond eyes; the snake seemed to her so amusing that she was ready to cover it with kisses.

Mrs Lubyantsev sang popular songs, nervously, with a sort of half-drunken abandon, and as though rubbing salt in somebody's wounds she chose sad, melancholy songs that spoke of lost hopes, the past, old age. 'And old age draws nearer and nearer . . .' she sang. But what did she care for old age?

'There's something awful going on inside me,' the thought sometimes occurred to her, as she laughed and sang.

The visitors left at twelve o'clock. Ilyin was the last to go. Mrs Lubyantsev had still enough of her feeling of abandon left to see him off as far as the lower step of the veranda. She wanted to tell him that she was going away with her husband and to see the effect this news would have on him.

The moon was hiding behind the clouds, but it was so bright that Mrs Lubyantsev could see the wind playing with the tails of his overcoat and with the hangings on the veranda. She could also see how pale Ilyin was and how he twisted his upper lip, trying to smile.

'Sonia, my darling,' he murmured, not letting her speak. 'Oh, my dear, my beautiful one!'

In an access of tenderness, with tears in his voice, he showered her with caressing words, each more tender than the other, and was already speaking to her as if she were his wife or mistress. Before she could stop him, he suddenly put one arm round her waist and seized her elbow with his hand.

'My dear one, my darling pet,' he whispered, kissing her neck. 'Be honest! Come to me now!'

She slipped out of his embrace and raised her head, intending to burst out in indignation and show him how exasperated she was; but somehow her indignation never came, and all that was left of her much-lauded virtue and purity was the phrase which all ordinary women use on an occasion like this:

'You must be mad!'

'Come along, really,' Ilyin continued. 'Just now, and over there by the seat, I felt convinced that you were as helpless as myself, Sonia. You too will have to pay dearly for it. You love me, and you are just wasting your time trying to come to terms with your conscience.'

Seeing that she was leaving him, he caught her by her lace sleeve and concluded rapidly:

'If not today, then tomorrow. You will have to give in. What's the good of putting it off? My dear, my darling Sonia, the sentence has been passed, why postpone the execution? Why deceive yourself?'

Mrs Lubyantsev broke away from him and darted into the house. She returned to the drawing-room, shut the piano mechanically, gazed for a long time at the vignette on the cover of the book of music, and sat down. She could neither stand nor think. All that was left of her excitement and her feeling of abandon was a terrible weakness, accompanied by indolence and tedium. Her conscience whispered to her that she had behaved badly and foolishly at the party, like a wild, loose woman, and that only a moment ago on the veranda and even now she felt uncomfortable round her waist and her elbow. There was not a soul in the drawing-room, only one candle was burning. Mrs Lubyantsev sat on the round piano stool without moving, waiting for something. And as though taking advantage of her extreme exhaustion and the darkness, a disturbing, irresistible desire began to possess her. Like a boa constrictor, it held her limbs and soul in a clasp of iron; it grew every second, and was no longer threatening, but stood before her as plain as plain could be in all its nakedness.

For half an hour she sat without moving and without preventing herself from thinking of Ilyin. Then she got up lazily and walked slowly into the bedroom. Mr Lubyantsev was in bed already. She sat down at the open window and gave herself up to her desire. There was no longer 'confusion' in her head. All her thoughts and feelings crowded amicably together round one clear purpose. She tried to fight against it, but gave up the struggle immediately. She understood now how strong and implacable the enemy was. To fight him she had to possess strength and determination, but her birth, her upbringing, and her life had given her nothing to fall back on.

'You're a slut, you're a vile creature,' she thought, tormenting herself for her weakness. 'That's what you really are!'

Her offended respectability had been so upset by this weakness of hers that she called herself all the bad names she could think of and told herself many unflattering and humiliating truths. She told herself that she had never really been an honest woman and that she had not fallen before only because there was no ostensible reason for it, that her day-long struggle had been nothing but a game and a comedy.

'Even suppose that I did struggle,' she thought, 'what sort of a struggle was it? Even prostitutes struggle before they sell themselves, but in the end they do sell themselves. Some struggle! Like milk, it turned in one day. In one day!'

She was convinced that what was drawing her from her home was not feeling, nor Ilyin's personality, but the sensations which awaited her. A woman on holiday looking for a bit of excitement – there were hundreds of them!

'Like a mo-o-ther murdered in her baby's nest,' someone sang under the window in a hoarse tenor voice.

'If I'm going,' thought Mrs Lubyantsev, 'then I'd better go at once.'

Her heart suddenly began throbbing violently. 'Andrey!' she almost shouted. 'Listen, are we going away together or not? Are we?'

'I've told you: go by yourself!'

'But listen,' she brought out with difficulty, 'if you don't come with me, you may lose me. You see, I – I think I am in love.'

'Who with?' asked Mr Lubyantsev.

'What does it matter to you who with?' cried Mrs Lubyantsev.

Mr Lubyantsev sat up in bed, put down his feet on the floor, and looked with amazement at the dark figure of his wife.

'Oh, you're imagining things,' he said with a yawn.

He found it hard to believe, but he was frightened all the same. After thinking it over and putting a few unimportant questions to his wife, he expressed his views on family life, on infidelity, spoke languidly for about ten minutes, and then lay down again. There are a great number of views and opinions in the world, and a good half of them belong to people who have been in some trouble or other.

In spite of the late hour, holiday-makers were still moving about behind their windows. Mrs Lubyantsev threw her long cloak round her shoulders and stood still for a while, thinking. She still had enough resolution to say to her sleepy husband:

'Are you asleep? I'm going out for a little walk. Would you like to come with me?'

It was her last hope. Receiving no answer, she went out. It was windy and fresh. She was not aware of the wind or the darkness, but walked on and on. An irresistible force drove her, and it seemed to her that if she stopped it would push her in the back.

'You slut!' she murmured mechanically. 'You vile creature!'

She was gasping for breath, she was burning with shame, she did not feel her feet under her, but the thing which pushed her forward was stronger than her shame, her reason, her fear. . . .

A Boring Story

(From an Old Man's Notebook)

I

THERE is in Russia an eminent professor, Nikolai Stepanovich, a privy councillor, who has been awarded many decorations in his lifetime; indeed, he possesses so many Russian and foreign orders that whenever he has to put them all on the students call him 'the iconostasis'. He moves in most distinguished circles – at least during the last twenty-five or thirty years there has not been a single famous scholar or scientist in Russia with whom he has not been intimately acquainted. There is no one now with whom he could be on friendly terms but, so far as the past is concerned, the long list of his eminent friends would end with such names as Pirogov, Kavelin, and the poet Nekrasov, all of whom bestowed on him their warmest and most sincere friendship. He is an honorary Fellow of all the Russian and three foreign universities. Etcetera, etcetera. All this, and a great deal more, makes up what is known as my name.

This name of mine is well known. It is known to every educated person in Russia and abroad, it is mentioned by university lecturers with the addition of the adjectives 'celebrated' and 'esteemed'. It is among those few fortunate names which it is considered bad taste to abuse or speak of disrespectfully in public or in print. And so it should be. For my name is closely associated with the idea of a man who is famous, richly endowed, and most certainly useful. I am as hard-working and as hardy as a camel, which is important, and I am talented, which is even more important. Besides I may as well add that I am a well brought up, modest, and honest fellow. I have never poked my nose into literature or politics, never sought popularity by engaging in polemics with ignoramuses, and never made speeches at dinners or at the graves of my colleagues. ... There is in fact not a single blot on my name as a scientist, and I have no complaints to make. It is fortunate.

The bearer of this name, that is myself, is a man of sixty-two, with a bald head, false teeth, and an incurable tic. My name is as brilliant and attractive as I myself am dull and unprepossessing. My head and hands tremble from weakness; my neck, like that of one of Turgenev's heroines, resembles the finger-board of a double-bass; my chest is hollow and my back narrow. When I speak or lecture my mouth twists to one side; when I smile my whole face is covered with ghastly wrinkles. There is nothing impressive in my wretched figure; it is only perhaps when I suffer from the tic that I get a peculiar expression which in anyone who happens to look at me at the time provokes the stern and impressive thought: 'That man will probably die soon.'

I can still lecture quite well; as before, I can hold the attention of my audience for two hours. My passionate nature, the literary form of my exposition and my humour make the defects of my voice almost unnoticeable, though it is dry and harsh, and though its sing-song tone is that of a sanctimonious bigot. But I write badly. The small area of my brain which is in control of my writing abilities refuses to function. My memory has become weak; there is not enough consistency in my thoughts, and when I put them down on paper it always seems to me that I have lost the flair for giving them organic connexion, the construction is monotonous, the sentences barren and timid. Quite often I do not write what I mean to; when I write the end, I cannot remember the beginning. I often forget the most common words, and I always have to waste a great deal of energy to avoid superfluous phrases and unnecessary subordinate clauses in my writing, both of which, beyond a per-adventure, prove the decline of my mental faculties. The remarkable thing is that the simpler the subject of my writing the more agonizing the strain. I feel much freer and much more intelligent when writing a scientific article than when writing a letter of congratulation or a report. One thing more: I find it much easier to write in German or English than in Russian.

As regards my present life, I must first of all mention the insomnia from which I have begun to suffer lately. If I were asked: 'What is now the chief and fundamental fact of your existence?' I would reply: 'Insomnia.' As before, from force of habit, I undress and get into bed exactly at midnight. I fall asleep quite soon, but shortly after one o'clock I wake up with the feeling that I have not slept at all. I have to get out of bed and light the lamp. For an hour or two I pace up and down my room, gazing at the long pictures and photographs. When I am tired of walking, I sit down at my desk. I sit there motionless, without thinking of anything and without feeling any desire for anything; if a book happens to lie in front of me, I draw it towards me mechanically and read without the slightest interest. Thus, quite recently I read mechanically a whole novel with the curious title *What the Swallow Sang Of*. To occupy my mind I sometimes make myself count to a thousand, or I call to mind the face of one of my colleagues and try to remember in what year and under what circumstances he joined the faculty. I like listening to sounds. Sometimes two doors away from me my daughter Lisa will say something rapidly in her sleep, or my wife will walk through the drawing-room with a candle and invariably drop a box of matches, or the warped wood of the wardrobe will creak, or the wick in the lamp will unexpectedly begin to hum — all these sounds for some reason excite me.

Not to sleep at night means to be conscious every minute that you are abnormal, and that is why I wait impatiently for the morning and the day, when I have the right not to sleep. Many wearisome hours pass before the cock crows in the yard. This is my first bringer of glad tidings. As soon as he has crowed, I know that an hour later the hall porter will wake up downstairs and will walk up the stairs for something or other, coughing irritably. And then it will gradually be getting lighter beyond the window, and the sound of voices will come from the street. . . .

The day begins for me with the coming of my wife. She enters my room in her underskirt, with her hair undone, but having already had a wash and smelling of eau-de-Cologne. She looks as though she had come in by accident, and every time she says the same thing: 'Sorry, I just looked in for a moment. You've slept badly again, haven't you?' Then she puts the lamp out, sits down at the table, and starts talking. I am no prophet, but I know beforehand what she will be talking about. Every morning the same thing. Usually, after anxious inquiries after my health, she suddenly remembers our officer son, who is serving in Warsaw. On the twentieth of each month we send him fifty roubles – which is usually the chief subject of our conversation.

'It's hard on us, of course,' sighs my wife, 'but until he can stand firmly on his own feet we must help him. The poor boy is in a strange country, his pay is small. Still, if you insist, we'll send him forty roubles next month instead of fifty. What do you think?'

Daily experience might have convinced my wife that expenses do not grow less by constantly talking about them; but my wife has no use for experience, and conscientiously every morning talks about our officer son and about bread being cheaper, thank God, while sugar has gone up two kopeks in price. And all this in a tone of voice as if she were telling me something new.

I listen to her, agreeing mechanically. And, probably because I have not slept all night, strange, inappropriate thoughts take hold of me. I look at my wife and wonder like a child. Bewildered, I ask myself: Is it possible that this very fat, clumsy old woman, whose dull expression is so full of petty cares and anxiety about a crust of bread, whose eyes are blurred with perpetual thoughts of debts and poverty, who can only talk of expenses and only smile when things get cheaper – is it possible that this woman was once that very slim Varya, whom I loved so passionately for her fine, clear intellect, her pure soul, her beauty, and – as Othello loved Desdemona – that she did pity me for the hardships of my scientific work? Is this woman really the same Varya, my wife, who once bore me a son?

I gaze intently at the face of this flabby, clumsy old woman, trying to discover my Varya in her, but nothing of the past remains about her except her anxiety about my health and her way of calling my salary *our* salary, and my hat *our* hat. It pains me to look at her, and to console her a little I let her talk about anything she pleases and don't say a word even when she is unfair to people or reproaches me for not taking up private practice and for not publishing textbooks.

Our conversation always ends in the same way. My wife suddenly remembers that I have not had my tea, and looks startled.

'What am I sitting here for?' she says, getting up. 'The samovar has been on the table for hours and I sit chattering here. Good gracious, what an awful memory I have!'

She walks away quickly, but stops at the door to say:

'We owe Yegor five months' wages. You realize that, don't you? How many times have I told you that one should never let the servant's wages run on? It is much easier to pay ten roubles every month than fifty roubles for five months.'

Outside the door she stops again.

'I'm not sorry for anyone as much as for our poor Lisa. The girl studies at the conservatoire, she's always in good society, and goes about in goodness only knows what. That fur coat of hers! Why, it's a disgrace to show herself in the street in it. If she were someone else it wouldn't matter so much, but everyone knows her father is a famous professor, a privy councillor!'

And having reproached me with my professional name and my rank, she goes away at last. Thus begins my day. It does not improve as it goes on.

While I am having breakfast, my daughter Lisa comes in, wearing her worn-out fur coat and hat and carrying her music, ready to go to the conservatoire. She is twenty-two. She looks even younger, pretty, a little like my wife when she was young. She kisses me tenderly on my temple and my hand.

'Good morning, Daddy. How are you?'

As a child she was very fond of ice-cream, and I often had to take her to the confectioner's. Ice-cream was the standard by which she judged all that was best. If she wanted to say something nice to me, she would say: 'You're a plum ice, Daddy!' One of her fingers she called pistachio, another plum, still another raspberry, and so on. Usually, when she came to say good morning to me, I put her on my knees, kissed her fingers, and said:

'Plum . . . pistachio . . . raspberry . . .'

And now, too, from force of habit, I kiss Lisa's fingers, murmuring: 'Pistachio . . . plum . . . lemon . . .', but it is not the same thing. I am as cold as ice-cream and I feel ashamed. When my daughter comes in and touches my temple with her lips, I start as though I had been stung by a bee, smile constrainedly, and turn my face away. Ever since I began suffering from insomnia, one question keeps worrying me continually. My daughter often sees me, an old man, a famous scientist, blushing painfully because I owe our servant his wages; she sees how often the worry of small debts forces me to stop working and start pacing the room for hours on end thinking. Why then hasn't she come to me even once, without telling her mother, and whispered: 'Father, here's my watch, my bracelets, my ear-rings, my dresses – pawn them, you need money. . . .' Why, seeing how her mother and I, in an attempt to keep up appearances, try to hide our poverty from people, does she not give up the expensive pleasure of studying music? Anyway I should not have accepted her watch, the bracelets, or any sacrifice from her – God forbid! – I don't want that.

Incidentally, this reminds me of my son, the Warsaw army officer. He is an intelligent, honest, and sober fellow. But that is not enough for me. I can't help thinking that if I had an old father, and if I knew that there were moments when my father was ashamed of his poverty, I would have resigned my commission and taken a job as a labourer. Such thoughts about my children poison my existence. What good are they? Only a narrow-minded and embittered person can bear a grudge against ordinary people for not being heroes. But enough of that.

At a quarter to ten I have to go and give a lecture to my dear boys. I dress and walk along the road I have known for thirty years, a road which has a history of its own for me. Here is the large grey building with the chemist's shop; a small building stood on the site before, and it had a beer shop, in which I thought over my thesis and wrote my first love letter to Varya. I wrote it in pencil, on a sheet of paper with the printed heading *Historia Morbi*. And there is the grocer's shop; it used to belong to a little Jew who sold me cigarettes on credit, and later to a fat woman who was fond of students because 'every one of them has a mother'. Now it is owned by a red-headed tradesman who does not seem to take any interest in anything and who keeps drinking tea from a copper teapot. And here are the grim gates of the university, which have not been repaired for ages; a bored caretaker in a sheepskin, a broom, heaps of snow. . . . Such gates can hardly produce a wholesome impression on a lad fresh from the provinces who imagines that the temple of science really is a temple. On the whole, the dilapidated state of the university buildings, the gloom of its corridors, the dinginess of its walls, the lack of light, the dismal appearance of the stairs, the coat-hooks and the benches, occupy one of the foremost places in the history of Russian pessimism, they are part of the diathesis. . . . And here is our park. Since my student days it does not seem to have grown any worse or any better. I do not like it. It would be much more sensible if tall pine trees and sturdy oaks grew here instead of the consumptive lime trees, yellow acacias, and thin, clipped lilac bushes. A student, whose state of mind is largely dependent on his surroundings, should at every step see before him only what is grand and strong and elegant in the place where he studies. Heaven preserve him from gaunt trees, broken windows, drab walls, and doors covered with torn oilcloth.

As I approach the wing of the building in which I lecture, the door is flung open and I am met by my old associate, the hall porter, my namesake Nikolai, who is the same age as I. Having let me in, he clears his throat and says:

'It's frosty, sir.'

Or, if my coat is wet:

'It's raining, sir.'

Then he runs ahead of me and opens all the doors on my way. In my room he carefully helps me off with my coat and at the same time manages to tell me some university news. Because of the good understanding that exists between the university hall porters and caretakers, he knows everything that is going on in the four faculties, the registrar's office, the rector's room, and the library. What doesn't he know? When, for instance, the resignation of the rector or one of the deans is the subject of general discussion, I hear him telling the junior caretaker who the likely candidates are and explaining that so-and-so will not be approved by the minister and that so-and-so will himself refuse the post, and then going into fantastic details about some mysterious documents received in the registrar's office about some alleged secret conversation between the minister and the permanent head of the education department, and so on. Apart from these details, he almost always turns out to be right. The descriptions he gives of the personality of each character are highly original, but they also happen to be true. If you want to know in what year a certain person read his thesis, joined the staff, resigned, or died, you have only to consult the prodigious memory of this veteran and he will not only name you the year, month, and day but will supply you with all the details of this or any other event. Only he who loves can remember so much.

He is the guardian of the university traditions. From his predecessors he has inherited a great number of legends of university life, has added to this store a great deal of his own, procured during his years of service, and if you like he will tell you many stories, long and short. He can tell you of extraordinary sages who knew *everything*, of remarkable scholars who could go on working without sleep for weeks, of innumerable martyrs and victims of science; in his stories good always triumphs over evil, the weak always defeat the strong, the wise man the fool, the modest the proud, the young the old. . . . It is not necessary to take all these legends and cock-and-bull stories at their face value, but put them through a filter and something of real importance will remain: our excellent traditions and the names of true heroes acknowledged by all.

In our society all that is known about the world of science and learning is limited to stories of the extraordinary absentmindedness of old professors and a few witty sayings ascribed to Gruber, Babukhin, and myself. For an educated society this is not enough. If we loved science, scientists, and students as Nikolai does, we would long ago have had a literature of epics, legends, and biographies — which unfortunately we have not got at present.

After he has told me the news, Nikolai's face assumes a stern expression and we embark on a business talk. If at the time an outsider could hear how freely Nikolai uses scientific terminology, he might be forgiven for thinking that he was a scholar disguised as an old soldier. By the way, the stories about the erudition of university porters are greatly exaggerated. It is true Nikolai knows more than a hundred Latin terms, can put a skeleton together, and occasionally prepare a slide or amuse the students with some long, learned quotation, but so simple a theory as, for instance, the circulation of the blood is still as great a mystery to him as it was twenty years ago.

At the table in my room, bent low over a book or some slide or other, sits my dissector Peter Ignatyevich, an industrious, modest, but mediocre man of thirty-five, already bald and with a big paunch. He works from morning to night, reads a terrific lot, and remembers everything he has read, and in this respect he is worth his weight in gold; but in all other respects he is just a cart-horse, or in other words a learned blockhead. The characteristic cart-horse features which distinguish him from a man of talent are narrowness of outlook and sharply limited specialization. Apart from his special subject he is as naïve as a child. I remember one morning going into my room and saying:

'Have you heard the bad news? Skobelev is dead.'

Nikolai crossed himself, but Peter Ignatyevich turned to me and asked:

'Who is Skobelev?'

Another time, a little earlier, I told him that Professor Petrov had died. Dear old Peter Ignatyevich asked:

'What was his subject?'

I suppose if Patti herself sang into his ear, if hordes of Chinese invaded Russia, if there were an earthquake, he would not turn a hair, but would go on looking into his microscope with one eye screwed up. In a word, 'What's Hecuba to him?' I'd give a lot to see how that dry stick goes to bed with his wife.

Another trait: a fanatical belief in the infallibility of science and above all in everything the Germans write. He is sure of himself and his slides, he knows the purpose of life and is completely ig-norant of the doubts and disappointments that turn talented men grey. A slavish worship of authority and a complete absence of independent thought. It is difficult to make him change his opinions and quite impossible to argue with him. How can you argue with a man who is firmly convinced that medicine is the best science, that doctors are the best people, and that medical traditions are the best traditions? The only thing that has sur-vived from the bad past of medicine is the white tie doctors still wear; to a scholar, an educated man, there is really nothing but the general university tradition, without splitting up the faculties into medical, legal, and so on. Peter Ignatyevich finds it difficult to agree with this, and he is ready to argue with you about it till doomsday.

I can imagine his future quite plainly. In the course of his life he will make a few hundred slides, perfect in every respect, write a great number of dry but quite tolerably good papers, make a dozen conscientious translations; but he won't invent gunpowder. To invent gunpowder one needs imagination, inventiveness, and a capacity for divining things, and Peter Ignatyevich has nothing of the sort. To put it in a nutshell, so far as science is concerned, he is not a foreman but a labourer.

Peter Ignatyevich, Nikolai, and I lower our voices when we talk. We feel a little ill at ease. You get a strange feeling when you hear an audience roaring like a sea behind the door. In thirty years I have not grown accustomed to that feeling, and I experience it every morning. I button up my frock-coat nervously, ask Nikolai unnecessary questions, get cross. . . . It looks as though I were afraid; but it is not fear, it is something else which I cannot name or describe. I glance at my watch as though I did not know the right time.

'Well,' I say, 'it's time to go.'

And we walk in procession, in the following order: Nikolai with the preparations or diagrams in front, myself after him; and after me, his head modestly bent, plods the cart-horse. Or, when necessary, a cadaver is carried in front on a stretcher, after the cadaver comes Nikolai, and so on. At my appearance the students get up, then sit down, and the roar of the sea suddenly dies down. A calm sets in.

I know what I am going to lecture about, but I do not know how I shall lecture, what I shall start and end with. There is not a single ready-made phrase in my head. But as soon as I glance at my audience, sitting round me in an amphitheatre, and utter the stereotyped 'At our last lecture we stopped at –', the sentences roll out in a long succession and – I am off! I speak with irresistible rapidity and passion, and it seems that no power on earth could interrupt the flow of my speech. To lecture well, that is to say, without boring your listeners, and to benefit them, you must possess not only talent but also the right kind of skill as well as experience, you must also have a perfectly clear idea both of your own abilities and the subject of your address. In addition, you must never be thrown off your guard, never relax your attention, and never for a moment lose sight of your audience.

A good conductor, while conveying the ideas of the composer, performs a dozen things all at once: he reads the score, waves his baton, keeps an eye on the singer, motions to the drummer, the French horns, etc. It is the same with me when I am lecturing. In front of me are a hundred and fifty faces, all different from one another, and three hundred eyes staring straight into my face. My aim is to conquer this many-headed hydra. If I never allow their attention to slacken for a moment during the whole of my lecture, and at the same time never talk above their heads, then they are in my power. My other enemy is within me. This is the endless variety of forms, phenomena, and laws, and the great multitude of thoughts, my own and those of others, which arise from them. Every moment I must be able to extract from this enormous mass of material what is most important and necessary, and I must do it as quickly as I talk; moreover, I must convey my thought in the form that is accessible to the hydra's mind and is capable of exciting its attention. I must, besides, take good care to see that my thoughts are communicated not as they accumulate, but in the order required for the correct composition of the picture I intend to draw. Furthermore, I do my best to make sure that I try to invest my speech in a literary form, make my definitions brief and exact and the sentences as simple and elegant as possible. Every moment I must check myself and try to remember that I have only one hour and forty minutes at my disposal. In a word, I have plenty to do. At one and the same time I have to be a scientist, a teacher, and an orator; and it's a poor outlook for me if the orator gets the better of the teacher and scientist, or vice versa.

After lecturing for fifteen or thirty minutes, I suddenly notice that the students are beginning to stare at the ceiling or at Peter Ignatyevich; one of them is fumbling for his handkerchief, another trying to settle himself more comfortably, and a third smiling at his own thoughts. This means that their attention is beginning to slacken. I have to do something about it. I take advantage of the first opportunity to make a pun. All the hundred and fifty faces smile broadly, their eyes sparkle merrily, for a brief moment one can hear the roar of the sea. . . . I join in the laughter. Their attention is refreshed and I can go on.

No debate, no entertainment, no game has ever given me so much pleasure as giving a lecture. Only while lecturing have I been able to give myself up wholly to passion, and to understand that inspiration is not an invention of poets, but really exists. And I can't help thinking that Hercules, after the most sensational of his exploits, never had such an exquisite feeling of lassitude as I experienced every time after a lecture.

That was in the past. Now at lectures I experience nothing but torture. Scarcely half an hour passes before I begin to feel a terrible weakness in my legs and shoulders; I sit down, but I am not used to lecturing sitting down. A minute later I am on my feet again and lecture standing; then I sit down again. My mouth is dry, my voice hoarse, my head dizzy.... To conceal my condition from my audience, I take a drink of water now and then, cough and blow my nose as though I am suffering from a cold in the head, make inopportune puns, and at last announce an interval sooner than I ought to. But the worst of it is that I feel ashamed.

Conscience and reason tell me that the best thing I could do now is to deliver a farewell lecture to the boys, say my last word to them, give them my blessing, and give up my post to a younger and stronger man than myself. But — God be my judge — I have not the courage to act according to what my conscience tells me I ought to do.

Unfortunately, I am neither a philosopher nor a theologian. I know perfectly well I have no more than six months to live; it would therefore seem that I should be chiefly occupied with questions of the darkness beyond the grave and the visions that may visit my sleep in the grave. But for some reason my soul does not want to know anything about these questions; only my mind realizes their importance. Now that death is so near, all I am interested in is science, just as I was twenty or thirty years ago. Even while breathing my last I shall still believe that science is the most important, most beautiful, and most necessary thing in the life of man, that it always has been and will be the highest manifestation of love, and that it alone will enable man to conquer nature and himself. This belief is perhaps naïve and fundamentally unsound, but it is not my fault that I believe as I do and not otherwise; it is not in my power to overcome this belief of mine.

But that is not the point. All I ask is that allowance should be made for my weakness, and that it should be understood that to tear away from his university chair and his students a man who is more interested in the development of the bone-marrow than in the final goal of creation is tantamount to nailing him down in his coffin without waiting for him to die.

As a result of my insomnia and the struggle against my growing weakness, something strange is happening to me. In the middle of my lecture tears rise to my throat, my eyelids begin to itch, and I feel an hysterical, passionate desire to stretch out my hands and complain aloud. I feel like shouting in a loud voice that fate has sentenced me, a famous man, to death, that in six months' time another man will be in charge of this lecture room. I feel like crying out that I have been poisoned, that new thoughts I did not know before have poisoned the last days of my life and keep stinging my brain like mosquitoes. At that moment my position seems so terrible to me that I should like all my students to be horrified, leap panic-stricken from their seats, and rush shrieking madly to the exit.

It is not easy to live through such moments.

II

After the lecture I work at home. I read periodicals and dissertations, prepare for my next lecture, and sometimes write something. My work is constantly interrupted, for I have to receive visitors.

The door bell rings. It is a colleague of mine who has come to talk over some business. He comes in with his hat and stick, and holding them out towards me says:

'I've just looked in for a moment. Don't get up, colleague. Only a couple of words.'

First we try to show each other how extraordinarily polite we are and how glad we are to see each other. I make him sit down in an armchair, and he insists on my resuming my seat; at the same time we carefully stroke each other's waists, touching each other's buttons, and it looks as if we are feeling each other and are afraid of burning ourselves. We both laugh, though we have not said anything funny. Having sat down, we both bend our heads towards each other and start talking in an undertone. However well disposed we may be towards one another, we cannot help gilding our conversation with all sorts of Chinese civilities like 'as you so justly observe' or 'as I've already had the honour to tell you', or laughing heartily if either of us makes a pun, even though a bad one. Having finished our business, my colleague gets up abruptly and begins to take his leave, waving his hat towards my work. We again feel each other and laugh. I accompany him to the hall and help him on with his fur coat, while he does his best to decline so great an honour. Then, when Yegor opens the front door to him, he expresses his concern about my catching a cold, while I pretend to be ready to follow him even as far as the street. And when at last I am back in my study, my face is still wreathed in smiles, I suppose from inertia.

A little later, another ring. Someone comes into the hall, spends a long time taking off his coat and galoshes, and coughs. Yegor announces that one of my students wishes to see me. I say: 'Show him in, please.' A moment later a young man of pleasant appearance enters my study. For nearly a year our relationship has been rather strained: he gives me most abominable answers at examinations, and I give him the lowest marks. Every year I get about seven of these fine fellows whom I 'persecute' or 'plough', in the language of the students. Those of them who do not pass their examinations because of their incapacity or illness usually bear their cross with patience, and do not bargain with me; only those come to bargain with me at home who are optimists by nature, fellows of wide though not very profound interests, whose failure in examinations spoils their appetites and prevents them from going regularly to the opera. The former I make allowances for; the latter I 'persecute' for a whole year.

'Sit down, please,' I say to my visitor. 'What can I do for you?'

'I am sorry to trouble you, sir,' he begins, stammering and not looking me in the face. 'I – er – shouldn't have taken the liberty of – er – troubling you sir, if – er . . . You see, sir, I've sat for your examination five times and – er – have not passed. I beg you, sir, to be so kind as to give me a pass, because . . .'

The argument which all sluggards bring forward in their favour is always the same: they have passed in all the other subjects with distinction, but failed only in mine, which is all the more surprising because they have always studied my subject most diligently and know it thoroughly. They have failed because of some quite inexplicable misunderstanding.

'I am very sorry, my friend,' I say to my visitor, 'but I cannot give you a pass. Go and read through your lecture notes again, and then come to me. Then we shall see.'

A pause. I cannot suppress a desire to torment the student a little for preferring beer and the opera to science and I say with a sigh:

'In my opinion, the best thing for you to do now is to give up medicine altogether. If a man of your ability is quite unable to pass the examination, then it is evident that you have neither the desire nor the vocation to be a doctor.'

The optimistic fellow pulls a long face.

'I'm sorry, sir,' he says with a laugh, 'but that would certainly be a strange thing for me to do. To study for five years and then – give it up!'

'Yes, why not? After all, it's better to waste five years than to do something you do not like for the rest of your life.'

But almost at once I feel sorry for him, and I hasten to say:

'However, just as you like. Read a little more, and then come to me.'

'When?' the sluggard asks, dully.

'Any time you like. Tomorrow, even.'

And I can read in his good-natured eyes: 'I can come all right, but then you'll throw me out again, you dirty dog.'

'Now, of course,' I say, 'you won't become a more learned person by sitting fifteen times for my examination, but it'll be good training for your character. That's something to be thankful for, too.'

Silence. I rise, waiting for my visitor to go, but he stands there looking out of the window, fingering his little beard and thinking. The thing is becoming a bore.

The optimistic fellow has a pleasant, mellow voice, intelligent ironical eyes, and a complacent face that is somewhat crumpled by overdoses of beer and by lying about on sofas for hours. I expect he could tell me a great many interesting things about the opera, his love affairs, his fellow-students, among whom he is popular, but unfortunately it is not the thing to do. And yet I would gladly listen to him.

'I give you my word of honour, sir, that if you give me a pass, I – er ...'

But as soon as it gets to 'my word of honour', I wave my hands and sit down at my desk. The student thinks for another minute and then says gloomily :

'In that case, good-bye.... I'm sorry, sir.'

'Good-bye, my friend. Good luck !'

He goes irresolutely out into the hall, slowly puts on his things, and, on going out into the street, no doubt meditates for a long time about his situation, but, unable to think of anything except calling me 'an old devil', goes to a cheap restaurant to drink beer and dine, and then back home to sleep. Peace to your ashes, you honest hard-working fellow!

A third ring. In comes a young doctor in a new black suit, gold-rimmed spectacles, and of course a white tie. He introduces himself. I ask him to take a seat, and inquire after his business. The young priest of science begins telling me, not without agitation, that he has passed his doctor's examination this year and that now he has only to write his dissertation. He would like to work with me, under my guidance, and I would greatly oblige him by suggesting a subject for his dissertation.

'I should be delighted to be of use to you, colleague,' I say, 'but let's first of all see if we agree about what exactly a dissertation is supposed to be. This word is usually understood to mean a written composition which is the result of independent work. Isn't that so? A work written on a subject suggested by someone else and under the supervision of someone else has a different name.'

The aspirant is silent. I lose my temper and jump out of my chair.

'Tell me why you all come to me?' I shout angrily. 'Do I keep a shop? I'm not a dealer in subjects for dissertations. For the hundredth time I ask you to leave me in peace. I'm sorry to be so outspoken, but I'm sick and tired of the whole thing!'

The aspirant is silent and only his face above his cheekbones colours slightly. His face shows a profound respect for my famous name and my erudition, but I can see from the expression in his eyes that he despises my voice, my pitiful figure, and my nervous gestures. In my anger, I strike him as an eccentric fellow.

'I don't keep a shop,' I repeat angrily. 'What an extraordinary business! Why don't you want to be independent? Why do you loathe freedom so much?'

I go on talking for a long time, but he keeps silent. In the end I gradually cool down and of course give in. The aspirant will receive a worthless subject from me and under my supervision write a dissertation which is of no earthly use to anyone, will defend it with dignity in a boring debate, and will get his useless doctorate of medicine.

The door bell can go on ringing for ever, but I will restrict myself to four. The bell rings for the fourth time and I hear familiar footsteps, the rustle of a dress, and the dear voice. . . .

Eighteen years ago a colleague of mine, an eye specialist, died, leaving a seven-year-old daughter, Katya, and sixty thousand roubles. In his will he appointed me as her guardian. Katya lived in my family till she was ten, then she was sent to a boarding school and only lived with us during the summer holidays. I had no time to look after her education and no opportunity of keeping an eye on her except occasionally, and can therefore say very little about her childhood.

The first thing I remember, the memory which I treasure, is the extraordinary trustfulness with which she came into my home and allowed the doctors to treat her when she was ill, a trustfulness which always irradiated her sweet face. She might be sitting somewhere by herself with a bandage round her head, and would be sure to be watching something intently; whether she was watching me writing and turning over the pages of a book, or my wife bustling about, or the cook peeling potatoes in the kitchen, or the dog playing about, her eyes invariably expressed the same thing: 'Everything that is going on in this world is wise and wonderful.' She was inquisitive and liked to talk to me very much. She would sit facing me at the table, watching my movements and asking questions. She was interested to know what I was reading, what I did at the university, whether I was not afraid of the cadavers, and what I did with my salary.

'Do the students fight at the university?' she would ask.

'Yes, they do, my dear.'

'And do you make them go down on their knees?'

'I do.'

And it seemed so funny to her that the students fought and I made them go down on their knees that she burst out laughing. She was a gentle, patient, and good child. I often happened to see how something was taken away from her, or how she was unjustly punished, or her curiosity was not satisfied; at such moments sadness would be added to her usual expression of trustfulness, but that was all. I did not know how to stick up for her and it was only when I saw her looking sad that I was overcome by a desire to draw her close to me and tell her how sorry I was for her in the words of an old nurse: 'You poor little orphan!'

I remember too that she was very fond of dressing up and sprinkling herself with scent. In this respect she was like me. I too like good clothes and fine scent.

I regret that I had neither the time nor the inclination to watch the beginning and the growth of the passion which took hold of Katya when she was fourteen or fifteen. I am talking of her passionate love for the theatre. When she came from her boarding school to live with us for the summer, there was nothing she spoke about with such pleasure and enthusiasm as plays and actors. She used to tire us with her constant talk about the theatre. My wife and children would not listen to her. I alone had not the courage to refuse her my attention. Whenever she felt like sharing her raptures, she would come to my study and say in an imploring voice:

'Do let me talk to you about the theatre.'

I used to show her my watch and say:

'I give you half an hour from – now!'

Later she began bringing home dozens of portraits of actors and actresses she worshipped; then she tried a few times to take part in amateur theatricals, and at last, when she left school, she told me that she was born to be an actress.

I never shared Katya's theatrical enthusiasms. In my opinion, if a play is good there is no need to trouble the actors for it to produce the desired impression: all you have to do is to read it. On the other hand, if the play is bad no acting will make it good.

When I was young I often went to the theatre, and now too my family takes a box twice a year and takes me there for 'an airing'. This, of course, is not enough to give me the right to express an opinion on the theatre, but I will say just a few words about it. In my opinion, the theatre has not improved in the last thirty or forty years. I am still unable to get a glass of clean water in the corridors or the foyer. I am still being fined twenty kopeks for my fur coat by the cloakroom attendants, although there is nothing reprehensible in wearing warm clothes in winter. Music is still quite unnecessarily being played in the intervals, adding something new and completely uncalled for to the impression received from the play. Men still go to the bar for a drink during the intervals. Since there is no progress in little things, it would be a waste of time to look for it in bigger things. When an actor, entangled from head to foot in theatrical traditions and prejudices, tries to give us a simple, ordinary monologue like 'To be or not to be' not at all simply, but for some reason always with hissings and convulsions, or when he tries to convince me at all costs that Chatsky, who is always talking with fools and is in love with a fool of a girl, is a very clever man and *The Misfortune of Being Clever* is not a boring play, then what I get from the stage is a whiff of the same old routine which I found so boring forty years ago when I was regaled with classical howlings and beatings of the breast. And every time I come out of the theatre I am a more confirmed conservative than when I entered it.

It is not difficult to persuade a sentimental and credulous crowd that the theatre in its present state is a school. But anyone who knows the real meaning of a school will not swallow this sort of bait. I do not know what it will be like in fifty or a hundred years, but under present conditions the theatre can serve only as a place of entertainment. But this place of entertainment is too expensive to be worth while. It deprives the state of thousands of young, healthy, and talented men and women, who if they were not dedicated to the theatre could have become good doctors, farmers, schoolmistresses, or army officers; it deprives the public of their evening hours – the best time for intellectual work and friendly conversations. Not to mention the waste of money and the moral injury suffered by the spectators when they see murder, adultery, and slander wrongly treated on the stage.

Katya, however, was of quite another opinion. She assured me that the theatre, even in its present state, was far superior to lectures, far superior to books, far superior to anything in the world. The theatre was a force, uniting in itself all the arts, and the actors were missionaries. No particular art or science was able to exert such a strong and beneficial influence on the human soul as the stage, and that was the real reason why even the mediocre actor enjoyed greater popularity in the country than the greatest scientist or artist. Indeed, no public activity could give such satisfaction and enjoyment as acting.

So one fine day Katya joined a theatrical company and went away, I believe, to Ufa, taking with her a great deal of money, thousands of rainbow-coloured hopes and grandiose views on the business of the theatre.

Her first letters, written during the journey, were wonderful. I read them, and was simply amazed that these small sheets of paper could contain so much youthful enthusiasm, purity of soul, divine naïveté, and at the same time so many subtle and sensible views, which would have done honour to a first-class masculine intelligence. The Volga, the countryside, the towns she visited, her fellow-actors, her successes and failures, she did not so much describe as glorify in song; every line breathed the trustfulness which I was used to seeing on her face – and with all this a mass of grammatical mistakes and an almost total absence of punctuation marks.

Six months had scarcely passed when I received a highly poetic and rapturous letter beginning with the words: 'I have fallen in love.' She enclosed a photograph of a young man with a clean-shaven face, in a wide-brimmed hat and a plaid thrown over one shoulder. The next letters were just as wonderful, but now punctuation marks began to make an appearance, there were no more grammatical mistakes, and they exuded a strong masculine odour. Katya began to write how splendid it would be to build a big theatre somewhere on the Volga, make it into a limited company, and get the rich businessmen and shipowners to join it as shareholders. There would be plenty of money, the box-office receipts would be enormous and the actors would work on a partnership basis. ... This might be a good thing, for all I know, but it seemed to me that such ideas could only come from a man's head.

Be that as it may, for a year or two everything was apparently all right: Katya was in love, had faith in her work, and was happy; but later on I began to be conscious of unmistakable signs of despondency in her letters. At first Katya began to complain to me about her fellow-actors – this was the first and most ominous sign. If a young scientist or writer begins his career by complaining bitterly about scientists or writers, it means that he is already worn out and no longer fit for his work. Katya wrote that her fellow-actors did not go to rehearsals and did not know their parts; that they showed an utter contempt for the public by their production of ridiculous plays and by the way they behaved on the stage; in the interests of the box-office receipts, which was the only topic of conversation among them, actresses of the legitimate stage degraded themselves by singing music-hall songs, while tragic actors sang similar songs in which they made fun of deceived husbands and the pregnancy of unfaithful wives, and so on. In fact, it was quite amazing that provincial theatres still existed and that they could carry on in so meagre and bad an art form.

In reply I sent Katya a long and, I am afraid, rather boring letter. Among other things, I wrote: 'I have often had the chance of talking with old actors, most honourable men, who have been good enough to be amiable to me. From talking to them I realized that their activities are guided not so much by reason and freedom of choice as by the prevalent social mood and fashion; the best of them have at one time or another had to act in tragedies, operettas, Parisian farces, and pantomimes, and they always considered that in every case they were following the right path and were of benefit to society. So, you see, the source of the evil must be sought not in the actors, but deeper down, in the art itself and in the attitude of society towards it.' This letter of mine only exasperated Katya. She wrote in reply: 'We are talking about different things. I did not write to you about those honourable men who have been good enough to like you, but of a gang of rogues who have no idea of honour. They are a horde of savages, who found themselves on the stage only because they wouldn't have been given a job anywhere else, and who call themselves actors out of sheer arrogance. Not a single talented person among them, but any number of mediocrities, drunkards, schemers, and scandalmongers. I can't tell you how bitter I feel that the art I love so much should have fallen into the hands of people I detest; it hurts me that the best men should only see evil from a distance and refuse to go nearer, and instead of doing something about it write platitudes in a ponderous style and dispense moral judgements nobody cares a rap about. . . .' And so on in the same vein.

A little later I received the following letter:

'I have been cruelly deceived. I can't go on living any more. Make use of my money as you think fit. I have loved you as a father and as my only friend. Forgive me.'

So it seemed that *he* belonged to 'the horde of savages', too. Afterwards I gathered from certain hints that there had been an attempt at suicide. Katya, it seems, tried to poison herself. I think she must have been seriously ill afterwards, for the next letter from her I received from Yalta, where the doctors had probably sent her. Her last letter to me contained a request to send her a thousand roubles to Yalta as quickly as possible, and concluded with the words: 'I am sorry my letter is so gloomy. Yesterday I buried my child.' After spending about a year in the Crimea, she came back home.

She had been away for about four years, and I must confess that during the whole of that time I played a rather strange and un-enviable part so far as she was concerned. When at the very begin-ning she told me that she was going on the stage and when later she wrote to me about her love, when every now and then she succumbed to fits of extravagance so that I had to send her one or two thousand roubles at her request, when she wrote to me of her intention to take her life and then of the death of her child, I was at a loss what to do every time, and all I did to help her was to think a lot about her and write her long boring letters which I need not have written at all. And yet I took the place of a father to her and I loved her like my own daughter.

At present Katya lives within half a mile of me. She has taken a five-roomed flat and furnished it very comfortably, with the good taste that is part of her nature. If anyone were to try to describe her way of life, then the predominant mood would have to be its indolence. Soft couches and soft chairs for her indolent body, thick carpets for her indolent feet, faded, dim, or soft colours for her indolent eyes; for her indolent soul, plenty of cheap fans on the walls, as well as small pictures in which originality of execution predominates over content; and an over-abundance of little tables and shelves, full of useless and worthless things, shapeless scraps of material in place of curtains. . . . All this, combined with a horror of bright colours, symmetry, and space, shows a perversion of natural taste, too, quite apart from spiritual indolence. Katya lies on a couch for days, reading books, mostly novels and short stories. She goes out only once a day, in the afternoon, to come and see me.

I am working, and Katya sits not far away from me on a sofa. She is silent and keeps wrapping herself in her shawl as though she were cold. Either because I like her, or because I got used to her frequent visits when she was still a little girl, her presence does not prevent me from concentrating. Occasionally I ask her something, without thinking, and she gives me a curt answer; or, for a moment's relaxation, I turn round and look at her as, lost in thought, she browses through a medical journal or a newspaper. It is then that I notice the absence of her former look of trustfulness. Her expression is now cold, indifferent, abstracted, like that of passengers who have to wait a long time for their train. She dresses as before, well and simply, but negligently; it is quite evident that her dress and hair suffer not inconsiderably from the couches and rocking-chairs on which she lies all day and every day. Neither is she as inquisitive as she used to be. She no longer asks me any questions, just as though she had experienced everything in life and did not expect to hear anything new.

At about five o'clock, people can be heard moving about in the large drawing-room and the sitting-room. It is Lisa, who has come back from the conservatoire and brought some of her friends with her. You can hear them playing the piano, trying out their voices, and laughing loudly. Yegor is laying the table in the dining-room, rattling the plates and dishes.

'Good-bye,' says Katya. 'I won't go in to see your people today. They must excuse me. I haven't time. Come and see me.'

When I see her to the front door, she looks me up and down sternly and says in a vexed tone of voice:

'You get thinner and thinner. Why don't you look after yourself? You ought to consult a doctor. I'll go to Sergey Fyodorovich and ask him to come and see you. Let him examine you.'

'No, Katya.'

'I can't understand why your family doesn't do anything about it. A fine family you've got!'

She puts on her coat furiously, and one or two hairpins invariably fall on the floor from her negligently done hair. She is too lazy and in too much of a hurry to tidy her hair; she pushes the straggling curls perfunctorily under her hat and goes away.

When I enter the dining-room, my wife asks me:

'Has Katya been with you? Why didn't she come to see us? It's really extraordinary....'

'Mother,' Lisa says to her reproachfully, 'if she doesn't want to come, she needn't. 'We're not going to go down on our knees to her, are we?'

'Say what you like, it's downright rude! To sit for hours in your father's study and forget all about us! Still, she can do as she likes, I suppose.'

Varya and Lisa both hate Katya. Their hatred is quite incomprehensible to me, but I expect that to understand it one must be a woman. I'm ready to bet anything you like that of the one hundred and fifty young students whom I see almost daily in my lecture room, and of the hundred or so middle-aged and elderly men I see every week, not one would be able to understand their hatred and their feeling of disgust for Katya's past, that is to say, for the fact that she has been pregnant without being married and has had an illegitimate child; at the same time I cannot think of a single woman or girl of my acquaintance who does not consciously or unconsciously entertain such feelings. And this is not because a woman is more virtuous or purer than a man: for virtue and purity, if they are not free from feelings of malice, differ very little from vice. I explain it simply by the backwardness of women. The uneasy feeling of compassion and the pricks of conscience a modern man experiences at the sight of unhappiness speak much more of culture and moral development than do hatred and disgust. A modern woman is as coarse at heart and as liable to burst into tears as a woman in the Middle Ages. In my opinion, those who advise her to get the same education as a man are very sensible.

My wife also dislikes Katya for having been an actress, for her ingratitude, her pride, her eccentricity, and for all those innumerable vices one woman can always discover in another.

Besides myself and my family, we have two or three of my daughter's girl friends to dinner, as well as Alexander Adolfovich Gnekker, Lisa's admirer and suitor. He is a fair young man of about thirty, of medium height, very stout, broad-shouldered, with reddish whiskers round his ears and a dyed moustache which gives his chubby, smooth face a doll-like look. He wears a very short jacket, a fancy waistcoat, large check trousers very wide at the top and very narrow at the bottom, and yellow, flat-heeled boots. He has bulging lobster-like eyes, his tie is like a lobster's tail, and in fact this young man seems to exude the smell of lobster soup. He visits us every day, but no one in the family knows where he comes from, where he was educated, or what he lives on. He does not play any musical instruments, nor does he sing, but he seems to have some connexion with music and singing, sells pianos somewhere, is often to be seen at the conservatoire, knows all the celebrities, and organizes concerts; he gives his opinion on music with the air of an authority, and I have noticed that everybody readily agrees with him.

Rich people always have hangers-on about them, and so have the arts and sciences. I believe there is no science or art in the world which is free from the presence of such 'foreign bodies' as this Mr Gnekker. I am no musician, and I may be wrong about Gnekker, whom I do not know very well, besides. But his authoritative air as well as the air of dignity he assumes when standing beside a grand piano and listening to the singing or playing, strikes me as a little suspicious.

You may be a man of excellent breeding and a privy councillor a hundred times over, but if you have a daughter you can never be absolutely secure against the petty middle-class atmosphere which is so often introduced into your house and your state of mind by courtships, engagements, and weddings. For instance, I can never reconcile myself to the solemn expression on my wife's face every time Gnekker pays us a visit, or to the bottles of Lafitte, port, and sherry which are on the table solely on his account, so that he shall see with his own eyes how grandly and sumptuously we live. Nor can I stand Lisa's laughter and her manner of screwing up her eyes when men come to our house. Above all, I simply cannot understand why a person utterly alien to my habits and the whole tenor of my life, a person who is quite unlike the people I am fond of, should come to visit me every day and have dinner with me. My wife and the servants whisper mysteriously that he is the 'fiancé', but I still can't understand why he is here. His presence bewilders me, just as much as though a Zulu were put next to me at table. I find it strange, too, that my daughter, whom I still look upon as a child, should love that tie, those eyes, those chubby cheeks. . . .

Before, I either enjoyed my dinner or was indifferent to it, but now it rouses in me nothing but boredom and irritation. Ever since I became a privy councillor and served my term as head of the faculty, my family has for some reason considered it necessary to make a thorough change in our menu and our arrangements at dinner. Instead of the plain dishes I was used to as a student and doctor, I am now fed on thick soup with some sort of white bits of something resembling icicles floating about in it, and kidneys in Madeira sauce. My high rank and fame have deprived me for ever of cabbage soup, delicious pies, goose and apple sauce, and bream with buckwheat. They have also deprived me of my maidservant Agasha, a talkative and amusing old woman, instead of whom Yegor, a stupid and supercilious fellow, now serves at dinner, with a white cotton glove on his right hand. The intervals between the courses are brief, but they seem terribly long, because there is nothing to fill them. Gone are the old gaiety, the unconstrained conversations, the jokes, the laughter, the mutual endearments, and the feeling of happiness which thrilled the children, my wife, and myself when we used to meet round the dinner table.

To a busy man like myself, dinner meant a time of rest in the family circle, and to my wife and children it was a festive occasion, brief, it is true, but bright and joyful, for they knew that for half an hour I belonged not to science, not to my students, but to them alone and no one else. No more getting tipsy on one glass of wine, no more Agasha, no more bream with buckwheat, no more of the gay uproar at table following slightly unconventional incidents such as a fight between the cat and the dog under the table or Katya's bandage falling off her cheek into her soup.

Our present dinner is as unappetizing to describe as it is to eat.

There's my wife's solemn face, with its assumed air of gravity and habitual worried expression as she nervously examines our plates.

'I see you don't like the roast meat,' she says, addressing Gnekker. 'You don't really, do you? Tell me, please.'

'Don't worry, my dear,' I feel obliged to say. 'The meat's delicious.'

'You always take my part, Nikolai,' she says. 'You never tell the truth. Why does Mr Gnekker eat so little?'

And this goes on all through the meal.

Lisa laughs her abrupt, staccato laugh and screws up her eyes. I look at both of them, and it is only now, at dinner, that I see quite clearly that their inner life has long ago escaped me completely. I have a feeling as though I had once – a long time ago – lived at home with a real family, but that now I am dining out with a woman who is not really my wife and looking at a girl who is not really my daughter Lisa. A great change has taken place in both of them, and I have failed to notice the long process that has led up to the change, so it's no wonder I'm unable to understand it now. Why did this change take place? I don't know. Perhaps the whole trouble is that the Lord has not given my wife and daughter the strength He gave me. From my childhood I have grown accustomed to resisting outside influences, and I have steeled myself properly to do so; such vicissitudes of life as fame, high rank, transition from comfort to living beyond my means, acquaintance with the aristocracy, and so on, have had no particular influence on me, and I have remained safe and sound; but on the weak, on my wife and Lisa, unsteeled as they were, all this has fallen like an avalanche and crushed them.

The young ladies and Gnekker talk of fugues, counterpoint, singers and pianists, Bach and Brahms; and my wife, afraid of being suspected to be an ignoramus in music, smiles as though she knows all about it and murmurs: 'Splendid, splendid. . . . Really. . . . No?' Gnekker eats sedately, jokes sedately, and listens condescendingly to the remarks of the young ladies. Occasionally he cannot resist his impulse to talk bad French, and then for some unknown reason he finds it necessary to address me grandly as 'Votre Excellence'.

And I am morose. Evidently I embarrass them, and they embarrass me. I have never before been aware of possessing any class antagonisms, but now I am worried by something of the kind. I try to find only bad traits in Gnekker, find them in no time at all, and am tormented by the thought that a man who does not belong to my social circle should have usurped the place of my daughter's fiancé. His presence has a bad effect on me in another way, too. As a rule, when I am left alone or find myself among people I am fond of, it never occurs to me to think of my own achievements, and if I do think of them they seem so trivial to me, as though I had become a scientist only yesterday; but in the company of people like Gnekker my achievements seem to tower like a cloud-capped mountain, at the foot of which the swarming Gnekkers are hardly visible to the eye.

After dinner I retire to my study and light my pipe, one for the whole day, the only survivor of my bad old habit of smoking from morning till night. While I am smoking, my wife comes in and sits down to talk to me. Just as in the morning, I know beforehand what our talk will be about.

'I must have a serious talk to you, Nikolai,' she begins. 'About Lisa, I mean. Why don't you pay any attention?'

'Oh? To what?'

'You pretend not to notice anything. It's not good enough. You can't just ignore everything. Gnekker will probably propose to Lisa. What do you say to that?'

'Well, I can't very well say he's a bad man because I don't know him well enough; but I've told you a thousand times that I don't like him.'

'But,' she says, getting up and pacing the room agitatedly, 'you can't take up such an attitude towards a serious step like that! You can't. When it concerns the happiness of your daughter, we must abandon all personal considerations. I know you don't like him. All right. But if we refuse him now, if we break it off, how can you be sure that Lisa won't bear a grudge against us all her life? There aren't many eligible young men nowadays, and it is quite likely that she won't get another chance. He is very much in love with Lisa, and I think she likes him. Of course, he has no definite position of any kind, but we can't do anything about it, can we? Let's hope that one day he will get some permanent job. He comes from a good family and is well off.'

'How do you know that?'

'He said so. His father has a big house in Kharkov and an estate nearby. I'm afraid, Nikolai, you'll have to go to Kharkov.'

'Why?'

'You'll be able to find out there. You know some of the professors there, and they'll help you. I'd go there myself, but I'm a woman. I can't. . . .'

'I won't go to Kharkov,' I say sullenly.

My wife looks frightened and an expression of agonizing pain appears on her face.

'For God's sake, Nikolai!' she implores me with a whimper. 'For God's sake, take this burden off my shoulders. I'm suffering!'

It hurts me to look at her.

'Oh, very well, Varya,' I say, tenderly. 'I'll go to Kharkov if you want me to. I'll do anything you want.'

She presses her handkerchief to her eyes and goes to her room to cry. I am left alone.

A little later a lamp is brought in. Familiar shadows I've long since come to dislike fall on the walls from the chairs and the lampshade, and when I look at them it seems to me that it is already night and my damned insomnia is about to begin. I lie down on my bed, then get up again and pace the room, and lie down again. . . . As a rule, my nervous tension reaches its climax after dinner, before the evening. I begin to cry for no apparent reason and hide my head under the pillow. At those moments I'm afraid someone may come in. I'm afraid of sudden death. I'm ashamed of my tears, and altogether something awful is going on inside me. I feel that I can't bear to look any longer at my lamp, my books, the shadows on the floor, that I can no longer bear to hear the voices in the drawing-room. A kind of invisible and incomprehensible force pushes me violently out of the house. I jump up, put on my hat and coat hurriedly, and go cautiously out into the street, taking every care not to be seen by anyone in the house. Where am I to go?

The answer to this question has long been in my head – to Katya.

III

As usual, she is lying on the ottoman or on a couch, reading a book. Seeing me, she raises her head indolently, sits up, and stretches out her hand to me.

'You're always lying down,' I say after a short pause for rest. 'It's not good for you. You ought to find something to do.'

'Oh?'

'Yes, you ought to find something to do.'

'What? A woman can become either a domestic servant or an actress.'

'Very well then. If you don't want to do domestic work, why not go on the stage?'

She makes no answer.

'You ought to get married,' I say, half in jest.

'There's no one I'd like to marry. Besides, I don't want to marry.'

'But you can't live like that.'

'Without a husband? What does that matter? There are lots of men, if that were what I wanted.'

'That's not nice, Katya.'

'What's not nice?'

'Why, what you just said.'

Noticing that I am upset and wishing to gloss over the bad impression, Katya says:

'Come, I'll show you something. This way.'

She takes me to a small and very cosy little room, points to the writing desk, and says:

'There it is. I got it ready for you. You will work here. Come every day, and bring your work with you. At home they only interfere with you. Will you work here? Would you like to?'

Not to hurt her feelings by a refusal, I tell her I will and that I like her room very much. Then we both sit down in the cosy little room and begin to talk.

Warm comfortable surroundings and the presence of an understanding companion arouse in me not a feeling of pleasure as before but a strong desire to complain and grumble. For some reason it seems to me that if I complained and grumbled I'd feel better.

'Things are bad, my dear,' I begin with a sigh. 'Very bad.'

'What's the matter?'

'You see, my dear, the highest and most sacred prerogative of kings is the right to pardon. I have always felt myself a king, for I have availed myself of that prerogative again and again. I have never judged, I have always made allowances, I have gladly granted free pardons right and left to everybody. Where others have protested and been indignant, I have only advised and persuaded. All my life I have tried my best to make my company tolerable to my family, my students, my colleagues, and my servants. And this attitude of mine towards people has, I know, had a salutary effect on everyone who has had anything to do with me. But now I am a king no longer. What is going on inside me now is something tolerable only in a slave: day and night evil thoughts fill my head, and feelings I never knew before have built a nest in my heart. I hate, I despise, I am filled with indignation, I am exasperated, and I am afraid. I have become quite excessively strict, demanding, irritable, rude, suspicious. Even the things which formerly used to make me perpetrate a pun, and laugh good-humouredly, merely make me feel sick at heart now. My sense of logic, too, has undergone a change: before, it was only money I despised, but what I loathe now is not money but the rich, as if they were to blame; before, I hated violence and tyranny, but now I hate the people who use violence, as though they alone were to blame, and not all of us who do not know how to educate one another. What does it mean? If my new thoughts and my new feelings are the result of a change in my convictions, how can this change have arisen? Has the world become worse? Have I become better? Or have I been blind and indifferent till now? If this change has arisen from a general decline in my mental and physical faculties – for I am sick, you see, I lose weight every day – then my position is pitiful indeed. For it can only mean that my new thoughts are morbid and abnormal, and that I ought to be ashamed of them and regard them as contemptible.'

'Sickness has nothing to do with it,' Katya interrupts me. 'It is simply that your eyes have been opened. That's all. You see things now which for some reason you did not want to notice before. In my opinion, you must first of all make a final break with your family and leave them.'

'You're talking nonsense.'

'You don't love them any more, do you? Then why be hypocritical about it? What sort of a family is it, anyhow? Nonentities! If they were to die today, by tomorrow no one would notice their absence.'

Katya despises my wife and daughter as much as they hate her. It is almost impossible nowadays to speak of people being entitled to despise one another. But if one accepts Katya's point of view and admits that they are entitled to, one has to admit that she is just as much entitled to despise my wife and daughter as they are to hate her.

'Nonentities,' she repeats. 'Did you have any dinner today? They didn't forget to call you to have your dinner? They still remember that you exist?'

'Katya,' I say severely, 'please don't talk like that.'

'Why, do you think I enjoy talking about them? I'd be glad not to know them at all! Listen to me, dear. Leave everything and go away. Go abroad. The sooner the better.'

'What nonsense! And the university?'

'And the university, too. What do you want it for? What's the use of it, anyway? You've been lecturing for thirty years, and where are your pupils? Are there many famous scientists among them? Count them! And to multiply the doctors who exploit ignorance and make fortunes you don't need to be a good and talented man. You're not wanted.'

'Dear me, how severe you are!' I exclaim, horrified. 'How severe! Not another word, or I'll go. I don't know what to reply to these bitter things you say.'

The maid comes in to tell us that tea is served. At the tea table our conversation, thank God, takes a different turn. Having uttered my complaints, I cannot resist giving way to another weakness of old age – reminiscences. I tell Katya about my past, and to my own great surprise expatiate on incidents I never suspected I remembered so well. She listens to me with deep emotion, with pride, with bated breath. I particularly like to tell her how I once studied at a theological college and how I dreamed of entering a university.

'I used to walk about in the grounds of the seminary,' I tell her, 'and whenever the wind brought the strains of a concertina and a song from some far-away country pub, or a *troika* dashed past the seminary fence with a jingle of bells, it was enough for a feeling of happiness to flood not only my breast, but also my belly, legs, and hands. . . . I would listen to the strains of the concertina or to the sounds of the harness bells dying away in the distance, and imagine myself a doctor, and paint all sorts of pictures – each one more thrilling than the next. And, as you see, my dreams came true. I have got more than I dared to dream of. For thirty years I have been a popular professor, have had excellent colleagues, enjoyed an honourable reputation. I loved, I married for passionate love, I had children. In short, looking back, the whole of my life seems a beautiful and ably made composition. All that remains for me to do now is not to spoil the ending. This makes it necessary that I should die like a man. If death is really a danger, then it must be met in a way worthy of a teacher, a scientist, and a citizen of a Christian state: boldly and in a calm spirit. But I'm afraid I am spoiling the ending. I am drowning, and I am calling to you for help, and you say: "Drown! That's how it should be!" '

At that moment the front door bell rings. Katya and I both recognize the ring and say:

'That must be Mikhail Fyodorovich!'

And indeed a minute later Mikhail Fyodorovich, a university colleague of mine, a philologist, comes in. He is a tall, well-built man of fifty, clean-shaven, with thick grey hair and black eyebrows. He is a good man and an excellent friend. He belongs to an old aristocratic family, rather fortunate and gifted, which has played an outstanding part in the history of our literature and education. He is himself clever, gifted, and highly educated, but not without certain oddities of character. To a certain extent all of us are a bit odd, all of us are eccentrics, but his oddities are rather exceptional and not without danger to his friends. Among the latter I know quite a few who are unable to see his many good points because of these oddities of his.

As he comes in, he slowly removes his gloves and says in his velvety bass:

'Good evening. Having tea? Excellent! It's hellishly cold.'

Then he sits down at the table, takes a glass of tea, and immediately starts talking. The most characteristic thing about his conversation is its invariably jocular tone, a sort of blend of philosophy and buffoonery, like Shakespeare's grave-diggers. He always talks about serious things, but never seriously. His opinions are always harsh and abusive, but his gentle, smooth, and jocular tone somehow prevents his harshness and abusiveness from grating on the ears, and you soon get used to them. Every evening he brings half a dozen stories of university life, and he usually starts with them when he sits down at the table.

'Oh dear,' he sighs, twitching his black eyebrows sardonically, 'what comical fellows there are in the world!'

'Why?' asks Katya.

'I was coming from my lecture today and who should I meet on the stairs but that silly old fool N. There he was, his horsy chin thrust out as usual, looking for someone to complain to about his headaches, his wife, and the students who won't go to his lectures. Good Lord, I thought, he's seen me and I'm in for it now, no escape . . .'

And so on in the same vein. Or he would begin like this:

'I was at our Z's public lecture yesterday. I am amazed how our *alma mater* (may she forgive me for mentioning her at this witching hour of night) dares to show the public such imbeciles and patent idiots as that Z fellow. Why, he's known all over Europe as a born fool. Good Lord, you wouldn't find another like him in the whole of Europe, not even if you went looking for him with a torch in daylight! He lectures – believe it or not – just as if he were sucking sweets, with a sort of lisp. Gets frightened, can't read his own writing, his insipid thoughts hardly moving at all, like a bishop riding a bicycle, and worst of all you can't make out what he's trying to say. You could die of boredom, which can only be compared to the boredom in the assembly hall at the annual conferment of degrees, when the traditional graduation speech – damn it – is made.'

And immediately an abrupt change of subject.

'About three years ago – Nikolai Stepanych here will remember – it was my turn to make that speech. Hot, close, my uniform tight under my arms – frightful! I spoke for half an hour, an hour, an hour and a half, two hours . . . Well, I thought to myself, thank God I've only ten more pages left. Actually I counted on leaving

79

out the last four pages, for they were quite superfluous. So, I said to myself, that leaves only six pages. At that moment I happened to look up and there in the front row I saw a general with a ribbon round his neck, and a bishop, sitting side by side. The poor fellows, stiff with boredom, were staring open-eyed to keep themselves from falling asleep, but trying to look as if they were following my speech closely, as if they understood it and liked it. Well, I thought, if you really like it, you shall have the whole damn lot! Just to teach you a lesson. So I read through all the last four pages!'

When he talks, only his eyes and eyebrows smile, as is the case with all sardonic people. There is neither hatred nor malice in his eyes at such moments, but a great deal of wit, and the sort of fox-like cunning which can only be seen in the faces of very observant people. Talking of his eyes, I have noticed another peculiarity about them. When he takes a glass from Katya, or listens to her remarks, or follows her with his eyes when she goes out of the room for a little while, I catch a look in his eyes of something gentle, beseeching, pure. . . .

The maid takes the samovar away and places on the table a big piece of cheese, fruit, and a bottle of Crimean champagne, a rather bad wine which Katya had got to like while living in the Crimea. Mikhail Fyodorovich takes two packs of cards from the bookcase and begins to lay out a game of patience. He assures us that some games of patience demand great concentration and attention, but he goes on talking nevertheless while laying out the cards. Katya keeps an attentive eye on his cards and helps him, more by dumb show than words. During the whole of the evening she drinks no more than two glasses of wine; I drink only a quarter of a glass; the rest falls to the lot of Mikhail Fyodorovich, who can drink any amount without getting drunk.

Over the game of patience we solve all sorts of problems, mostly of the lofty order, and most of our sharpest criticism is directed against our dearest love – science.

'Science, thank heavens, has had its day,' says Mikhail Fyodorovich. 'It's goose is cooked. Yes, sir. Mankind is beginning to feel the need of putting something else in its place. It grew up in the soil of prejudice, it was nourished on prejudice and is now itself the quintessence of prejudice, like its defunct grandmothers' alchemy, metaphysics, and philosophy. And, really, what has science given to man? The difference between the learned Europeans and the Chinese, who get along without science, is trifling, purely external. The Chinese have no knowledge of science, and what have they lost?'

'Flies have no knowledge of science, either,' I say, 'but what does it prove?'

'You needn't get angry, Nikolai Stepanych. I'm only saying it between ourselves. I'm much more careful than you think. I wouldn't dream of saying so in public. The great majority of people still cherish the prejudice that the arts and sciences are superior to agriculture and commerce, superior to industry. Our sect makes a living out of that prejudice, and I'm the last man in the world to destroy it. God forbid!'

During the game of patience the younger generation, too, gets it in the neck.

'Our student audiences, too, are degenerating rapidly,' Mikhail Fyodorovich declares with a sigh. 'I'm not speaking of ideals and so on – if only they knew how to work and think properly. Yes, indeed, "Sadly I behold our younger generation", as the poet said.'

'Yes, they're terribly degenerate,' agrees Katya. 'Tell me, has there been even one outstanding personality among your students during the last five or ten years?'

'I don't know about the other professors, but I can't think of anyone among my own students.'

'I've met many students and young scholars in my time, as well as a great number of actors, and, well, I don't think I've ever been fortunate enough to come across a single interesting person among them, let alone demigods or men of real talent.'

All this talk about degeneracy always makes me feel as if I had accidentally overheard some unpleasant remark about my daughter. What I find so offensive is that these accusations are utterly unfounded and are based on such hackneyed commonplaces and such scarifying phantoms as degeneracy, lack of ideals, or references to the glorious past. Any accusation, even if made in the presence of ladies, should be formulated with the utmost definitiveness, otherwise it is no accusation but mere gossip, unworthy of decent people.

I am an old man; I've been a university teacher for thirty years and I have not noticed any degeneration or lack of ideals, and I don't find that things are worse now than before. My caretaker Nikolai, whose experience in this case is not without value, maintains that students today are neither better nor worse than those of former times.

If I were asked what it was I did not like about my present students, I should not give an immediate answer or say much, but whatever I said would be sufficiently definite. I know their shortcomings, and I need not therefore resort to some hazy commonplaces. What I don't like about them is that they smoke and drink too much and get married too late, that they are feckless, and often so callous that they do not seem to notice that some of their fellow-students are starving, and that they don't pay their debts to the Students' Aid Society. They are ignorant of modern languages and express themselves incorrectly in Russian; only yesterday, my colleague the professor of hygienics complained to me that he had to give twice as many lectures because of their unsatisfactory knowledge of physics and complete ignorance of meteorology. They are readily influenced by the latest writers, even those who are not the best, but are completely indifferent to classics like Shakespeare, Marcus Aurelius, Epictetus, and Pascal, and their lack of experience of everyday life is perhaps best seen in this inability to distinguish between the great and the small. All the difficult questions of a more or less social character (for instance, the question of land settlement in distant provinces) they solve by subscription lists, and not by scientific investigation and experiment, though that is at their disposal and corresponds entirely with their vocation. They readily become house physicians, assistant lecturers, laboratory assistants, non-resident physicians, and they are quite willing to occupy these posts till they are forty, though independence, a sense of freedom, and personal initiative are not less necessary in science than they are, for instance, in art or commerce. I have pupils and students, but no assistants and successors, and that is why I love them and feel for them but am not proud of them. Etc., etc. . . . .

But such shortcomings, however numerous, can give rise to pessimistic or abusive moods only in a timid and pusillanimous man. They are all of an accidental and transitory nature, and depend entirely on circumstances; in ten or so years they will most probably disappear or give way to other and fresh shortcomings, which are inevitable and which will in turn frighten the faint-hearted. The sins of students often annoy me, but this annoyance is nothing compared to the joy I have felt these thirty years when talking to my students, lecturing to them, watching their relationships, and comparing them to people who do not belong to their social group.

Mikhail Fyodorovich goes on with his disparaging talk, Katya listens to him, and neither of them notices the deep abyss into which such a seemingly innocent pastime as talking ill of their neighbours is leading them. They do not seem to realize how an ordinary conversation can gradually turn into mockery and derision, and how both of them even stoop to defamation and slander.

'You certainly come across some queer types,' says Mikhail Fyodorovich. 'I went to see Yegor Petrovich yesterday and found one of your medicos there. A third-year student, I believe. A curious face. Reminded me of Dobrolyubov: a stamp of profound thought on his brow. We started talking. "Wonders will never cease, young man," I said to him. "I've just read that some German – I forget his name – has extracted a new alkaloid from the human brain – idiotine." And what do you think? He really believed me – there was an expression of reverential awe on his face: "See what our scientists can do!" And the other day I went to the theatre. I took my seat. In front of me two students were sitting, one apparently a law student, one of the "comrades", and the other, a hirsute fellow, a medical student. The medical student was as drunk as a cobbler. He just sat there dozing and nodding. But as soon as an actor began to recite some soliloquy in a loud voice or simply raised his voice, our medico gave a start, nudged his neighbour, and asked: "What did he say! Was it noble?" "Yes, very noble," our "comrade" replied. "Bravo!" roared the medical student. "Noble! Bravo!" You see, the drunken sot didn't go to the theatre for the sake of art, but for noble sentiments. It's noble sentiments he wants.'

Katya listens and laughs. Her laughter is rather strange: inhalation followed rapidly and rhythmically by exhalation. It is as though she were playing a mouth-organ, and in her face only her nostrils seem to laugh. I lose heart and don't know what to say. I flare up, jump up from my seat, and shout:

'Shut up, will you? What are you sitting there like a couple of toads for, poisoning the air with your breath? Enough!'

And without waiting for them to stop their slanderous talk, I get up to go home. It is time, anyway – eleven o'clock.

'I'll stay a little longer,' says Mikhail Fyodorovich. 'You don't mind, do you, Yekaterina Vladimirovna?'

'Not in the least,' replies Katya.

'*Bene*. In that case, let's have another bottle.'

They see me off to the hall, with candles in their hands, and while I am putting on my fur coat Mikhail Fyodorovich says:

'You're looking awfully thin and old today, Nikolai Stepanych. What's the matter? Are you ill?'

'Yes, a little.'

'He won't see a doctor,' Katya puts in gloomily.

'Why don't you? You can't go on like this. The Lord helps those who help themselves, my dear chap. Give my regards to your wife and daughter and my apologies for not coming to see them. I shall be going abroad shortly and I'll come to say good-bye before I leave. I shan't forget. I'm leaving next week.'

I come away from Katya's feeling irritated, frightened by the talk of my illness, and dissatisfied with myself. I ask myself why really I don't consult one of my colleagues. But immediately I can see my colleague, after examining me, going silently over to the window, standing there for a while thinking, then turning round to me and saying casually, trying to prevent me from reading the truth on his face: 'I don't see anything special so far. But all the same, my dear colleague, I'd advise you to give up your work.' And that will deprive me of my last hope.

Which of us doesn't have hopes? Now, when I diagnose and treat myself, I sometimes hope that my ignorance deceives me, that I am mistaken about the albumen and sugar I find in my urine, about my heart, and about the oedematose swellings which I have already noticed in the morning; when, with the eagerness of a hypochondriac, I again read through the text-books on therapy and change my medicine every day, it always seems to me that I shall come across something comforting. The triviality of it all!

Whether the sky is covered with clouds or the moon and stars shine in it, on returning home I always look up at it and think that I shall soon be dead. It would seem that at such moments my thoughts ought to be as deep as the sky, bright and striking. . . . But no! I think about myself, my wife, Lisa, Gnekker, the students, and about people in general; my thoughts are mean and trivial. I try to deceive myself, and my view on life might be expressed in the words of the famous Arakcheyev, who wrote in one of his private letters: 'No good thing in the world can be without some evil, and there is always more bad than good.' In other words, everything is disgusting, there is nothing to live for, and the sixty-two years of my life must be regarded as wasted. I catch myself in these thoughts and try to convince myself that they are accidental and transient and not deeply rooted in me, but immediately I think:

'If that is so, then why do I long to go to those two toads every evening?'

And I vow never to go and see Katya again, though I know very well that I will go to her again the next day.

As I pull my front-door bell and then go upstairs, I feel that I have no family and have no desire to get it back. It is clear that these new Arakcheyev thoughts of mine are neither accidental nor transient, but have taken possession of all my being. With a sick conscience, dejected, languid, scarcely able to move my limbs, as though carrying an enormous weight on my shoulders, I go to bed and soon fall asleep.

And then – insomnia.

IV

Summer comes and life changes.

One fine morning Lisa comes into my room and says in a jesting tone:

'Come on, your excellency! Everything's ready.'

My excellency is led out into the street, put into a cab, and driven away. Having nothing to do, I read the signboards backwards as I am being driven past. The word for 'tavern', *Traktir*, beomes Ritkart. That would make a very good name for a German nobleman's family – Baroness von Ritkart. Further on I drive across open country, past a cemetery, which makes no impression on me whatsoever, although I shall be lying there soon. Then we are driven through a wood and once more through open country. Nothing interesting. After two hours' drive my excellency is taken to the ground floor of a country cottage and placed in a small but very cheerful room with blue wallpaper.

At night insomnia again, but in the morning I do not keep awake and do not listen to my wife, but stay in bed. I am not asleep. I am in that somnolent state when one is hardly conscious of one's surroundings, and when one knows that one is not asleep and yet has dreams. At noon I get up and sit down at my desk from force of habit, though I don't work but amuse myself with yellow French paperbacks sent by Katya. No doubt it would be more patriotic to read Russian authors, but to tell the truth I am not particularly fond of them. With the exception of one or two classics, the whole of our modern literature strikes me not as literature but as a kind of home industry which only exists because of being encouraged and whose products are only reluctantly purchased. The best of these home products can hardly be described as in any way remarkable, and one cannot praise them sincerely without a qualifying 'but'; the same can be said about all the literary novelties I have read during the last ten or fifteen years. Clever, noble, but not talented; talented, noble, but not clever; or finally, talented, clever, but not noble.

I cannot honestly say that French books are talented, clever, and noble, and they do not really satisfy me; but they are not as boring as Russian books, and it is not rare to find in them the most important element of creative art – the sense of personal freedom, which Russian authors do not possess. I cannot remember a single new book in which the author does not do his best from the very first page to entangle himself in all sorts of conventionalities and compromises with his conscience. One writer is afraid to speak of the naked body, another has bound himself hand and foot by psychological analysis, a third must have 'a warm attitude towards his fellow-men', a fourth purposely fills his pages with descriptive passages so as not to be suspected of tendentiousness. . . . One is absolutely set on appearing in his works as a member of the middle classes, another as a nobleman; and so on. Deliberateness, cautiousness, craftiness, but no freedom, no courage to write as one likes, and therefore no creative art.

All this refers to works of fiction.

As for serious articles by Russian writers, on sociology, for instance, on art, and so on, I don't read them, out of mere timidity. As a boy and a young man I was for some reason afraid of hall porters and theatre attendants, and that fear has remained with me to this day. I am still afraid of them. People say that it is very difficult to understand why hall porters and theatre attendants look so self-important, so haughty, so grandly impolite. When I read serious articles I feel the same kind of vague apprehension. Their extraordinary self-importance, their magisterial playfulness, the familiarity with which they treat foreign authors, the pompous way in which they utter their clichés – all this I find utterly incomprehensible and frightening, and quite unlike the modesty and the calm gentlemanly tone to which I am used when reading our writers on medicine and the natural sciences. It is not only articles. I find it as hard to read even the translations made or edited by serious Russian writers. The arrogantly self-assured and complacent tone of the prefaces, the multitude of footnotes by the translator which prevent me from concentrating, the question marks and parenthetical 'sics' scattered by the generous translator throughout the book or article, seem to me an unwarranted intrusion both on the author's independence and on my own as a reader.

I was once invited in my capacity as an expert to the assize court; during a break in the proceedings, one of the other experts called my attention to the rude way in which the public prosecutor treated the defendants, among whom were two educated women. I don't think I exaggerated at all when I replied that this rudeness was no worse than the way authors of serious articles treat one another. Indeed, they treat one another so rudely that one can only speak of it with pain. They treat each other or the writers they criticize either with excessive respect, without regard to their own dignity, or on the other hand with less reserve than I have treated my future son-in-law Gnekker in these notes and in my thoughts. Accusations of irresponsibility, of ulterior motives, and even of all sorts of crimes are the usual embellishments of serious articles. And that is, as young doctors like to say in their papers, quite *ultima ratio*. Such an attitude cannot but have an effect on the morals of the younger generation of writers, and I am therefore not at all surprised to find that in the new novels added to our literature during the last ten or fifteen years the heroes drink a great deal of vodka and the heroines are anything but chaste.

I read French novels and keep glancing through the open window. I can see the toothed palings of the fence of my front garden, a couple of gaunt trees, and beyond the fence the road, a field, then a wide strip of pine forest. I am often amused to watch a boy and a girl, both ragged and almost white-haired, climbing the fence and laughing at my bald pate. In their sparkling eyes I can read: 'Come on, baldy!' These are almost the only human beings who do not seem to care a damn about my reputation or my high rank.

I don't have visitors every day now. I will mention only the visits of Nikolai and Peter Ignatyevich. Nikolai usually comes to see me on holidays, apparently on business but actually because he likes to see me. When he arrives, he is more than a bit tight, which never happens to him in the winter.

'Well, how are things?' I ask, coming out into the hall.

'Sir,' he says, pressing his hand to his heart and looking at me with the rapture of a lover, 'may the Lord strike me dead where I stand! May I drop dead! *Gaudeamus igitur juvenestus . . .*'

And he kisses me eagerly on the shoulders, the sleeves, the buttons.

'Is everything all right over there?' I ask.

'Sir, as before God . . .'

He never stops invoking the deity, without rhyme or reason, and I soon get bored with him and send him off to the kitchen, where he is given dinner. Peter Ignatyevich also comes on holidays specially to see me and share his thoughts with me. He usually sits down near the table, modest, clean, sensible, not daring to cross his legs or lean on the table. And all the time he goes on talking to me in his quiet, even, thin voice about what he considers the highly interesting and piquant items he has gleaned from periodicals and books. These are alike and follow the same pattern: a Frenchman has made a discovery, someone else – a German – has shown him up, proving that the discovery was made as long ago as 1870 by some American, and a third, also a German, has outwitted them both, showing that they have made fools of themselves by mistaking air bubbles under a microscope for a dark pigment. Even when he wants to amuse me, Peter Ignatyevich tells his stories at great length and in detail, as though he were defending a thesis, with a most detailed enumeration of the bibliographical sources he has used, taking particular care not to make mistakes in his dates, the number of the journal, or names, never saying Petit but always Jean-Jacques Petit. If he happens to stay to dinner, he tells the same piquant stories all through the meal, boring us all to death. If Gnekker and Lisa start talking in his presence about fugues, counterpoint, Bach, or Brahms, he lowers his head modestly and looks embarrassed: he feels ashamed that people should be talking of such trivial things in the presence of such serious people as myself and him.

In my present mood, five minutes are enough to bore me as much as though I had been seeing and listening to him for an eternity. I hate the poor wretch. His quiet even voice and his pedantic language make me wilt, and his stories dull my senses. He cherishes the most kindly feelings towards me, and talks to me only to give me pleasure; and I repay him by staring fixedly at him as though I wanted to hypnotize him, and keep saying to myself: 'Go, go, go! . . .' But he is proof against suggestion and sits, sits, sits. . . .

While he is with me I cannot get rid of the thought that when I die, he will most probably be appointed in my place, and my poor lecture-room appears to me like an oasis in which the well-spring has dried up; and I am uncivil, silent, morose with Peter Ignatyevich, as though it were his fault and not mine that I am having such thoughts. When, as is his wont, he starts extolling the German scientists, I no longer answer him jokingly, but mutter glumly:

'Your Germans are donkeys. . . .'

This reminds me of the late Professor Nikita Krylov, who, when bathing in Reval with Pirogov, got angry with the water, which was very cold, and swore: 'Bloody Germans!' I behave badly to Peter Ignatyevich, and it is only when he is gone and I catch a glimpse of his grey hat on the other side of the fence that I feel like calling him back and saying: 'I'm sorry, my dear fellow!'

Dinner is much more boring than in the winter. The same Gnekker, whom I now hate and despise, dines with us almost every day. Before, I used to put up with his presence in silence, but now I direct all sorts of uncomplimentary remarks at him, which make my wife and Lisa blush. Carried away by malicious feeling. I often say silly things, and I don't know why I say them. Thus, one day, after looking at Gnekker contemptuously for a long time, I blurted out for no reason at all:

> Eagles may often lower than chickens fly
> But never will chickens fly up to the sky. . . .

And what's so annoying is that the chicken Gnekker turns out to be much more intelligent than the eagle professor. Knowing that my wife and daughter are on his side, he employs the following tactics: replies to my uncomplimentary remarks with a condescending silence (the old man has gone off his head, what's the use of talking to him?), or keeps pulling my leg goodhumouredly. It really is amazing how petty a man may become. During the whole of the meal I am capable of imagining that Gnekker will turn out to be an adventurer, that my wife and daughter will realize their mistake, that I will tease them — and similar ridiculous fantasies, when I have one foot in the grave!

There are misunderstandings now, too, which I was previously aware of only by hearsay. Greatly as I am ashamed of it, I will describe one of them, which occurred after dinner the other day.

I was sitting in my room, smoking my pipe. My wife came in as usual and began telling me how nice it would be if I went to Kharkov, now that it was so warm and I was free, and made inquiries about Gnekker.

'All right,' I said, 'I'll go.'

My wife, looking pleased with me, got up and went to the door, but turned back at once.

'Incidentally,' she said, 'there's something I want to talk to you about. I'm sorry, but you see all our friends and neighbours have been remarking on the way you see Katya every day. Now I agree she's a clever and well-educated girl, and I daresay you find it agreeable to be with her, but don't you think that for a man of your age and your position it's a bit odd to take pleasure in her company? Besides, her reputation, you know ...'

All my blood suddenly rushed from my brain, my eyes flashed, I jumped to my feet, and clutching at my head and stamping, I screamed in a frenzy:

'Leave me alone! Leave me alone! Leave me!'

I expect my face must have looked terribly distorted, and my voice must have sounded very strange, for my wife turned pale and also uttered a kind of frenzied desperate scream. At our cries, Lisa and Gnekker came rushing in, followed by Yegor.

'Leave me!' I kept shouting. 'Get out! Leave me!'

My feet grew numb, as if they did not exist. I felt myself falling into somebody's arms, for a few moments I heard someone sobbing, then I sank into a faint which lasted for two or three hours.

Now about Katya. She comes to see me every day, which of course our friends and neighbours could not help noticing. She comes in for a few minutes and then takes me out for a drive. She has her own horse and a new carriage she bought this summer. Altogether she lives in grand style. She has rented an expensive country residence with a large garden and moved her furniture into it, keeps two maids and a coachman. . . .

'What will you live on, Katya, after you've squandered all the money your father left you?'

'I'll worry about it when it happens,' she replies.

'That money, my dear, deserves to be treated with more respect. It was earned by a good man and by honest labour.'

'You've told me that before. I know.'

At first we drive through open country, then through the pine wood I can see from my window. The countryside looks as beautiful to me as ever, though the devil does whisper in my ear that all those pines and firs, those birds and white clouds, will not notice my absence in three or four months after I am dead. Katya likes taking the reins, she enjoys the fine weather and my sitting beside her. She's in a good mood and does not say disagreeable things.

'You're a very good man, Nikolai,' she says. 'You're a rare specimen, and there's no actor who could represent you on the stage.

Even a bad actor could manage me or Mikhail Fyodorovich, but no one could do you. And I envy you. I envy you terribly. But what do I represent? What?'

She thinks for a moment, then asks me:

'Tell me, I am a negative phenomenon, aren't I?'

'Yes,' I reply.

'I see. So what am I to do?'

What answer can I give her? It is easy to say 'work' or 'give your property to the poor' or 'know thyself', and because it is so easy to say that, I don't know what answer to give.

My therapeutist colleagues, when teaching, tell their students 'to individualize each separate case'. One has only to take this advice to realize that the remedies recommended in textbooks as the best, and entirely suitable as a standard rule, are quite unsuitable in individual cases. The same applies to moral ailments.

But I have to give her an answer, so I say:

'You've too much time on your hands, my dear. You ought to find some occupation. Why shouldn't you go on the stage again, if that's your vocation?'

'I can't.'

'You talk and look as if you'd been hard done by. I don't like it, my dear. It's all your own fault. Remember you began by getting angry with people and things, but you did nothing to improve the one or the other. You didn't struggle against evil, you got tired, and you're the victim of your own weakness, not of the struggle. I realize, of course, that you were young and inexperienced then. Now everything can be different. Go back to the stage – do! You will work, serve the sacred cause of art. . . .'

'Don't try to pull the wool over my eyes, my dear sir,' Katya interrupts me. 'Let's agree once and for all to talk about actors, actresses, and writers, and let's leave art out of it. You're a rare and excellent person, but I don't think your knowledge of art is so thorough as to justify you in calling it sacred with a clear conscience. You have neither the ear nor the flair for art. You have been busy all your life, and haven't had the time for acquiring the flair. And as a matter of fact I don't like all this talk about art,' she goes on nervously. 'I don't like it. Art has been vulgarized enough already, thank you very much!'

'Who vulgarized it?'

'The actors by drunkenness, the papers by their over-familiar treatment, clever people by philosophy.'

'Philosophy has nothing to do with it.'

'Besides, anyone who philosophizes shows that he understands nothing.'

To prevent our conversation from turning into an interchange of sharp words, I hasten to change the subject, and then I am silent for a long time. It is only when we emerge from the woods and approach Katya's house that I return to our former subject of conversation.

'You didn't answer me,' I say. 'Why don't you want to go back to the stage? Or do you?'

'My dear sir, that really is cruel!' she cries, and suddenly blushes all over. 'Do you want me to tell you the truth? By all means if that's — if that's what you want. I have no talent, you see. I have no talent and . . . and lots of vanity! That's all there is to it.'

Having made this admission, she turns her face away from me, and to conceal her trembling hands tugs at the reins violently.

As we drive up to her house, from a distance we can see Mikhail Fyodorovich walking about near the gate waiting for us impatiently.

'There's that Mikhail Fyodorovich again!' says Katya in vexation. 'Take him away from me, please. I'm sick and tired of him. He's played out. To hell with him!'

Mikhail Fyodorovich should have gone abroad long ago, but he keeps putting off his departure every week. A change has come over him lately: his face looks pinched; he has begun to be affected by drink, something that has never happened to him before, and his black eyebrows have begun to go grey. When our carriage draws up at the gate he cannot conceal his joy and impatience. He fussily helps Katya and myself to get out, he is in a hurry, laughs, rubs his hands; and the gentle, beseeching, pure expression which I noticed before only in his eyes is now spread all over his face. He is happy and at the same time ashamed of his happiness, ashamed of his habit of coming to see Katya every evening, and he finds it necessary to explain his visit by some such obvious absurdity as: 'I was passing on business and I thought to myself why not drop in for a minute.'

The three of us go into the house. At first we have tea, then the long-familiar two packs of cards appear on the table, followed by a big piece of cheese, fruit, and a bottle of Crimean champagne. The subjects of our conversation are not new, but the same as they were in the winter. The university, the students, literature, and the theatre all come in for their share of abuse; the air grows thick and close with spiteful gossip, and it is poisoned not as in the winter by the breath of two toads, but of three. In addition to the deep velvety laugh and the high-pitched reedy laughter that reminds one of a mouth-organ, the maid who waits on us hears the unpleasant jarring laugh of comic generals in stage farces: Heh – heh – heh . . .

V

There are terrible nights with thunder, lightning, rain, and high winds, which the peasants call 'sparrow' or 'equinoctial' nights. There was one such equinoctial night in my private life too.

I woke up after midnight and suddenly leapt out of my bed. It seemed to me for some reason that I was about to die suddenly. Why? There was not a single sensation in my body which pointed to a rapid end, but my heart was seized with a feeling of horror just as though I had suddenly seen a vast ominous glow in the sky.

I lighted my lamp hastily, took a sip of water straight from the decanter, and then rushed over to the open window. It was a magnificent night. There was the scent of new-mown hay in the air, and some other delicious smell. I could see the serrated tops of the fence, the sleepy gaunt trees near the window, the road, and the dark strip of woods; a bright calm moon in the sky, and not a single cloud. Perfect stillness, not a leaf stirred. It seemed to me as if the whole world was looking at me, listening, intent on hearing how I was going to die.

I felt terrified. I shut the window and rushed back to my bed. I felt my pulse and, unable to find it in my wrist, began feeling for it in my temples, my chin, and again in my wrist, and all the time I was bathed in a cold sweat and everything I touched was cold and clammy. My breathing grew more and more rapid, my body trembled, everything inside me was in motion, and my face and bald head felt as though they were covered by a cobweb.

What was I to do? Call my family? No, I mustn't do that. I did not see what my wife and daughter could do if they came in.

I hid my head under the pillow, shut my eyes, and waited, waited. . . . My back was cold, and it seemed almost as if it were drawn inwards. I had a curious feeling that death was quite certain to approach me from behind, very quietly. . . .

'Kee-wee! Kee-wee!' A loud squeak suddenly resounded in the stillness of the night, and I could not tell whether it was coming from my chest or from outside.

'Kee-wee!'

God, how awful! I wanted to have another drink of water, but I was too terrified to open my eyes, afraid to raise my head. It was an unaccountable animal terror, and I was absolutely at a loss to understand what I was so afraid of : was it because I wanted to live, or that some new pain, never before experienced, awaited me?

In the room upstairs someone was groaning or laughing. . . . I listened. A little later there was the sound of footsteps on the stairs. Someone was coming down quickly, then running up again. A minute later footsteps could be heard again coming down; some-one stopped outside my door and listened.

'Who's there?' I shouted.

The door opened; I opened my eyes boldly and saw my wife. Her face was pale and her eyes blotchy with crying.

'You're not asleep?' she asked.

'What do you want?'

'For God's sake, go and see Lisa. Something's terribly wrong with her.'

'Very well . . . gladly. . . .' I muttered, pleased not to be alone. 'Very well. . . . One moment. . . .'

I followed my wife, listened to what she told me, but I was too agitated to understand a word of what she said. Bright spots of light danced on the stairs from her candle, our long shadows trembled, my feet got entangled in the long skirt of my dressing gown. I was out of breath, and I felt as if someone were chasing me and trying to seize me from behind. 'Any moment now I shall die here on the stairs. . . . Now, now! . . .' But the stairs were behind us; we were walking along a dark corridor with an Italian window at the end, and at last entered Lisa's room. Lisa was sitting moaning on the bed in her chemise, her bare feet hanging down.

'Oh dear, oh dear,' she was muttering, screwing up her eyes because of our candle. 'I can't, I can't . . .'

'Lisa, my child,' I said, 'what's the matter with you?'

Seeing me, she uttered a cry and flung her arms round my neck.

'Daddy, darling Daddy,' she sobbed, 'dear, dear Daddy. . . . Oh, darling, I don't know what's the matter with me. . . . I feel so awful!'

She was embracing me, kissing me, murmuring the endearing names I used to hear from her when she was still a child.

'Come, come, my child, calm yourself,' I said. 'Don't cry. I don't feel so well myself.'

I tried to cover her, my wife gave her something to drink, and both of us jostled about confusedly round the bed; my shoulder brushed against hers, and I remembered how we used to bath our children together.

'Do something for her, do something,' my wife implored me.

But what could I do? There was nothing I could do. There was some heavy load on the poor girl's heart, but I understood nothing, knew nothing, and could only murmur: 'It's nothing, nothing. It'll pass. Go to sleep, go to sleep. . . .'

As though on purpose, a dog suddenly began howling in our yard just then, at first quietly and irresolutely, then loudly, in two voices. I had never before attached any significance to such omens as the howling of dogs or the hooting of owls, but at that moment my heart contracted painfully, and I hastened to explain the reason for that howling.

'It's a lot of nonsense,' I thought. 'The influence of one organism on another. My violent nervous tension communicated itself to my wife, to Lisa, to the dog, that's all. . . . Transmissions like that explain premonitions, previsions. . . .'

When a little later I returned to my room to write out a prescription for Lisa, I no longer thought that I would die soon. I simply felt so sick at heart and so wretched that I was even sorry I had not died suddenly. I stood for a long time motionless in the middle of the room, thinking what to prescribe for Lisa, but the moans upstairs ceased and I decided not to prescribe anything. But I still remained standing there. . . .

There was a dead silence, the sort of silence which, as some writer put it, seemed to ring in the ears. Time passed slowly, the shafts of moonlight on the window-sill did not change their position, just as if they were frozen. . . . It was still a long time till dawn.

Suddenly the garden gate creaked; someone was stealing towards the house and, breaking a twig from one of the gaunt trees, began tapping cautiously on the window.

'Nikolai Stepanych,' I heard someone whisper, 'Nikolai Stepanych!'

I opened the window and thought I was dreaming: under the window, clinging close to the wall, stood a woman in a black dress, brightly lit by the moon, looking at me with wide-open eyes. Her face was pale, austere, and looked unreal in the moonlight, like marble.

'It's me,' she said. 'Me – Katya.'

In moonlight all women's eyes look big and black, everyone looks taller and paler, and that was probably why I did not recognize her at first.

'What's the matter?'

'I'm sorry,' she said, 'but I suddenly felt so unbearably wretched. I couldn't stand it any longer and drove over here. There was a light in your window and – and I decided to knock. . . . I'm awfully sorry. . . . Oh, if you knew how sick at heart I felt! What are you doing now?'

'Nothing. . . . Insomnia. . . .'

'I had a kind of premonition. Still, it's all nonsense. . . .'

Her eyebrows lifted, her eyes gleamed with tears, and her whole face glowed as though with light, with the familiar expression of trustfulness I had not seen on it for such a long time.

'Nikolai Stepanych,' she said in a beseeching voice, holding out both hands to me, 'my dear, I beg you . . . if you don't scorn my friendship and my respect for you, please do what I ask.'

'What is it?'

'Take my money.'

'What will you be thinking of next! What do I want your money for?'

'You could go away for treatment somewhere. You must get good medical treatment. Will you take it? Will you? Darling, will you?'

She looked eagerly into my face and repeated:

'Will you? Will you take it?'

'No, my dear friend, I won't take it,' I said. 'Thanks all the same.'

She turned her back on me and lowered her head. I must have refused in a tone of voice that did not admit of any further talk about money.

'Go back to bed,' I said. 'I'll see you tomorrow.'

'So you don't consider me your friend?' she asked despondently.

'I didn't say that. But your money is no use to me now.'

'I'm sorry,' she said, lowering her voice a whole octave. 'I understand. To be beholden to a person like me . . . a retired actress. . . . Oh well. Good-bye.'

And she went away so quickly that I had no time even to say good-bye to her.

VI

I am in Kharkov.

Since it would be useless, besides being beyond my strength, to fight against my present state of mind, I have decided that the last days of my life shall be irreproachable – outwardly, at any rate; if I have been unfair towards my family, as I realize very well, I shall do my best to do what they want. If I am to go to Kharkov, to Kharkov I shall go. Besides, of late I have become so indifferent to everything that it is absolutely all the same to me where I go – to Kharkov, to Paris, or to Berdichev.

I arrived here at noon and put up at a hotel not far from the cathedral. I felt sick in the train, chilled through and through by draughts, and now I sit on the bed, holding my head between my hands and waiting for the tic. I ought really to have paid a visit to the local professors, I know, but I have neither the will nor the strength.

The old hotel waiter comes in to ask whether I have brought my own bed linen. I keep him for about five minutes and question him about Gnekker, on whose account I have come here. The waiter turns out to be a native of Kharkov; he knows the town like the back of his hand but cannot recall a family by the name of Gnekker. I ask him about estates, and get the same answer.

The clock in the corridor strikes one, then two, then three. . . . The last months of my life, while I wait for death, seem much longer than the whole of my life to me. Never before, though, have I been able to submit with a good grace to the slow passage of time, as I do now. Before, when waiting at the station for a train or invigilating at an examination, a quarter of an hour would seem an eternity to me, but now I can sit motionless on my bed all night, thinking with complete indifference that tomorrow and the day after tomorrow the nights will be just as long and as ghastly. . . .

The clock in the corridor strikes five, six, seven. . . . It is getting dark.

I feel a dull pain in my cheek – the beginning of the tic. To distract myself by thinking of something, I try to adopt the point of view I used to hold when I was not indifferent to everything, and I ask myself why I, a famous man, a privy councillor, am sitting in this small hotel room, on this bed covered by a strange grey blanket. Why am I looking at that cheap tin washstand and listening to the jarring chimes of the wretched clock in the corridor? Is this worthy of my fame and my high position in society? And I reply to these questions with an ironical smile. The naïveté with which in my youth I exaggerated the importance of fame and the exceptional position famous men apparently occupy seems ridiculous to me now. I am famous, my name is spoken with reverence, my portrait has appeared in the illustrated weekly *Niva* and in the *Universal Illustrated Monthly*, I have even read my biography in a German journal – and what does it all amount to? Here I am all alone in a strange town, on a strange bed, rubbing my aching cheek with my hand. . . . Family troubles, the callousness of creditors, the rudeness of railway guards, the inconvenience of the passport system, the expensive and unwholesome food in the refreshment rooms, the general ignorance and coarseness of the people — all this, and a great deal more that would take too long to enumerate, concerns me no less than it does any tradesman who is known only in his own little street. In what way is my position so exceptional? Suppose I were a thousand times more famous, suppose I were a hero of whom my country is proud, all the papers publishing bulletins of my illness, every post already bringing me letters of sympathy from my colleagues, my students, and the public; yet all that would not prevent me from dying in a strange bed, in misery and total loneliness. . . . No one can be blamed for this, of course; but, miserable sinner that I am, I do not like my popular name. I feel that it has deceived me.

At about ten I fall asleep, and in spite of my tic sleep soundly and would have slept a long time if I had not been wakened. Soon after one o'clock there is a sudden knock at my door.

'Who's there?'

'A telegram, sir.'

'You could have waited till tomorrow,' I mutter angrily, as I take the telegram from the night porter. 'I shan't fall asleep again now.'

'Very sorry, sir. There was a light in your room, so I thought you were awake.'

I open the telegram and first of all look at the signature. It's from my wife. What does she want?

'Gnekker and Lisa were married secretly yesterday stop come back.'

I read the telegram, but my alarm does not last long. It is not so much what Gnekker and Lisa have done that frightens me as the fact that I am so completely indifferent to the news of their marriage. Philosophers and sages are said to be indifferent. It isn't true. Indifference is paralysis of the soul, premature death.

I go back to bed and try to think of some ideas to occupy my mind. What am I to think about? It seems to me that everything has already been thought of and there is nothing new that is capable of arousing my thoughts.

Daybreak finds me sitting on the bed, clasping my knees and trying, having nothing better to do, to know myself. 'Know thyself' is most excellent and useful advice; the pity is the ancients did not think it necessary to show us the way to avail ourselves of this advice.

When I felt like trying to understand someone or myself before, I used to take into consideration desires and not actions, about which everything is conditional. Tell me what you want and I will tell you what you are.

And now, too, I examine myself: what do I want?

I want our wives, our children, our friends, our students to love not our name, our firm, our label, but ourselves, ordinary human beings. What else? I should like to have assistants and successors. What else? I should like to wake in a hundred years and take a look, even if only with one eye, at what has happened to science. I should like to live another ten years. . . . What more?

Nothing more. I think and think, and cannot think of anything. And however much I were to think and however far I were to scatter my thoughts, it is clear to me that the main thing, something very important, is lacking in my desires. In my partiality for science, in my desire to live, in my sitting here on a strange bed and in my longing to know myself, in all my thoughts, feelings, and concepts about everything, there is no common link, there is nothing that might bind it together in one whole. Each thought and each feeling lives in me separately, and the most skilful analyst could not discover what is known as a ruling idea or what might be called the god of the living man in all my opinions of science, the theatre, literature, students, and all the pictures my imagination conjures up.

And if that is not there, nothing is there.

In view of such poverty, any serious illness, the fear of death, the influence of circumstances and people, is quite sufficient to turn upside down and smash into smithereens everything which I have hitherto regarded as my view of things and in which I have seen the meaning and joy of life. There is nothing surprising, therefore, in my having darkened the last months of my life by thoughts and feelings worthy of a slave and a barbarian, in my being indifferent now and not noticing the dawn. When a man lacks the things that are higher and stronger than all external influences, a bad cold in the head is enough to upset his equilibrium and make him see an owl in every bird and hear a dog's howl in every sound. And all his pessimism or optimism, all his thoughts, great or small, are in this case merely a symptom and nothing more.

I am beaten. If that is so, there is no point in going on thinking, no point in going on talking. I shall sit and wait in silence for what is to come.

In the morning the porter brings me tea and a copy of the local newspaper. I read mechanically through the advertisements on the first page, the editorial, the extracts from other newspapers and periodicals, the news items. Among the news items I find the following piece of information: 'Yesterday our famous scientist, Professor Nikolai Stepanovich so-and-so, arrived by express train and is staying at the — Hotel.'

Big names are evidently created to live by themselves, apart from those who bear them. Now my name is walking unworried all over Kharkov, and in three months' time it will shine in golden letters on a tombstone as bright as the sun itself – and that's when I myself will be covered with earth. . . .

A light knock at the door. Someone still wants me, it seems.

'Who's there? Come in.'

The door opens, and I step back in astonishment and quickly draw my dressing-gown more tightly round me. Katya stands before me.

'Good morning,' she says, out of breath with walking up the stairs. 'You didn't expect me, did you? I – I've come here too.'

She sits down and goes on, stammering and not looking at me.

'Why don't you ask me how I am? I – I came here too – today. I found out you were at this hotel and I came to see you.'

'I'm delighted to see you,' I say, shrugging my shoulders, 'but I must say I am surprised. You seem to have dropped from the sky. What are you doing here?'

'Me? Oh, I just came, you know. . . .'

Silence. Suddenly she gets up impulsively and walks up to me.

'Nikolai Stepanych,' she says, turning pale and pressing her hands to her breast, 'I can't go on living like this. I can't! I can't! For God's sake tell me quickly, this minute, what am I to do? Tell me, what am I to do?'

'What can I tell you?' I say, looking bewildered at her. 'I can't tell you anything.'

'Say something, I implore you,' she goes on, gasping for breath and trembling all over. 'I swear I can't go on like this any more! It's more than I can bear.'

She collapses on a chair and starts sobbing. She throws her head back, wrings her hands, stamps her feet; her hat falls off and dangles by its elastic band, her hair comes undone.

'Help me! Help me!' she implores. 'I can't go on like this any more!'

She takes a handkerchief out of her bag and pulls out a few letters, which fall from her knees on to the floor. I pick them up, and on one of them I recognize Mikhail Fyodorovich's handwriting and accidentally read part of a word, 'passionate . . .'

'I'm sorry, I can't tell you anything, Katya,' I say.

'Help me!' she cries, sobbing. And catching me by the hand, she begins to kiss it. 'Why, you're my father, my only friend! You're clever, you're well educated, you've lived so long. You've been a teacher. Tell me – what am I to do?'

'Honestly, Katya, I don't know. . . .'

I am at a loss, embarrassed, touched by her sobs, and can hardly stand on my feet.

'Come, Katya, let's have breakfast,' I say, with a strained smile. 'Do stop crying.'

And immediately I add in a weak voice:

'I shall soon be dead, Katya.'

'Just one word, only one word,' she says, crying and holding out her hands to me. 'What shall I do?'

'What a strange girl you are,' I murmur. 'So intelligent, and suddenly tears, if you please!'

A pause. Katya puts her hair to rights, puts on her hat, then crumples the letters and puts them back in her bag. She does it all in silence and without hurry. Her face, her bosom, and her gloves are wet with tears, but her face already looks cold and severe. I look at her, and feel ashamed that I am happier than she. The absence in myself of what my philosopher colleagues call a ruling idea I noticed only shortly before my death, in the evening of my life; and the soul of this poor girl has never known and will not find a place of refuge all her life – all her life.

'Come, Katya, let's have breakfast,' I say.

'No, thanks,' she replies coldly.

Another minute passes in silence.

'I don't like Kharkov,' I say. 'Too dull. A dull sort of town.'

'I suppose so. Ugly. I'm not staying here long. Just passing through. Leaving today.'

'Where are you going?'

'To the Crimea. I mean the Caucasus.'

'I see. For long?'

'Don't know.'

Katya gets up and holds out her hand to me, smiling coldly and not looking at me.

I want to ask her: 'So you won't be at my funeral?' But she does not look at me; her hand is cold, like the hand of a stranger. I accompany her to the door in silence. She goes out of my room and walks along the long passage without looking back. She knows I am following her with my eyes, and I expect she will look round when she gets to the turning.

No, she does not look round. I catch a glimpse of her black dress for the last time, the sound of her footsteps dies away. . . . Good-bye, my treasure.

The Grasshopper

I

ALL Olga's friends and acquaintances were at her wedding.

'Look at him! Don't you think there's something about him?' she said to her friends, motioning towards her husband, as though wishing to explain why she had married such a plain, ordinary, and in no way remarkable man.

Her husband, Osip Stepanych Dymov, was a doctor with the lowest rank of titular counsellor. He worked in two hospitals: in one as a supernumerary house physician and in another as the doctor who did the post-mortems. From nine to twelve in the morning he received out-patients and visited his ward and in the afternoons he went by horse tram to the other hospital, where he performed post-mortems on the patients who had died there. His private practice was insignificant, bringing in about five hundred roubles a year. That is all. There is nothing more one can say about him. And yet Olga and her friends were not altogether ordinary people. Each of them was distinguished in one way or another, was not entirely unknown, had won a name for himself, was already considered a celebrity, or if not exactly a celebrity gave promise of a brilliant future. One was an actor, whose great histrionic gifts had long won general recognition, an eloquent, intelligent, and modest man, famous for his public readings, who gave Olga lessons in elocution. Another was an opera singer, a good-humoured fat man who assured Olga with a sigh that she was ruining herself, for if she were not so lazy and took herself in hand she would make a fine singer. Then there were several artists, and chief among them Ryabovsky, a genre, animal, and landscape painter, a very handsome fair-haired young man of twenty-five who won success at exhibitions and whose latest picture sold for five hundred roubles; he helped Olga with her sketches and expressed the view that one day perhaps she'd get somewhere. Then there was the cellist, who used to make his cello 'weep' and who frankly admitted that of all the women he knew only Olga was capable of accompanying him. There was also the writer, a young man already well known as the author of novels, plays, and short stories. Who else? Why, Vasily Vasilyich, a landed gentleman, and amateur illustrator and drawer of vignettes, endowed with a strong feeling for Russian style and for Russian ancient epic poems and tales, who could produce veritable miracles on paper, on china, and on smoked plates. These free, artistic, spoilt favourites of fortune, as they were, tactful and unpretentious, only knew of the existence of doctors when they fell ill; and among them Dymov, whose name sounded as ordinary as the names of Sidorov or Tarasov, seemed like a stranger, superfluous and small, though he was very tall and broad-shouldered. It seemed as though his frock coat had been made for someone else and that his beard was like a shop-assistant's. However, if he had been a writer or an artist, they would have said that his beard made him look like Zola.

The artist told Olga that with her flaxen hair and in her wedding dress she was exactly like a slender cherry tree when covered with delicate white blossoms in spring.

'No, but listen,' Olga said to him, seizing him by the arm. 'You are wondering how it could have happened? Listen, listen. You see my father and Dymov worked at the same hospital. When poor father fell ill, Dymov spent days and nights at his bedside. Such self-sacrifice! Listen, Ryabovsky, and you, too, as a writer, will find it very interesting. Come nearer. Such sacrifice! Such true sympathy! I didn't sleep at night, either. I, too, sat at father's bedside; and, suddenly – what do you think? – I had made a conquest of the strapping young fellow! Dymov fell head over ears in love with me. Fate certainly is sometimes quite fantastic. Anyway, after my father died he came to see me sometimes; I used to meet him in the street, and one fine evening – bang! – he proposed to me! Like a bolt from the blue. I cried myself sick all night and fell madly in love too. And now, as you see, I'm a lawful wedded wife. There is something strong, powerful, bear-like about him, don't you think? Now he's three-quarter face to us, and the light's all wrong, but when he turns full face you have a good look at his forehead. What do you say of a forehead like that, Ryabovsky? Dymov, we're talking about you,' she shouted to her husband. 'Come here. Hold out your honest hand to Ryabovsky. Like that. I'd like you to be friends.'

Dymov smiled good-humouredly and naïvely and held out his hand to Ryabovsky.

'Very pleased to meet you,' he said. 'There was a Ryabovsky with me in the final year at the university. He's not a relation of yours, is he?'

II

Olga was twenty-two and Dymov thirty-one. After their wedding they lived well. Olga covered the walls of the drawing-room with sketches by herself and her friends, some framed and some unframed, and the empty spaces near the piano and the furniture she crammed with Chinese parasols, easels, many-coloured bits of material, daggers, small busts, photographs. ... She covered the dining-room walls with cheap, popular prints, bast shoes, and sickles, put a scythe and rake in a corner; she got up the dining-room in the Russian style. To make the bedroom look like a cave, she draped the ceiling and walls with dark cloth, hung a Venetian lantern over the bed, and placed a figure holding a halberd at the door. And everyone declared that the newly-weds had a very charming little nook.

Olga got up at eleven o'clock every day and played the piano or, if it was a sunny day, painted in oils. At about one o'clock she drove to her dressmaker's. Since she and Dymov had very little money, only just enough for their needs, she and her dressmaker had to resort to all sorts of stratagems for her to be able to appear frequently in new dresses and to create the right kind of impression. Very often an old dyed dress, some cheap old bits of tulle, lace, velvet, and silk, were used for the creation of something well-nigh miraculous, something enchanting, not a dress, but a dream. From her dressmaker's, Olga usually called on an actress friend to learn the latest theatrical news and at the same time see if she could get tickets for the first night of a new play or somebody's 'benefit'.

From the actress's she had to go to the studio of some painter or to an exhibition, and afterwards to some celebrity to invite him to her house or to return a visit or just for a chat. Everywhere she received a gay and friendly welcome, and they all assured her that she was good, charming, one in a million. Those whom she called famous and great received her as one of themselves and declared unanimously that in view of her gifts, her taste, and her intelligence she would make a great name for herself, provided she did not try to do several things at once. She sang, played the piano, painted in oils, sculpted, acted in amateur theatricals, and not just anyhow, but showing real talent. Whether she made little lanterns for illuminations or dressed up or just tied somebody's tie, everything she did turned out exceedingly artistic, graceful, and charming. But it was in her ability to strike up an acquaintance and get on intimate terms with celebrated people in the shortest possible time that she really excelled. The moment anyone cut a figure in public, however small, and got talked about, she made his acquaintance, became his close friend on the same day, and invited him to her house. Every time she made a new acquaintance it was a red letter day to her. She worshipped the famous, was proud of them, and dreamed of them every night. She thirsted for them and could never assuage her thirst. Old ones went away and were forgotten, new ones came to take their place, but these too she soon got used to or they disappointed her, and she began to look eagerly for more and more new great men, found them, and began looking for others. Whatever for?

At about five o'clock she had dinner at home with her husband. His simplicity, common-sense, and good nature delighted and moved her deeply. She was continually jumping up, flinging her arms round his neck impulsively, and covering his face with kisses.

'You're an intelligent and high-minded man, Dymov,' she said, 'but you have one very bad fault. You aren't interested in art at all. You refuse to recognize the validity of music and painting.'

'I don't understand them,' he replied meekly. 'I've spent all my life studying natural sciences and medicine and I've had no time for art.'

'But that's awful, Dymov!'

'Why? Your friends know nothing about natural sciences and medicine, but you don't blame them for that, do you? Everyone to his own. I don't understand landscapes or operas, but what I think is that if intelligent people devote their whole lives to them and other intelligent people pay enormous sums for them, then they must be necessary. I don't understand, but that doesn't mean that I refuse to recognize their validity.'

'Come, let me press your honest hand!'

After dinner Olga paid visits, then she went to the theatre and returned home after midnight. This is how it was every day.

On Wednesdays she gave parties. At these parties the hostess and her guests did not play cards or dance, but amused themselves with all sorts of artistic pastimes. The actor recited, the singer sang, the artists made drawings in Olga's innumerable albums, the cellist played, the hostess herself also made drawings, modelled in clay, sang, and played accompaniments. In the intervals between the recitals, the music, and the singing, they talked and argued about literature, the theatre, and art. There were no women among her guests because Olga considered all women, except actresses and her dressmaker, boring and vulgar. Not a single party passed without the hostess giving a start at every ring at the door and saying with a triumphant expression: 'It's him!' By which she meant some new celebrity she had specially invited. Dymov was never in the drawing-room, and no one so much as remembered his existence. But exactly at half past eleven the door of the dining-room would open, Dymov would appear in the doorway, and with his good-natured gentle smile he would say, rubbing his hands:

'Ladies and gentlemen, supper is served.'

They would all troop into the dining-room and every time they saw the same dishes on the table: oysters, roast pork or veal, sardines, cheese, caviare, mushrooms, vodka, and two decanters of wine.

'My darling *maître d'hôtel*,' Olga would say, clasping her hands ecstatically, 'you're simply charming! Gentlemen, look at his forehead! Dymov, turn your profile to us. Gentlemen, look! The face of a Bengal tiger, but an expression as kind and charming as a deer's. Oh, you sweet darling!'

The guests ate and, glancing at Dymov, thought: 'He really is a nice fellow!' But they soon forgot all about him and went on talking about the theatre, music, and art.

The young couple were happy, and there seemed to be nothing to disturb the even tenor of their life. The third week of their honeymoon, though, was not spent very happily; rather sadly, in fact. Dymov caught erysipelas at the hospital, stayed in bed for six days, and had his beautiful black hair cropped to the roots. Olga sat at his bedside and wept bitterly; but when he got a little better she put a white handkerchief on his cropped head and began painting a Bedouin with him as a model. Both of them thought it great fun. Three days after he had got well and begun going to the hospital again, something else happened to him.

'I'm afraid I'm unlucky, darling,' he said one day at dinner. 'I had to do four post-mortems today, and I cut two fingers at once. I only noticed it when I got home.'

Olga looked frightened. He smiled and said that it was nothing and that he often cut his hands during post-mortems.

'I get carried away, darling, and become careless.'

Olga was worried that he might get blood poisoning, and prayed every night; but all was well, and once more their life flowed on happily without grief or anxiety. The present was wonderful, and spring was coming and smiling at them from a distance, promising a thousand joys. There would be no end to their happiness! In April, May, and June a country cottage a long way from town, walks, sketches, fishing, nightingales; and then from July till autumn the excursion of the artists on the Volga, in which excursion Olga was to take part as a permanent member of their *société*. She had already made herself two travelling costumes of linen crash, and had bought paints, brushes, canvases, and a new palette for the trip. Ryabovsky came to see her almost every day to watch the progress she was making in her painting. When she showed him her pictures, he would thrust his hands deep into his pockets, compress his lips tightly, breathe hard, and say:

'I see ... your cloud there screams: it doesn't shine with an evening light. The foreground is a bit chewed up; and there's something – you see – not quite ... And your hut seems to have been crushed by something. It's moaning pitifully.... The corner should have been a little darker. But on the whole it's not too bad. Quite a good effort. . . .'

And the more incomprehensible his speech was, the better Olga understood him.

III

On the afternoon of Whit Monday, Dymov bought some snacks and sweets for his wife, who was in the country. He had not seen her for a fortnight, and had missed her very much. In the railway carriage, and while looking for his cottage in the woods, he felt exhausted and hungry and was dreaming of how he would have a leisurely supper with his wife and then have a good sleep. And it made him happy to look at his parcel, which contained caviare, cheese, and white salmon.

By the time he had found and recognized his cottage, the sun was setting. The old maid told him that the mistress was not at home, but that she would probably be back soon. The cottage, which looked extremely unsightly, had low ceilings papered with sheets of foolscap, and uneven floors with gaps between the boards. There were only three rooms in it. In one was a bed; in another the chairs and window-sills were piled with canvases, brushes, dirty bits of paper, and men's coats and hats; and in the third Dymov found three men he had never seen before. Two of them were dark and had beards, and the third was fat and clean-shaven, apparently an actor. On the table a samovar was boiling.

'What do you want?' the actor asked in a bass voice, looking Dymov up and down in a rather unfriendly fashion. 'D'you want to see Olga Ivanovna? Please wait, she'll be here soon.'

Dymov sat down and waited. One of the dark men cast a sleepy, languid glance at him, poured himself out a glass of tea, and said:

'Would you care for a glass of tea too?'

Dymov would have liked to eat and drink, but as he was anxious not to spoil his appetite, he refused the tea. Soon he heard footsteps and the familiar laugh; a door banged, and Olga ran into the room in a wide-brimmed hat and carrying a box, followed by Ryabovsky, red-cheeked and jovial, with a large umbrella and a folding chair.

'Dymov!' cried Olga, flushing with delight. 'Dymov!' she repeated, laying her head and both her hands on his chest. 'It's you! Why haven't you come for such a long time? Why? Why?'

'When could I, darling? I'm always busy. And when I'm free, it always happens that there's no suitable train.'

'Oh, but I'm so glad to see you! I dreamt of you all night, all night, and I was afraid that you might have fallen ill. Oh, if you knew how sweet you are, and how glad I am you came today! You're the only one who can save me. Tomorrow,' she went on, laughing and tying her husband's cravat, 'a most original wedding is going to take place here. The young telegraphist at the railway station, a man called Chikeldeyev, is getting married. He is a handsome young man, not at all stupid, and, you know, there's something strong and bear-like about his face. He would make a lovely model for a young Varangian. All the holiday-makers here are taking an interest in him, and we've given him our word we'll be at his wedding. He's not exactly rolling in money, he's lonely and poor and shy; it would be a shame not to be kind to him. The wedding will be just after the morning service, and then everyone's going from the church to the bride's house. You see? The woods, the birds singing, patches of sunlight on the grass, and all of us – multicoloured spots against a green background! Wonderfully original, in the French impressionist style. But Dymov, what am I going to wear in church?' said Olga, looking at though she were going to burst into tears. 'I have nothing here, absolutely nothing! No dresses, no flowers, no gloves. You must save me! The fact that you've come today means it's fate's wish that you should save me. Darling, take my keys. Go home and get me my pink dress. You'll find it in the wardrobe. Remember? It's hanging in front. And in the pantry, on the floor on the right, you'll see two cardboard boxes. When you open the top one, you'll see lots of tulle, tulle, tulle, and bits of material, and underneath them flowers. Be very careful how you take the flowers out, darling. Try not to crumple them! I'll choose which ones I want afterwards. Oh, and bring me a pair of gloves.'

'Very well,' said Dymov. 'I'll go back tomorrow and send them.'

'Tomorrow?' Olga repeated, and looked at him in surprise. 'But when? You won't have time! The first train leaves at nine o'clock tomorrow, and the wedding's at eleven. No, darling, you must go today. You simply must! If you can't come tomorrow yourself, send the things by a messenger. Go now, please. The train's due any minute! Don't miss it, darling.'

'Very well.'

'Oh, I am sorry, darling, to let you go,' said Olga; and tears started to her eyes. 'Oh, what a fool I was to promise the telegraphist!'

Dymov gulped down his cup of tea, picked up a roll, and smiling meekly went to the station. The caviare, the cheese, and the white salmon were eaten by the two dark men and the fat actor.

IV

On a calm, moonlit night in July, Olga stood on the deck of a Volga steamer, looking at the water and the beautiful banks of the river. Ryabovsky stood beside her. He was telling her that the black shadows on the water were not shadows but a dream — that in the presence of that magical water with its lambent sheen, of that fathomless sky and the sad, pensive river banks, speaking to us of the vanity of our lives and the existence of something higher, something eternal and beatific, it would be good to forget everything, to die, to become a memory. The past was trivial and void of interest; the future was of no importance; and this wonderful night, the never-to-be-forgotten night of their lives, would soon come to an end and merge into eternity — why, then, live?

Olga listened to Ryabovsky's voice and to the stillness of the night, and told herself that she was immortal and would never die. The turquoise colour of the water, which she had never seen before, the sky, the banks of the river, the black shadows, and the unaccountable joy that filled her heart told her that one day she would be a great artist and that somewhere, far, far away beyond the moonlit night, in infinite space, success, fame, and the love of the people awaited her. . . . When she gazed long, open-eyed, into the far-away distance, she seemed to see crowds of people, lights, sounds of solemn music, shouts of enthusiasm, herself in a white dress, and flowers showering upon her from all sides. She told herself, too, that beside her, leaning on the rail, stood a man who was truly great, a genius, one of God's elect. . . . All he had done till now was beautiful, new, and unusual, but what he would create in time, when his rare gifts developed as he grew more mature, would be striking, tremendously great. That could be seen in his face, in the way he expressed himself, and in his attitude to nature. He talked in quite an unusual way, in a language all his own, about the shadows, the evening tones, the moonlight, so that you could not help feeling the charm of his power over nature. He was very handsome himself, as well as original; and his life, free, independent, and alien to the humdrum things of everyday life, was the life of a bird.

'It's getting chilly,' said Olga, shivering.

Ryabovsky wrapped his cloak round her and said sadly:

'I feel I'm in your power. I'm your slave. Why are you so adorable today?'

He looked at her all the time without taking his eyes off her, and his eyes were terrible and she was afraid to look at him.

'I'm madly in love with you,' he whispered, breathing on her cheek. 'Say the word and I'll stop living, I'll give up art,' he murmured, in violent agitation. 'Love me, love me. . . .'

'Don't talk like that,' said Olga, closing her eyes. 'This is awful. What about Dymov?'

'What's Dymov got to do with it? Why Dymov? What do I care about Dymov? The Volga, the moon, beauty, my love, my ecstasy, but no Dymov. . . . Oh, I know nothing. . . . I don't want the past. Give me only one moment, one moment. . . .'

Olga's heart began beating violently. She tried to think of her husband, but all her past, her wedding, Dymov, her parties, seemed small, insignificant, dull, unnecessary, and far, far away. . . . And, indeed, what had Dymov got to do with it? Why Dymov? What did she care about Dymov? Did he exist at all, wasn't he just a dream?

'For him, for a plain, ordinary man like him, the happiness he has had is quite enough,' she thought, covering her face with her hands. 'Let them condemn me *there*, let them curse me. I'll go to my ruin, bring disgrace and dishonour upon myself, just to spite them. . . . One must experience everything in life. Goodness, how terrifying and how lovely!'

'Well? Well?' the artist murmured, embracing her and eagerly kissing the hands with which she feebly tried to push him away. 'Do you love me? Yes? Yes? Oh, what a night! What a wonderful night!'

'Yes, what a night!' she whispered, gazing into his eyes, which were gleaming with tears, then she looked round quickly, flung her arms round him, and kissed him on the mouth.

'We're approaching Kineshma,' they heard someone say on the other side of the deck.

There was a sound of heavy footsteps. It was the waiter from the refreshment room passing.

'I say,' Olga said to him, laughing and crying with happiness, 'bring us some wine, please.'

The artist, pale with excitement, sat down on a bench, looked at Olga with adoring and grateful eyes, then closed his eyes and said with a languorous smile:

'I'm tired.'

And he rested his head on the rail.

V

The second of September was a warm, calm day, but overcast. Early in the morning there was a light mist over the Volga, and after nine o'clock it began to drizzle. There was no hope at all of its clearing up. At tea, Ryabovsky was telling Olga that painting was a most ungrateful and most boring art, that he was not a painter, that only fools thought he had talent; and suddenly, for no reason at all, he snatched up a knife and slashed his best sketch. After tea he sat gloomily at the window looking at the Volga. And the Volga, no longer sparkling, looked dull, lustreless, and cold. Everything, everything reminded them of the approach of dreary, lowering autumn. It seemed that nature had taken from the Volga the luxuriant green carpets on her banks, her diamondlike reflections of the sun's rays, her transparent blue distances, and all her gala splendour and smartness, and put it away in chests till next spring, and that the crows flew over the river teasing her: 'Naked! Naked!' Ryabovsky listened to their cawing and thought that he was played out and had lost his talent; that everything in the world was conditional, relative, and stupid; and that he should not have got himself involved with this woman. In a word, he was in a bad mood and felt depressed.

Olga sat on the bed on the other side of the partition and, running her fingers through her beautiful flaxen hair, imagined that she was in her drawing-room, in her bedroom, in her husband's study; her imagination took her to the theatre, to her dressmaker's, to her celebrated friends. What were they all doing at that moment? Did they think of her? The season had begun and it was time she started planning her parties. And Dymov? Dear Dymov! How humbly and how plaintively, like a child, he was imploring her in his letters to come home as soon as possible. Every month he sent her seventy-five roubles, and when she wrote to him that she had had to borrow a hundred roubles from the artists, he had sent her the hundred roubles, too. What a kind, generous man! The journey had tired Olga; she was bored, she was longing to get away from these peasants, from the smell of dampness rising from the river, to throw off this feeling of physical uncleanliness which never left her while living in the peasant cottages and wandering from village to village. If Ryabovsky had not promised the other artists, on his word of honour, to stay with them till the twentieth of September, they could have gone away that very day. And how glorious that would have been!

'Dear, oh dear,' Ryabovsky groaned, 'when will that sun come out? I can't go on painting a sunlit landscape without the sun!'

'But you've got a sketch with a cloudy sky,' said Olga, coming out from behind the partition. 'Remember? With the wood in the right foreground and a herd of cows and geese on the left. You could finish it now.'

'Oh.' The artist frowned. 'Finish it! Do you really imagine I'm such a fool as not to know what I ought to do?'

'How you've changed to me!' said Olga with a sigh.

'And a jolly good thing, too!'

Olga's face began to twitch; she went over to the stove and burst into tears.

'Oh Lord, tears are all we want now! For heaven's sake, stop crying. I have a thousand reasons for crying, but I don't cry, do I?'

'A thousand reasons, indeed!' Olga sobbed. 'The chief reason is that you're tired of me. Oh yes,' she said, sobbing aloud. 'The truth is that you are ashamed of our love! You're trying to conceal it from the artists, though it can't be done, for they've known about it for ages.'

'Olga,' the artist said in an imploring tone of voice, laying his hand on his heart, 'do one thing for me, I beg you – just one thing. Stop torturing me! That's all I want from you.'

'But swear you still love me!'

'Oh, this is impossible!' the artist hissed through clenched teeth. 'It'll end by my throwing myself into the Volga or going off my head! Leave me alone!'

'All right, kill me! Go on, kill me!' cried Olga. 'Kill me!'

She burst into sobs again and went behind the partition. The rain rustled on the thatched roof of the cottage. Ryabovsky clutched his head and began pacing the room; then, looking determined, as though he were going to prove something to someone, he put on his cap, threw his gun across his shoulder, and went out of the cottage.

After he had gone, Olga lay crying on her bed for a long time. At first she thought what a good thing it would be if she took poison, so that on his return Ryabovsky would find her dead; then her thoughts carried her to her drawing-room and her husband's study, and she saw herself sitting motionless beside Dymov and enjoying the feeling of physical rest and cleanliness, and then sitting in the theatre in the evening and listening to Mazzini. And her longing for civilization, for the noise of the city, and for celebrated men, wrung her heart. A peasant woman came into the room and began lighting the stove unhurriedly, in preparation for cooking dinner. There was a smell of burning, and the air turned blue with smoke. The artists came back in their muddy high boots, their faces wet with rain, looked at each other's sketches, and to console themselves remarked that even in bad weather the Volga was not without charm. The cheap clock on the wall went on ticking monotonously. Flies, feeling the cold, crowded in the front corner near the icons, buzzing, and cockroaches could be heard crawling about busily in the thick files of paper under the benches . . . .

Ryabovsky returned at sunset. He flung his cap on the table and, looking pale and exhausted and still in his muddy boots, sank lower on the bench and closed his eyes.

'I'm tired,' he said, twitching his brows in an effort to raise his eyelids.

To show how much she loved him and that she was not angry, she went up to him, kissed him in silence, and ran a comb through his fair hair. She just felt like combing his hair.

'What's this?' he asked with a shudder, as though something cold had touched him, and opened his eyes. 'What's this? Leave me alone, I beg you!'

He pushed her away and moved off, and she thought she caught a look of disgust and annoyance on his face. Just then the peasant woman came in, carefully carrying a plateful of cabbage soup, which she handed to him. Olga saw that she had dipped her thumbs in the soup; and the dirty peasant woman with her skirt drawn tight over her belly, and the cabbage soup which Ryabovsky began eating so greedily, and the peasant cottage, and the life she had at first loved for its simplicity and artistic disorder, seemed horrible to her now. She suddenly felt herself insulted.

'We must part for a time,' she said coldly, 'or we shall quarrel in real earnest from sheer boredom. I'm sick and tired of it all! I'm leaving today.'

'How? Riding on a broomstick?'

'Today's Thursday, and the steamer's due at half past nine.'

'Eh? So it is! All right, go by all means,' he said gently, wiping his mouth with a towel instead of a napkin. 'You're bored here, and you've nothing to do. I'd have to be an awful egoist to try to detain you. Go. And we'll meet again after the twentieth.'

Olga packed her things gaily, and her cheeks even glowed with pleasure. Could it really be true, she asked herself, that she would soon be painting in her drawing-room, sleeping in her bedroom, and dining with a cloth on the table? She felt relieved and was no longer angry with the artist.

'I'm leaving you my paints and brushes, Ryabovsky,' she said. 'You'll bring back what's left over, won't you? Don't be lazy or depressed when I'm not here. And work! You're one of the best, Ryabusha, you old stick!'

At ten o'clock Ryabovsky kissed her good-bye — so as not to

have to kiss her on deck in front of the artists, she thought – and saw her off to the landing stage. Soon the steamer arrived and took her away.

She was back home in two and a half days. Without taking off her hat and waterproof, and panting with excitement, she went into the drawing-room and from there to the dining-room. Dymov sat at the table in his shirtsleeves, his waistcoat unbuttoned, sharpening a knife on a fork. On the plate before him was a roast grouse. Olga had entered the flat determined to conceal everything from her husband, and she was sure she possessed the ability to do this; but now, when she caught sight of his broad, gentle, happy smile and his shining happy eyes, she felt that it would be as contemptible, detestable, and as impossible and beyond her capacity, for her to conceal anything from such a man as it would be to slander, to steal, or to murder. And she decided then and there to tell him everything. Letting him kiss and embrace her, she went down on her knees before him and covered her face.

'What's the matter, darling?' he asked her tenderly. 'Did you miss me so much?'

She raised her face, red with shame, and looked at him guiltily and beseechingly, but fear and shame prevented her from telling him the truth.

'It's nothing,' she said. 'I'm just . . .'

'Let's sit down,' he said, raising her and seating her at the table. 'So . . . Have some grouse. You must be famished, poor thing. . . .'

She inhaled the familiar air avidly and ate the grouse, while he looked at her with tender emotion, laughing happily.

VI

It was apparently by the middle of winter that Dymov began to suspect that he was being deceived. He could no longer look his wife straight in the eyes, just as though his conscience were not clear, he no longer smiled happily when meeting her, and, in order to remain as little as possible alone with her, he often brought home to dinner his friend Korostelev, a crop-headed little man with a crumpled face, who when talking to Olga kept buttoning and unbuttoning his coat from embarrassment and then began tweaking the left side of his moustache with his right hand. At dinner the two doctors talked shop, such as that when the diaphragm was too high palpitations sometimes occurred, or that there had been many cases of neuritis recently, or that when performing a post-mortem the day before on a patient diagnosed to have died of pernicious anemia, Dymov had discovered cancer of the pancreas. And it looked as though the two were carrying on a medical conversation to give Olga an excuse for not talking, that is, for not telling lies. After dinner Korostelev would sit down at the piano, and Dymov would say with a sigh:

'Why, hang it all, my dear fellow, let's have something really sad!'

Raising his shoulders and spreading out his fingers, Korostelev would strike a few chords and start singing in a tenor voice, 'Show me, oh show me, the place where the Russian peasant has not groaned. ...' While Dymov would fetch another sigh, prop his head on his fist and sink into thought.

Olga had been behaving with singular lack of caution lately. Every morning she woke up in the worst possible mood, convinced that she was no longer in love with Ryabovsky and that, thank God, all was over between them. But after she had had her coffee it would occur to her that since Ryabovsky had deprived her of her husband, she was now left without a husband and without Ryabovsky. Then she would remember the talk among her friends about some wonderful picture Ryabovsky was about to finish for an exhibition, a mixture of genre and landscape, something in the style of Polenov, which threw everyone who visited his studio into a paroxysm of delight. But, she told herself, he had created that picture under her influence, and altogether he had greatly changed for the better thanks to her influence. Her influence had, indeed, been so beneficial and considerable that if she were to leave him he would most probably be a failure. She remembered, too, that the last time he had been to see her he had come wearing a kind of shot-silk grey coat and a new tie, and had asked her languorously: 'Don't I look handsome?' And indeed, in his elegant coat, with his long wavy hair and blue eyes, he was very handsome (or perhaps it might have seemed so to her), and he was very affectionate with her.

Remembering many more things, and taking everything into consideration, Olga would dress and, in a state of great agitation, take a cab to Ryabovsky's studio. There she would find him in high spirits and full of admiration for his really splendid picture; he would jump about, play the fool, and counter serious questions with jokes. Olga was jealous of the picture and hated it, but out of politeness she stood before it in silent contemplation for five minutes and sighing, as one sighs before something holy, she would say:

'No, you never painted anything like that before. You know, it simply terrifies me.'

Then she would begin to implore him to go on loving her, not to leave her, to have pity on her, poor unhappy thing. She would weep, kiss his hands, demand that he should swear that he loved her, try to convince him that without her good influence he would stray from the path and perish. Having spoilt the day for him and humiliated herself, she would go to her dressmaker's or to an actress she knew from whom she hoped to get a free theatre ticket.

If she did not find Ryabovsky in his studio, she left him a note in which she threatened to take poison if he did not come to see her and stay to dinner that very day. Afraid of a scandal, he would go and stay to dinner. Unabashed by the presence of her husband, he would speak insolently to her, and she would do the same to him. Both felt that they were getting too involved with one another, that they were despots and enemies, and they were furious with one another, and in their fury they did not notice that they were both behaving badly and that even Korostelev with the cropped hair understood everything. After dinner Ryabovsky would hasten to take his leave and go.

'Where are you going?' Olga would ask him in the hall, looking at him with hatred.

Frowning and screwing up his eyes, he would name some woman, a mutual acquaintance, and she could see that he was making fun of her jealousy and merely wanted to annoy her. She would go to her bedroom and lie down on the bed; in her jealousy, spite, humiliation, and shame she would bite the pillow and burst into loud sobs. Dymov would leave Korostelev in the drawing-room, go into the bedroom disconcerted and perplexed, and say softly:

'Don't cry so loudly, darling. What's the use? One must keep quiet about it. One mustn't let people suspect. ... What's done can't be undone, you know.'

Not knowing how to subdue her pangs of jealousy, which even made her temples ache, and still believing that things could be mended, she would wash, powder her tear-stained face, and rush off to the woman he had mentioned. Not finding Ryabovsky there, she would take a cab to another, then to a third. At first she was ashamed to rush from one acquaintance to another like that, but later she got used to it; and sometimes she would call on all the women she knew in a single evening, in the hope of finding Ryabovsky, and they all realized it.

One day she said to Ryabovsky, referring to her husband:

'That man is killing me with his magnanimity!'

This phrase pleased her so much that every time she met any of the artists who knew of her affair with Ryabovsky she would refer to her husband and say with a dramatic gesture:

'That man is killing me with his magnanimity!'

The pattern of their life was the same as the year before. On Wednesday she gave her parties. The actor recited, the artists drew, the cellist played, the singer sang, and invariably at half past eleven the dining-room door opened and Dymov said with a smile:

'Ladies and gentlemen, supper is served!'

As before, Olga kept looking for great men, found them, grew dissatisfied, and went looking for others. As before, she came back home late at night, but Dymov was no longer asleep as he had been the year before, but sat in his study working at something. He went to bed at three and got up at eight.

One evening when Olga was standing before the glass in the bedroom having a last look at herself before going to the theatre, Dymov came in wearing a frock coat and white tie. He smiled gently and, as he used to do formerly, looked straight into his wife's eyes. His face was radiant.

'I've just defended my thesis,' he said, sitting down and stroking his knees.

'*Have* you defended it?' asked Olga.

'Oho!' he laughed, craning his neck to catch sight of his wife's face in the glass, for Olga remained standing with her back to him arranging her hair. 'Oho!' he repeated. 'You know, it's quite on the cards that I shall be offered a lectureship in general pathology. It looks very much like it.'

It could be seen from his blissful, radiant face that had Olga shared his joy and triumph, he would have forgiven her everything, present and future, and would have forgotten everything; but she did not realize what a lectureship in general pathology meant, and besides she was afraid to be late for the theatre, and so she said nothing.

He sat there for another two minutes, smiled guiltily, and went out.

VII

It had been a most disturbing day.

Dymov had a violent headache. He had no breakfast in the morning; he did not go to the hospital, but lay all day on the low ottoman in his study. As usual, Olga went to see Ryabovsky at one o'clock to show him her sketch for a still life and to ask him why he had not been to see her the day before. She knew her sketch was awful, and she had only painted it so as to have another pretext for going to see the artist.

She went in without ringing. When she was taking off her galoshes in the hall she heard someone running quietly across the studio. It must have been a woman, for she could distinctly hear the rustling of her dress, and indeed when she hastily glanced into the studio she was just in time to catch a glimpse of a brown skirt disappearing behind a large canvas on an easel covered to the floor by a sheet of black calico. There could be no doubt that a woman was hiding there. How often had Olga herself had to take refuge behind that very picture! Ryabovsky, obviously very embarrassed, pretended to be surprised to see her and held out his hands to her, saying with a forced smile:

'A-a-a-h! How nice to see you. What's your news?'

Olga's eyes filled with tears. She felt ashamed and miserable and if she had been offered a million, she would not have spoken in the presence of another woman, a rival of hers, the liar who was at that very moment standing behind the picture and no doubt giggling maliciously to herself.

'I've brought you this sketch,' she said timidly in a thin voice, and her lips trembled. 'It's a still life.'

'A-a-a-h! A still life.'

The artist took the sketch, and as he examined it he walked into the next room as though without noticing what he was doing. Olga followed him meekly.

'A still life,' he murmured, trying to find a suitable rhyme, 'strife, knife, rife, wife . . .'

The sound of hurried footsteps and the rustling of a skirt came from the studio. So *she* had gone. Olga felt like screaming, hitting the artist on the head with something heavy, and running away; but she was blinded with tears, crushed with shame, and felt that she was neither Olga nor an artist any longer, but some insignificant insect.

'I'm tired,' the artist said languourously, looking at the sketch and shaking his head to dispel his drowsiness. 'It's charming, of course. But it's a sketch today, a sketch last year, and another sketch in a month's time. . . . Don't you find it rather boring? In your place I'd give up painting altogether and take up music or something seriously. You see, you're not really a painter but a musician. Still, you know, I'm awfully tired! I'll tell them to bring us some tea. . . . Eh?'

He went out of the room and Olga could hear him giving orders to his manservant. Not to have to say good-bye, to avoid having it out with him, and above all to prevent herself bursting into sobs, she rushed out into the hall before Ryabovsky had time to come back, put on her galoshes, and went out. In the street she breathed freely and felt that at last she had rid herself for good of Ryabovsky, art, and the painful feeling of shame which had weighed so heavily on her in the studio. It was all over.

She took a cab to her dressmaker's, then to Barnay, who had only arrived the day before, and from Barnay to a music shop; and all the time she was thinking of the cold, harsh, dignified letter she would write to Ryabovsky, and how in the spring or summer she would go to the Crimea with Dymov, shake off her past completely there, and begin a new life.

When she came back home, very late, she sat down at once in the drawing-room, without changing, to compose her letter to Ryabovsky. He had told her that she was no artist, so in revenge she would tell him in her letter that year in, year out, he painted the same picture, said the same things day after day, that he had got into a rut, and that he would never be anything better than what he was already. She also wanted to tell him that he owed a great deal to her influence, and that if he was behaving badly now it was only because her influence was being undermined by certain disreputable creatures like the one who had been hiding behind the picture today.

'Darling,' Dymov called from his study, without opening the door. 'Darling!'

'What do you want?'

'Don't come in, darling. Just come to the door. What I want to say is that I caught diphtheria at the hospital the day before yesterday, and now I'm feeling ... rotten. Send for Korostelev straight away.'

Olga always called her husband by his surname, as she did all the men she knew. She did not like his Christian name Osip, which reminded her of the servant Osip in Gogol's comedy. But now she cried out:

'Osip, it isn't true, is it?'

'Send for Korostelev. I'm not feeling at all well,' said Dymov from behind the door, and she could hear him walking up to the ottoman and lying down. 'Send for him!' he repeated in a dull voice.

'Good heavens,' thought Olga, cold with horror. 'That's dangerous!'

She took a candle, though she did not need one, and went into her bedroom; while wondering what to do, she accidentally glanced at herself in the looking glass. With her pale, frightened face, in her jacket with high, puffed sleeves, yellow flounces at her breast, and the usual diagonal stripes on her skirt, she looked ghastly and revolting. She suddenly felt terribly, agonizingly sorry for Dymov, for his boundless love of her, for his young life and even for that bed of his which he had not slept in for so long; and she remembered his invariably meek and gentle smiles. She wept bitterly, and wrote an imploring letter to Korostelev. It was two o'clock in the morning.

VIII

When Olga came out of her bedroom at about eight o'clock the next morning, her head heavy from lack of sleep, her hair undone, unattractive, and with a guilty expression, a man with a black beard who looked like a doctor went past her into the hall. There was a smell of medicines. Near the door of the study stood Korostelev, twisting the left side of his moustache with his right hand.

'I'm sorry, I can't let you go into his room,' he said morosely to Olga. 'You might catch the infection. And anyway there isn't really any point in your being there. He's delirious.'

'Has he really got diphtheria?' Olga asked in a whisper.

'Those who play with fire unnecessarily should be put under arrest and tried!' muttered Korostelev, without answering Olga's question. 'Do you know how he got infected? On Tuesday he sucked through a tube the fibrinous exudations from the throat of a little boy with diphtheria. What for? Just because he was a damn fool. The stupidity of it!'

'It is dangerous? Very dangerous?' asked Olga.

'Yes, I'm afraid it's a very acute form. We really ought to send for Schreck.'

A red-haired little man with a long nose and a Jewish accent came, then a tall, stooping, shaggy man looking like a deacon, and then a very corpulent young man with a red face and wearing glasses. These were doctors, who came to keep watch by the bedside of their colleague. When his watch was over Korostelev did not go home, but stayed behind and wandered like a shadow about the rooms. The maid made tea for the doctors and was always running to the chemist's, and there was no one to tidy the rooms. It was quiet and dismal.

Olga sat in the bedroom telling herself that God was punishing her for having been unfaithful to her husband. The silent, uncomplaining, incomprehensible human being, deprived of individuality by his gentleness, lacking firmness, feeble from an excess of goodness, was now suffering as he lay helpless on the ottoman in his room without uttering a word of complaint. For if he had complained, even in delirium, his doctors would have realized that it was not only diphtheria that was to blame. Let them ask Korostelev. He knew everything, and it was not for nothing that he looked at the wife of his friend with eyes that seemed to say that it was she who was the chief and real culprit and that the diphtheria was merely her accomplice. She no longer remembered the moonlit night on the Volga, or Ryabovsky's declarations of love, or the poetic life in a peasant's cottage. All she remembered was that for a foolish whim, for sheer mischievousness, she had got herself covered from head to foot with something filthy and sticky, and that she would never be able to wash it off.

'Oh, what a terrible liar I've been!' she thought, recalling her turbulent love affair with Ryabovsky. 'Damn it! Damn it!'

At four o'clock she had dinner with Korostelev. He ate nothing. He only drank red wine and frowned. She too ate nothing. She either prayed silently, promising God that if Dymov recovered she would love him again and be a faithful wife to him, or, forgetting herself for a moment, looked at Korostelev and thought: 'Surely it must be awfully dull to be such an ordinary, such a totally undistinguished and obscure person, with such a crumpled face, too, and with such execrable manners!' Again, it seemed to her that God would strike her dead any minute for having never once been in her husband's study from fear of infection. Altogether, she felt dull and miserable, and she was quite certain that her life was ruined and that there was nothing she could do about it. . . .

After dinner it began to grow dark. When Olga went into the drawing-room she found Korostelev asleep on the settee with his head on a silk cushion embroidered in gilt thread. He was snoring.

The doctors who came to sit at the patient's bedside and went away again did not notice the disorder in the house, either. The stranger asleep and snoring in the drawing-room, the sketches on the walls, the curious interior, the mistress of the house going about with her hair undone and untidily dressed – all this no longer aroused any interest. One of the doctors happened to laugh at something, and his laughter sounded so timid and strange that everyone felt horrified.

When Olga went into the drawing-room again Korostelev was no longer asleep. He was sitting up and smoking.

'The diphtheria has spread to the nasal cavities,' he said softly. 'His heart is getting weaker, too. Things don't look too good, I'm afraid.'

'Have you sent for Schreck?' Olga asked.

'He's already been. It was he who noticed the spread of the diphtheria. Oh, but what can Schreck do? He can't do a thing! He's Schreck, I'm Korostelev – that's all.'

Time was dragging on terribly slowly. Fully dressed, Olga lay dozing in her bed, which had not been made since the morning. It seemed to her that the whole flat was filled from floor to ceiling with an enormous piece of iron, and that if the iron were removed everyone would feel happy. Waking up, she realized that it was not a piece of iron but Dymov's illness.

'Still life – strife, wife . . .' she thought, dozing off again. 'Knife, rife . . . and what about Schreck? Schreck, treck, peck, reck . . . And where are my friends now? Do they know about my trouble? Lord, save and have mercy. . . . Schreck, treck . . .'

There was that piece of iron again. . . . Time dragged on endlessly, though the clock on the floor below was striking the hour again and again and again. Now and again the doorbell rang – the doctors coming to see the patient. The maid came in with an empty glass on a tray.

'Shall I make up your bed, ma'am?' she asked.

Getting no reply, she went out. The clock on the floor below struck the hour. She dreamt it was raining on the Volga, and again someone came into the bedroom, a stranger this time, it seemed. Olga sat up with a start and recognized Korostelev.

'What's the time?' she asked.

'About three.'

'Well?'

'Well what? I came to tell you he's dying.'

He gave a whimper, sat down on the bed beside her, and wiped away a tear with a sleeve. At first she did not quite understand, then she turned cold all over and began to cross herself slowly.

'He's dying,' he repeated in a thin voice, and whimpered again. 'He's dying because he sacrificed himself. What a loss to science!' he said, bitterly. 'Compared to all of us, he was a great man, a remarkable man. What gifts! What hopes he inspired in all of us!' Korostelev went on, wringing his hands. 'Good Lord, you wouldn't find another scientist like him if you looked all over the world. Osip Dymov, Osip Dymov what have you done? Dear, oh dear!'

Korostelev shook his head and covered his face with both hands in despair.

'And what moral force!' he went on, getting more and more furious with someone. 'A kind, loving, pure soul – spotless! You could see through him as through a glass. Served science, and died in the cause of science. Worked like a horse, day and night, no one spared him; and a young scientist like him, a future professor, had to look for private patients and sit up all night doing translations to be able to pay for – for these rotten rags!'

Korostelev looked at Olga with hatred, seized the sheet in both his hands, and pulled at it angrily, as if it were to blame.

'He didn't spare himself, and others didn't spare him. Oh well, what does it really matter now?'

'Yes, he was a very remarkable man,' someone said in the drawing-room, in a bass voice.

Olga recalled her whole life with him, from beginning to end, in all its details, and suddenly realized that Dymov really had been a most remarkable man, and a great man, compared with the men she knew. And remembering what her late father and all his colleagues had thought of him, she realized that they had all seen in him a future celebrity. The walls, the ceiling, the lamp, and the carpet winked mockingly at her as if wishing to say: 'You've missed your chance! You've missed your chance!' She rushed weeping out of the bedroom, darted past some stranger in the drawing-room, and ran into her husband's study. He lay motionless on the ottoman, covered up to the waist by a blanket. His face looked terribly thin and drawn, and had that greyish-yellow colour never seen on the living; only by his forehead, his black brows, and his familiar smile could one recognize him as Dymov. Olga rapidly felt his chest, his forehead, and his hands. His chest was still warm, but his hands and forehead were horribly cold. And his half-closed eyes looked not at Olga, but at the blanket.

'Dymov!' she called loudly. 'Dymov!'

She wanted to explain to him that it had all been a mistake, that everything was not yet lost, that life could still be beautiful and happy, that he was a most rare and remarkable man, a great man, and that she would worship him all her life, pray to him, and feel a sacred awe of him. . . .

'Dymov!' she called him, shaking him by the shoulder and unable to believe that he would never awake again. 'Dymov! Dymov-v-v!'

In the drawing-room Korostelev was saying to the maid:

'What's there to ask about? Go round to the church and ask where the almswomen live. They'll wash the body and lay it out. They'll do all that's necessary.'

Ward 6

THERE is a small annexe in the hospital yard surrounded by a whole forest of burdock, stinging nettles, and wild hemp. The roof is rusty, half the chimney has collapsed, the front steps have crumbled away and are overgrown with grass, and only traces of plaster remain. It faces the hospital, and its back looks into a field from which it is separated only by the grey hospital fence studded with nails. The nails, their sharp points sticking upwards, the fence, and the annexe itself have that special kind of depressing, baneful air which is so characteristic of our hospitals and prison buildings.

If you do not mind being stung by nettles, let us go along the narrow path leading to the annexe and see what is going on inside. On opening the front door, we enter the hall. Here, against the walls and near the stove, mattresses are piled up, mountains of hospital odds and ends, old tattered dressing-gowns, drawers, striped blue shirts, useless, worn-out footwear — all this rubbish lies in tangled and jumbled-up heaps, rotting and exhaling a suffocating smell.

On top of this heap of rubbish, a pipe always between his teeth, lies the caretaker Nikita, an old retired soldier with faded brownish stripes on the sleeves of his shirt. He has a coarse drink-sodden face, beetling eyebrows which make him look like a steppe sheep-dog, and a red nose; short, thin, and wiry, there is something impressive about his carriage, and his fists are powerful. He is one of those simple-minded, intolerant, obtuse people who can be relied on to carry out an order and who value order above everything and are therefore convinced of the efficacy of blows. He beats his charges in the face, in the chest, in the back, in fact anywhere, in the firm belief that there is no other way to keep order in the ward.

From the entrance hall you enter a large spacious room which takes up all the rest of the annexe. The walls of this room are painted a muddy blue, the ceiling is black with soot just as in a hut without a chimney – it is plain that in the winter the stoves smoke and the room is full of poisonous fumes. The windows are disfigured on the inside with iron bars. The floor is discoloured and full of splinters. The place smells of sour cabbage, unsnuffed wicks, bed-bugs, and ammonia, and this mixture of smells at first gives you the impression of entering a menagerie.

There are beds in the room, screwed to the floor. Men in blue hospital dressing-gowns and wearing old-fashioned night-caps are sitting or lying on them. They are the lunatics.

There are altogether five of them. Only one of them is of a higher station in life, the rest are all artisans and tradesmen. The one nearest to the door, a tall lean tradesman with a shiny red moustache and eyes wet with tears, sits with his head propped up on his hand, staring fixedly at one point. Day and night he grieves, shaking his head, sighing, and smiling bitterly; he seldom joins in conversations and, as a rule, refuses to answer questions. He eats and drinks mechanically whenever food is brought to him. To judge by his painful, hacking cough, his emaciated appearance, and the flush on his cheeks, he is in the early phases of consumption.

The next bed is occupied by a little, active, and very agile old man with a pointed beard and black frizzly hair like a negro. He spends all day walking about the ward from window to window or sitting on the bed cross-legged, Turkish fashion, incessantly whistling like a bullfinch or humming a song or giggling. He displays his childlike gaiety and lively character at night, too, getting up to say his prayers, that is to smite his breast with his fists or pick at the door with a finger. This is Moseyka, a Jew, an imbecile, who went out of his mind about twenty years ago when his cap workshop was destroyed by fire.

He is the only inmate of Ward 6 who is allowed to leave the building and even to go out of the hospital yard into the street. He has enjoyed this privilege for years, probably because he is the oldest patient of the asylum and a quiet, harmless fool, the town idiot, whom the townspeople have long been used to seeing in the streets surrounded by street urchins and dogs. In his threadbare hospital gown, absurd nightcap, and slippers, or often barefoot and even without trousers, he walks about the streets, stopping at gates and small shops and begging for a kopek. At one place he would be given *kvass*, at another bread, and at a third a kopek, so that he usually returns to the ward rich and replete. Everything he brings back is taken from him by Nikita. The old soldier does it roughly, angrily, turning Moseyka's pockets inside out and calling God to witness that he will never again let the dirty Jew go out into the streets, for disorder is the worst thing in the world to him.

Moseyka loves to do people a good turn. He fetches water for his fellow-patients, covers them up when they are asleep, promises to bring each of them a kopek when he returns from the town and to make them new caps; he also spoon-feeds his neighbour on the left – a paralytic. He does this not from compassion or from any other humane motive, but simply following the example of Gromov, his neighbour on the right, to whose authority he submits unquestioningly.

Ivan Dmitrich Gromov, a man of about thirty-three, of good family, a civil servant of the twelfth and lowest grade, used to be a court bailiff. He suffers from persecution mania. He either lies curled up on his bed or paces the ward from corner to corner as though taking a constitutional. Only very rarely can he be seen sitting down. He is always in a state of great excitement and agitation, tense with some vague, obscure feeling of suspense. At the slightest noise in the passage or sound in the yard he raises his head and listens intently. Are they coming for him? Are they looking for him? And at such a moment his face expresses extreme alarm and abhorrence.

I like his broad face with the prominent cheekbones, always pale and unhappy, reflecting as in a mirror a mind tormented by incessant struggle and fear. His grimaces are strange and morbid, but the delicate lines traced on his face by profound and genuine suffering reveal sensibility and intelligence, and there is a warm and healthy glow in his eyes. I like the man himself, so polite, obliging, and considerate in his treatment of everyone except Nikita. If anyone drops a button or a spoon, he jumps quickly out of bed and picks it up. When he gets up in the morning he says 'good morning' to everyone, and when he goes to bed he wishes them 'good night'.

Apart from his grimaces and continual mental tension, his madness shows itself in the following way: sometimes in the evening he wraps his dressing-gown very tightly round him and, trembling all over, his teeth chattering, he walks rapidly from corner to corner and between the beds. He looks as though he were suffering from a violent fever. From the way in which he suddenly stops and stares at his fellow-patients it is plain that he has something very important to say, but evidently realizing that they will not listen to him or understand him, he shakes his head impatiently and continues to walk. But very soon his desire to talk overrides all other considerations and he lets himself go and talks and talks, warmly and passionately. His speech, confused and febrile, like the ramblings of a man in a delirium, is impetuous and not always intelligible, but there is something in his words and inflexions that betrays quite extraordinary goodness. When he speaks, you become aware of both the madman and the man in him. It is difficult to put his mad ravings down on paper. He speaks of human meanness, of coercion trampling upon justice, of the beautiful life that will one day come on earth, of the barred windows that remind him every moment of the stupidity and cruelty of the oppressors. What it all comes to is a confused and incoherent mixture of stories which are as old as the hills but are still unfinished.

II

Some twelve or fifteen years before there had lived in his own house in the main street of this town a civil servant by the name of Gromov, a well-to-do man of good repute. He had two sons, Sergey and Ivan. In his fourth year at the university, Sergey contracted galloping consumption and died, and his death seemed to be the beginning of a whole series of calamities which suddenly descended upon the Gromov family. A week after Sergey's funeral, the old man was put on trial for forgery and embezzlement, and soon after he died in prison of typhus. His house and property were sold by auction, and Ivan Gromov and his mother were left without means of subsistence.

Before, while his father was alive, Ivan Gromov had lived in Petersburg, where he had studied at the university, received an allowance of sixty or seventy roubles a month, and had no idea of the meaning of poverty; but now he had to introduce drastic changes in his way of life. He had to give private lessons for next to nothing from morning till night, copy manuscripts, and still go hungry, for he had to send all his earnings to his mother. This life was more than Ivan Gromov could bear; he lost heart, fell ill, and, leaving the university, went home. Here, in the small provincial town, he got a teaching job in the district school through influential friends, but as he could not get on with his colleagues and was not very popular among his pupils, he soon gave up the post. His mother died. For six months he was without a job, subsisting on bread and water, and then he accepted the post of court bailiff. This post he held till he was discharged for reasons of health.

He had never, even in his student days, given the impression of being a strong, healthy man. He was always pale and thin and subject to colds; he ate little and slept badly. One glass of vodka made him feel dizzy and become hysterical. He was always drawn to people, but because of his fastidiousness and irritable character he never got on intimate terms with anyone and he had no friends. He always spoke of the townspeople with contempt, declaring that their gross ignorance and torpid animal existence struck him as loathsome and disgusting. He had a high-pitched voice and he spoke loudly and passionately, always either acrimoniously and resentfully or in a state of rapture and amazement, and always sincerely. Whatever you talked to him about, he always turned the conversation to one and the same subject: life in this town was stifling and boring, society had no higher interests, it led a dull and senseless existence, veering between violence, coarse debauchery, and hypocrisy; scoundrels were well fed and clothed, while honest men had to be satisfied with a few crumbs; what they wanted was schools, a local newspaper with an honest political programme, a theatre, public readings, solidarity among all intellectual forces; it was necessary that society should become aware of its own shortcomings and be horrified by them. In his opinions of man he laid on the colours thickly, white or black, admitting no shades of any kind. Men were either honest or rogues – there was nothing in between. Of women and love he always spoke passionately and with enthusiasm, but he had never been in love.

In spite of his extreme views and his nervous disposition he was liked in the town, and behind his back he was affectionately called Vanya. His delicacy, considerateness, decency, and moral purity and his shabby old coat, sickly appearance, and family misfortunes inspired a warm, friendly feeling for him, tinged with sadness. Besides, he was well educated and well read; in the opinion of the townsmen he knew everything and was looked upon by everyone in the town as a kind of walking encyclopedia.

He read a great deal. He used to sit in the club for hours, pulling nervously at his little beard and turning over the pages of periodicals and books; and it was clear from his face that he was not so much reading as devouring their contents, without giving himself enough time to find out their meaning. Reading had apparently become one of his morbid habits, for he fell upon everything he came across with equal avidity, even last year's newspapers and almanacs. At home he always read lying down.

III

One autumn morning, the collar of his coat turned up, splashing through the mud, Gromov made his way along side streets and back alleys to the house of a tradesman to collect money on a writ of execution. As always in the morning, he was in a dismal mood. In one of the side streets he met two prisoners in chains escorted by four soldiers armed with rifles. Before, too, Gromov had often met prisoners; and every time they aroused in him a feeling of compassion and embarrassment, but that morning this meeting made a quite special and unusual impression on him. For some reason it occurred to him that he too might be put in irons and dragged to prison through the mud in the same way. After his visit to the tradesman, on his way back home, he met a police inspector of his acquaintance, near the post office. The police inspector exchanged greetings with him and walked a few yards down the street with him. For some reason this seemed to him suspicious. At home he was haunted all day by the thought of the prisoners and the soldiers with rifles, and an incomprehensible mental disquiet prevented him from reading and concentrating on his thoughts. In the evening he did not light his lamp and at night he did not sleep. The thought that he too might be arrested, put in irons, and thrown into prison never left him for a moment. He knew he was not guilty of any crime, and was quite confident that he would never commit murder or arson, or steal; but then it was not so difficult to commit a crime by accident, without meaning to. And is there not such a thing as wrongful accusation or miscarriage of justice? After all, long experience has taught the common people that one is never safe from poverty or prison. And in the present state of the law, a miscarriage of justice is more than likely and there is nothing unusual about it. People such as judges, policemen, and doctors, whose attitude to human suffering is strictly official and professional, become so callous in the course of time and from force of habit that they cannot treat their clients in any but a formal way even if they want to; in this respect they are not at all different from the peasant who slaughters sheep and calves in his backyard and does not give a thought to the blood. Granted this formal and callous attitude to human personality, a judge requires only one thing to deprive an innocent man of his civil rights and sentence him to hard labour – time. Only the time necessary for the observance of certain formalities, for which the judge is paid a salary, and then – all is over. Just try to look for justice and protection in this small, filthy town, one hundred and fifty miles from the nearest railway station! Besides, is it not absurd even to think of justice when every form of violence is regarded by society as a rational and expedient necessity and every act of clemency, for instance an acquittal, produces a veritable explosion of dissatisfied, vindictive feelings?

Next morning Gromov got out of his bed in a state of terror and with cold sweat on his forehead. He was absolutely certain that he might be arrested any minute. The fact that the painful thoughts of the previous day would not leave him, he concluded, must mean that there was a grain of truth in them. After all, they could not have entered his head without some reason.

A policeman walked slowly past his window. There must be some good reason for it. Two men stopped outside his house without uttering a word. Why were they silent?

Gromov spent the days and nights that followed in a state of anguish. He thought the people who passed his windows or entered his yard were spies or detectives. The police superintendent usually drove past his house in his carriage and pair every day at twelve o'clock; he was driving from his country house to the police department, but every time Gromov could not help thinking that he was driving too fast, and that there was a peculiar expression on his face: it was quite obvious that he was in a hurry to announce the presence of a dangerous criminal in the town. Every time the door bell rang or there was a knock at the gate, Gromov gave a start; and he was terribly worried when someone he had not met before came to see his landlady. When he met a policeman or a gendarme he smiled and whistled to appear indifferent. He did not sleep a wink at night, expecting to be arrested, but he snored loudly and breathed like a sleeping man to make his landlady believe that he was asleep; for if he were not asleep, it could only mean that he was suffering the pangs of remorse – and what evidence of guilt that would be! Facts and common sense persuaded him that all his fears were absurd and irrational, that there was nothing terrible in being arrested and imprisoned, if one took a broad view of things – so long as one's conscience was clear. But the more sensible and logical his reasoning was, the stronger and more tormenting became his mental anguish. He was like the hermit who tried to clear himself a spot in a primeval forest: the harder he wielded his axe, the denser and more impenetrable did the forest become. In the end, realizing the futility of it all, he gave up reasoning altogether and resigned himself to terror and despair.

He began to keep to himself and shun people. His job, which he had always detested, now became intolerable to him. He was afraid of a frame-up, of someone slipping some money in his pocket without his being aware of it and then accusing him of taking bribes; or that he would himself unwittingly make some mistake in an official document, which would be tantamount to forgery; or that he would lose money that did not belong to him.

The strange thing was that never at any other time was his mind so subtle and inventive as now that he had to think of thousands of different reasons every day for being seriously concerned about his honour and freedom. On the other hand, his interest in the outside world and particularly in books was weakening considerably, and his memory too was beginning to fail him perceptibly.

In the spring, after the snow had melted, two bodies, an old woman's and a little boy's – both in a state of advanced decomposition and bearing the signs of foul play – were discovered in a ravine near the cemetery. The whole town talked of nothing but these bodies and the unknown murderer. To make sure that people did not think that he was the murderer, Gromov walked about the streets and smiled; and when he met acquaintances, he went pale and blushed and began to assure them that there was no crime so vile as the murder of weak and defenceless people. But he soon got tired of this lie and, after thinking it over, he decided that the best thing for him to do was to hide himself in his landlady's cellar. He spent a day, a night, and another day in the cellar, and got chilled to the bone and, waiting till it was dark again, he crept secretly back into his own room like a thief. He stood motionless in the middle of the room till daybreak, listening. Early in the morning just before daybreak, some stove-fitters came to the landlady. Gromov knew very well that they had come to reset the stove in the kitchen, but his fear prompted the belief that they were policemen disguised as stove-fitters. He crept quietly out of the house and, gripped by panic, ran along the street without cap or coat. Dogs ran after him barking, a peasant shouted something after him, the wind whistled in his ears, and Gromov felt that all the violence in the world had accumulated behind his back and was chasing him.

He was stopped and brought home, and his landlady was sent to get a doctor. Dr Adrey Yefimych Ragin, of whom more later, prescribed cold compresses for his head and laurel drops, shook his head sadly, and went away, telling the landlady that he would not come again because one should not prevent people from going out of their minds. As he had no money to live on and pay for his medical treatment, he was soon sent to the hospital and put into the ward for V.D. patients. He did not sleep at night, was capricious and disturbed the other patients, and soon he was transferred to Ward 6 at the order of Dr Ragin.

In a year everybody in the town had forgotten all about Ivan Gromov; and his books, dumped by his landlady into a sledge under an awning, were gradually carried off by street urchins.

IV

The neighbour on the left of Gromov is, as I have already said, the Jew Moseyka; on the right is an obese, almost spherical peasant, with a stupid, almost inane face – an inert, gluttonous, unclean animal who has long lost the ability to think or to feel. He exudes a sharp, suffocating stench.

Nikita, who looks after him, beats him terribly, striking him with all his might and without sparing his own fists; but what is so awful is not so much the fact that he is beaten – one can get used to that – as that the torpid animal does not respond to the blows by a sound or movement or the flicker of an eye, merely rocking from side to side like a heavy cask.

The fifth and last inmate of Ward 6 is a townsman who was once a sorter at the post office, a thin, fair-headed little man with a kind but somewhat cunning face. To judge by the serene and cheerful look in his clever, tranquil eyes, he knows which side his bread is buttered on and has some highly important and agreeable secret. He has something under his pillow and under his mattress that he refuses to show to anyone, not because he is afraid that it might be taken away from him or stolen, but because he feels ashamed. Sometimes he walks up to the window and, turning his back upon his fellow-patients, puts something on his chest, lowers his head, and looks at it; if anyone should walk up to him at that moment, he will look embarrassed and tear something off his chest. But it is not difficult to guess his secret.

'Congratulate me,' he often says to Gromov. 'I have been recommended for the Order of St Stanislaus, second class, with a star. The order of second class with a star is only conferred on foreigners, but for some reason they want to make an exception in my case,' he declares with a smile, shrugging his shoulders and looking perplexed. 'I admit I never expected it.'

'I'm afraid I know nothing about it,' Gromov says gloomily.

'But do you know what I shall most certainly get sooner or later?' continues the ex-sorter, narrowing his eyes cunningly. 'I shall get the Swedish Order of the Pole Star! It's the sort of order worth taking a lot of trouble over. A white cross and a black ribbon. Very beautiful.'

Nowhere in the world, probably, was life as monotonous as it was in this hospital annexe. In the morning the patients, with the exception of the paralytic and the obese peasant, would go out into the passage and have a wash in a large wash-tub and dry themselves on the skirts of their dressing-gowns; after that they drank tea out of tin mugs brought from the main building by Nikita. Each was allowed one mugful. At noon they had sour cabbage soup and porridge, and for supper in the evening they had the porridge left over from dinner. Between meals they lay on their beds, slept, looked out of the windows, and paced the room from one corner to another. And so every day. Even the ex-sorter talked of the same two orders all the time.

Fresh faces were rarely seen in Ward 6. The doctor had long stopped admitting any new mental patients, and there are not many people in this world who go to visit lunatic asylums. Once every two months Semyon Lazarich, the hairdresser, paid a visit to the annexe. How he cut the patients' hair, and how Nikita assisted him, and the consternation among the patients at the appearance of the tipsy smiling barber, is best left untold.

Apart from the hairdresser nobody looked into the annexe. Day after day the patients were condemned to see only Nikita.

A strange rumour, though, had of late been circulating throughout the hospital.

It was rumoured that the doctor had been paying regular visits to Ward 6.

V

A strange rumour, indeed!

Dr Ragin was a remarkable man in his way. He was said to have been very religious as a young man and to have thought of taking holy orders. On finishing his studies at the secondary school in

1863 he had intended to enter a theological college, but his father, a doctor of medicine and a surgeon, had poured scorn on his plans and had declared that he would disown him if he became a priest. How much of this was true I don't know, but I have often heard it said that he never felt any vocation for medicine or for any specialized branch of science.

Be that as it may, he did not take holy orders after graduating from the medical faculty. He showed no sign of religiosity, and was as little like a priest at the beginning of his medical career as he is now.

He looked like a heavily built, coarse-featured peasant; his face, beard, straight hair, and strong, ungainly build reminded one of an innkeeper on the highway – well fed, intemperate, and harsh. His stern face was covered with blue veins, his eyes were small, his nose red. Being very tall and broad-shouldered, he had enormous hands and feet; one blow with his fist and you would be as good as dead. Yet he walked softly, cautiously, insinuatingly; meeting someone in a narrow passage, he was the first to stop and give way, saying 'Sorry' not in a deep bass voice, as you might expect, but in a soft, thin treble. He had a small tumour on his neck which prevented him from wearing stiff starched collars, and that was why he always went about in soft linen or cotton shirts. He did not dress like a doctor at all. He wore the same suit for ten years, and when he did buy new clothes, which he usually bought at a Jewish shop, they looked just as worn and crumpled on him as the old suit; he received patients, dined, and paid visits in one and the same coat; he did it not because he was a miser but because he was completely indifferent to his personal appearance.

When Dr Ragin arrived in our town to take up his post, the 'charitable institution' was in an appalling state. It was quite impossible to breathe in the wards, the corridors, and the hospital yard for the stench. The male hospital attendants, the nurses, and their families slept in the wards together with the patients. Everybody complained that cockroaches, bedbugs, and lice made life in the hospital unbearable. The surgical ward was never free from erysipelas. In the whole hospital there were only two scalpels and not a single thermometer; the baths were used for storing potatoes. The superintendent, the matron, and the doctor's assistant robbed the patients, and of the old doctor, Ragin's predecessor, it was said that he had engaged in illegal sales of the hospital spirits and had kept a veritable harem recruited from the nurses and the female patients. In the town they knew perfectly well of the disgraceful goings-on in the hospital and exaggerated them, but it did not seem to worry anyone; some justified it by saying that it was after all only peasants and tradesmen who went to hospital and that they could not possibly be dissatisfied since they were much worse off at home. They did not expect to be fed on grouse, did they? Others argued that the town could not be expected to run a good hospital without assistance from the rural council; they ought to be grateful for any hospital, even a bad one. As for the rural council, which had only recently come into being, it did not open a hospital in the town or its vicinity on the ground that the town had one already.

After inspecting the hospital, Dr Ragin came to the conclusion that it was an immoral institution, highly detrimental to the health of those who lived in it. In his opinion the best thing to do was to discharge the patients and close down the hospital. But he realized that he had not the authority to do so, and that it would be no good, anyhow; for clearing away all the physical and moral uncleanliness from one place would merely transfer it to another; it was necessary to wait till it disappeared of itself. Besides, if people opened a hospital and kept it going, it meant that there was a need for it; prejudices and all sorts of foul and abominable things which one came across in life were necessary, for in the course of time they were converted into something useful, just as manure was converted into fertile black earth. There was nothing good on earth that had not originally had something vile in it.

Having taken up his duties, Dr Ragin seems to have regarded these abuses with apparent indifference. He merely asked the male hospital attendants and nurses not to spend the night in the wards and installed two cupboards of surgical instruments; the superintendent, the matron, the medical assistant, and the erysipelas stayed where they were.

Dr Ragin was a great believer in intelligence and honesty, but he lacked the strength of character and the confidence in his own right to assert himself in order to see to it that the life around him should be honest and intelligent. He simply did not know how to give orders, to prohibit, or to insist. It was almost as though he had taken a vow never to raise his voice or to use the imperative mood. He found it difficult to say 'Give me —' or 'Bring me —'. When he felt hungry, he cleared his throat irresolutely and said to his cook: 'I wonder if I could have a cup of tea. . . .' Or: 'I wonder if I could have my dinner now. . . .' But to tell the superintendent to stop stealing and give him the sack, or to abolish the unnecessary, parasitical office altogether, was quite beyond his strength. When deceived or flattered or handed a quite obviously fraudulent account for signature, he turned as red as a lobster and felt guilty, but he signed the account all the same; when the patients complained that they were not given enough to eat or that the nurses ill-treated them, he looked embarrassed and muttered guiltily: 'All right, all right, I'll look into it later. . . . I expect there must be some misunderstanding. . . .'

At first Dr Ragin worked very hard. He received patients every day from morning till dinner-time, performed operations, and even did a certain amount of midwifery. Among the women he gained a reputation for being very conscientious and very good at diagnosing illnesses, especially those of women and children. But as time passed he got tired of the monotony and the quite obvious uselessness of his work. One day he would receive thirty patients, the next day thirty-five, the next day after that forty, and so on from day to day, from one year to another, though the death-rate in the town did not decrease and the patients continued to come. To give any real assistance to forty patients between morning and dinner-time was a physical impossibility, which meant that his work was a fraud, necessarily a fraud. He received twelve thousand out-patients in a given year, which bluntly speaking meant that he had deceived twelve thousand people. To place the serious cases in the wards and treat them in accordance with the rules of science was also impossible, for although there were rules, there was no science; on the other hand, if he were to leave philosophy alone and follow the rules pedantically, like the other doctors, he would above all require cleanliness and fresh air and not filth, wholesome food and not stinking sour cabbage soup, good assistants and not thieves.

Besides, why prevent people dying if death was the normal and legitimate end of us all? Did it really matter if some huckster or government clerk lived an extra five or six years? And if the aim of the medical profession was to alleviate suffering by the administration of medicine, the question inevitably arose: why alleviate suffering? For in the first place it was argued that man could only achieve perfection through suffering, and, secondly, if mankind really learnt to alleviate suffering by pills and drops it would give up religion and philosophy, in which it had hitherto found not only protection from all misfortunes but even happiness. Pushkin suffered terribly before he died, and poor Heine lay paralysed for several years; why then should some Andrey Yefimych or a Matryona Savishna not be ill, particularly if but for suffering their lives would be as meaningless and insipid as the life of an amoeba?

Crushed by such arguments, Dr Ragin lost heart and stopped going to the hospital every day.

VI

This is how he spent his days. He usually got up at eight in the morning, dressed, and had his breakfast. Then he sat in his study and read, or went to the hospital. There, in a dark, narrow corridor, the out-patients were waiting to be received. Nurses and male attendants ran past them with a clatter of boots on the brick floor; emaciated patients in their dressing-gowns sauntered by; corpses and bedpans were carried out; children cried, and every time a door was opened an icy wind blew through the corridor. Dr Ragin knew, of course, that these surroundings were a torment to feverish, consumptive, or just nervous patients; but what was to be done about it? In the reception room he was met by his assistant Sergey Sergeyich, a little fat man, with a shaven, well-washed, chubby face, with easy, polished manners, wearing a new loose-fitting suit and looking more like a high-court judge than an assistant doctor. He had a very large practice in the town, wore a white tie, and believed himself to be much more experienced than the doctor, who had no practice. In the corner of the reception room was a large icon in a case, with a heavy lamp in front, and next to it a large candlestick in a slip-cover of white linen; on the walls hung portraits of bishops, a view of the Svyatogorsk Monastery, and wreaths of dried cornflowers. Sergey Sergeyich was a pious man and was fond of grandeur in anything of a religious nature. The large icon had been put up at his expense; on Sundays, at his express orders, a patient chanted a hymn, and Sergey Sergeyich himself went round the wards with a censer spreading clouds of incense.

There were many patients but little time, and that was why the examinations had to be limited to a few short questions and the dispensing of some medicaments, such as an ointment or castor oil. Dr Ragin sat lost in thought, his cheek resting on a fist, questioning the patients mechanically. Sergey Sergeyich, too, sat there, rubbing his plump hands and putting in a word from time to time.

'We are ill and poor,' he would say, 'because we pray too little to our merciful God. Yes, sir!'

During surgery hours Dr Ragin performed no operations; he had long got out of practice, and the sight of blood upset him. When he had to open a child's mouth to examine its throat and the child cried and tried to push him away with its little hands, the noise in his ears made his head swim and tears start to his eyes. He hastened to write out a prescription and waved his hands for the peasant woman to take her child away.

During the visiting hours he soon got tired of the timidity of the patients and their muddle-headedness, the proximity of the sanctimonious Sergey Sergeyich, the portraits on the walls, and his own questions, the same questions he had been asking his patients for over twenty years. And he went home after having received five or six patients. The rest were received by his assistant.

On returning home, agreeably conscious of the fact that, thank God, he had long given up private practice and that no one would interfere with him, Dr Ragin immediately settled down in his study and began to read. He read a great deal and always with pleasure. He spent half his salary on the purchase of books, and three of the six rooms of his flat were cluttered up with books and old periodicals. He liked books on history and philosophy most of all; the only medical magazine he subscribed to was *The Physician*, which he always began reading from the end. He would read without interruption for several hours without feeling tired. He did not read as quickly and eagerly as Ivan Gromov had once read, but slowly, absorbedly, often stopping at passages which either pleased him or which he did not understand. Beside his book there was always a decanter of vodka and next to it, on the tablecloth and never on a plate, a salted cucumber or a pickled apple. Every half hour he poured himself out a glass of vodka, drank it, and, still without raising his eyes from the book, felt for the cucumber and took a bite from it.

At three o'clock he walked cautiously up to the kitchen door, cleared his throat, and said:

'What about dinner, Darya?'

After dinner, never too good and always badly served, Dr Ragin walked about his rooms, arms folded on his chest, thinking. The clock struck four, then five, but he was still walking and thinking. Occasionally the kitchen door creaked and Darya's red, sleepy face appeared.

'Isn't it time for your beer, doctor?' she would ask, with a worried look.

'No, not yet, thank you,' he would reply. 'I'll wait . . . I'll wait a little. . . .'

In the evening the postmaster, Mikhail Averyanych, usually turned up. He was the only man in the whole town whose company the doctor did not find wearisome. The postmaster had once been a rich country gentleman and served in a cavalry regiment, but he had squandered his fortune and been forced to take a job in the post office in his old age. He looked cheerful and in good health; he had magnificent white whiskers, well-bred manners, and a loud but pleasant voice. He was kindhearted and sensitive, but short-tempered. If a member of the public protested, refused to agree with him, or simply began to argue, he turned crimson, shook all over, and roared 'Silence!' at the top of his voice, so that the post office had for a long time earned the reputation of an establishment you entered at your peril. The postmaster liked and respected Dr Ragin for his intellectual attainments and his noble sentiments, but he looked down upon the rest of the inhabitants and treated them as inferiors.

'Well, here I am, my dear sir!' he would say on entering the room. 'How are you? I expect you must be sick and tired of me, eh?'

'On the contrary, I'm very glad to see you,' answered the doctor. 'I'm always glad to see you.'

The friends would sit down on the sofa in the study, smoking in silence for a while.

'I say, Darya,' said Dr Ragin, 'what about some beer?'

The first bottle was also drunk in silence; the doctor drank with an abstracted air and the postmaster with the gay and lively air of a man who had something highly interesting to say. It was always the doctor who opened the conversation.

'What a pity,' he began slowly and quietly, without looking at his friend's face (he never looked anyone in the face), 'what a pity, my dear fellow, that there is not a soul in this town who cares to engage in interesting and intelligent conversation, or is capable of it. It's a great loss to us. Even the educated classes do not rise above the commonplace. The level of their mental development, I assure you, is no higher than that of the lower classes.'

'Quite right. I agree.'

'You know, of course,' the doctor went on quietly and without haste, 'that everything in this world is unimportant and uninteresting save the highest spiritual manifestations of the human mind. The mind draws a sharp line between man and animal, gives an intimation of the former's divine nature, and to a certain extent even takes the place of immortality, which does not exist. The mind is therefore the only possible source of pleasure. But we neither see nor hear any evidence of the existence of minds around us, which means that we are deprived of enjoyment. It is true we have books, but that is quite a different matter from live conversation and true communion. If I may use a not very apt simile, I should say that books are the musical score and conversation the singing.'

'Quite true.'

There was a pause. At that moment Darya came out of the kitchen and stopped in the doorway to listen, with an expression of mute grief, her face resting on her fist.

'Good gracious,' the postmaster said with a sigh, 'you don't expect people of today to have minds, do you?'

And he went on to speak of the old days when life was wholesome, gay, and interesting, when the educated classes displayed a high level of intelligence and set a high value on honour and friendship. They used to lend money without promissory notes, and thought it disgraceful not to hold out a helping hand to a friend in need. And what campaigns there were, what adventures, what skirmishes, what comrades, what women! And the Caucasus — what a wonderful country! There was the wife of a battalion commander, an extraordinary woman who dressed up as an officer and made off into the mountains in the evenings, alone without a guide. It was rumoured that she had an affair with some Circassian prince in a mountain village.

'Holy mother of God!' sighed Darya.

'And how we drank! How we ate! And what desperate liberals we were!'

Dr Ragin listened, but heard nothing; he was thinking of something else, sipping his beer.

'I often dream of intelligent people and have conversations with them,' he said unexpectedly, interrupting the postmaster. 'My father gave me an excellent education, but he was influenced by the ideas of the 1860s and forced me to become a doctor. I can't help feeling that if I had not obeyed him I should now be in the very midst of an intellectual movement, a member of some faculty perhaps. No doubt the intellect too is not eternal but transitory, but of course you know why I think so highly of it. Life is a snare and a delusion. When a thinking man reaches maturity and becomes capable of forming his own ideas, he cannot but face the fact that he is caught in a trap from which there is no escape. And indeed he is summoned against his will from non-existence to life as a result of some accidental circumstances. . . . Why? If he tries to find out the meaning and aim of his existence, he receives no answer, or is told some absurd nonsense. He knocks, but no one opens to him; then death comes to him, also against his will. And as men in prison are united by common misfortune and feel comforted when they come together, so in life, too, when men who possess a flair for analysis and generalizations come together and spend their time in the exchange of great, free ideas, they don't notice that they are in a trap. In that sense the mind is an irreplaceable source of enjoyment.'

'Quite true.'

Without looking at his companion, Dr Ragin would go on

talking, quietly, and pausing continually, about intelligent people and the satisfaction of exchanging ideas with them, while the postmaster listened to him attentively, expressing agreement: 'Quite true.'

'Don't you believe in the immortality of the soul?' the postmaster asked suddenly.

'I do not, my dear sir. I neither believe in it nor do I see any reason for believing in it.'

'Well, I must say, I too have my doubts. Though, mind you, I have a feeling that I will never die. Good gracious me, I say to myself, surely it's time you were dead, you old dodderer! But deep inside me, you know, a little voice whispers: "Don't you believe it, you will never die!" '

Soon after nine the postmaster usually left. Putting on his fur coat in the hall, he would say with a sigh:

'Dear me, what a God-forsaken hole fate has thrown us into! The awful thing is that we shall have to die here, too. Oh dear, oh dear! ...'

VII

After seeing his friend off, Dr Ragin would sit down at his desk again and resume his reading. The stillness of the evening, followed by the stillness of the night, was unbroken by a single sound. Time seemed to stand still and hover with the doctor over the book, and one got the impression that there was nothing in the world but that book and the lamp with its green shade. Gradually a smile of tender emotion and rapture lit up the doctor's coarse peasant-like face as he thought of the continuous progress of the human mind. 'Oh,' he thought, 'why isn't man immortal? Why the brain centres and convolutions? Why eyesight, speech, self-awareness, genius, if they are all doomed to pass into the earth and at last go cold with the earth's crust, and then whirl round the sun together with the earth for millions of years without rhyme or reason?' To grow cold and then go whirling round the sun it was surely not necessary to drag man with his high, almost divine mind out of non-existence and then, as though in mockery, turn him into clay. Transmutation of matter! But what cowardice it was to console oneself with that makeshift immortality! The unconscious processes which went on in nature were lower even than human stupidity, for there was at any rate some consciousness and will in stupidity, while there was nothing at all in those processes. Only a coward whose fear of death was greater than his self-respect could console himself with the thought that his body would go on living in a blade of grass, in a stone, in a toad. . . . To see immortality in the transmutation of matter is just as absurd as to predict a brilliant future to a violin case after the costly violin has been broken and become useless.

Every time the clock struck the hour Dr Ragin leaned back in his armchair and closed his eyes to think a little. And almost in spite of himself, under the influence of the admirable thoughts he had just been reading, he began to review his life – past and present. The past was horrible; better not to think of it. And the present was not much different from the past. He knew that while his thoughts were whirling round the sun together with the cooling earth, in the large hospital building next to his flat people were languishing in disease and filth; some of them were at that very moment unable to sleep for fighting with the insects, while others had been infected with erysipelas or were moaning because of a tight bandage; some of the patients were perhaps playing cards with the nurses and drinking vodka. Twelve thousand persons had been treated in the current year; the whole work of the hospital was based on theft, squabbles, gossip, favouritism, and gross charlatanism, just as twenty years before; and as in those days the hospital was nothing but an immoral institution, highly detrimental to the health of the inmates. Dr Ragin knew that behind the bars of Ward 6 Nikita beat the patients with his fists and that Moseyka went out begging into the streets every day.

On the other hand, he knew perfectly well that during the past twenty-five years medicine had undergone a miraculous change. When he was studying at the university it had seemed to him that medicine would soon share the fate of alchemy and metaphysics, but now, when he read his books at night, he felt that medicine moved him deeply, that the advances made by medical science amazed him and even sent him into raptures. And, indeed, what unexpected brilliance, what a revolution! Thanks to antiseptics, operations were performed which the great Pirogov had considered impossible even *in spe*. Ordinary rural-district doctors did not hesitate to perform a resection of the knee joint, only one person in a hundred died after an abdominal operation, and gallstones were regarded as too trivial to write about. Syphilis was being given radical treatment. And what about the theory of heredity, hypnotism, the discoveries of Pasteur and Koch, hygiene, statistics, and our Russian rural medical service? Psychiatry, with its modern classification of ailments, methods of diagnosis, and treatment — compared with what it used to be it was a gigantic achievement. No longer was cold water poured over the heads of lunatics, nor were they any longer put into strait-jackets; they were treated like human beings, and even had theatrical performances and dances organized for them, so the newspapers reported. Dr Ragin knew that according to modern ideas and tastes such an abomination as Ward 6 was only possible in a small town one hundred and fifty miles away from a railway, where the mayor and the town councillors were semi-literate tradesmen who looked upon a doctor as a highpriest who had to be believed uncritically, even though he were to pour molten lead into a patient's throat; in any other place the public and the press would have torn that little Bastille to shreds.

'But what about it?' Dr Ragin asked himself, opening his eyes. 'What does it prove? Antiseptics, Koch, and Pasteur — but essentially nothing has changed. Disease and mortality are still the same. Theatrical performances and dances are organized for lunatics, but they are not let out of the asylums all the same. Which means that it is all nonsense and vanity, and there is virtually no difference at all between the best Vienna clinic and my hospital.'

But grief and a feeling akin to envy made it impossible for him to remain indifferent. Perhaps it was due to exhaustion. His weary head dropped on to the page. Resting his face on his hands for greater comfort, he went on thinking:

'I am serving a bad cause, and I receive a salary from people whom I deceive. I am dishonest. But then I am nothing by myself, I am only a small part of a necessary social evil: all district officials are bad and draw their salaries for doing nothing. Which means that I am not to blame for my dishonesty. It is the fault of the

time I live in. . . . If I were to be born two hundred years later, I'd
be a different man.'

When the clock struck three, he put out his lamp and went to
his bedroom. But he did not feel at all sleepy.

VIII

About two years ago, in a moment of wild extravagance, the district rural council had decided to allocate three hundred roubles annually towards increasing the hospital medical staff until such time as a rural district hospital should be opened, and the district doctor Yevgeny Fyodorovich Khobotov was invited by the town council to act as assistant to Dr Ragin. Khobotov was still a very young man, under thirty, tall, dark, with broad cheekbones and small eyes; his forebears were probably of Asiatic origin. He arrived in the town penniless, with a small trunk and a plain young woman whom he called his cook and who had a baby. Khobotov wore a peaked cap and high boots, and in the winter a sheepskin coat. He soon became great friends with the doctor's assistant and the hospital treasurer; the rest of the officials he shunned and for some reason dubbed 'aristocrats'. He had only one book in his flat – *The Latest Prescriptions of the Vienna Clinic for 1881*. He took this book with him every time he went to see a patient. He played billiards at the club in the evenings. He did not care for cards. In conversation he was very fond of such expressions as 'don't muck about', 'mantifolia with vinegar', 'stop casting nasturtiums', and so on.

He visited the hospital twice a week, made the rounds of the wards, and received out-patients. The complete absence of antiseptics and the abundance of cupping glasses aroused his indignation, but he did not introduce any changes for fear of offending Dr Ragin. He regarded his colleague Dr Ragin as an old rogue, suspected him of being rich, and secretly envied him. He would gladly have taken over his post.

IX

One spring evening towards the end of March, when there was no more snow on the ground and the starlings were singing in the hospital garden, the doctor had gone out to the gate to see off his friend the postmaster. At that very moment the Jew Moseyka entered the yard, returning from one of his foraging expeditions. He wore no cap and had a pair of galoshes on his bare feet. In his hand he carried a small bag with the alms he had collected.

'Give me a kopek, sir,' he said to the doctor, shivering with cold and smiling.

Dr Ragin, who could never refuse anyone anything, gave him a silver ten-kopek piece.

'How horrible,' he thought, looking at the bare feet and the thin old ankles. 'And it's wet, too.'

And prompted by a feeling of mingled pity and disgust, he followed the Jew into the ward, casting glances at his bald head and his ankles in turn. At the entrance of the doctor, Nikita jumped up from his rubbish heap and stood at attention.

'Good evening, Nikita,' said Dr Ragin mildly. 'I think the Jew ought to be given a pair of boots, don't you? He might catch cold, you know.'

'Very good, sir. I'll report it to the superintendent.'

'Please do. Ask him in my name. Tell him I asked.'

The door of the ward was open. Lying on his bed, propped up on an elbow, Gromov listened with alarm to the stranger's voice and suddenly recognized the doctor. Shaking with anger, he jumped off his bed and, with a vicious look on his reddened face and bulging eyes, he ran out into the middle of the ward.

'The doctor has come!' he shouted, roaring with laughter. 'At last! Gentlemen, I congratulate you. The doctor has been so good as to pay us a visit. Damned rotter! No, killing is not enough! Drown him in the latrine!'

Dr Ragin, who had heard it all, put his head in at the door and asked mildly:

'What for?'

'What for?' cried Gromov, going up to him with a menacing look and wrapping his dressing-gown round him convulsively. 'What for? Thief!' he shouted with disgust, puckering his lips as if he were going to spit. 'Quack! Hangman!'

'Compose yourself,' said Dr Ragin with a guilty smile. 'I assure you I have never stolen anything. As for the rest, you are probably exaggerating. I can see you are angry with me. Compose yourself, I beg you, if you can, and tell me calmly why you are so angry.'

'Why do you keep me here?'

'Because you are ill.'

'Yes, I am ill. But surely there are scores of madmen, hundreds, walking about unmolested, simply because in your ignorance you're incapable of distinguishing them from healthy people! Why then should I and these unhappy wretches be kept here, like so many scapegoats for the others? You, your assistant, the superintendent, and the rest of the scoundrels employed in the hospital – you're morally infinitely lower than any of us! Why then must we be kept here and not you? Where's the logic?'

'I'm afraid morality and logic have nothing to do with it. It's all a matter of chance. Those who are put here stay here, and those who are not put here are free to live as they like. That's all. There's neither morality nor logic in the fact that I am a doctor and you are a mental patient. It's just mere chance.'

'I don't understand this nonsense,' Gromov said in a dull voice, sitting down on his bed.

Moseyka, whom Nikita could not bring himself to search in the doctor's presence, spread out his crusts, bits of paper, and bones on his bed and, still shivering with cold, began saying something in Yiddish in a rapid singsong. He probably imagined he had opened a shop.

'Let me out,' said Gromov, and his voice shook.

'I can't.'

'Why can't you? Why not?'

'Because it isn't in my power. Just think: what good would it do you if I let you go? Suppose I let you go. You would be stopped by the townspeople or the police and brought back here.'

'Yes, yes, that's true,' said Gromov and wiped his forehead. 'It's terrible! But what am I to do? What?'

Gromov's voice and his young, intelligent, grimacing face pleased Dr Ragin. He wished to be nice to the young man and calm him. He sat down on the bed beside him and after a moment's thought said:

'You ask what's to be done. The best thing in your position would be to run away. But unfortunately it would be useless. You'd be detained. When society decides to protect itself against criminals, mentally sick people, and people it considers generally inconvenient, it is invincible. There's only one thing you can do: reconcile yourself to the idea that your stay here is necessary.'

'It isn't necessary to anyone.'

'Once prisons and lunatic asylums exist, there must be someone to be there. If it's not you, it's me; if it's not me, then it's someone else. Have patience – when in the far-away future prisons and lunatic asylums cease to exist, there won't be any more barred windows or hospital gowns. Such a time will of course come, sooner or later.'

Gromov smiled sarcastically.

'You're joking,' he said, screwing up his eyes. 'What do gentlemen like you and your assistant Nikita care for the future? But you can rest assured, sir, that better times will come. I may be expressing myself vulgarly, you may laugh at me, but a new life will dawn one day, and justice will triumph and – we, too, will have something to celebrate! I may not live to see it, I shall have kicked the bucket by then, but someone's great-grandchildren will see it. I salute them with all my heart and I rejoice for them. Forward! May God help you, friends!'

Gromov rose, his eyes shining, and stretching out his arms to the window he went on in an agitated voice:

'From behind these bars I bless you! Long live Justice! I rejoice!'

'I see no special reason for rejoicing,' said Dr Ragin, who thought Gromov's gesture theatrical but could not help admiring it. 'There will be no prisons and lunatic asylums, and justice will triumph, as you put it; but substantially things will remain as they are, and the laws of nature will be the same. People will fall ill, grow old, and die – just as they do now. However magnificent the dawn that lights up your life, in the end you will be nailed in your coffin and flung into a hole in the ground.'

'But immortality?'

'Oh, for goodness sake!'

'You do not believe, but I do. Dostoevsky – or was it Voltaire? – said that if there had been no God men would have had to invent him. Well, I believe – no, I'm sure – that if there's no immortality, man's great intellect will invent it sooner or later.'

'Well said,' remarked Dr Ragin, smiling with pleasure. 'It's a good thing you have faith. With such faith one can live happily, even when immured in a wall. You had a higher education, didn't you?'

'Yes. I was a university student. But I didn't take my degree.'

'You're an intelligent and thoughtful man. You can discover peace of mind within yourself in any environment. Free and profound thought which aspires to a comprehension of life, and utter contempt for the vanity of the world — those are the two blessings than which man has known nothing higher. And you may possess them even if you live behind triple bars. Diogenes lived in a barrel and yet he was happier than all the kings on earth.'

'Your Diogenes was a damn fool,' Gromov declared gloomily. 'Why are you talking to me about Diogenes and some kind of comprehension of life?' he said angrily, jumping to his feet. 'I love life! I love it passionately. I suffer from persecution mania, I am constantly in an agony of terror; but there are times when I am seized with a thirst for life — and it's then that I'm afraid of going mad. I want to live, terribly. Terribly!'

He walked up and down the ward in agitation and said, lowering his voice:

'When I dream, I'm visited by apparitions. Strange men come to see me. I hear voices, music. And it seems to me that I'm walking somewhere in a wood or on the seashore, and I long so much for the bustle and worries of life. Tell me, please, what's the news there?' Gromov asked. 'What's going on there?'

'Do you mean in the town or in the world generally?'

'Tell me about the town first and then about the world in general.'

'Well, why not? It's terribly boring in the town. No one to talk to. No one to listen to. No new people. We've got a new doctor, though. Khobotov, a young chap.'

'I know. He arrived while I was still living in the town. A boor, I suppose?'

'Yes, an uncultured man. It's funny, you know. To the best of my knowledge, there's no intellectual stagnation in our capital cities. There's plenty of activity there, which means that there are real people there. And yet for some reason they always send us people one wouldn't like to see around, let alone talk to. Unhappy town!'

'Yes, indeed, unhappy town!' Gromov said with a sigh and laughed. 'And what's doing in general? What do they write about in the newspapers and periodicals?'

It was already dark in the ward. The doctor rose, and standing up, he told Gromov what was being written in Russia and abroad and what was the trend of contemporary thought. Gromov listened attentively and asked questions. But all of a sudden, as though he had just remembered something terrible, he clutched at his head and lay down on his bed with his back to the doctor.

'What's the matter?' asked Dr Ragin.

'You won't hear another word from me!' Gromov said rudely. 'Leave me alone!'

'Why?'

'I tell you, leave me alone! What the hell do you want?'

Dr Ragin shrugged his shoulders, sighed, and went out. As he passed through the corridor, he said:

'This place ought to be tidied up a bit, Nikita. A horrible smell.'

'Very good, sir.'

'What a nice young man,' thought Dr Ragin as he walked home. 'He's the first man worth talking to that I've met all the time I've been here. He can reason and he takes an interest in the things that really matter.'

While reading that night and later as he was going to bed, he kept thinking all the time about Ivan Gromov, and on waking next morning he remembered that he had made the acquaintance of a clever and interesting man and made up his mind to pay him another visit at the first opportunity.

X

Gromov was lying in the same pose as on the day before, cross-legged and clutching his head. Dr Ragin could not see his face.

'Good afternoon, my friend,' the doctor said. 'You're not asleep, are you?'

'In the first place, I'm not your friend,' said Gromov, his face buried in the pillow. 'And secondly, you're wasting your time. You won't get another word out of me.'

'Strange,' murmured Dr Ragin, taken aback. 'Yesterday we were talking so peaceably, but suddenly you took offence for some reason and broke off. ... I expect I must have expressed myself awkwardly, or perhaps said something that conflicts with your views. ...'

'You don't expect me to believe you, do you?' said Gromov, sitting up and looking sarcastically and with alarm at the doctor. His eyes were bloodshot. 'You can go spying and interrogating somewhere else. You're just wasting your time here. Already yesterday I realized what you'd come here for.'

'What a curious idea,' said the doctor with a smile. 'Do you really think I'm a spy?'

'I do! A spy, or a doctor who's been instructed to interrogate me – what difference does it make?'

'Good lord. I'm sorry, but what a funny fellow you are, to be sure!'

The doctor sat down on a stool beside the bed and shook his head reproachfully.

'Well, suppose you're right,' he said. 'Suppose I am trying to catch you out, in order to betray you to the police. You'll be arrested and put on trial. But do you really think that you'll be much worse off in court or prison than here? And even if they sentence you to exile or hard labour in Siberia, would you be worse off than in this annexe? I don't think so. What are you afraid of, then?'

These words apparently made an impression on Gromov. He sat down quietly.

It was after four o'clock in the afternoon, when Ragin usually walked up and down his study and Darya came in to ask him whether it was time for his beer. The weather was calm and clear.

'I went out for a walk after dinner,' said the doctor, 'and as you see, I've come to see you. Real spring weather.'

'What month is it? March?' asked Gromov.

'Yes, the end of March.'

'Muddy outside?'

'No, not very. The paths in the garden are already dry.'

'It would be nice to drive out of town in a carriage on a day like this,' said Gromov, rubbing his bloodshot eyes, as though he had only just woken up, 'and then go home to a warm, cosy study, and – er – get a decent doctor to treat me for my headaches. . . . I've not lived like a human being for a long time. It's foul here – unbearably foul.'

After his excitement of the day before he felt tired and languid and reluctant to talk. His fingers trembled and you could see by his face that his head was aching badly.

'There is no difference between a warm, cosy room and this ward,' said Dr Ragin. 'A man's peace of mind and contentment are not outside him, but within him.'

'You mean?'

'An ordinary man expects to find good or evil outside him, that is, from his marriage or his studies; but a thinking man expects to find them within himself.'

'You'd better go and preach that philosophy in Greece, where it's warm and the air is full of the perfume of orange blossoms. Here it doesn't agree with the climate. Who was I talking about Diogenes to? Was it you?'

'Yes, yesterday.'

'Diogenes was not in need of a study and warm rooms. There it's hot, anyhow. Lie in your barrel and eat oranges and olives. But if he had lived in Russia, he would have been glad to be taken to a room, not only in December but even in May. He would have been doubled up with cold, I shouldn't wonder.'

'No, sir. It is possible not to feel cold, like any other pain. Marcus Aurelius said: "Pain is merely the vivid conception of pain: change this conception by an effort of will, shake it off, stop complaining, and the pain will disappear." That's true. A sage, or simply the thinking, inquiring man, is distinguished by his contempt of suffering; he's always content and isn't surprised at anything.'

'Then I must be an idiot, for I'm suffering, I'm discontented, and I'm surprised at human baseness.'

'You shouldn't be, you know. If you thought more deeply about it, you'd realize how trivial all the external things that agitate you are. One must strive to comprehend life, for in that comprehension is true happiness.'

'Comprehension . . .' Gromov repeated with a frown. 'External, internal . . . I'm sorry, but I don't understand it. All I know is,' he said, getting up and looking crossly at the doctor, 'all I know is that God created me of warm blood and nerves. Yes, sir. And organic tissue, if it's live tissue, must react to every kind of irritation. And I do react! I respond to pain with tears and cries, to baseness with indignation, to abomination with disgust. To my mind that is really what's called life. The lower the organism, the less it responds to irritation; the higher, the more sensitively and energetically it reacts to reality. How is it you don't know that? You, a doctor, don't know such elementary things! To despise suffering, to be always content and not be surprised at anything, a man has to get to *that* sort of state,' Gromov said, pointing to the fat peasant, 'or else have become so hardened by suffering as to have lost all susceptibility to it – or, in other words, to have ceased to live. I'm sorry, I'm not a sage or a philosopher,' Gromov went on irritably, 'and I don't understand anything about those things. I'm not in a position to argue.'

'On the contrary, you argue very well indeed.'

'The stoics, whose ideas you misrepresent, were remarkable men. But their teaching became petrified two thousand years ago, and it hasn't advanced an inch, it can't advance, because it's not practical, it doesn't answer to the demands of life. It was successful only with a minority who spent their lives in study and savouring all sorts of doctrines. The majority never understood it. A doctrine that preaches indifference to riches and comforts, contempt for suffering and death, is utterly incomprehensible to the vast majority, who've never known either riches or comforts. To them, despising suffering can only mean despising life itself. Man's whole existence consists of the sensations of hunger, cold, insults, bereavements, and a Hamlet-like horror of death. The whole of life is made up of these sensations! One may hate it or find it tiresome, but one can't *despise* it. . . . I tell you the teachings of the stoics can never have a future, and, as you see, from the dawn of time to this day the things that show any progress are strife, sensitivity to pain, and the ability to react to irritation.'

Gromov suddenly lost the thread of his thoughts and stopped short, rubbing his forehead in vexation.

'I was about to say something important,' he remarked, 'but it's gone right out of my head. What was I talking about? Oh, yes. It's this. One of the stoics sold himself into slavery to redeem a friend. So you see, even a stoic reacted to something that was irritating him, for such a generous act as the destruction of oneself for the sake of another requires that a man should possess a compassionate heart that's capable of a feeling of indignation. Here, in this prison, I've forgotten everything I learnt. Or I should have remembered something else. But what about Christ? Christ responded to reality by weeping, smiling, grieving, being angry, and even by feeling miserable. He didn't go forth to meet suffering with a smile. He didn't despise death. He prayed in the garden of Gethsemane that the cup might pass from him!'

Gromov laughed and sat down.

'Suppose that peace of mind and contentment are not outside but within a man,' he said. 'Suppose we must despise suffering, and be surprised at nothing. What grounds have you for preaching this doctrine? Are you a sage? A philosopher?'

'No, I'm not a philosopher, but I think everyone should preach that doctrine, because it's rational.'

'Oh, but I should like to know why you consider yourself competent to judge about comprehension, contempt for suffering, and so on. Have you ever suffered? Have you any idea of the meaning of suffering? Tell me, were you ever flogged as a child?'

'No, my parents strongly disapproved of corporal punishment.'

'Well, my father flogged me brutally. My father was a stern disciplinarian. A government official, worn out by work. He had a long nose and a yellow neck. He suffered from piles. But let's talk about you. All through your life, no one has ever laid a finger on you, or intimidated you, or bullied you. You're as strong as a horse. You grew up under your father's wing, you studied at his expense. And then all at once you got a sinecure. For over twenty years you've lived without paying anything for your flat or your heating, lighting, and service. In addition, you enjoy the right to work as and when you like, or even not to work at all. You're a lazy man by nature with a fat flabby body; and for that reason you've tried to organize your life in such a way as to avoid trouble and unnecessary movement. You've turned over your duties to your assistant and the rest of the scum here, while you sit at home in quiet and warmth, saving up money, reading books, indulging yourself in reflections about all sorts of lofty drivel, and' (Gromov shot a glance at the doctor's red nose) 'overcharged with drunkenness. In short, you've seen nothing of life. You don't know it at all. You've only a theoretical knowledge of reality. You despise suffering and are not surprised at anything, for a very simple reason. Vanity of vanities; internal and external; contempt for life, suffering, and death, comprehension, true happiness – all that philosophy best suits a Russian lie-abed! You see a peasant beat his wife, for instance. Why interfere? Let him beat her; they'll both die sooner or later, anyway. And, besides, the man who beats his wife degrades himself by his blows, not his victim. To get drunk is stupid and indecent; but whether you drink or not you'll die all the same. A peasant woman comes to you with toothache ... Well, what of it? Pain is merely our conception of pain and, besides, we can't expect to go on living without falling ill; we shall all die; so go away, woman, and let me think and drink in peace! A young man comes to you for advice – what should he do, how ought he to live? Anyone else would try to think before giving his answer. But you have your answer ready: strive to achieve comprehension or true happiness. But what *is* this fantastic "true happiness"? There's no answer, of course. We're kept here behind iron bars, tortured, allowed to rot, but all this is wonderful and rational, for there's no *real* difference between this ward and a warm, comfortable study! An expedient philosophy. You can't do anything about it. Your conscience is clear. And you feel you're a real sage. ... No, sir, that isn't philosophy. That isn't thought. That isn't breadth of view. It's laziness! Mumbo-jumbo! Deadly nightshade! Yes, indeed!' cried Gromov, flying into a rage again. 'You despise suffering – but squeeze your finger in the door and you'll scream at the top of your voice!'

'Perhaps I won't,' said Dr Ragin with a smile.

'Won't you? Now if you had a stroke or if some fool or some impudent fellow were to take advantage of his rank and social position and insult you in public and you knew that he could do so with impunity – well, you would then know what it means to tell people to achieve comprehension and true happiness!'

'This is original,' said Dr Ragin, laughing with delight and rubbing his hands. 'I'm pleasantly surprised by your turn for generalizations and the way you've just analysed my character is simply brilliant! I don't mind admitting that talking to you gives me great pleasure. Well, sir, I've been listening to you, and now I'd be glad if you'd be so good as to listen to me. . . .'

XI

This conversation went on for about another hour and apparently made a great impression on Dr Ragin. He began visiting the annexe every day. He went there in the morning and after dinner, and he often sat talking to Gromov till dark. At first Gromov was shy with him, suspected him of evil intentions, and openly expressed his dislike of him. Then he got used to him and changed his sharp tone to one of condescending irony.

Soon the rumour spread through the hospital that Dr Ragin had begun visiting Ward 6. No one – neither his assistant, nor Nikita, nor the nurses – could understand why he went there, why he stayed there for hours, what he was talking about, and why he did not write out any prescriptions. His behaviour seemed strange. The postmaster very often did not find him at home when he called, which had never happened before, and Darya was very upset because the doctor did not drink his beer at the usual time and was even late for dinner sometimes.

One day – it was at the end of June – Dr Khobotov went to see Dr Ragin on some business. Not finding him at home, he went to look for him in the yard; there he was told that the old doctor had gone to Ward 6. Going into the annexe and stopping in the passage, Khobotov overheard this sort of conversation:

'We shall never agree and you'll never succeed in converting me to your faith,' Gromov was saying irritably. 'You have no idea of reality, you've never suffered. You've only fed on the sufferings of others, like a leech. Whereas I have suffered uninterruptedly, from the day I was born. Therefore I tell you frankly I consider myself much higher and more competent than you in all respects. It's not for *you* to teach *me*!'

'I most certainly have no desire to convert you to my way of thinking,' said Dr Ragin quietly, feeling sorry that Gromov did not want to understand him. 'That's not the point, my friend. The point is not that you have suffered and I have not. Suffering and joys are transient things. Let's forget them. They are of no account. The point is that you and I are thinking individuals. We see in one another men who are capable of thought and argument, and this creates a bond between us, however different our views may be. If you knew, my friend, how sick and tired I am of the universal rudeness, mediocrity, and stupidity, and how glad I am to talk to you. You are an intelligent man, and it's a pleasure to be with you.'

Khobotov opened the door an inch and looked into the ward. Gromov in his nightcap and Dr Ragin were sitting side by side on the bed. The madman made faces, shuddered, and kept convulsively wrapping his dressing-gown round him, while the doctor sat motionless, lowering his head, his face flushed, helpless, sad. Khobotov shrugged his shoulders, smirked, and exchanged glances with Nikita. Nikita, too, shrugged his shoulders.

Next day Khobotov came to the wing together with the assistant doctor. Both stood in the passage eavesdropping.

'Our old man seems to have gone nuts,' said Khobotov, going out of the annexe.

'The Lord have mercy on us, miserable sinners,' pious Sergey Sergeyich said with a sigh, careful to avoid stepping into the puddles so as not to soil his brightly polished boots. 'To tell you the truth, my dear doctor, I've long been expecting it.'

XII

After this incident Dr Ragin began to notice that he was surrounded by an air of mystery. The servants, the nurses, and the patients looked questioningly at him when they met him and then whispered among themselves. The superintendent's little girl Masha, whom he liked meeting in the hospital grounds, for some reason ran away from him now when he went up smilingly to her to stroke her head. The postmaster no longer said 'Quite true' as he listened to him, but muttered in incomprehensible embarrassment, 'Yes, yes, yes. . . .' and looked at him wistfully and sadly; for some unknown reason he began advising his friend to give up vodka and beer, but being a tactful man he did not say it in so many words, but dropped hints, telling him about a certain battalion commander, an excellent fellow, or about a regimental padre, a fine chap, who had made themselves ill by drinking and recovered completely as soon as they gave it up. Once or twice his colleague Khobotov paid him a visit; he too advised him to give up liquor, and without apparent reason suggested he might take potassium bromide.

In August Dr Ragin received a letter from the mayor with a request to go and see him on some very important business. When he arrived at the town hall at the appointed time, Dr Ragin found awaiting him the chief of the military garrison, the superintendent of the district school, a member of the council, Khobotov, and a fair and corpulent gentleman who was introduced to him as a doctor. This doctor, who had an unpronounceable Polish name, lived at a stud farm about twenty-five miles away and was now only passing through the town.

'Here's a – er – communication which concerns your department,' the member of the council said, addressing Dr Ragin. 'Dr Khobotov says here that there is not enough room for the dispensary in the hospital building and that it ought to be transferred to one of the annexes. There is of course no reason why it should not be transferred, but the trouble, you see, is that in that case the annexe will have to be repaired.'

'Yes, I'm afraid it will certainly have to be repaired,' said Dr Ragin after a moment's pause. 'For instance, if the corner wing is to be used for the dispensary, I suppose at least five hundred roubles will have to be spent. It's unproductive expenditure.'

They were all silent for a few moments.

'I believe,' Dr Ragin went on in a quiet voice, 'I submitted a report ten years ago in which I pointed out that in its present state this hospital is a luxury our town cannot afford. It was built in the eighteen-forties, but the position was different in those days. The town is spending too much on unnecessary buildings and superfluous appointments. With the money spent on them, we could, I think, keep two model hospitals going, given a different order of things, that is.'

'Well,' the member of the council said promptly, 'let's have a different order of things!'

'I have already, I believe, submitted a recommendation that the medical department should be taken over by the rural council.'

'Yes, transfer our funds to the rural council and it will steal them,' said the fair-haired doctor with a laugh.

'That's the way it is, I'm afraid,' the member of the council also laughingly agreed.

Dr Ragin gave the fair-haired doctor a dull and languid look.

'We must be fair,' he said.

There was another pause. Tea was served. The military gentleman, for some reason looking very embarrassed, touched Dr Ragin's hand across the table and said:

'You've quite forgotten us, doctor. But, then, you're a regular hermit: you don't play cards, you don't love women. You're bored with us, I am afraid.'

They all began saying how a decent man must find it boring to live in this town. No theatre, no music, and at the last dance at the club there had been twenty women and only two men. The young people did not dance, but crowded round the bar or played cards. Dr Ragin began to say, slowly and quietly, without looking at anyone, how sad, how very sad it was that the townspeople should be wasting their vital energy, their hearts and their minds on cards and gossip, and should be unable and unwilling to spend their time in interesting conversation and in reading, or making use of the pleasures that the mind alone gave. The mind alone was interesting and remarkable, the rest was petty and trivial. Khobotov, who was listening attentively to his colleague, suddenly asked:

'Tell me, Dr Ragin, what's the date today?'

Having received the answer, he and the fair-haired doctor began to ask Dr Ragin, in the tone of examiners who are aware of their incompetence, what day of the week it was, how many days there were in a year, and whether it was true that there was a remarkable prophet in Ward 6.

In reply to the last question Dr Ragin blushed and said:

'Yes, he is sick, but he is a very interesting young man.'

No more questions were put to him.

As Dr Ragin was putting on his coat in the hall, the military governor put his hand on the doctor's shoulder and said with a sigh:

'It's time we old men took a rest.'

On leaving the town hall, Dr Ragin realized that he had been before a commission appointed to examine his mental state. He recalled the questions which had been put to him and blushed. For some reason he felt for the first time in his life very sorry for the science of medicine.

'Good Lord,' he thought, as he recalled the way the doctors had examined him, 'it was only a short time ago that they attended their lectures on psychiatry, passed their exams. Then why this utter ignorance? They have no idea of psychiatry.'

And for the first time in his life he felt insulted and angry.

The same evening the postmaster came to see him. Without a word of greeting, the postmaster went up to him, took hold of both his hands, and said in an agitated voice:

'My dear friend, prove to me that you believe in the sincerity of my affection for you, that you consider me your friend. My dear, dear friend,' he went on excitedly, not letting Dr Ragin put in a word, 'I love you for your learning and the nobility of your mind. Listen to me, dear friend. Medical etiquette compels the doctors to conceal the truth from you, but as an old soldier I'm telling you bluntly that you are not well. I'm sorry, dear friend, but that's the truth. It has been noticed by everybody round you for some time. Dr Khobotov has just been telling me that for the benefit of your health you must have rest and distraction. It's absolutely true. Now, what is so splendid is that I shall be taking my leave in a few days and going off for a change of air. Now, prove to me that you're really my friend, and come with me. Come, let's recall the old days!'

'I feel perfectly well,' said Dr Ragin after a moment's thought. 'I'm afraid I can't come with you. Let me prove my friendship to you in some other way.'

To go away for some unknown reason, without his books, without Darya, without his beer, to disturb the daily routine which had been established for twenty years — the idea seemed wild and fantastic to him at first. But, recalling the conversation at the town hall and how depressed he had felt on the way home from the town hall, the idea of leaving the town, where stupid people thought he was mad, for a short time appealed to him.

'And where,' he asked, 'do you intend to go?'

'To Moscow, Petersburg, Warsaw. . . . In Warsaw I spent five of the happiest years of my life. What a wonderful town! Come with me, my dear friend!'

XIII

A week later it was suggested to Dr Ragin that he should take a rest, that is, should send in his resignation. He treated the suggestion with the utmost indifference, and after another week he and the postmaster were sitting in the open post-office carriage and driving to the nearest railway station. The days were cool and sunny, the sky blue, distant objects plainly visible in the clear air. It took them two days to travel the one hundred and fifty odd miles to the station, and they spent two nights at posting stations. When they were served tea in dirty glasses or when it took a long time for their carriage to be driven up to the door, the postmaster grew purple, shook all over, and shouted: 'Shut up! Don't argue!' In the carriage he talked incessantly about his travels in the Caucasus and Poland. The number of adventures he had had! The people he had met! He talked so loudly and stared at Dr Ragin with eyes so round with astonishment that one might have thought that he was lying. Moreover, when he talked he breathed in Dr Ragin's face and roared with laughter in his ear. This embarrassed the doctor and prevented him from thinking and concentrating on his thoughts.

To save money they travelled third class and in a non-smoking carriage. Half of the passengers were as neatly dressed as themselves. The postmaster soon became acquainted with all of them and, going from bench to bench, declared loudly that one ought not to travel on those outrageous railways. Such swindling all round! Now riding on horseback was a different matter altogether:

you covered a hundred miles a day and you felt as fresh as a daisy. And the bad harvests were of course caused by the draining of the Pinsk marshes. A frightful mess everywhere. He got excited, talked loudly, and let no one else get a word in. This incessant chatter alternating with bursts of loud laughter and expressive gesticulation wearied Dr Ragin.

'Which of us is the madman?' he thought in vexation. 'I, who do my best not to worry the passengers? Or this egoist, who thinks that he is cleverer and more interesting than anyone else here, and for that reason gives no one a moment's peace?'

In Moscow the postmaster donned his military tunic, but without shoulder-straps, and trousers with red piping. Out of doors he wore a military cap and greatcoat and was saluted by the soldiers. Dr Ragin now looked upon him as a man who had wasted all the good qualities of a gentleman that he had once possessed, retaining only the bad ones. He liked people to dance attendance on him even when it was quite unnecessary. Matches lay on the table in front of him, he saw them, and yet he shouted to the waiter to let him have some matches; he did not mind walking about in his underclothes in front of the maid; he was rude to waiters, even if they were old men, and when angry called them fools and blockheads. That, Dr Ragin could not help thinking, might be behaving like a gentleman, but it was disgusting nevertheless.

First of all the postmaster took his friend to the small chapel in which the icon of the Iversky Holy Virgin was kept. He prayed fervently, prostrating himself and shedding tears, and when he had finished he fetched a deep sigh and said:

'You may be an unbeliever, but somehow you can't help feeling more at peace with yourself after saying your prayers. Kiss the icon, my dear fellow.'

Dr Ragin felt embarrassed but kissed the icon, while his friend the postmaster pursed his lips and, shaking his head, prayed in a whisper, and again tears started in his eyes. Then they went to the Kremlin, had a look at the Tsar Cannon and the Tsar Bell, actually touching them with their fingers. They admired the view across the Moskva river, and paid visits to the Cathedral of the Saviour and the Rumyantsev Museum.

They dined at the celebrated Testov restaurant. The postmaster studied the menu for a long time, stroking his side-whiskers, and said to the waiter in the tone of a gourmet who feels very much at home in a restaurant:

'Let's see what you've got to regale us with today, my good man.'

XIV

The doctor went about, looked, ate and drank, but he always had the same feeling, a feeling of vexation with his companion the postmaster. He longed to have a rest from his friend, to go away from him, to hide from him, while his friend considered it his duty not to let him out of his sight and to provide him with as many diversions as possible. When there was nothing to look at, he tried to divert him by his conversation. Dr Ragin put up with it for two days, but on the third day he told his friend that he felt ill and wished to stay at home all day. His friend said in that case he would stay at home too. And, indeed, he added, they needed a good rest, for otherwise they'd be walked off their feet. Dr Ragin lay down on a sofa with his face to the wall and, clenching his teeth, listened to his friend eagerly assuring him that France would sooner or later defeat Germany, that Moscow was teeming with swindlers, and that it was impossible to judge a horse from its appearance alone. The doctor's heart began to throb and his ears to ring, but he was too good-mannered to ask his friend to go away or to shut up. Fortunately, the postmaster got tired of staying in the hotel room and went for a walk after dinner.

Left by himself, Dr Ragin gave himself up to the feeling of restfulness. How pleasant it was to lie motionless on the sofa and be conscious that you are alone in the room. True happiness is impossible without solitude. The fallen angel probably betrayed God because he longed for solitude, which angels do not know. Dr Ragin wanted to think about the things he had seen and heard during the last few days, but he could not get his friend the postmaster out of his head.

'And yet he obtained leave and came with me out of pure friendship and generosity,' the doctor thought in vexation. 'There is nothing worse than to be under a friend's tutelage. He's kind and generous and gay, but what a bore! A crashing bore. So, there are people who always talk cleverly and well, but who, you cannot help feeling, are stupid nevertheless.'

During the following days Dr Ragin pretended to be ill and did not leave his hotel room. He lay on the sofa with his face to the wall, feeling wretched when his friend tried to divert him by his conversation and resting when the postmaster was away. He was vexed with himself for having come on this journey and with his friend, who was becoming more garrulous and familiar every day. He simply could not manage to concentrate his thoughts on any serious and lofty subject.

'It is the reality Gromov spoke of that is getting the better of me,' he thought, angry with himself for his own pettiness. 'But that's nonsense. . . . When I get back home, things will be as before. . . .'

In Petersburg it was the same: he did not leave his hotel room for days on end, lying on the sofa and only getting up to drink beer. All the time the postmaster kept urging him to go to Warsaw.

'Why should I go to Warsaw, my dear fellow?' said Dr Ragin imploringly. 'Go by yourself and let me go home! Please, I beg you!'

'Not for anything in the world!' protested the postmaster. 'It's a wonderful town. I spent five of the happiest years of my life there.'

Dr Ragin had not enough strength of character to insist, and reluctantly agreed to go to Warsaw. There too he did not leave his hotel room, lay on the sofa, and was furious with himself, his friend, and with the hotel servants, who stubbornly refused to understand Russian – while the postmaster, as usual cheerful, gay, and the picture of health, went about the town from morning till night looking up his old friends. Several times he stayed out all night. Once, after a night spent goodness only knew where, he returned early in the morning in a state of great excitement, red-faced and dishevelled. He walked up and down the room for a long time, muttering under his breath, then he stopped and said:

'Honour above everything!'

After walking up and down a little longer, he clutched at his head and said in a tragic voice:

'Yes, honour above everything! Cursed be the hour when the idea of going to this Babylon first entered my head! My dear friend,' he addressed Dr Ragin, 'you may well despise me: I've lost all my money. Lend me five hundred roubles!'

Dr Ragin counted out five hundred roubles and handed them to his friend in silence. The postmaster, still purple with shame and anger, uttered some incoherent and unnecessary vow, put on his cap, and went out. Returning two hours later, he sank into an armchair, sighed loudly, and said:

'Honour is saved! Let's go, my friend. I don't want to stay another minute in this accursed town. Rogues! Austrian spies!'

When the friends returned, it was November and the streets were covered in deep snow. Dr Khobotov now filled Dr Ragin's post; he was still living in his old flat, waiting for Dr Ragin to come back and move out of the flat at the hospital. The plain woman he called his cook had already been installed in one of the hospital wings.

New hospital rumours were circulating in the town. It was said that the plain woman had quarrelled with the superintendent and that the superintendent had crawled before her on his knees, begging her to forgive him.

Dr Ragin had to look for a new flat on the first day of his arrival in the town.

'My dear friend,' the postmaster said to him diffidently, 'forgive the indiscreet question, but how much money have you?'

Dr Ragin counted his money in silence and said:

'Eighty-six roubles.'

'I'm afraid you've misunderstood me,' said the postmaster, not understanding the doctor's answer and looking embarrassed. 'What I want to know is how much money you have altogether.'

'But I've just told you: eighty-six roubles. That's all I have.'

The postmaster considered the doctor to be an honest and honourable man, he was under the impression that he was worth at least twenty thousand roubles, but having now discovered that he was a poor man and had nothing to live on, he suddenly burst out crying and flung his arms round his friend.

XV

Dr Ragin went to live in a little house, its only windows looking out on to the street. It belonged to a Mrs Belov, a woman of the artisan class and it had only three rooms, not counting the kitchen. Two of them, with the windows looking out on to the street, were occupied by the doctor and Darya; the landlady and her three children lived in the third room and the kitchen. Sometimes the landlady's lover came to spend the night, a drunken peasant who created an uproar at night and terrified Darya and the children. When he came and sat down in the kitchen and began demanding vodka, they all felt cramped, and the doctor would take the crying children into his room out of compassion, making up a bed for them on the floor; and this gave him great satisfaction.

He got up at eight o'clock, as before, and after breakfast sat down to read his old books and periodicals. He had no money to buy new ones. But whether it was because his books were old or because of the change in his environment, the reading no longer held his attention and in fact tired him. So as not to waste his time, he compiled a detailed catalogue of his books and stuck labels on their backs, and this mechanical, laborious work seemed to him much more interesting than reading. The monotonous laborious work seemed to lull his thoughts in some inexplicable way; he did not think of anything, and time passed quickly. He found an absorbing interest even in sitting in the kitchen and helping Darya peel potatoes or pick the dirt out of buckwheat meal. On Saturdays and Sundays he went to church. Standing at the wall and screwing up his eyes, he listened to the singing and thought of his father and mother, the university, and religion; he felt peaceful and melancholy and, on leaving the church, he was sorry the service was over so soon.

Twice he went to the hospital to have a talk with Gromov. But on both occasions Gromov was quite unusually angry and excited; he begged to be left alone because he had long ago got tired of empty prattle, and said that all he asked the accursed base people as a reward for all the sufferings he had undergone was solitary confinement. Would they refuse him even that? When Dr Ragin took leave of him and wished him good night, Gromov snapped viciously:

'Go to hell,'

Ragin was undecided now whether he should go and see him a third time or not. He wished to go very much.

In former days Dr Ragin used to spend the time after dinner in walking about the room and thinking; now from dinner to tea-time he lay on the sofa with his face to the wall, giving himself up to trivial thoughts which he could not suppress, hard as he tried. He felt hurt that after more than twenty years of service he was not given a pension or a grant. True, he had not done his duties as honestly as he should, but then all who served were given a pension, irrespective of whether they were honest or not. Modern ideas of fairness consisted of the fact that rank, orders, and pensions were awarded not for moral qualities or abilities but for service, whatever it had been like. Why then should he alone be the exception? He was penniless. He was ashamed to pass the shop and look at the woman who owned it. For beer alone he owed thirty-two roubles. He also owed the landlady. Darya had been secretly selling his old clothes and books, and she lied to the landlady, telling her that the doctor was to come into a lot of money soon.

He was angry with himself for having spent a thousand roubles on his holiday trip: all the money he had saved up. How useful the thousand roubles would have been now! He was vexed at not being left in peace. Khobotov thought it his duty to visit his sick colleague from time to time. Dr Ragin loathed everything about him: his well-nourished face, his condescending bedside manner, the word 'colleague' which he used in addressing him, and his high boots; but what disgusted him most was that Khobotov should consider it his duty to prescribe treatment for him, and that he should imagine that he really did give him medical treatment. For every time he visited Dr Ragin he brought with him a bottle of potassium bromide and gregory powders.

The postmaster too considered it his duty to visit his friend and try to amuse him. Every time he entered Dr Ragin's room, with an affected air of familiarity, he burst into forced laughter and began assuring him that he looked very well and that his affairs, thank God, were taking a turn for the better, from which it could be concluded that he considered his friend's case hopeless. He had not yet paid back the money he had borrowed in Warsaw and, overcome by a sense of shame, he laboured under a constant strain and for this reason laughed more loudly and tried to tell funnier stories. His stories and anecdotes now seemed endless and were a torture both to Dr Ragin and himself.

During his visits Dr Ragin usually lay on the sofa with his face to the wall and listened with clenched teeth; he felt the resentment in his heart accumulating in layer after layer, and every time after the postmaster's visit these layers of resentment grew and grew till they reached to his very throat.

To stifle his petty feelings, he made haste to reflect that Khobotov, the postmaster, and he himself would sooner or later perish without leaving as much as a trace of their existence behind them. If one were to imagine some spirit flying through space past the earth a million years hence, he would see nothing but clay and bare rocks. Everything – civilization and moral law – would have perished and not even be buried under burdock. What then did his feeling of shame towards the shopkeeper matter, or the insignificant Khobotov, or the postmaster's painful friendship? It was all a lot of nonsense.

But such reflections were no longer of any help to him. In the moment when he imagined what the earth would look like a million years hence, he saw Khobotov appearing in his high boots from behind a bare rock, or the postmaster with his constrained laugh, and he even heard the sheepish whisper: 'About that Warsaw loan, old man, I will pay it back in a few days ... without fail.'

XVI

One day the postmaster arrived after dinner when Dr Ragin was lying on the sofa. It so happened that Khobotov arrived at the same time with his potassium bromide. Dr Ragin rose heavily and sat down, supporting himself on the sofa with his hands.

'Today, my dear friend,' began the postmaster, 'your colour is much better than yesterday. You look fine! Really fine!'

'It's high time you were getting better, colleague, high time,' said Khobotov. 'I expect you must be fed up mucking about like this.'

'We'll be getting better!' the postmaster cried gaily. 'We'll live for another hundred years, damned if we won't!'

'I don't know about a hundred,' Khobotov put in consolingly, 'but he's good for another twenty. Don't worry, colleague, don't worry. Keep your spirits up.'

'We'll show them,' the postmaster said, roaring with laughter and slapping his friend on the knee. 'We'll show them the stuff we're made of! Next year, God willing, we'll be off to the Caucasus, and gallop all over it – hop, hop, hop! And when we come back from the Caucasus – who knows? – we may dance at your wedding.' The postmaster gave a sly wink. 'We'll marry you off, my dear friend, I'm damned if we won't!'

Dr Ragin suddenly felt that the layers of his resentment were reaching to his throat: his heart began to thump terribly.

'This is vulgar!' he said, getting up hastily and walking to the window. 'Don't you realize the vulgar things you are saying?'

He wanted to go on quietly and civilly, but in spite of himself he clenched his fists and raised them above his head.

'Leave me!' he screamed hysterically, going red in the face and trembling all over. 'Get out! Both of you! Both of you! Out!'

The postmaster and Khobotov got up and stared at him, first in perplexity, then in terror.

'Get out both of you!' Dr Ragin went on shouting. 'Stupid idiots! Fools! I don't want your friendship or your medicine, you fools! Vulgar! Disgusting!'

Exchanging bewildered glances, Khobotov and the postmaster backed to the door and went into the passage. Dr Ragin seized the bottle of potassium bromide and flung it after them; the bottle broke with a clatter on the threshold.

'Go to blazes!' he shouted in a sobbing voice, running out into the passage. 'To blazes with you!'

After his visitors had gone, Dr Ragin, shaking as though in a fever, lay down on the sofa, repeating over and over again:

'Stupid idiots! Fools!'

When he calmed down, it first of all occurred to him that the poor postmaster must be feeling terribly ashamed and greatly distressed. The whole thing was so awful. Such a thing had never happened to him before. Where was his intelligence and tact? Where was his comprehension of things, his philosophic indifference?

The doctor could not sleep all night for the shame and annoyance with himself, and about ten o'clock next morning he went to the post office and offered his apologies to the postmaster.

'Oh,' said the postmaster with a sigh, looking deeply moved and pressing Dr Ragin's hand warmly. 'Forget what's happened. Let bygones be bygones. Lyubavkin!' he shouted, so loudly that all the post office clerks and the customers started. 'Bring a chair! And you wait!' he shouted to a peasant woman who was handing him a registered letter through the bars. 'Can't you see I'm busy? Let's forget it all,' he went on gently, addressing the doctor. 'Do sit down, my dear fellow.'

For a minute he sat stroking his knees, then he said: 'I never thought of being offended with you. Illness is something you can't do much about. I understand that. The doctor and I were greatly alarmed by your attack yesterday and we had a long talk about you. My dear fellow, why do you refuse to get proper treatment for your illness? You can't go on like this, can you? Forgive the plain speaking of a friend,' the postmaster went on in a whisper, 'but you live in such unfavourable surroundings: cooped up in such a little space, filth, no one to look after you, no means to get decent medical treatment. . . . My dear friend, the doctor and I both beg you with all our hearts to take our advice and go to the hospital. There you'll get wholesome food, good nursing and medical treatment. Dr Khobotov may be a bit of a boor – that's strictly between you and me – but he's a knowledgeable fellow and one can rely on him entirely. He gave me his word he'd look after you.'

Dr Ragin was touched by the sincere concern of his friend and the tears which suddenly gleamed on the postmaster's cheeks.

'My dear friend,' he whispered, putting his hand on his heart, 'don't believe them! The whole thing's a fraud! All my illness amounts to is that in twenty years I have found only one intelligent man in our town, and he too is a madman. I'm suffering from no illness. I've simply got myself into a vicious circle from which there's no escape. But I don't care, I'm ready for anything.'

'Go to the hospital, my dear fellow.'

'I don't care, even to my grave.'

'My dear fellow, promise me that you'll obey Dr Khobotov in everything.'

'By all means. I promise. But I repeat, my dear friend, I've got myself into a vicious circle. Now everything, even the sincere concern of my friends, can lead only to one thing – my destruction. I'm on the point of destroying myself and I've the courage to realize it.'

'My dear fellow, you'll get cured.'

'What's the use of talking like that?' said Dr Ragin testily. 'There's hardly a man who hasn't to go through the same thing towards the end of his life. When you're told that you're suffering from a disease of the kidneys and an enlarged heart, or that you are a madman or a criminal, in short, when people suddenly turn their attention on you, then it simply means that you've got yourself into a vicious circle from which there's no escape. The more you try to get out of it, the more certain you are to lose your way. Give in, for no human efforts will save you. That's how it seems to me, anyway.'

Meanwhile a queue had formed at the other side of the grating. Not wishing to be in the way, Dr Ragin got up and began to take his leave. The postmaster made him promise again and saw him off to the door.

Later in the afternoon of the same day, Khobotov came to see Dr Ragin unexpectedly, in his sheepskin coat and high boots, and said, just as if nothing had happened the day before:

'I've come to you on business, colleague. I'd like to invite you to a consultation – care to come?'

Thinking that Khobotov wanted him to go for a walk or actually give him a chance of earning some money, Dr Ragin put on his hat and coat and went out with him. He was glad of the opportunity to make amends for the way he had behaved the day before and he was grateful to Khobotov, who did not say a word about the incident, evidently wishing to spare his feelings. From an uncultured man like him one could hardly have expected such tactfulness.

'Where is your patient?' asked Dr Ragin.

'At the hospital. I've been wanting to show him to you for some time. A most interesting case....'

They went into the hospital yard, skirted the main building, and went to the annexe where the lunatics were kept. When they entered the hall, Nikita, as usual, jumped to his feet and stood at attention.

'One of the patients here has a complication in the lungs,' Khobotov said in an undertone as he entered the ward with Dr Ragin. 'Wait here, I'll be back in a minute. I'll go and fetch my stethoscope.' And he went out.

XVII

It was getting dark. Gromov lay on his bed, his face buried in the pillow; the paralytic sat motionless, weeping quietly and moving his lips. The fat peasant and the ex-sorter were asleep. It was quiet in the room.

Dr Ragin sat on Gromov's bed and waited. But half an hour passed, and instead of Khobotov, Nikita came in, carrying under his arm a hospital gown, some underclothes, and a pair of slippers.

'Please put these on, sir,' he said softly. 'There's your bed,' he added. 'This way, please.' And he pointed to an unoccupied bed, which had evidently been brought there a short time before. 'Don't worry, sir. God willing, you'll soon get well.'

Dr Ragin understood everything. Without uttering a word, he went over to the bed indicated by Nikita and sat down on it; seeing that Nikita was waiting for him, he stripped naked, and felt ashamed. Then he put on the hospital clothes: the drawers were too short, the shirt too long, and the dressing-gown smelt of smoked fish.

'You'll get well, God willing,' repeated Nikita.

He took up Dr Ragin's clothes, went out, and closed the door behind him.

'It's all the same,' thought Dr Ragin, wrapping the dressing-gown round him shamefacedly and feeling that in his new rig-out he looked like a convict. 'It's all the same ... all the same — frock coat, uniform, or this dressing-gown....'

But his watch? His note-book in his side pocket? His cigarettes?

Where had Nikita taken his clothes? To his dying day he would probably never again wear trousers, a waistcoat, or boots. All this seemed so strange, and even incomprehensible at first. Even now Dr Ragin was convinced that there was not the slightest difference between Mrs Belov's house and Ward 6, that everything in this world was nonsense and vanity of vanities, and yet his hands trembled, his feet turned cold, and he was terrified of the thought that soon Gromov would get up and see him in the hospital gown. He got up, took a turn around the room, and sat down again.

He had been sitting for half an hour, and he felt sickened and weary of sitting there. Was it really possible to live here a day, a week, or even years as these people had done? Well, he had sat there, taken a turn round the room, and sat down again. He could look out of the window, take another turn round the room, and then what? Sit here all the time like a stone idol, and think? No, he could not do that.

Dr Ragin lay down, but got up at once, wiped the cold sweat from his forehead with a sleeve, and felt that his whole face smelt of smoked fish. He took another turn round the room.

'This is some misunderstanding,' he said, spreading out his arms in bewilderment. 'It must be cleared up. . . . It's a misunderstanding. . . .'

At that moment Gromov woke up. He sat down and propped up his cheeks on his hand. He spat. Then he looked sleepily at the doctor, and apparently at the first moment did not understand anything; but the next moment his sleepy face assumed a malicious and sarcastic expression.

'Aha, so they got you here too, my dear fellow,' he said in a voice hoarse with sleep, screwing up one eye. 'I'm very glad. You've been sucking other men's blood, now they'll be sucking yours. Excellent!'

'It's some misunderstanding,' said Dr Ragin, alarmed by Gromov's words. He shrugged his shoulders and repeated: 'Some misunderstanding. . . .'

Gromov spat again and lay down.

'Damn this life!' he muttered. 'And what's so galling and annoying is that all this life will end not with a reward for suffering, not with an apotheosis, as in an opera, but in death. The attendants will come and drag away the dead body by the arms and legs to the cellar. Ugh! Well, never mind. We shall have a grand party in the next world to make up for it. I shall come back regularly here as a ghost from the next world and frighten these swine to death. I'll make their hair turn white. . . .'

Moseyka came back to the ward at that moment and, seeing the doctor, stretched out his hand.

'Spare a kopek, sir,' he said.

XVIII

Dr Ragin went up to the window and looked out at the field. It was getting quite dark, and on the horizon, on the right side, a cold crimson moon was rising. Not far from the hospital fence, about eight hundred feet away, was a tall white building surrounded by a stone wall. It was the prison.

'There's reality for you!' thought Dr Ragin, and he felt terrified.

Everything was terrifying: the moon, the prison, the nails in the fence, and the far-away flames coming out of the bone mills. Behind his back someone sighed. Dr Ragin looked round and saw a man with glittering stars and orders on his chest. The man was smiling and winking slyly. This too seemed terrifying.

Dr Ragin tried to assure himself that there was nothing peculiar in the moon or the prison, that even sane men wore orders, and that in time everything would rot and turn into dust, but he was suddenly seized by despair and, getting hold of the bars of the windows with both hands, he began to shake them with all his strength. The firm grating did not give way.

Then, in an attempt to banish his terror, he went up to Gromov's bed and sat down on it.

'I lost heart, my dear chap,' he murmured, trembling and wiping the cold sweat off his forehead. 'Lost heart.'

'You'd better try philosophizing,' said Gromov sarcastically.

'Dear Lord, dear Lord. . . . Yes, yes. . . . I believe you said once that there's no philosophy in Russia, but that we all like philosophizing, even the small fry. But then there's no harm in the philosophizing of the small fry, is there?' said Dr Ragin, his voice sounding as if he were going to cry or were trying to make Gromov sorry for him. 'Why, my dear fellow, this malignant laugh? Why shouldn't the small fry philosophize, if they're dissatisfied? An intelligent, well-educated, proud, freedom-loving man, created in the image of God, has no choice but to become a doctor in some filthy and stupid little town and spend his whole life in applying cupping-glasses, leeches, and mustard plasters. The quackery, narrow-mindedness, vulgarity! Oh, my God!'

'You're talking nonsense. If you feel so awful about being a doctor, why not become a cabinet minister?'

'You can't do it. You just can't do it. We're weak, my friend. I was indifferent, I reasoned cheerfully and sanely, but the moment I felt the rough touch of life, I lost heart . . . utter prostration. . . . We're weak, we're worthless. . . . You too, my dear fellow. You're intelligent, honourable, you imbibed noble impulses with your mother's milk, but you'd hardly begun life when you got tired and fell ill. . . . We're weak, weak. . . .'

Apart from his terror and his resentment, Dr Ragin had had a strange, persistent feeling of irritation ever since the approach of evening. At last he realized that what he wanted was to have his beer and his smoke.

'I'm going out, my dear fellow,' he said. 'I'll tell them to give us a light. I can't like that – I – I – can't. . . .'

Dr Ragin went up to the door and opened it, but immediately Nikita jumped up and barred the way.

'Where are you going?' he said. 'You can't go, you can't! It's bedtime now.'

'But only for a minute . . . just for a walk in the yard,' Dr Ragin said, taken aback.

'You can't, you can't. It's not allowed. You know it yourself.'

Nikita slammed the door and put his back against it.

'But what harm will it do if I go out for a minute?' asked Dr Ragin, shrugging his shoulders. 'I can't understand. Nikita, I have to go out,' he said in a faltering voice. 'I have to.'

'Don't you start any trouble here,' said Nikita, admonishingly. 'It's not nice.'

'It's disgraceful!' Gromov suddenly cried, jumping up. 'What right has he to refuse to let you go out? How dare they keep us here? The law states clearly that no man can be deprived of his freedom without a fair trial. It's coercion! Tyranny!'

'Of course it is,' said Dr Ragin, encouraged by Gromov's outburst. 'I have to go out! I must! He has no right! Let me out, I tell you!'

'Do you hear, you stupid brute?' shouted Gromov, knocking on the door with his fist. 'Open up or I'll break the door open! You hell-hound!'

'Open the door!' cried Dr Ragin, trembling all over. 'I order you!'

'Do you now?' said Nikita behind the door. 'Do you indeed?'

'At least go and call Dr Khobotov. Tell him I'd like to see him – er – for a minute.'

'He'll be coming to see you himself tomorrow.'

'They'll never let us out,' Gromov was saying in the meantime. 'They'll let us rot here. Oh, Lord, is there really no hell, and will these scoundrels be forgiven? Where is justice? Open up, you scoundrel! I'm suffocating!' he cried in a hoarse voice, flinging himself against the door. 'I'll bash my brains out! Murderers!'

Nikita flung the door open, pushed Dr Ragin back roughly with both hands and his knee, swung back his arm, and struck him with his clenched fist across the face. A huge salt wave seemed to precipitate itself over his head and drag him towards his bed; and indeed there was a salty taste in his mouth: his gums were evidently bleeding. As though wishing to swim away, he waved his arms and caught hold of someone's bed, but at the same time felt two more blows on his back.

Gromov screamed loudly. He too was evidently being beaten.

Then all was quiet. The moon shed its liquid light through the iron bars, and on the floor lay a shadow which looked like a net. It was terrifying. Dr Ragin lay down, holding his breath and waiting in a panic for more blows. He felt as if someone had thrust a scythe into his body and twisted it several times in his chest and bowels. The pain made him bite his pillow and clench his teeth. Suddenly the terrible, unbearable thought flashed through his mind, in the midst of all this chaos, that all those people in the ward, who looked like dark shadows in the moonlight, must have experienced the same kind of pain day after day for years and years. How was it that for over twenty years he had not known of it, had not wished to know of it? He had not known, he had had no idea of the pain, therefore he could not be blamed; but conscience, as rough and intractable as Nikita, sent a cold shiver through him from head to foot. He jumped up, wanted to scream at the top of his voice and rush out to kill Nikita, Khobotov, the superintendent, and the assistant doctor, and then himself; but not a sound came out of his breast, and his legs would not obey him. Panting for air, he pulled his dressing-gown and shirt from his chest, tearing them, and fell unconscious on his bed.

XIX

Next morning his head ached, his ears throbbed, and his whole body felt crushed. He was ashamed to think of his weakness on the day before. He had behaved like a coward, he had been afraid even of the moonlight, had expressed in all sincerity thoughts and feelings he had never suspected in himself. For instance, the idea of the dissatisfaction of the philosophizing small fry. But now nothing mattered to him any more.

He neither ate nor drank, but lay motionless and silent on his bed.

'I don't care,' he thought, when they asked him questions. 'I shan't answer. . . . I don't care.'

After dinner the postmaster came to see him, bringing a quarter of a pound of tea and a pound of sweets. Darya also came, and stood for an hour at his bedside with an expression of dumb grief on her face. Khobotov visited him too. He brought a bottle of potassium bromide and told Nikita to fumigate the ward with something or other.

Towards evening Dr Ragin died from an apoplectic stroke. At first he felt a numbing chill and nausea; something horrible seemed to be spreading all over his body, even over his fingers, extending from his stomach to his head and flooding his eyes and ears. Everything turned green before his eyes. Dr Ragin realized that his end had come, and remembered that Gromov, the postmaster, and millions of people believed in immortality. What if it did exist? But he did not want immortality, and he thought of it only for a moment. A herd of deer, extraordinarily beautiful and graceful, which he had been reading about on the previous day, raced past him; then a peasant woman stretched out a hand to him with a registered letter. . . . The postmaster said something. Then everything vanished, and Dr Ragin lost consciousness for ever.

The attendants came, seized him by the arms and legs, and took him to the chapel. There he lay on the table with open eyes, and the moon shed its light on him at night. In the morning the assistant doctor came, offered up a devout prayer before the crucifix, and closed the eyes of his former chief.

A day later Dr Ragin was buried. Only the postmaster and Darya were present at the funeral.

Ariadne

A RATHER handsome young man with a little round beard came up to ask me for a light on the deck of a steamer bound from Odessa to Sebastopol.

'Take a look at those Germans sitting near the deck cabin,' he said. 'When Germans or Englishmen meet, they talk about the price of wool, the crops, or their personal affairs. But for some reason when Russians come together they only discuss women or sublime truths, but women most of all.'

The face of this man was already familiar to me. The day before we had returned from abroad in the same train, and at Volochisk I had seen him standing in the customs shed with a young woman, his travelling companion, before a veritable mountain of trunks and baskets filled with women's clothes, and I could not help noticing how embarrassed and dispirited he looked when he had to pay duty for some silk finery, while his companion protested and threatened to lodge a complaint with someone; then, on the way to Odessa, I had seen him carrying pastries and oranges to the ladies' compartment.

It was rather damp, the boat rocked a little, and the women passengers retired to their cabins. The young man with the little round beard sat down beside me.

'Yes,' he repeated, 'when Russians come together they only discuss women and sublime truths. We are so highly intellectual, we are so pompous that we utter nothing but truths and can solve only problems of a high order. A Russian actor does not know how to be funny, he puts on an air of profundity even when acting in a light comedy. We are the same: when we happen to talk of trifles we treat them only from a lofty point of view. This shows a lack of boldness, sincerity, and simplicity. We talk so often about women because, I think, we feel dissatisfied. We regard women too idealistically and put forward demands that are out of all pro-

187

portion to what reality can give us. We get something which is quite different from what we want, and the result is dissatisfaction, shattered hopes, heartaches; and if something hurts someone he can't help talking about it. I don't bore you with my talk, do I?'

'No, not at all.'

'In that case, let me introduce myself,' said the young man, rising from his seat a little: 'Ivan Ilyich Shamokhin, a Moscow landowner of sorts. I know you very well.'

He sat down and gave me a frank and friendly look.

'A middling philosopher like Max Nordau,' he said, 'would explain this perpetual talk about women as a kind of exotic obsession, or ascribe it to the fact that we have been serf-owners, and so forth. But I look on it differently. I repeat, we are dissatisfied because we are idealists. We want the beings who bear us and our children to be superior to us and to everything else in the world. When we are young we worship those with whom we fall in love, and endow them with poetic qualities. With us, love and happiness are synonymous. In Russia we despise people who do not marry for love, we regard sensuality as ridiculous and revolting, and our best-sellers are novels and stories in which women are beautiful, poetic, and exalted. I assure you there is not a scintilla of affectation about the way the Russian has for years been in raptures over Raphael's Madonna or worried about women's emancipation. But the trouble is that when we get married or have an affair with a woman it takes us only two or three years to feel disappointed and deceived; we have affairs with others and once more suffer disappointment, horror; and in the end we become convinced that women are liars, that they are trivial, vain, unjust, mentally undeveloped, cruel, in fact, that, far from being superior, they are infinitely inferior to us men. And dissatisfied and deceived as we are, there is nothing left for us but to grumble and talk about what we have been so cruelly deceived in, without thinking deeply.'

While Shamokhin was talking, I noticed that the Russian language and the Russian surroundings gave him great pleasure. I expect it was because he had been very homesick abroad. While praising the Russians and ascribing to them a rare idealism, he did not speak slightingly of foreigners, and that spoke in his favour.

It was also noticeable that he was unhappy, that he wanted to talk more about himself than about women, and that I would have to listen to a long story in the nature of a confession.

And, to be sure, when we had ordered a bottle of wine and had each drunk a glass, he began as follows:

'I think it's in one of Weltman's novels that someone says: "What a story!" and someone else replies: "No, sir, it's not a story, it's merely an introduction to a story." So, too, what I've just been saying is only an introduction, for what I really want to tell you is the story of my last love affair. I'm sorry, I must ask you again: you won't be bored listening, will you?'

I told him I would not be bored, and he went on.

The action takes place in the province of Moscow, in one of its northern districts. The countryside there, I must tell you, is wonderful. Our estate lies on the high bank of a rapid stream, at a so-called water-hole, where the water roars day and night. Imagine a big old garden, neatly arranged flower beds, an apiary, a kitchen garden, the river below with leafy willow bushes, which after a heavy dew look a little as though they had turned grey, and on the other side a meadow, and on a hill beyond the meadow a terrible dark pine wood. This pine wood is full of orange-brown mushrooms, thousands of them, and elks still live in its depths. When I die and am nailed up in my coffin, I think I shall still dream of those early mornings, when the sun hurts your eyes, you know, or of the wonderful spring evenings when the nightingales and the landrails call in the garden and beyond the garden, and the sounds of a concertina float across from the village, while in the house someone plays the piano, and the river roars – in short, such music as to make you wish to sing and cry aloud both at once. We don't own a great deal of arable land, but we are saved by our meadows, which together with the woods bring in about two thousand a year. I am an only son, and my father and I are unpretentious people. With my father's pension and that income we have enough for our needs. After graduating from the university I spent the first three years on our estate; I looked after it, always expecting to be elected to some local council. But what really kept me there was that I had fallen violently in love with a ravishingly beautiful and fascinating girl. She was the sister of a neighbour of ours, a ruined landowner by the name of Kotlovich; on his estate he had pineapples, marvellous peaches, lightning conductors, a fountain in the middle of the courtyard – and at the same time not a kopek in his pocket. He did nothing, didn't know how to do anything; a flabby sort of individual, as though made out of boiled turnip. He used to treat his sick peasants by homoeopathy, and was a practising spiritualist. On the whole, however, he was an extremely considerate, gentle, and far from stupid man; but I'm afraid I can't stomach people who talk to spirits and cure peasant women by magnetism. First, because people who are not intellectually free are always confused about their ideas and it is very difficult to talk to them, and secondly because they usually do not like anyone and do not live with women, and this mysterious sort of life they lead has an unpleasant effect on sensitive people. I did not care for his appearance, either. He was tall, fat, with a white skin and a little head, small shining eyes, and chubby white fingers. He did not shake hands with you, but kneaded your hands in his. And all the time he kept apologizing. If he asked for anything: 'I'm sorry.' If he gave you anything, again: 'I'm sorry.' His sister was quite different. I ought perhaps to tell you that I did not know the Kotloviches in my childhood and early youth, for my father had been a professor at N— and we had lived in the provinces for many years. When I did get to know them, the girl was twenty-two, had left her boarding school long before, and had spent two or three years in Moscow with a rich aunt who had brought her out into society. When I made her acquaintance and had to talk to her for the first time, what struck me most of all was her unusual and beautiful name – Ariadne. It suited her so marvellously! She was a brunette, very thin, very slender, supple, shapely, extraordinarily graceful, with refined and exceedingly noble features. Her eyes were shining, too, but while her brother's shone coldly and with a cloying sweetness, like clear transparent fruit-drops, hers glowed with youth, proud and beautiful. I fell in love with her on the first day of our acquaintance, and it couldn't have been otherwise. My first impressions were so overwhelming that I still cannot get rid of my illusions, I still cannot help thinking that nature had some sweepingly grand

and wonderful design when she created that girl. Ariadne's voice, her footsteps, her hat, even her footprints on the sandy bank where she used to fish for gudgeon, filled me with joy and a passionate hunger for life. I judged of her spiritual qualities from her beautiful face and her beautiful figure; and every word, every smile of Ariadne's sent me into raptures, fascinated me, and made me believe that she possessed a lofty soul. She was affectionate, talkative, gay, simple in her manners; she had a poetic belief in God, she talked in a poetic vein about death, there was such a wealth of nuances in her turn of mind that she could impart some kind of special, charming qualities even to her faults. Suppose she wanted a new horse and had no money – well, what did that matter? One could sell or pawn something. And if the steward swore that there was nothing to sell or pawn any more, one could tear off the iron from the roofs of the cottages in the grounds and sell it to a factory, or at the busiest time drive the farm horses to market and sell them there for next to nothing. These unbridled desires at times reduced the whole estate to despair; but she expressed them with such refinement that in the end everything was forgiven her and everything was permitted her, as to a goddess or a Roman empress. My love was passionate, and soon everyone – my father, the neighbours, and the peasants – noticed it. They all sympathized with me. When I treated the farm labourers to vodka, they would bow and say: 'God grant you may marry the Kotlovich young lady, sir.'

Ariadne herself knew that I loved her. She often rode over on horseback or drove over in a barouche, and sometimes she spent whole days with me and my father. She made great friends with the old man, and he even taught her to bicycle – it was his favourite pastime. One evening they were getting ready to go riding and I helped her to get on the bicycle. She was so lovely just then, I remember, that I felt as though I were burning my hands when I touched her. I was trembling all over with rapture. When the two of them, the old man and she, both looking so handsome and elegant, cycled side by side on the road, a black horse ridden by the steward shied away on meeting them, and it seemed to me that it did so because it too was struck by her beauty. My love, my worship, touched Ariadne and moved her deeply. She desired passionately to be as smitten as I was and to respond with the same kind of love. It was so poetic, you see.

But she could not love as truly as I did because she was frigid and already sufficiently corrupted. Already there was a demon in her who whispered day and night that she was a ravishing, divine creature; and she, who had no idea what she had been created for and for what purpose life had been given her, imagined herself in the future as rich and as moving in the highest aristocratic circles. She dreamed of balls, races, liveries, sumptuous drawing-rooms, her own *salon*, and a whole swarm of counts, princes, ambassadors, famous painters and actors, all of them adoring her and admiring her beauty and her dresses. . . . This craving for power and personal success, and this continual concentration of all one's thoughts in one direction, dampen people's ardour, and Ariadne was cold – to me, to nature, and to music. Meanwhile time was passing and still there were no ambassadors in sight. Ariadne went on living with her brother, the spiritualist; things went from bad to worse, till in the end she had no money to buy hats and dresses with and she had to resort to all kinds of tricks and stratagems to conceal her poverty.

As luck would have it, a certain Prince Maktuyev, a wealthy but utterly worthless man, had proposed to her when she was living at her aunt's in Moscow. She had refused him point-blank. But now she was sometimes tortured by a growing sense of regret: why had she refused him? Just as our peasant blows with disgust on a mug of *kvass* with cockroaches floating about in it and yet drinks it, so she frowned disdainfully at the recollection of the prince and yet would say to me: 'Say what you like, but there is something inexplicable, something fascinating, about a title!'

She dreamed of a title, of cutting a great figure in high society, but at the same time she did not want to let me slip through her fingers. However you may dream of ambassadors, your heart is not a stone and you can't help being indulgent towards your own youth. Ariadne tried hard to fall in love, she pretended to, she even swore she loved me. But I am a nervous and extremely sensitive man; when I am loved, I can feel it even at a distance, without vows and assurances, but with Ariadne I immediately felt a coldness in the air, and when she talked to me of love I seemed to be listening to the singing of a nightingale made of metal. Ariadne herself felt that she was lacking in conviction. She was vexed, and more than once I saw her burst into tears. Why, one evening on the river bank she flung her arms round me impulsively and kissed me, but I could see from her eyes that she did not love me, that she had embraced me merely out of curiosity, to test herself, to see what came of it. And I was horrified. I took her hand and cried in despair:

'These caresses without love make me unhappy!'

'What a – strange fellow you are!' she said with vexation, and walked away.

In all probability I would have married her after a year or two, and that would have been the end of my story; but fate decided to arrange our romance differently. It so happened that a new person appeared on our horizon. Ariadne's brother had a visit from an old university friend, Mikhail Ivanovich Lubkov, a charming man whom coachmen and footmen described as 'a proper card'. He was of about medium height, rather lean, bald, with the face of a good-natured shopkeeper, not interesting but impressive, pale, with a stiff, carefully tended moustache, the skin on his neck covered with goose pimples, and a big Adam's apple. He wore a pince-nez on a wide black ribbon and could not pronounce either *r* or *l*, so that, for instance, the word 'really' sounded 'weawy'. He was always cheerful and he thought everything funny. He had married rather foolishly at twenty, getting two houses in Moscow for his dowry, had started converting them and building a bath-house, and had gone bankrupt, and now his wife and four children lived in a tenement house in poverty and he had to support them – and he thought it was funny. He was thirty-six and his wife was already forty-two – and that too was funny. His mother, a conceited, haughty personage with aristocratic pretensions, despised his wife and lived apart with a whole swarm of cats and dogs, and he had to make her an additional allowance of seventy-five roubles a month; he was a man of taste, too, liked lunching at the Slav Bazaar and dined at the Hermitage; he needed a lot of money, and his uncle only allowed him two thousand roubles a year, which was not enough, so that he would run all over Moscow with his tongue hanging out for days looking for someone to borrow from – and this, too, was funny. He had come to stay with Kotlovich for a bit of fresh air and for a rest from family life. At dinner, at supper, and on our walks he talked to us about his wife, his mother, his creditors, the bailiffs, and laughed at them; he laughed at himself, and assured us that thanks to his ability to raise loans he had acquired many agreeable acquaintances. He laughed without stopping, and we laughed too. In his company we too spent our time differently. I was more inclined to quiet and, so to speak, idyllic pleasures; I liked fishing, evening walks, gathering mushrooms; but Lubkov preferred picnics, fireworks, hunting. He would organize picnics three times a week, and Ariadne, with a serious and inspired face, would write down a list of oysters, champagne, sweets, and send me to Moscow to get them, without, of course, bothering to ask me whether I had any money. At the picnics there were toasts, laughter, and more funny stories of how old his wife was, what fat lapdogs his mother had, what charming people his creditors were. . . .

Lubkov loved the country, but he looked upon it as something long familiar, something that was in essence infinitely beneath him and had only been created for his pleasure. He would, for instance, stop dead before some magnificent view and say: 'A lovely place for a cup of tea!' One day, seeing Ariadne walking in the distance with a parasol, he motioned towards her and said: 'She's thin, and that's what I like. I don't like fat women.'

This made me wince. I asked him not to speak like that about women in my presence. He looked up at me in surprise.

'What's wrong about my liking thin women and disliking fat ones?'

I made no answer. On another occasion, being in an excellent frame of mind and a little tipsy, he said:

'I've noticed Ariadne likes you. I'm surprised you don't do something about it.'

His words made me feel embarrassed, and I explained to him my views on love and women.

'I don't know,' he said with a sigh. 'In my opinion a woman's a woman and a man's a man. Ariadne, as you say, may be poetic and noble-minded, but that doesn't mean that she is above the laws of nature. You can see for yourself that she has reached an age when she must have a husband or a lover. I respect women no less than you do, but I do not think that certain relations exclude poetry.

Poetry is one thing and a lover is another. It's the same as in farming: the beauty of nature is one thing and the income from forests and fields is another.'

When Ariadne and I were fishing, Lubkov lay on the sand near us and cracked jokes at my expense or gave me lessons on how to live.

'I am surprised, my dear sir, how you can live without a love affair,' he would say. 'You're young, handsome, interesting, in short a man in a thousand, and yet you live like a monk. Dear me, these old men of twenty-eight! I am nearly ten years older than you, and which of us is the younger? Ariadne, which do you think?'

'You, of course,' Ariadne said.

And when he got tired of our silence and the attention with which we stared at our floats, he went home; and she said, looking angrily at me:

'Indeed, you're not a man but, God forgive me, a namby-pamby, spineless creature. Men must fall in love, rave, make mistakes, suffer! A woman will forgive audacity and impudence, but she'll never forgive reasonableness.'

She was angry in good earnest.

'To be successful with women,' she went on, 'one has to be resolute and bold. Lubkov is not as handsome as you, but he is more interesting, and he'll always be successful because he's not like you, he's a man!'

There was even a note of bitterness in her voice.

One evening at supper she began saying, without addressing herself to me, that if she had been a man she would not have vegetated in the country, but would have travelled, spent the winter somewhere abroad, in Italy, for instance. Oh, Italy! At this point my father unwittingly put the fat in the fire. He began telling us at length about Italy, how wonderful it was, what lovely scenery, what museums! Ariadne was suddenly filled with a burning desire to go to Italy. She even banged her fist on the table, and her eyes flashed as she cried: 'Let's go!'

Then they started talking about how wonderful it would be in Italy. Italy! Oh, Italy! And so it went on every day, and when Ariadne fixed her eyes at some invisible point over my shoulder, I could see from her cold and obstinate expression that in her dreams she had already conquered Italy with all her *salons*, her aristocratic foreigners and tourists, and that there was no holding her back now. I advised her to wait a little, to put off her trip for a year or two, but she puckered her face disdainfully.

'You're as sensible as an old woman,' she said.

Lubkov was in favour of the trip. He declared it could be done very cheaply and that he would be only too glad to go to Italy and have a rest from his family life. I admit I behaved as naïvely as a schoolboy. Not from jealousy, but from a presentiment of something terrible and out of the ordinary, I tried as much as possible not to leave them alone together, while they kept pulling my leg; for instance, when I came into the room they pretended they had just been kissing, and so on.

Then, one fine morning, her chubby-faced white-skinned brother, the spiritualist, came to see me and expressed the wish to have a talk with me in private.

He was a man without a will of his own; in spite of his tactfulness and good education he could never resist reading someone else's letter if he found it lying in front of him on the table. And now he admitted that he had by chance read a letter Lubkov had written to Ariadne.

'From this letter I learned that she is very shortly going abroad. My dear fellow, I'm terribly upset. Explain to me, for goodness' sake! I'm completely in the dark.'

When he said this he breathed hard straight in my face, and his breath smelled of boiled beef.

'I'm sorry I'm letting you into the secret of this letter,' he went on, 'but you're Ariadne's friend. She respects you. Perhaps you know something of her plans. She wants to go abroad, but with whom? Mr Lubkov is planning to go with her, too. I'm sorry, but it certainly is a little strange of Mr Lubkov. He's a married man, he has children, and yet he tells Ariadne that he loves her, writes to her as if she were already his mistress. I'm sorry, but it is strange, isn't it?'

I turned cold, my hands and feet went numb. I felt a pain in my chest, as if a three-cornered stone had been placed there. Kotlovich sank exhausted in a chair, his hands drooping limply at his sides.

'What can I do?' I asked.

'Make her realize how frightful it all is. ... Persuade her. ... Just think, what use is Lubkov to her? Is he a match for her? Oh Lord, this is terrible, terrible!' he went on, clutching at his head. 'She's had such wonderful offers, Prince Maktuyev and — and others. The prince adores her, and only last Wednesday week her late grandfather Ilarion declared positively — I mean, it was as plain as plain could be — that Ariadne would be his wife. Positively! Her grandfather Ilarion, you understand, is dead, but he's an amazingly intelligent person. We call up his spirit every day.'

After this conversation I did not sleep all night, and I thought of shooting myself. Next morning I wrote five letters and tore them all up. Then I sobbed in the threshing barn, then I got my father to give me some money, and I left for the Caucasus without saying good-bye.

Now of course a woman's a woman and a man's a man, but is it really as simple in our day as it was before the Flood? And is it really possible that I, a civilized man, endowed with a complex spiritual organization, have to explain my strong attraction to a woman merely by the fact that the structure of her body is different from mine? Oh, how terrible that would be! I'd like to think that in his struggle with nature the genius of man has also struggled with physical love, as with an enemy, and that if it has not conquered it, it has at any rate succeeded in entangling it in a net of illusions of brotherhood and love; for me, at any rate, it is not simply a function of my animal organism, as with a dog or a frog, but real love; and every embrace is sublimated by a pure impulse of the heart and respect for the woman. Indeed, disgust for the animal instinct has been instilled for centuries in hundreds of generations, it is inherited by me in my blood and is part of my nature, and if I idealize love now, is it not as natural and necessary as that the lobes of our ears are immobile or that I am not covered with fur? It seems to me that this is how the majority of civilized people think of it, for today absence of the moral and poetic element in love is treated as an atavistic phenomenon; it is said to be a symptom of degeneration and of many forms of insanity. It is true that by idealizing love we assume the presence in those we love of qualities that are often not to be found in them, and no doubt that is a source of continual mistakes and continual suffering. But in my opinion it is much better to suffer than to acquiesce in the proposition that a woman's a woman and a man's a man.

In Tiflis I received a letter from my father. He wrote that Ariadne had gone abroad with the intention of spending the whole winter there. A month later I returned home. It was already autumn. Every week Ariadne sent my father very interesting letters, on scented paper, written in excellent literary language. In my opinion, every woman can be a writer. Ariadne described in great detail how it had not been easy for her to make it up with her aunt and persuade her to give her a thousand roubles for the trip abroad and how it had taken her a long time to find an old lady in Moscow, a distant relative, and get her to accompany her as chaperon. Such a superfluity of details made me smell a rat at once, and I realized that she had no woman companion with her. A few days later I too had a letter from her, also scented and literary. She wrote that she had missed me, missed my beautiful, intelligent, tender eyes, reproached me, as one of my oldest friends, for wasting my youth vegetating in the country while like her I could be living in paradise beneath palm trees inhaling the aroma of orange blossoms. She signed herself 'your forsaken Ariadne'. Two days later came another letter in the same vein, signed 'your forgotten Ariadne'. I was at a loss what to do. I loved her passionately, I dreamed of her every night, and then this 'forsaken', 'forgotten' – what for? What did she mean? And then the boredom of the country, the long evenings, the depressing thoughts of Lubkov. The uncertainty tortured me, it poisoned my days and nights, life became unbearable to me. I could not stand it any longer and went abroad.

Ariadne wanted me to join her in Abbazzia. I arrived there on a bright, warm day. It had been raining and the raindrops were still hanging on the trees. I got a room in the same huge, barrack-like annexe of the hotel where Ariadne and Lubkov were staying. They were not at home. I went to the park, wandered about the avenues, then sat down. An Austrian general walked past with his hands crossed behind him and the same kind of red stripes on his trousers as those worn by our generals; a baby in a pram was wheeled by, the wheels squeaking on the wet sand. A decrepit old man with jaundice passed, followed by a crowd of Englishwomen, a Catholic priest, and the Austrian general again. A military band, just arrived from Fiume, marched by to the bandstand, its brass instruments glittering in the sun – it struck up some tune. Have you ever been in Abbazzia? It is a filthy little Slav town with only one street, which stinks and in which one can't walk after rain without galoshes. I had read so much and every time with such deep emotion about this earthly paradise that I felt vexed and ashamed when afterwards I had cautiously to cross the narrow street with rolled-up trousers; when from sheer boredom I bought hard pears from an old peasant woman who, recognizing me as a Russian, tried to speak in broken Russian; when I asked myself in perplexity where to go or what to do there; and when I invariably met Russians who had been as deceived as I had been. There is a calm bay there, crossed by steamers and boats with sails of all colours; you can see Fiume and the distant islands, covered in a lilac haze, and that would have been picturesque if the view over the bay had not been obstructed by hotels and their annexes, built in the same vulgar and incongruous architectural style as the other buildings with which this green shore has been covered by greedy hucksters, so that for the most part you see nothing in this paradise except windows, terraces, and little squares with white tables and the black frock coats of waiters. There is a park here, which is like any other park you can find in every watering-place abroad. In about ten minutes you get sick and tired of the dark, motionless, silent foliage of the palm trees, the bright green seats, the glitter of the blaring brass instruments, and the red stripes on the generals' trousers; and yet for some reason you feel obliged to spend ten days or even ten weeks there! Having dragged myself reluctantly from one of these holiday places to another I have grown more and more convinced of the discomfort and monotony of the life led by the well-fed and the rich, the dullness and feebleness of their imagination, the timidity of their tastes and desires. How much happier are those tourists, young and old, who are unable to afford hotels and live where they can, admire the view and the sea from the tops of mountains, lying on the green grass, travel on foot, see the woods and villages at close quarters, observe the customs of the country, listen to its songs, fall in love with its women. . . .

While I was sitting in the park it began to grow dark, and in the twilight my Ariadne appeared, elegant and smart, like a princess; behind her walked Lubkov, wearing a loose-fitting suit, probably bought in Vienna.

'Why are you so angry?' he was saying. 'What have I done to you?'

Catching sight of me, she uttered a joyous cry, and if we had not been in the park she would have flung herself on my neck. She pressed my hands warmly and laughed. I laughed too, and nearly cried with emotion. She overwhelmed me with questions: how were things on the estate, how was my father, had I seen her brother, and so on. She insisted that I should look her straight in the eyes and kept asking me whether I remembered our fishing, our little quarrels, our picnics. . . .

'Oh dear,' she said with a sigh, 'how wonderful it all was! But we're not exactly bored here, either. We've lots of acquaintances, my dear one, my sweet. Tomorrow I'll introduce you to a Russian family here. Only please buy yourself another hat!' She looked me up and down, and frowned. 'Abbazzia is not a village,' she said. 'Here one must be *comme il faut.*'

Then we went to a restaurant. Ariadne laughed and was full of fun all the time. She kept calling me 'dear', 'sweet', 'clever', and looked as though she could not believe that I was with her. We sat like that till eleven o'clock and parted very satisfied both with the dinner and with each other. Next day Ariadne introduced me to a Russian family: 'The son of a distinguished professor, our estates are next to each other.' She talked to this family only about estates and crops, and kept referring to me for confirmation. She wanted to appear to be a very rich landowner, and indeed she succeeded in doing so. She carried herself splendidly, like a real aristocrat, which as a matter of fact she was by birth.

'But what do you think of my aunt?' she said suddenly, looking at me with a smile. 'We had a little disagreement, and off she went to Morano! How do you like that?'

A little later, when we were walking in the park, I asked her what aunt she was talking about.

'I didn't know you had an aunt,' I said.

'Oh,' Ariadne laughed, 'I had to tell that lie to save my reputa-

tion. You see, they mustn't know that I'm without a chaperon.'
After a moment's silence, she snuggled up to me and said: 'Darling, please be friends with Lubkov. He's so unhappy. His wife and mother are simply awful!'

She was very formal in her mode of address when speaking to Lubkov, and when going to bed said good night to him exactly as she did to me; and their rooms were on different floors. All this made me hope that it was all nonsense and that there was no question of any love affair between them, and I felt at ease when meeting them. When one day he asked me for a loan of three hundred roubles I gave it to him with pleasure.

Every day we spent in enjoying ourselves. All we did was to have a good time. We went for walks in the park, we ate, we drank. Every day we met and talked to the Russian family. I gradually got used to the fact that if I went to the park I was bound to meet the old gentleman with jaundice, the Catholic priest, and the Austrian general, who carried a pack of little cards and sat down wherever it was convenient and laid out a game of patience, nervously twitching his shoulders. The military band, too, played the same tunes over and over again. At home in the country I used to feel ashamed when I met peasants on week-days while I was on my way to do some fishing or to a picnic; here too I was ashamed when I met workmen, coachmen, or waiters, for it seemed to me that they were looking at me and thinking: 'Why aren't you doing any work?' And I experienced this feeling of shame every day from morning till night. It was a strange, unpleasant, monotonous time, relieved only by the constant requests for loans by Lubkov, who, when he got his hundred or fifty gulden from me, would suddenly cheer up, like a morphia addict after a dose of morphine, and begin to laugh noisily at his wife, at himself, or at his creditors.

But the rains came and it got cold. We went to Italy, and I wired my father 'for God's sake' to send me eight hundred roubles to Rome. We stayed in Venice, Bologna, and Florence, and in every town invariably put up at an expensive hotel, where we were fleeced for lights, for service, for heating, for bread at lunch, and for the privilege of dining in a private room. We ate enormously. In the morning they served us *café complet*. At one o'clock, lunch:

meat, fish, some kind of omelette, cheese, fruit, and wine. At six o'clock, a dinner of eight courses, with long intervals during which we drank beer and wine. At nine o'clock, tea. Before midnight Ariadne would declare that she was famished and ask for ham and soft-boiled eggs. We too would eat to keep her company. Between the meals we used to rush about to museums and exhibitions, always worrying about being late for lunch or dinner. The pictures bored me, I was anxious to go back to our hotel for a rest, I felt exhausted, I kept looking for a chair, and I hypocritically repeated after the others: 'What an exquisite picture! How much air!' Like overfed boa constrictors, we paid attention only to things that sparkled. The shop windows hypnotized us and we went into raptures over imitation brooches and bought masses of useless and worthless things.

It was the same in Rome, where it rained and where a cold wind kept blowing. After a sumptuous lunch we went to have a look at St Peter's, but as a result of feeling heavy after eating so much at lunch, or perhaps because of the bad weather, it made no impression whatever on us, and we nearly quarrelled after accusing each other of being indifferent to art.

The money arrived from my father. I went to get it, I remember, in the morning. Lubkov went with me.

'The present cannot be full and happy when one has a past,' he said. 'I'm wearing a big load round by neck from the past. Still, it wouldn't be so bad if I had money; but as it is I am striding the blast like a naked new-born babe. You see, I've only eight francs left,' he went on, lowering his voice, 'and yet I have to send my wife a hundred and my mother as much. And we have to live here, too. Ariadne's like a child, she just ignores our desperate position and throws money about like a duchess. What did she buy a watch for yesterday? And, tell me, why on earth do we go on playing at being good children? You see, she and I conceal our relationship from the servants and from our friends, and that costs us another ten or fifteen francs a day, for I have a separate room. What is it all for?'

I felt as though a sharp stone was turned round in my chest. There was no longer any uncertainty, everything was clear to me; I turned cold all over and at once made up my mind not to see them any more, to run away from them, to go back home at once.

'It's easy to have an affair with a woman,' went on Lubkov. 'All you have to do is to undress her. But what a nuisance it is afterwards, what a silly business!'

When I was counting over the money, he said to me:

'If you don't lend me a thousand francs, I'm done for. Your money is my only hope.'

I gave him the thousand francs and he cheered up at once and began to laugh at his uncle, the stupid fellow, who could not keep his address secret from his wife. When I came back to the hotel, I packed and paid my bill. I had only to say good-bye to Ariadne.

I knocked at her door.

'*Entrez!*'

Her room was in disorder, as it was still early in the morning: on the table were the tea things, an unfinished roll, an eggshell; there was a strong overpowering smell of scent. The bed had not been made, and it was clear that two had slept in it. Ariadne herself had only got up a short while before: her hair was undone and she was wearing a flannel jacket.

We exchanged the usual greetings, and then I sat in silence for a minute until she did up her hair.

'Why,' I broke the silence, trembling all over, 'why did you send for me to come abroad?'

She must have guessed what was in my mind, for she took me by the hand and said:

'I want you to be here. You're so pure.'

I was ashamed of my agitation, of my trembling. What if I were suddenly to burst into tears! I went out without saying another word, and an hour later I was already sitting in a train. All the way home, for some reason, I thought of Ariadne as pregnant; and she was loathsome to me, and all the women I saw in the carriages and at the stations also for some reason looked pregnant to me, and they too were loathsome and pathetic. I was in the position of a greedy, obsessed miser who all of a sudden discovers that all his gold coins are false. The pure, graceful images my love-stimulated imagination had cherished so long, my views on love and women – all were now jeering and putting out their tongues at me. Ariadne, I asked myself in horror, that young, well-educated and remarkably beautiful girl, the daughter of a high-court judge, having a sordid affair with such an ordinary, uninteresting vulgarian? But then, why shouldn't she be in love with Lubkov? In what way is he worse than I? Oh, let her love anyone she likes, but why lie to me? But then, why on earth should she be frank with me? And so on, all in the same vein, till I felt stupefied. It was awfully cold in the train. I travelled first class, but even so there were three passengers to a side, there were no double windows, the outer door opened straight into the compartment, and I felt as though I were in the stocks, cramped, abandoned, miserable. My feet were frozen, and at the same time I kept calling to mind how ravishing she had looked that morning in her flannel jacket and with her hair down, and I was suddenly seized by such a violent feeling of jealousy that I kept jumping up from my seat in anguish, so that my fellow-passengers looked at me in wonder and even in terror.

At home I found snowdrifts and twenty degrees of frost. I love the winter, I love it because at that time, even in the hardest frosts, I feel particularly warm there. On a bright frosty day it is pleasant to put on one's sheepskin and felt boots and potter about in the garden or in the yard, or to read in one's well-heated room, or to sit in father's study in front of the fireplace, or to wash in one's country bath-house. Except, of course, that if there is no mother in the house, no sister and no children, it is somehow frightening on winter evenings, and they seem extraordinarily long and quiet. The warmer and cosier it is, the more strongly is their absence felt. In the winter when I returned from abroad the evenings were interminably long, I felt very miserable, and from sheer misery I could not even read. During the day it was not so bad, I could clear away the snow in the garden or feed the chickens and the calves, but in the evening it was damn awful!

I had never cared for visitors before, but now I was glad of them, because I knew that I was certain to hear something of Ariadne. Kotlovich, the spiritualist, often came to see us, as he wished to have a talk about his sister, and he sometimes brought with him his friend Prince Maktuyev, who was as much in love with Ariadne as I was. To sit in Ariadne's room, to finger the keys of her piano, to look at her music, was simply a necessity for the prince, he could not live without it, and the spirit of grandfather Ilarion was still predicting that sooner or later she would be his wife. The prince usually spent hours at our house, from lunch to midnight, and he never opened his mouth; he drank two or three bottles of beer in dead silence, and only from time to time, to show that he too was taking part in the conversation, he laughed an abrupt, melancholy, rather stupid laugh. Before departing for home, he always took me aside and said in an undertone: 'When did you see Ariadne last? Is she well? She is not getting tired of being there, is she?'

Spring came. There was snipe shooting, then the sowing of spring crops and clover. I felt sad, but it was a spring sadness: I longed to be reconciled to what I had lost. Working in the fields and listening to the larks, I asked myself whether it would not be best to finish once and for all with this question of personal happiness and marry a simple peasant girl. Suddenly, just when the work on the estate was in full swing, I received a letter with an Italian stamp. The clover, the apiary, the calves, and the peasant girl – everything vanished into thin air. This time Ariadne wrote that she was terribly unhappy. She reproached me for not holding out a helping hand to her, for looking down at her from the heights of my virtue and abandoning her in the hour of peril. All this was written in a large nervous hand, with blots and smudges, and it was quite clear that she wrote in a hurry and that she was in real distress. In conclusion, she implored me to come and save her.

Again I slipped anchor and rushed off. Ariadne lived in Rome. I arrived late in the evening, and when she saw me she burst into sobs and flung herself on my neck. She had not changed at all during that winter and she was still as young and lovely. We had supper together, then drove about Rome till dawn, and all the time she was telling me what she had been doing. I asked where Lubkov was.

'Don't remind me of that creature,' she cried. 'I loathe and detest him.'

'But you did love him, didn't you?'

'Never! At first I found him rather original and I was sorry for him – that was all. He's impudent, he takes a woman by storm, and that's exciting. But don't let's talk about him. That's a sad page of my life. He's gone to Russia to get money – good riddance! I told him not to dare come back.'

She was no longer living at a hotel, but in a two-roomed flat, which she had decorated and furnished to her own taste, coldly and sumptuously. After Lubkov had gone, she had borrowed about five thousand francs from her acquaintances, and my arrival was in truth her salvation. I had counted on taking her back to the country, but I did not succeed in that. She longed to be back, but her memories of the poverty she had been through there, of privations, of the rusty roof on her brother's house, made her shudder with disgust; and when I suggested going home, she squeezed my hands convulsively and said:

'No, no! I shall die of boredom there!'

Then my love entered upon its last phase, into its last quarter.

'Be the darling you used to be and love me a little,' said Ariadne, leaning over to me. 'You're sullen and reasonable, you're afraid to yield to impulse, you're always thinking of the consequences, and that's boring. Please, I ask you, I implore you, be nice to me! Oh, my pure one, my holy one, my dearest darling, I love you so!'

I became her lover. For one month, at any rate, I was like a madman, in a state of absolute ecstasy. To hold a young and lovely body in your arms, to delight in it, to feel its warmth every time you wake from sleep! And to remember that she was there, she – my Ariadne – oh, it was not so easy to get used to that! But I did get used to it all the same and gradually began to take up a rational attitude to my new position. First of all I realized that Ariadne, as before, was not in love with me. But she did want to be seriously in love, she was afraid of loneliness and, above all, I was young, strong, and healthy, while she was sensuous like all frigid people – and we pretended that we had become lovers because we were both passionately in love with one another. Soon I realized something else.

We stayed in Rome, Naples, Florence; we even went to Paris, but we thought it was too cold there and we returned to Italy. We gave ourselves out to be husband and wife, wealthy landowners, and we found no difficulty in making many acquaintances. Ariadne was a great success. As she was taking lessons in painting, she was called an artist and – believe it or not – that suited her very well, though she hadn't any talent at all. She slept every day till two or three in the afternoon; she had her coffee and lunch in bed. At dinner she ate soup, lobster, fish, meat, asparagus, game; and after she had gone to bed I usually brought her something, for instance roast beef, and she ate it with a sad and worried expression. And waking up at night, she ate apples and oranges.

The chief and as it were fundamental quality of that woman was her amazing cunning. She was never straightforward, she tried to deceive you every moment, and apparently without any need, as though by instinct, by the same sort of urge as makes the sparrow chirrup and the cockroach move its feelers. She tried to get the better of me, of the waiters, of the porter, of the saleswomen in the shops, of her acquaintances; not one conversation, not one meeting, took place without her putting on airs and affectations. A man had only to enter our hotel room – whoever he might be, a waiter or a baron – for her eyes, her expression, her voice, and even the lines of her figure to change. If you had seen us even once, you would have said there were no more aristocratic and wealthy people in Italy than we. She did not let go of a single musician or artist without first telling him all sorts of nonsensical lies about his remarkable talent.

'You're a genius!' she would say in her sugary sing-song voice, 'I feel terrified to be in the same room with you. I think you must see right through people.'

And all this in order to create an impression, to be successful, to be fascinating! She woke up every morning with only one thought in her mind: 'to create an impression'. And that was the aim and object of her life. If I had told her that in a certain house and in a certain street there lived a man who did not like her, she would have been really upset about it. Every day she simply had to enchant, to fascinate, to drive men crazy. The fact that I was in her power and was reduced to a complete nonentity by her charms gave her the same kind of satisfaction as the victors used to enjoy in tournaments. My own humiliation was not enough. At night, sprawling naked on the bed like a tigress – she was always too hot – she would read the letters Lubkov sent her; he implored her to return to Russia, vowing that if she did not he would rob or murder someone just to get the money to come to her. She hated him, but his passionate, slavish letters excited her. She had an extraordinary opinion of her own charms. She imagined that if at some crowded assembly men could see what a wonderful figure and what a beautiful skin she had, the whole of Italy, the whole of the world would be at her feet. This talk about her wonderful figure and her beautiful skin offended me, and to spite me she would say all sorts of vulgar things, just to provoke me; and this went so far that one day, at the country house of a woman acquaintance of ours, she flew into a rage with me and said:

'If you don't stop annoying me with your sermons, I'll undress this minute and lie down naked on the flowers here!'

After looking at her asleep, or eating, or trying to assume an innocent expression, I thought to myself: 'Why has God given her this extraordinary beauty, grace, and intelligence? Surely not for her to sprawl on the bed, eat, and tell lies, tell lies all the time.' And was she really intelligent? She was afraid of three candles in a row, and of the number thirteen; she was terrified of the evil eye and bad dreams; she talked of free love and freedom, in general, like a sanctimonious old woman; and she declared that a mediocrity like Boleslav Markevich was a better writer than Turgenev. But she was diabolically cunning and sharp, and knew how to appear in society as a highly educated woman of advanced views. Even when in the best of spirits she thought nothing of insulting a servant or killing an insect; she loved bull fights; she loved to read about murders and was angry when a defendant was acquitted.

For the sort of life Ariadne and I were leading, we needed a great deal of money. My poor father sent me his pension, all the meagre income from his estate, he borrowed for me wherever he could; and when one day he answered me: '*Non habeo*', I sent him a desperate telegram in which I implored him to mortgage the estate. A little later I asked him to get some money somewhere on a second mortgage. He carried out both my requests without a murmur and sent me the money to the last kopek. Ariadne despised the practical aspect of life, it was no concern of hers; and when, flinging away thousands of francs for the satisfaction of her mad desires, I groaned like an old tree, she would be lightheartedly humming '*Addio, bella Napoli*'. Little by little my love for her disappeared, and I began to be ashamed of our life together. I dislike pregnancy and confinements, but now I sometimes dreamed of a child, which would at least have been a formal justification of our life. Not to become utterly repulsive to myself, I began visiting museums and galleries and reading books. I gave up drinking and was eating as little as possible. To drive oneself round and round, like a horse on a lunge-rope, from morning till night, makes one somehow feel easier in mind.

Ariadne got tired of me, too. Incidentally, the people with whom she was a great success were all of the middling sort; as before, there were no ambassadors and there was no *salon*, there was not enough money for that, which outraged her and made her burst into sobs, and at last she told me that she would not mind going back to Russia. And so here we are. During the last months before our departure she was zealously corresponding with her brother; she quite obviously has some secret plans, though goodness only knows what they are. I am sick and tired of trying to find out what she is scheming to do next. But we are not going back to the country, but to Yalta and from there to the Caucasus. She can only live in watering-places now; and if only you knew how I hate all these watering-places, and how suffocated and ashamed I feel in them. Oh, if I could be back in the country now! Now I should really be working, earning my bread by the sweat of my brow, atoning for my mistakes. I feel a tremendous access of energy, and it seems to me that were I now to make full use of that energy I could redeem my estate in five years. But, as you see, there are all sorts of complications. We're no longer abroad, but in dear old Russia; and we have to think of lawful wedlock. Of course my infatuation is all gone, there is no trace left of my old love, but, be that as it may, I'm in duty bound to marry her. . . .

Excited by his story, Shamokhin and I went below and continued talking about women. It was late. It appeared that he and I shared the same cabin.

'For the time being,' Shamokhin was saying, 'it's only in the villages that woman does not lag behind man. There she thinks and feels the same as a man and struggles with nature in the name of civilization as zealously as he. The educated middle-class woman in the towns has long since dropped behind and is returning to her primitive condition. She is half human and half beast already, and it's due to her that a great deal of what has been won by human genius has been lost again. The woman is gradually disappearing and her place is taken by the primitive female. This backwardness of the educated woman is a serious danger to civilization, for in her regressive movement she is trying to drag man after her and impedes his progress. There's no doubt about that.'

I asked him why he was generalizing and why he judged all women by Ariadne alone. I pointed out that women's very desire for education and equality of rights, which I understand as a desire for justice, precluded any theory of a retrogressive movement. But Shamokhin scarcely listened to me and merely smiled sceptically. He had become a passionate and convinced misogynist and it was impossible to change his opinion.

'Oh, I don't think you really mean it,' he said. 'The moment a woman regards me not as a man, not as an equal, but merely as a male, and is all her life thinking only of how she can make me fall in love with her, or in other words how she can get possession of me, there can be no talk of equality of rights. Oh, don't you believe them! They're devilishly cunning. We men are doing our best to secure their emancipation, but they don't really want it, they merely pretend to. They're awfully cunning, dreadfully cunning!'

I was getting tired of this discussion. I was feeling sleepy, and turned over with my face to the wall.

'Yes, sir,' I heard as I was falling asleep, 'yes, sir! And who is to blame for it all, my dear sir? Why, our educational system! In our towns the whole system of woman's upbringing and education boils down to making her into a human beast, that is to making her attractive to the male so as to enable her to subdue him. Yes, sir,' Shamokhin went on with a sigh. 'What we want is a system of co-education, so that girls and boys should always be together. A woman must be educated so as to be always conscious, like a man, that she might be wrong; otherwise she always thinks she is right. Instil into the girl from a very early age that a man is not first and foremost a cavalier or a prospective husband, but a human being like her, her equal in everything. Train her to think logically, to draw general conclusions, and don't try to convince her that because her brain weighs less than a man's she can be indifferent to the sciences, the arts, and the problems of civilization in general.

A young apprentice to a shoemaker or to a house painter also has a smaller brain than a grown-up, yet he takes part in the general struggle for existence, he works and he suffers. We must also give up appealing to physiology, to pregnancy and childbirth, to bolster up our arguments, for in the first place a woman does not give birth every month, secondly, not all women have babies, and, finally, a normal countrywoman works in the fields up to the day of her confinement and is not a whit the worse for it. If a man offers a woman his chair or picks up her handkerchief, let her do the same for him. I don't mind if a girl of good family helps me on with my coat or hands me a glass of water. . . .'

I heard no more, for I fell asleep. Next morning the weather was unpleasant and damp as we were approaching Sebastopol. The boat rocked. Shamokhin sat on deck with me, sunk in thought and silent. Men with turned-up coat collars and women with pale, sleepy faces began going below as soon as the bell rang for tea. A young and very beautiful woman, the one who had been furious with the customs officers in Volochisk, stopped before Shamokhin and said to him, with the expression of a naughty pampered child:

'Jean, your little birdie has been seasick!'

Afterwards, in Yalta, I saw this beautiful woman on horseback, galloping so fast that two army officers could hardly keep pace with her. One morning I saw her in a pretty apron and Phrygian cap, sitting on the front and painting a seascape, with a large crowd admiring her from a distance. I too was introduced to her. She pressed my hand very warmly and, looking rapturously at me, thanked me in a sugary, sing-song voice for the pleasure I had given her by my writings.

'Don't believe her,' Shamokhin whispered to me. 'She hasn't read a thing of yours.'

As I was walking on the sea front one evening, I ran into Shamokhin; he had his arms full of large parcels of snacks and fruit.

'Prince Maktuyev is here,' he cried joyfully. 'He arrived yesterday with her brother, the spiritualist. Now I understand what she was writing to him about. Lord,' he went on, raising his eyes to the heavens and pressing his parcels to his breast, 'if she comes to an arrangment with the prince, it means freedom and I can go back to the country, to my father!'

And he rushed off.

'I'm beginning to believe in spirits,' he called to me, looking back. 'The spirit of Ilarion seems to have uttered a true prophecy. Oh, if only . . .'

The day after this meeting I left Yalta, and how Shamokhin's love affair ended I don't know.

The House with an Attic

(An Artist's Story)

THIS happened six or seven years ago, when I was living in one of the districts of the province of T— on the estate of Belokurov, a young landowner who used to get up very early in the morning, go about in a long, close-fitting, pleated peasant coat, drink beer in the evenings, and always complain to me that he never met with sympathy anywhere from anyone. He lived in a cottage in the grounds, and I in the mansion in a vast drawing-room with columns and without furniture except for a wide sofa on which I slept and a table on which I laid out games of patience. Here even on a calm day there was a strange roaring noise in the old Amos stoves, and during a thunderstorm the whole house shook and seemed about to split into pieces; this was rather alarming, especially at night when all the ten big windows were suddenly lit up by lightning.

Doomed as I was to perpetual idleness, I did absolutely nothing. I spent hours looking out of the window at the sky, the birds, the avenues, read everything that was brought to me from the post, and slept. Sometimes I left the house and went for walks till late at night.

One day, as I was returning home, I found myself by sheer chance on an estate I had never been to before. The sun was already low on the horizon and the evening shadows lay over the flowering rye. Two rows of very tall, closely planted old fir trees stood like solid walls, forming a beautiful dark avenue. I climbed easily over a hedge and walked along this avenue, slipping on the fir needles which lay an inch thick on the ground. It was still and dark, and only very high up, on the tops of the fir trees, the bright golden light of the setting sun shimmered and flecked the spiders' webs with the colours of the rainbow. There was a strong, over-powering smell of fir trees. Then I turned into a long avenue of lime trees. Here too were neglect and old age; last year's leaves rustled mournfully under my feet and shadows lurked between the trees in the twilight. On the right, in an old orchard, an oriole – an old lady, too, no doubt – was singing listlessly in a weak voice. But at last the lime trees, too, came to an end; I walked past a white house with a terrace and an attic, and suddenly there stretched before me a view of the courtyard, a large pond with a bathing pavilion, a cluster of green willows, and a village on the other side of the pond with a high, narrow belfry on which a cross glittered, reflecting the setting sun. For a moment I stood spell-bound and enchanted by something familiar, something that was very near and dear to me, just as though I had seen exactly the same landscape at some time in my childhood.

At the white stone gates, which led from the courtyard into the fields, at those ancient, sturdy gates adorned with lions, stood two girls. The older of the two, slender, pale, very pretty, with a great shock of chestnut hair and a small, obstinate mouth, had a very severe expression and scarcely took any notice of me; the other, a very young girl – she could not have been more than seventeen or eighteen – also pale and slender, with a large mouth and big eyes, looked at me with surprise as I passed by, said something in English, and was overcome with embarrassment; and it seemed to me that I had known those two charming faces, too, a long, long time. I returned home feeling as though I had had a delightful dream.

A few days later, about noon, Belokurov and I were walking near the house when quite unexpectedly a well-sprung light carriage drove into the yard, rustling over the grass, and in it was sitting one of the girls I had seen. It was the elder one. She had come with a subscription list in aid of peasants whose houses had been burnt down. Without looking at us, she told us very earnestly and in great detail the number of houses that had been burnt in the village of Siyanovo, the number of men, women, and children left homeless and what immediate steps the relief committee, of which she was a member, proposed to take. After giving us the list to sign, she put it away and at once began to take leave of us.

'You've quite forgotten us,' she said to Belokurov, as she shook hands with him. 'Do come, and if Mr — ' (she named me) 'would like to see how some of his admirers live and will come and see us, my mother and I will be delighted.'

I bowed.

When she had gone, Belokurov began to tell me about her. He said the girl was of a good family and her name was Lydia Volchaninov. The estate on which she lived with her mother and sister, like the large village on the other side of the pond, was called Shelkovka. Her father had occupied an important post in Moscow and had died with the rank of privy councillor. Though they were well-off, the Volchaninovs lived on their estate all the year round, both summer and winter. Lydia was a teacher at the rural council school in her village of Shelkovka and received a monthly salary of twenty-five roubles. She spent nothing but this money on herself and was proud of earning her own living.

'An interesting family,' said Belokurov. 'Why not pay them a visit one day? They would be very pleased to see you.'

One day after dinner, it happened to be a holiday, we remembered the Volchaninovs and went to Shelkovka to call on them. The mother and the two daughters were at home. The mother, Yekaterina Pavlovna, once evidently good-looking but now grown much too stout for her age, short-winded, melancholy, and absent-minded, tried to entertain me with conversation about art. Having heard from her daughter that I might call on them, she had hurriedly recalled two or three of my landscapes she had seen at exhibitions in Moscow and now asked what I had intended to express by them. Lydia, or, as she was called at home, Leda, spoke more to Belokurov than to me. Looking serious and unsmiling, she asked him why he did no work for the rural council and why he had not been at a single one of its meetings.

'It's not good enough,' she said reproachfully. 'Not good enough. You ought to be ashamed of yourself.'

'Quite true, Leda, quite true,' her mother agreed. 'It isn't good enough.'

'The whole of our district,' Lydia said, addressing me, 'is in the hands of Balagin. He himself is the chairman of the local board and he has filled all the posts in the district with his nephews and sons-in-law, and he does as he likes. We must fight him. The young people of the district must form a strong party – but you see what our young people are like. You ought to be ashamed of yourself, Mr Belokurov!'

While the affairs of the rural council were being discussed, Zhenya, the younger sister, said nothing. She took no part in serious conversations. She was not as yet considered grown up by the family, who still called her by her pet name of Missie, because that was what she had called her English governess when she was a little girl. She was all the time looking at me with curiosity, and when I was examining the photographs in the album, she explained to me: 'That's my uncle . . . that's my godfather,' passing a finger over the portraits, touching me with her shoulder like a child, so that I got a close view of her delicate, undeveloped breasts, her slender shoulders, her plait, and her slim body tightly drawn in at the waist by her sash.

We played croquet and tennis, went for a walk in the grounds, drank tea, then sat a long time over supper. After the huge, empty ballroom, I felt at ease in this small, cosy house in which there were no oleographs on the walls and the servants were treated with civility, and thanks to the presence of Leda and Missie everything seemed young and pure to me and everything had an air of decency. At supper Leda again talked to Belokurov about the rural council, Balagin, and school libraries. She was a vivacious and sincere girl who held strong views and who was interesting to listen to, though she talked a great deal too much and too loudly, but that was perhaps because she was accustomed to talking to school-children. Belokurov, on the other hand, retained from his days as a university student the habit of turning every conversation into an argument, and he spoke boringly, listlessly, and at great length, trying all too obviously to show what an advanced and clever man he was. Gesticulating, he upset a sauce-boat with his sleeve and a large pool formed on the tablecloth, but no one except myself seemed to notice it.

When we walked home it was dark and still.

'Good breeding is shown not by not upsetting a sauce-boat on a tablecloth, but by not noticing it if someone else does,' said Belokurov, with a sigh. 'Yes, a splendid, cultured family. I've lost touch with decent people — it's simply dreadful to be so out of touch! Always work, work, work!'

He went on to speak of the hard work that had to be done if one wanted to be a model farmer. But I thought: 'What a difficult, lazy fellow you are!' When he spoke of some serious matter, he drawled with a great effort, 'er — er — er'; and he did his work as he spoke — slowly, always late, never finishing anything at the right time. I had little faith in his business ability, if only because he carried about in his pockets for weeks the letters I gave him to post.

'What is so damnable,' he muttered as he walked beside me, 'is that however hard you work, you meet with no sympathy from anyone. No sympathy whatever.'

II

I began to visit the Volchaninovs frequently. I usually sat on the lower step of the terrace: I was depressed by a feeling of discontent with myself, I was sorry that my life was passing so rapidly and so uninterestingly, and I kept thinking how wonderful it would be to tear out of my breast the heart which had grown so heavy. On the terrace they were talking; I could hear the rustle of dresses and pages of a book being turned. I soon got used to the fact that during the day Leda received patients, gave out books, and often went to the village with a parasol over her bare head and in the evening talked loudly about the rural council and school. Every time the conversation turned on some serious subject, this slim, pretty, invariably severe girl said to me drily:

'You won't find this interesting.'

She did not like me. She did not like me because, being a landscape painter, I did not depict the hard life of the common people on my canvases, and because she thought I was indifferent to what she believed in so firmly. I remember once driving along the shore of Lake Baikal and meeting a Buriat girl on horseback, wearing a shirt and blue Chinese cotton trousers; I asked her to sell me her pipe and, while we were talking, she gazed contemptuously at my

European face and at my hat, and in a moment she got tired of talking to me and galloped off with a whoop. Leda too despised me as someone who was alien to her. She never outwardly showed her dislike of me, but I felt it and, sitting on the lower step of the terrace, I felt irritated and said that to treat peasants without being a doctor was to deceive them, and that it was easy to dispense charity when one was the owner of six thousand acres.

Her sister, Missie, had not a care in the world and, like myself, spent her life in complete idleness. As soon as she got up in the morning she took up a book and sat down to read on the terrace in a deep armchair, her feet hardly touching the ground, or hid herself with her book in the lime-tree avenue, or went through the gate into the fields. She read all day, eagerly scanning the pages, and only her tired and dazed eyes and the extreme pallor of her face showed that this reading overtaxed her brain. When I arrived, she would blush a little when she caught sight of me, put down her book, and, looking into my face with her big eyes, tell me eagerly what had happened in the house, for instance that the chimney had caught fire in the kitchen or that one of their servants had caught a big fish in the pond. On week-days she usually wore a white blouse and a dark blue skirt. We went for walks together, picked cherries for making jam, went for a sail in a boat, and when she jumped up to reach a cherry or plied the oars, her thin, weak arms showed through her wide sleeves. Or I would sketch and she would stand beside me and look on rapturously.

One Sunday at the end of July I called on the Volchaninovs at about nine o'clock in the morning. I walked about the park, keeping as far from the house as possible, looking for white mushrooms, which were very plentiful that summer, and placing marks near them so that I could gather them later with Zhenya. A warm breeze was blowing. I saw Zhenya and her mother, both in light Sunday dresses, coming home from church, Zhenya holding on to her hat to prevent it from blowing off. Then I heard them having tea on the terrace.

To a carefree person like me, trying to find an excuse for perpetual idleness, these Sunday mornings in our country houses in summer always had a particular attraction. When the green garden, still wet with dew, is all sparkling in the sun and looks happy, when the air near the house is full of the scent of mignonette and oleander, and the young people have just returned from church and are having tea in the garden, when all are so charmingly dressed and so gay, and when you know that all these healthy, well-fed, handsome people are going to do nothing all day long, you can't help wishing that life would always be like this. Now, too, I was thinking the same, and as I walked through the park I was ready to walk about like that, aimlessly, and do no work all day, all the summer.

Zhenya came out with a basket; she looked as if she knew or had a feeling that she would find me in the park. We gathered mushrooms and talked, and every time she asked me something she walked ahead of me so as to see my face.

'A miracle happened in the village yesterday,' she said. 'Lame Pelageya has been ill the whole year, no doctors or medicine did her any good, but yesterday an old wise-woman came and whispered over her, and her illness was gone.'

'That's nothing,' I said. 'You needn't look for miracles among the sick or among wise-women. Isn't health a miracle? And life itself? Everything we cannot understand is a miracle.'

'But aren't you terrified of what you cannot understand?'

'No, I'm not. Phenomena I do not understand I approach boldly. I do not submit to them. I am above them. Man must regard himself as higher than lions, tigers, and stars, higher than anything in nature, even higher than the things we do not understand and which seem miraculous to us, for otherwise he is not a man but a mouse, afraid of everything.'

Zhenya thought that, being an artist, I knew a lot and could divine correctly what I did not know. She longed for me to introduce her into the sphere of the eternal and the beautiful, into that higher world in which, as she imagined, I was quite at home, and she spoke to me of God, of eternal life, of miracles. And I, who refused to admit that myself and my imagination would perish for ever after death, would reply: 'Yes, men are immortal' or 'Yes, eternal life awaits us.' She listened and believed, and did not ask for proofs.

As we were going back to the house, she suddenly stopped and said:

'Our Leda is a remarkable person, isn't she? I love her very much, and I would gladly sacrifice my life for her any minute. But tell me,' she went on, touching my sleeve with her finger, 'tell me, why are you always arguing with her? Why are you so irritable?'

'Because she's wrong.'

Zhenya shook her head and tears came into her eyes.

'I can't understand it,' she said.

At that moment Leda, who had just returned from somewhere, was standing by the front steps with a riding-crop in her hand, slim and beautiful in the sunlight, giving orders to a farm labourer. Talking loudly and in a great hurry, she received two or three patients, then walked through the rooms with a preoccupied and businesslike air, opening one cupboard, then another, and then going up to the attic. They looked for her a long time to call her to dinner, but she only came after we had had our soup. For some reason I remember all these small details with affection. I remember the whole of that day vividly, though nothing particular happened. After dinner Zhenya read, reclining in her deep armchair, while I sat on the bottom step of the terrace. We were silent. The whole sky was covered with clouds, and soon it began to drizzle a little. It was hot, the wind had long dropped, and it seemed as if this day would never end. Yekaterina Pavlovna came out to us on the terrace, looking sleepy and carrying a fan.

'Oh, Mother,' said Zhenya kissing her hand, 'it's bad for you to sleep in the daytime.'

They adored each other. When one of them went into the park, the other would be sure to stand on the terrace and, looking in the direction of the trees, call out: 'Zhenya, come!' or 'Mummy, where are you?' They always said their prayers together, both had the same faith, and they understood each other perfectly even when they never uttered a word. Their approach to people was also the same. Yekaterina Pavlovna also soon got used to me and became attached to me, and when I did not come for two or three days she would send someone to find out if I were well. She too looked rapturously at my sketches and told me, as frankly and as volubly as Missie, everything that had happened while I was away, and often confided her domestic secrets to me.

She worshipped her elder daughter. Leda did not care for caresses and talked only about serious things; she lived her own life, and to her mother and sister was as sacred and somewhat enigmatic a figure as an admiral, always sitting in his cabin, is to sailors.

'Our Leda is a remarkable person, isn't she?' the mother would often say.

Now, too, when it was raining, we talked of Leda.

'She's a remarkable person,' said the mother, adding in a conspiratorial undertone as she looked around apprehensively: 'You wouldn't meet people like her if you were to scour the earth for them, though, you know, I'm beginning to be worried a little. The school, the dispensary, books – all this is very well, but why go to extremes? She's nearly twenty-four, you know, and it's time she began thinking seriously about her own future. Spending all her time with her books and dispensaries, she might not notice that life was passing her by. It's time she got married.'

Zhenya, pale from reading, and her hair in disarray, raised her head and said as though to herself, looking at her mother:

'Everything's in God's hands, Mummy!'

And again buried herself in her book.

Belokurov came, in his pleated peasant coat and embroidered shirt. We played croquet and tennis and then, when it grew dark, sat a long time over the supper table. Leda talked again about school and Balagin, who had got the whole district in his grasp. When I left the Volchaninovs that evening, I carried away the impression of a long, long, idle day and I thought sadly that everything came to an end in this world, however long it might be. Zhenya saw us to the gate, and perhaps because she had spent all day with me, from morning till night, I felt that without her life was rather dull and that all that charming family was near and dear to me; and for the first time that summer I felt that I wanted to paint.

'Tell me,' I said to Belokurov, as we walked home together, 'why is your life so dull and colourless? My own life is dull, hard, and monotonous because I am an artist, because I am a strange sort of fellow, because from my earliest days I've been harried by envy and dissatisfaction with myself, lack of belief in my work. I'm always poor, I'm a tramp; but you – you're a healthy, normal man, a landowner, a gentleman. Why do you live such an uninteresting life? Why do you take so little out of life? Why, for instance, haven't you fallen in love with Leda or Zhenya?'

'You forget that I love another woman,' replied Belokurov.

He was speaking of his mistress, Lyubov Ivanovna, who lived with him in the cottage. Every day I saw this lady, very stout, chubby-faced, dignified, looking like a fattened goose, walking about the garden in a Russian national dress and beads, always with a parasol over her head, and continually being called by a maid to a meal or tea. Three years ago she had rented one of the cottages in the grounds for the summer and had settled there with Belokurov, apparently for good. She was ten years older than he and she kept him so well in hand that he had to ask her permission every time he went out of the house. She often sobbed, in a man's voice, and I used to send word to her that if she did not stop I would have to give up my room, and she did stop.

When we got home, Belokurov sat down on the sofa and, knitting his brows, sank into thought, while I began pacing the room, overcome by a quiet feeling of unrest, as though I were in love. I wanted to talk about the Volchaninovs.

'Leda could only fall in love with a rural councillor as mad on hospitals and schools as she is herself,' I said. 'Oh, for such a girl one would gladly not only become a rural councillor, but wear out a pair of iron boots like the hero in the fairy-tale. And Missie? What a sweet girl that Missie is!'

Belokurov, drawling and interspersing his speech with 'er – er', embarked on a long-winded disquisition on the disease of the age – pessimism. He spoke confidently, in a tone that implied that I was disagreeing with him. Hundreds of miles of desolate, monotonous, parched steppe cannot make you feel so depressed as a man who sits and talks and talks and you don't know when he will get up to go.

'It isn't a question of pessimism or optimism,' I said, irritably. 'It's simply that ninety-nine men out of a hundred have no brains.'

Belokurov interpreted this as referring to himself, took umbrage, and went away.

'The prince is staying in Malozyomovo and sends you his regards,' said Leda to her mother, having just come back from somewhere and taking off her gloves. 'He told me lots of interesting things. Promised to raise the question of a medical centre in Malozyomovo at the meeting of the provincial council again, but he says there's not much hope.' And turning to me, she said: 'I'm sorry, I'm always forgetting that you can't find this very interesting.'

I felt irritated.

'Why not?' I asked, shrugging my shoulders. 'You don't care to know my opinion, but I assure you this question interests me very much.'

'Oh?'

'Yes. In my opinion, a medical centre in Malozyomovo is quite unnecessary.'

My irritation communicated itself to her; she looked at me, screwing up her eyes, and asked:

'What *is* necessary? Landscapes?'

'Landscapes aren't necessary, either. They don't need anything there.'

She finished taking off her gloves and opened the newspaper, which had just been brought from the post; a minute later she said quietly, evidently trying to restrain herself:

'Last week Anna died in childbirth; if there had been a medical centre there she would be alive now. It seems to me that even landscape painters ought to have some convictions on this point.'

'I have most definite convictions on this point, I assure you,' I replied, while she concealed herself behind the newspaper, as though not wishing to listen to me. 'In my opinion, medical centres, schools, village libraries and dispensaries, under present conditions, merely serve the cause of enslavement. The people are entangled in a great chain, and you are not cutting through the chain but merely adding new links to it – there you have my conviction.'

She raised her eyes, looked at me, and smiled sardonically, but I went on, trying to elucidate my main idea.

'What is important,' I said, 'is not that Anna died in childbirth, but that all these Annas, Mavras, and Pelageyas break their backs from morning till night, fall ill from work which is beyond their strength, are all their lives worrying over their sick and starving children, are all their lives afraid of death and disease, are all their lives looking for remedies for their illnesses, fade early, age early, and die in filth and stench. When they grow up, their children start the same thing all over again; and so centuries pass, and millions of people live worse than beasts, and all for a crust of bread — living in a state of continual fear. The whole horror of their situation is that they have no time to think of their souls, no time to remember that they've been created in the image of God. Hunger, cold, animal fear, never-ending toil, have, like avalanches of snow, barred their way to spiritual activities, to the very thing that distinguishes man from the dumb beast and makes life worth living. You go to their aid with hospitals and schools, but you don't free them from their fetters by that. On the contrary, you enslave them still more, for by introducing new standards into their life, you increase the number of their needs, not to mention the fact that they have to pay the rural council for their blister-flies and their books, and so are obliged to do more back-breaking work.'

'I'm not going to argue with you,' said Leda, putting down the paper. 'I've heard all this before, I will say only one thing: you can't just sit about and do nothing. It's true we are not saving humanity, and perhaps we make a great many mistakes; but we do all we can, and — we're right. The highest and most sacred task of civilized man is to serve his neighbours, and we try to serve them as best we can. You don't like it, but then one can't please everybody.'

'That's true, Leda,' said her mother, 'that's true.'

In Leda's presence she was always timid, glancing nervously at her when making some remark, afraid of saying something she shouldn't. She never contradicted her, but always agreed: 'True, Leda, true.'

'Peasant literacy,' I said, 'books full of all sorts of wretched precepts and stupid sayings, and medical centres, cannot reduce either their ignorance or their mortality rate. Just as the light from your window cannot light up this huge park. You give nothing by your interference in the lives of these people. You're merely creating new needs, a new reason for working.'

'But, good heavens, one has to do something, hasn't one?' said Leda with vexation, and from the tone of her voice it was clear that she regarded my arguments as worthless and contemptible.

'People must be freed from heavy physical labour,' I said. 'You have to lighten their burden. You have to give them a breathing-space, to make sure they don't spend their whole lives at the stove, at the wash-tub, or in the fields, but also have time to think of their souls, of God, to be given a chance to display their spiritual abilities in all sorts of fields. Every man's vocation lies in spiritual activity, in the constant search for truth and the meaning of life. Make hard physical labour unnecessary for them, give them the opportunity of feeling themselves free, and then you'll realize what a mockery these books and dispensaries are. Once a man becomes conscious of his real vocation, he can only be satisfied by religion, science, and art, not by these absurd trifles.'

'Free them from labour!' Leda said, with a sarcastic laugh. 'Do you really think that is possible?'

'Yes, I do. Take part of their labour on yourself. If all of us, town and country dwellers, all without exception, agreed to divide among ourselves the labour which mankind as a whole spends on the satisfaction of its physical needs, then each of us would have to work for no more than two or three hours a day. Imagine that all of us, rich and poor, worked only three hours a day and had the rest of the time free. Imagine, further, that to make ourselves more independent of our bodies, and to work still less, we invent machines to do our work for us and try to cut down our needs to a minimum. We should harden ourselves and our children so that they would no longer be afraid of hunger and cold and we shouldn't be constantly worrying about their health as Anna, Mavra, and Pelageya are. Imagine that we are no longer anxious about our health, that we don't keep dispensaries, tobacco factories, distilleries — what a lot of spare time we should have at our disposal! Then we should all be able to devote our leisure to science and art. As our peasants sometimes repair the roads by agreeing to share the work on a communal basis, so too we could all search for the truth of the meaning of life together on a communal basis, and

— I am quite sure of this — truth would be discovered very quickly. Man would rid himself of his constant, agonizing and oppressive fear of death, and even of death itself.'

'But you seem to contradict yourself,' said Leda. 'You say: science, science, and yet you deny the usefulness of literacy.'

'The literacy which makes it possible for a man to read sign-boards on pubs and occasionally books he doesn't understand — such literacy we have had since the days of Prince Rurik. Petrushka in Gogol's *Dead Souls* has long been able to read, and the country-side has remained practically the same as in Rurik's time. It isn't literacy we want, but freedom for the widest possible manifestation of our spiritual abilities. It isn't schools we need, but universities.'

'But you also deny the usefulness of medicine, don't you?'

'Yes. Medicine would be necessary only for the study of diseases as natural phenomena, not for their cure. If one must cure, then let us concentrate not on the treatment but on the prevention of disease. Do away with the main cause of disease, physical labour, and there will be no more diseases. I do not recognize the science that seeks to heal,' I continued excitedly. 'Real science and art aim not at temporary and private but at eternal and universal ends. They seek for the truth and the meaning of life, they search for God, for the soul, and when they are forced to deal with trivial, everyday affairs, with silly little dispensaries and silly little libraries, they only complicate and encumber life. We have plenty of doctors, pharmacists, and lawyers, in other words, plenty of literate people, but we have no biologists, mathematicians, philosophers, poets. All our intelligence, all our spiritual energy is spent on the satisfaction of temporary and transient needs. Scientists, writers, and artists are hard at work; thanks to them the comforts of life are increasing daily, our physical demands multiply, and yet we are still far from truth and justice, man still remains the most pre-datory and unclean of animals, and everything seems to point to the ultimate degeneration of mankind as a whole and the per-manent loss of man's will and ability to live. In such conditions the life of an artist is meaningless, and the greater his talent, the stranger and more incomprehensible his role, for on close examina-tion it appears that by supporting the existing order of things he is working merely for the entertainment of a predatory and unclean animal. And I don't want to work and I won't. . . . Nothing is wanted. Let the world go to blazes!'

'Missie, I think you'd better leave the room,' said Leda to her sister, apparently considering what I was saying harmful for a young girl.

Zhenya looked sorrowfully at her mother and sister and left the room.

'People usually say such charming things when they wish to justify their indifference,' said Leda. 'To deny the usefulness of hospitals and schools is easier than to cure or to teach.'

'True, Leda, true!' said her mother.

'You threaten to stop working,' Leda went on. 'You evidently think very highly of your work. Let's stop arguing; we shall never agree, anyway, for I consider the most imperfect of the libraries and dispensaries you spoke of so contemptuously just now far superior to all the landscape paintings in the world.' And turning abruptly to her mother, she went on in quite a different tone of voice: 'The prince has grown very thin and has changed very greatly since he was last here. They're sending him to Vichy.'

She was telling her mother about the prince so as not to talk to me. Her face was flushed, and to conceal her agitation she bent low over the table, as if she were shortsighted, and pretended to read the newspaper. I was out of favour. I said good-bye and went home.

IV

It was very still outside the house; the village on the other side of the pond was already asleep; not a single light was to be seen, and only the pale reflections of the stars glimmered faintly on the surface of the pond. At the gate with the lions Zhenya stood motionless, waiting for me.

'They're all asleep in the village,' I said to her, trying to descry her face in the darkness, and I saw her dark, mournful eyes fixed on me. 'The publican and the horse thieves are peacefully asleep, while respectable people like us irritate one another and argue.'

It was a sad August night, sad because autumn was in the air; the moon was rising from under a crimson cloud, faintly illuminating the road and the fields of winter corn on either side of it. Shooting stars fell frequently. Zhenya walked beside me along the road and tried not to look at the sky so as not to see the shooting stars, which for some reason frightened her.

'I think you're right,' she said, shivering in the slight damp night air. 'If people could all unite in devoting themselves to spiritual activities, they would soon find out everything.'

'Of course. We are higher beings, and if we were really conscious of the whole force of human genius and lived only for higher ends we should at last become like gods. But that will never happen. Mankind will degenerate, and there will not be a trace of genius left.'

We were out of sight of the gates; Zhenya stopped and shook hands with me hastily.

'Good night,' she said, shivering; her shoulders were only covered by a thin blouse and she shrank with cold. 'Come tomorrow.'

The thought of being left alone, irritated and dissatisfied with myself and other people, frightened me; and I too tried not to look at the shooting stars.

'Stay with me a little longer,' I said. 'Please.'

I loved Zhenya. I loved her perhaps because she met me and saw me off, because she looked at me so tenderly and with such rapture. Her pale face, her slender neck, her slender arms, her weakness, her idleness, her books – everything about her was so touchingly beautiful. And her mind? I suspected that she was quite exceptionally intelligent; I greatly admired the breadth of her views, perhaps because her ideas were so different from those of the severe and beautiful Leda, who disliked me. Zhenya liked me as an artist, I had conquered her heart by my talent, and I desired passionately to paint only for her; I dreamed of her as my little queen, who together with me would possess those trees, those fields, this mist, this sunset, this exquisite, wonderful countryside in the midst of which I had till now felt so hopelessly lonely and unwanted.

'Stay a little longer,' I begged her. 'I implore you.'

I took off my coat and put it over her shivering shoulders; afraid of looking ridiculous and uncomely in a man's coat, she laughed and threw it off, and at that moment I put my arms round her and covered her face, shoulders, and hands with kisses.

'Till tomorrow,' she whispered, and she embraced me softly, as though afraid of disturbing the stillness of the night.

'We have no secrets from one another, and I must tell my mother and my sister everything at once. Oh, I'm so terrified. Mother is all right, mother is fond of you, but Leda!'

She ran to the gates.

'Good-bye,' she called out.

For about two more minutes I heard her running. I did not want to go home, and there was no particular reason for going there. I stood still for a few minutes wondering what to do, then I walked back slowly to have another look at the house in which she lived, the dear, naïve old house, which seemed to be gazing at me with its attic windows, as with eyes, and understanding everything, I walked past the terrace, sat down on the seat near the tennis court, in the darkness under an old elm, and looked at the house from there. A bright light appeared in the windows of the attic in which was Missie's room, then it changed to a discreet green – the lamp had been covered with a shade. Shadows began to move about. . . . I was full of tenderness, calm, and satisfaction with myself, satisfaction at having been capable of being carried away and falling in love, and yet at the same time I felt uneasy at the thought that at this very moment, within a few yards of me, Leda lived in one of the rooms of this house, Leda who disliked and perhaps hated me. I sat there waiting for Zhenya to come out, straining my ears, and it seemed to me that I could hear people talking in the attic.

About an hour passed. The green light went out and I could see no more shadows. The moon now stood high above the house, lighting up the sleeping garden and the paths; the dahlias and the roses could be seen clearly in the flower-beds in front of the house, and all seemed to be of the same colour. It was getting very cold. I went out of the garden, picked up my coat on the way, and walked home slowly.

When next day after dinner I called on the Volchaninovs, the glass door into the garden was wide open. I sat down on the terrace, waiting for Zhenya to appear any moment from behind the flower-beds on the lawn or from one of the avenues of the park, or for the sound of her voice from one of the rooms. Then I walked into the drawing-room, the dining-room. Not a soul was to be seen. From the dining-room I walked along the long passage to the entrance hall and back. There were several doors in the passage and from behind one of them I could hear the voice of Leda.

'The crow ... a piece of ...' she was saying loudly and with frequent pauses between words (she was probably dictating Krylov's fable to someone), 'a piece of cheese ... had somewhere ... found ... Who's there?' she suddenly called out, hearing my steps.

'It's me.'

'Oh! I'm sorry I can't come out to you. I'm giving Dasha her lesson.'

'Is your mother in the garden?'

'No, she and my sister left this morning on a visit to our aunt in the province of Penza. I expect they'll be going abroad in the winter,' she added after a pause. 'The crow a piece of cheese ... had somewhere found ... Have you written it down?'

I went out into the hall and stood there staring vacantly at the pond and the village, and I could hear Leda dictating: '... A piece of cheese ... The crow a piece of cheese had somewhere found ...'

I left the estate by the road I had first taken, only the other way round: first from the courtyard into the garden, past the house, then along the lime-tree avenue. Here a small boy caught up with me and handed me a note. 'I told my sister everything, and she insists that we should never see each other again,' I read. 'I had not the strength to grieve her by disobeying. God grant you happiness – forgive me. If you only knew how bitterly my mother and I are crying!'

Then the dark fir avenue, the broken-down fence ... In the field where the rye had been in flower and the quail were calling there were now cows and hobbled horses. Here and there on the hills there was a bright green patch of winter corn. A sober, prosaic mood came over me and I was ashamed of all I had said at the Volchaninovs' and I felt bored with life once more. When I came home, I packed my things and left for Petersburg that evening.

I never saw the Volchaninovs again. Not so long ago I met Belokurov in the train on my way to the Crimea. He was still wearing the long, pleated peasant coat and an embroidered shirt, and when I asked him how he was he replied: 'Very well, thanks to your prayers.' We began talking. He had sold his estate and bought another smaller one in Lyubov Ivanovna's name. He had not much to tell me about the Volchaninovs. Leda still lived in Shelkovka and taught in the village school. She had gradually succeeded in gathering round her a circle of people who agreed with her ideas. Together they had formed a strong party, and at the last elections to the rural council they had 'blackballed' Balagin, who had till then held the whole district in the hollow of his hand. All Belokurov could tell me of Zhenya was that she did not live at home and that he did not know where she was.

I have almost forgotten the house with the attic, and it is only occasionally, while painting or reading, that for no apparent reason I suddenly remember the green light in the window, the sound of my footsteps when I walked home across the fields that night, in love and rubbing my cold hands. More rarely still, at moments when I am overcome by loneliness and am feeling sad, it all comes back to me rather vaguely and for some reason I begin to feel that she too remembers me, that she is waiting for me and that we shall meet one day. . . .

Missie, where are you?

Ionych

I

WHEN people who had lived only a short time in the town of S——
complained of boredom and the monotony of life there, the local
inhabitants, as though in self-justification, claimed that on the
contrary there was nothing wrong with S——, that it had a public
library, a theatre, a club, that balls were given there, and, last but
not least, that there were quite a number of intelligent, interesting,
and pleasant families with whom one could strike up an acquaintance. And they would point to the Turkin family as one of the
most cultivated and talented.

The Turkins lived in their own house in the main street, next
door to the Governor's official residence. Ivan Petrovich, a stout,
handsome, dark-haired man with side-whiskers, organized amateur
theatricals in aid of charity and played old generals, in which roles
he used to cough most amusingly. He knew a great many amusing stories, riddles, and proverbs, was fond of making jokes
and delivering himself of witticisms, and it was quite impossible to
tell whether he was serious or joking. His wife, Vera Yosifovna, a
thin, good-looking woman who wore a *pince-nez*, wrote stories and
novels which she was not at all reluctant to read aloud to visitors.
The daughter Yekaterina, a young girl, played the piano. In short,
each member of the family had some talent or other. The Turkins
gave their guests a cordial welcome and were only too glad to show
off their talents, which they did with the utmost frankness and
simplicity. Their big, stone-built house was spacious and cool in
the summer, half of its windows looked out on to an old shady
garden in which nightingales sang in the spring; when they had
visitors, knives made a terrific clatter in the kitchen, and the yard

was full of the smell of fried onions — all of which gave promise of an abundant and appetizing meal.

Dr Dmitry Ionych Startsev, too, when he was appointed rural district medical officer and took up his residence in Dyalizh, about five miles from S—, was told that as a cultured man he must make the acquaintance of the Turkins. One day in winter he was introduced to Mr Turkin in the street; they had a chat about the weather, the theatre, and the cholera epidemic, and an invitation followed. In the spring, on one of the church holidays — it was Ascension day — Startsev went to the town after surgery hours in search of relaxation and to do some shopping. He walked unhurriedly (he had not yet acquired a carriage and pair of his own), humming to himself the whole way:

'The tears I drained from life's bitter cup . . .'

In town he dined, took a walk in the park, and then, all of a sudden remembering Mr Turkin's invitation, he decided to call on the Turkins to see what kind of people they were.

'Good afternoon, how are you, please?' said Mr Turkin, meeting Startsev on the front steps. 'Delighted to see such a welcome visitor. Let me introduce you to my better half. I've told him, Vera,' he went on, after introducing the doctor to his wife, 'that he had no right under Roman Law to spend all his time at the hospital, that he had to dedicate his leisure hours to society. Don't you agree, darling?'

'Sit here, please,' said Mrs Turkin, inviting the visitor to sit beside her. 'You can flirt with me. My husband is as jealous as Othello, but we'll try to behave in such a way that he doesn't notice anything.'

'Oh, you sweet darling,' Mr Turkin murmured affectionately, imprinting a kiss on her forehead. 'You've called just at the right time,' he addressed the doctor again. 'My better half has just finished a hugely enormous novel, and she is going to read it aloud this evening.'

'Jean, my sweet,' Mrs Turkin said to her husband, '*dites que l'on nous donne du thé.*'

Startsev was then introduced to Yekaterina, a girl of eighteen, who looked amazingly like her mother and was just as thin and good-looking. Her expression was still childish, her waist slender and delicate, and her already fully developed virginal bosom, healthy and beautiful, held promise of spring, real spring. A little later they had tea with jam, honey, sweets, and very delicious pastries which melted in your mouth.

With the approach of evening, more visitors began to arrive, and to everyone of them Mr Turkin turned his smiling eyes and said:

'Good evening how are you, please?'

Then they all sat down in the drawing-room, looking very serious, and Mrs Turkin read them her novel. It began: 'The frost was getting harder. . . .' The windows were wide open, the knives made a terrific clatter in the kitchen, and there was an overpowering smell of fried onions. It was very restful sitting in the deep, soft armchairs, the candles blinked so enchantingly in the twilight of the drawing-room, and now, on a summer evening, when the sound of voices and laughter was coming from the street and the smell of lilac was blowing in from the garden, it was difficult to imagine how the frost was getting harder or how the setting sun's cold rays could be lighting up the snow-covered plain and the lonely wayfarer on the road. Mrs Turkin read how a beautiful young countess opened up schools, hospitals, and libraries on her vast estates, and how she fell in love with a wandering artist — read of things that never happened in life, and yet it was quite pleasant and comforting to listen to her, and such calm, delightful thoughts passed through one's mind — one simply did not want to get up.

'Not so horridiferous,' Mr Turkin said softly.

And one of the visitors, listening and carried far, far away in his thoughts, said in a scarcely audible voice:

'Yes . . . indeed . . .'

One hour passed, and another. In the park nearby a band was playing and a choir was singing. When Mrs Turkin closed her manuscript, they all sat in silence for five minutes listening to a folk song the choir was singing, which told them more of life than the novel they had just heard.

'Do you publish your works in periodicals?' Startsev asked Mrs Turkin.

'No,' she replied, 'I don't publish them anywhere. I write them and put them away in a cupboard. Why publish them?' she exclaimed. 'We're well enough off.'

And for some reason they all heaved a sigh.

'And now, Kitty, you play something,' said Mr Turkin to his daughter.

The lid of the grand piano was raised, the music books lying there in readiness were opened, and Yekaterina sat down and struck the keys with both hands; then she struck them again with all her might, and again and again; her shoulders and bosom shuddered, she went on striking the keys in the same place, and one could not help feeling that she would go on hitting the keys till she had driven them into the piano. The drawing-room filled with thunder; everything thundered – the floor, the ceiling, the furniture. Yekaterina was playing a difficult passage, interesting just because it was difficult, long and monotonous. Listening to it, Startsev imagined rocks falling from the top of a high mountain, falling and falling, and he wished they would stop falling quickly, while he found Yekaterina, rosy with the exertion, strong and energetic, a lock of hair falling over her forehead, very attractive indeed. After a winter spent in Dyalizh among peasants and patients, to be sitting in a drawing-room looking at this young, exquisite, and probably pure creature and listening to these noisy, tiresome, but none the less cultivated sounds, was as pleasant as it was novel.

'Well, Kitty, you played as never before tonight,' said Mr Turkin with tears in his eyes after his daughter had finished, and he quoted the words addressed to the Russian eighteenth-century playwright Denis Fonvisin: 'You can die now, Denis, you'll never write anything better!'

They all surrounded her, congratulated her, expressed their admiration, assured her that they had not heard such music for a long time, while she listened in silence, a faint smile playing on her lips, and her whole figure expressed triumph.

'Wonderful! Excellent!'

'Excellent!' Startsev said too, giving in to the general enthusiasm. 'Where did you study music?' he asked Yekaterina. 'At the conservatoire?'

'No, I'm only just now trying to get into the conservatoire. For the time being I'm taking lessons from Mrs Zavlovsky.'

'Were you at the secondary school here?'

'Oh, no,' Mrs Turkin replied for her, 'we had tutors for her at home. At a secondary school or at a boarding school there might be bad influences. While a girl is growing, she must be under the influence of her mother alone.'

'I'll go to the conservatoire all the same,' said Yekaterina.

'No, Kitty, you love your mother, don't you? Kitty won't do anything to grieve her mother and father, will she?'

'I will go, I will!' said Yekaterina, half in earnest and half in jest, stamping her little foot.

At supper Mr Turkin showed off his talents. He told funny stories, smiling only with his eyes, he showered witticisms, set humorous problems and solved them himself, spoke all the time in his peculiar lingo, acquired by long practice in trying to say something funny, which had obviously become second nature to him: hugely enormous, not so horridiferous, thanks ever so mustily. . . .

But that was not all. When the visitors, sated and contented, crowded in the entrance hall, sorting out their coats and sticks, the footman Pavel, or Pava as they called him, a boy of fourteen with a cropped head and chubby cheeks, used to bustle about them.

'Now then, Pava,' said Mr Turkin, 'perform!'

Pava struck a pose, raised one hand, and said in a tragic tone of voice :

'Die, unhappy woman!'

And everyone roared with laughter.

'Amusing!' thought Startsev, as he went out into the street.

He went to a restaurant, had some beer, and walked back to Dyalizh. All the way home, he hummed:

'Thy voice so tender and so langorous . . .'

After a five-mile walk he did not feel in the least tired as he went to bed. Indeed, he felt he could have walked another twelve miles with pleasure.

'Not so horridiferous,' he remembered as he dozed off, and laughed.

II

Startsev had been intending to visit the Turkins again, but he was kept so busy at the hospital that he could never find any time to spare. In this way over a year passed in work and solitude. Then one day a letter in a blue envelope arrived from the town.

Mrs Turkin had long suffered from migraine, but more recently, with Kitty threatening every day to leave for the conservatoire, her attacks had become more and more frequent. All the doctors in the town had called on the Turkins, and now at last came the turn of the rural district doctor. Mrs Turkin wrote him a moving letter in which she begged him to come and relieve her suffering. Startsev went, and after that visit he could be found often, very often, at the Turkins'. He did in fact help Mrs Turkin a little, and she was already telling all her visitors that he was an exceptional and a quite marvellous doctor. But he was not calling on the Turkins because of Mrs Turkin's migraine.

It was a holiday. Yekaterina had finished her long tedious exercises on the piano. Then they all sat for hours at the dining table drinking tea, and Mr Turkin was telling some of his funny stories. Then there was a ring at the front door and Mr and Mrs Turkin had to go out to meet some visitor. Startsev availed himself of the momentary confusion to whisper to Yekaterina in great agitation:

'For God's sake, don't torture me, I beg you, let's go into the garden.'

She shrugged her shoulders as though she were puzzled and did not understand what he wanted from her, but she got up and went out with him.

'You play the piano for three or four hours,' he said, following her, 'then you sit with your mother, and it's quite impossible to have a talk with you. Let me have just one quarter of an hour, I implore you.'

Autumn was approaching, and everything in the old garden was still and melancholy; dark leaves lay thick on the paths. The evenings were drawing in.

'I haven't seen you for a whole week,' went on Startsev, 'and if you knew how much that means to me. Let's sit down. Please, listen to what I've got to say.'

They had their favourite place in the garden: a seat underneath an old spreading maple tree. Now they sat down on that seat.

'What do you want?' asked Yekaterina in a cold, businesslike voice.

'I haven't seen you for a whole week, I haven't heard your voice for such a long time. I want to hear your voice passionately, I yearn for it. Please, speak.'

She entranced him by her freshness, by the innocent expression of her eyes and face. Even in the way she wore her dress he saw something extraordinarily charming, something that was touching in its simple and naïve grace. At the same time, notwithstanding this naïveté, she seemed to him very clever and extraordinarily intelligent for her age. He could talk to her about literature, art, or anything else, he could complain to her about life and people, though it did happen sometimes that in the middle of a serious conversation she would suddenly burst out laughing quite irrelevantly or run into the house. Like almost all the girls in S—, she read a lot. (Generally speaking, people in S— were not great readers, and the local librarians declared that but for the girls and young Jews the library might just as well be closed.) Startsev liked that very much and he used to ask her excitedly every time what she had been reading the last few days and listen entranced when she told him.

'What have you been reading this week since we last met?' he asked her now. 'Please, tell me.'

'I've been reading Pisemsky.'

'What exactly?'

'*A Thousand Souls,*' Kitty replied. 'What a funny patronymic Pisemsky had: Alexey Feofilaktych!'

'Where are you going?' Startsev cried in alarm, when she suddenly got up and went towards the house. 'I must have a talk with you. There's something I must say to you. At least stay with me for five minutes, I beg you!'

She stopped as if wishing to say something, then she thrust a note awkwardly into his hand and ran into the house, where she sat down at the piano again.

'Tonight at eleven o'clock,' read Startsev, 'be at the cemetery at Demetti's tomb.'

'Now, this isn't clever at all,' he thought, on recovering from his surprise. 'What has the cemetery to do with it? Why?'

It was quite clear: Kitty was making a fool of him. Who, indeed, would seriously think of asking a man to come to a rendez-vous at night in a cemetery a long way from town, when they could so easily have met in the street or in the park? And did it become him, a rural district doctor, an intelligent, respectable member of society, to play the love-lorn swain, to receive notes, to hang about cemeteries, to do all sorts of silly things which even school-boys would laugh at nowadays? What could this romance lead to? What would his colleagues say if they found out? So thought Startsev, as he wandered about among the tables in the club; but at half past ten he suddenly made up his mind and drove off to the cemetery.

He now had his own carriage and pair and a coachman called Panteleimon who wore a velveteen waistcoat. The moon was shining. It was still and warm, though only a warm night in autumn. In the suburb of the town, near the slaughterhouses, dogs were howling. Startsev left his carriage at the outskirts of the town, in a side-street, and walked to the cemetery. 'Everyone has his own idiosyncrasies,' he thought. 'Kitty is a strange girl, too, and – who knows? – perhaps she was not joking, perhaps she will come.' And he gave himself up to this feeble, vain hope and succumbed to its intoxicating spell.

For about half a mile he walked across a field. The cemetery could be seen like a dark strip in the distance, giving the impression of a wood or a large park. Then its white stone wall appeared and a gate. In the moonlight the inscription over the gate could be read: 'Behold, the hour is at hand.' ... Startsev went through the wicket gate, and the first thing he saw was a wide avenue lined with poplars, and white crosses and monuments on either side of it, all of them casting black shadows: all around and stretching far into the distance only black and white was visible, and the drowsy trees spread their branches over the white monuments. It seemed to be much lighter here than in the field; the paw-like leaves of the maples stood out sharply against the yellow sand of the avenues and the tombstones, and the inscriptions on the monuments were clearly visible. At first Startsev was struck by the fact that he was seeing something he had never seen before and would probably never see again: a world that was unlike any other world, a world in which the moonlight was as beautiful and as soft as though this were its cradle, a world where there was no life, none at all, but where in every dark poplar and in every grave one felt the presence of a mystery which held out the promise of a quiet, beautiful, and everlasting life. From the tombstones and the faded flowers and the autumnal smell of leaves there came a breath of forgiveness, sorrow, and peace.

All round was silence; the stars gazed from the sky in profound humility, and Startsev's footsteps sounded harsh and discordant. It was only when the church clock was striking the hour and he imagined himself dead and buried here for ever, that he had the odd feeling that someone was looking at him, and for a moment it occurred to him that this was not peace and stillness but the dull anguish of non-existence, suppressed despair. . . .

Demetti's tomb was in the form of a chapel with an angel on top of it. Many years before an Italian operatic company had passed through the town of S—, one of the singers had died and been buried there, and this monument had been erected in her memory. Nobody in the town remembered her any more, but the lamp over the entrance to her tomb reflected the moonlight and seemed to be burning.

There was no one there. And who would be coming to the cemetery at midnight? But Startsev waited, and waited ardently, as though the moonlight was merely inflaming his passion, and in his imagination he saw kisses, embraces. He sat beside the monument for half an hour, then took a walk through the side paths, his hat in his hand, waiting and wondering how many of the women and girls buried in those graves had been beautiful and fascinating, had loved, burning with passion at night as they yielded to the caresses of their lovers. What a silly joke mother nature really played on man, and how humiliating to be conscious of it! Startsev was thinking thus, but at the same time he felt like shouting aloud that he wanted love, that he waited for love, that he must have it at all costs; he no longer saw before him slabs of white marble but beautiful bodies, he saw shapes that hid bashfully in the shadows of trees, he felt their warmth, and this agony of unfulfilled desire was becoming unbearable. . . .

Suddenly it was as though a curtain had been lowered: the moon disappeared behind a cloud and everything around grew dark. Startsev could hardly find the gate, it was as dark as on an autumn night. Then he wandered about for an hour and a half looking for the side-street in which he had left his carriage.

'I'm so tired I can hardly stand,' he told Panteleimon. And as he got gratefully into his carriage, he thought: 'Oh, I've been putting on too much weight!'

III

The next day he went to the Turkins' in the evening to propose to Yekaterina. But he could not do it because Yekaterina was just then in her room having her hair done by her hairdresser. She was going to a dance at the club.

Startsev had once more to sit in the dining-room for a long time, having tea. Seeing that his guest was pensive, Mr Turkin took some notes out of his waistcoat pocket and read out a highly amusing letter from a German steward who had only an elementary knowledge of the Russian language.

'I expect they'll give her a pretty good dowry,' thought Startsev, listening abstractedly.

After his sleepless night he was in a state of stupefaction, just as though he had been given some sweet narcotic; there was an obscure but joyful and warm feeling in his heart, and yet a cold and heavy bit of his brain kept warning him to stop before it was too late. 'Is she a match for you? She is spoilt, capricious, sleeps till two in the afternoon, while you're a sacristan's son, a district doctor. . . .'

'Well, what about it?' he thought. 'Let her!'

'Besides,' the recalcitrant bit of his brain went on, 'if you marry her, her relations will make you give up your rural district job and open a practice in town.'

'Well, what's wrong with that?' he thought. 'Why not open a practice in town? They'll give her a good dowry and we'll set up house. . . .'

At last Yekaterina came in, wearing her low-cut ball dress and looking so sweet and lovely that Startsev could not take his eyes off her and was so enraptured that he could not utter a word, but just looked at her and laughed.

She began saying good-bye and, as there was no point in staying any longer, he got up, saying that he must go home as his patients were waiting for him.

'Well,' said Mr Turkin, 'if you must, you must; but you might as well give Kitty a lift to the club.'

It was dark and drizzling out of doors, and it was only from the sound of Panteleimon's cough that they knew where the carriage was. The hood of the carriage was raised.

'I go on the snow, you go on your toe,' said Mr Turkin as he helped his daughter into the carriage, 'he goes on his nose. Off with you. Good-bye, please!'

They drove off.

'I did go to the cemetery last night,' said Startsev. 'How ungenerous and cruel it was of you. . . .'

'You were at the cemetery?'

'Yes, and I waited for you almost till two o'clock. I suffered agonies . . .'

'You deserve to suffer, if you can't understand a joke.'

Yekaterina, pleased to have played such a clever trick on her admirer and to be loved so ardently, burst out laughing and suddenly uttered a cry of alarm, for at that very moment the carriage lurched violently as it turned sharply in at the club gates.

Startsev put his arm round Yekaterina's waist and in her fright she leaned against him. Unable to restrain himself, he kissed her passionately on the lips and chin and embraced her more tightly.

'That'll do,' she said coldly.

A moment later she was no longer in the carriage, and the policeman at the lighted entrance of the club began shouting in a repulsive voice at Panteleimon.

'What are you gaping at, fathead? Move on!'

Startsev went home, but was soon back. Wearing somebody else's frock coat and stiff white tie, which somehow seemed to pucker up and slip down from the collar, he was sitting at midnight in the drawing-room of the club, talking with great animation to Yekaterina.

'Oh, how little do those know who have never loved,' he said. 'It seems to me that no one has ever described love truthfully, and indeed I don't think it is possible to describe this tender, joyous, agonizing feeling; and anyone who has experienced it even once will never try to put it into words. Why waste time on introductions or descriptions? Why all this quite unnecessary eloquence? My love is boundless. I beg you,' Startsev brought out at last, 'I implore you to be my wife.'

'Dmitry Ionych,' said Yekaterina with an extremely serious expression, after thinking it over for a moment, 'Dmitry Ionych, I am very grateful to you for the honour, I respect you, but . . .' She got up and went on speaking standing up. '. . . but, I'm sorry, I cannot be your wife. Let's discuss it seriously. You know that I love art more than anything in the world; I love music madly, I adore it, I want to devote my whole life to it. I want to be an artist, I want fame, success, freedom. And you want me to go on living in this town, to carry on with this empty, useless life, which has become unbearable to me. To become a wife – no, thank you! A human being must aspire to some lofty, brilliant goal, and family life would bind me for ever. Dmitry Ionych,' she went on, with a hardly perceptible smile (in pronouncing 'Dmitry Ionych' she had remembered 'Alexey Feofilaktych'), 'Dmitry Ionych, you are a good, honourable, intelligent man, you're better than anyone I know. . . .' Here tears welled up in her eyes. 'I feel for you with all my heart, but – but I know you will understand. . . .'

And, not to burst into tears, she turned away and walked out of the drawing-room.

Startsev's heart was no longer beating uneasily. On going out of the club into the street he first of all tore off the tight collar and took a deep breath. He was a little ashamed, and his vanity was wounded, and he still could not believe that all his dreams, his agonies, and hopes, had petered out so stupidly, an ending worthy of a silly little play performed by some amateur company. But above all he pitied his feelings, this love of his, so much that he felt like sobbing or bringing his umbrella down with all his strength on Panteleimon's broad back.

For about three days he had not the heart to do anything, he neither ate nor slept, but when the news reached him that Yekaterina had gone to Moscow to enter the conservatoire he calmed down and carried on as before.

Afterwards, when he sometimes recalled how he had wandered

about the cemetery or how he had driven all over the town in search of a frock coat, he stretched lazily and said:

'What a fuss, to be sure!'

IV

Four years passed. Startsev had a big practice in the town. Every morning he received patients hastily at his surgery in Dyalizh, then he drove to his town patients, and he no longer drove in a carriage and pair but in a carriage drawn by a team of three horses with harness bells, and he returned home late at night. He put on weight and was no longer keen on walking, because he suffered from breathlessness. Panteleimon too put on weight, and the more he grew in breadth the more mournfully he sighed and complained of his bitter lot: this constant driving was getting too much for him!

Startsev visited many houses and met many people, but he did not strike up a close friendship with any of them. The townspeople exasperated him by their conversation, their views on life, and even by their appearance. Experience had gradually taught him that so long as one played cards or had a meal with any of them, the man was bearable, good-humoured, and even quite intelligent, but the moment one started talking about anything inedible, such as politics or science, for instance, he would either be completely at a loss or start airing views which were so stupid and spiteful that all one could do was give him up as a bad job and go away. When Startsev tried to talk even with a liberal-minded townsman, for instance, about the fact that mankind was progressing, thank God, and in time might carry on without passports and capital punishment, he would be met with a suspicious sidelong glance and the question: 'Do you mean to say that those people would be allowed to cut the throat of anyone they liked in the street?' And when at supper or at tea Startsev said in company that everyone had to work hard, for without hard work it was impossible to live, everyone interpreted it as a personal accusation and grew angry and began arguing heatedly. And yet these philistines did nothing, absolutely nothing, showed no interest in anything, and it was quite impossible to think of anything to talk to them about. Consequently Startsev avoided conversation; he just ate and played bridge with them, and when he happened to be in a house at some family celebration and was invited to dinner, he would sit down and eat in silence, staring at his plate; for all they said on these occasions was uninteresting, unjust, and stupid, and it inflamed and irritated him. But he never opened his mouth, and because he was always sternly silent and stared at his plate he was nicknamed in the town 'a stuck-up Pole', though there was not a drop of Polish blood in his veins.

He avoided such entertainments as the theatre and concerts, but he played bridge every evening for about three hours, and enjoyed it greatly. There was another occupation he greatly enjoyed, into which he was gradually and imperceptibly drawn – this was to draw out of his pockets in the evening the banknotes he had received during his rounds; and sometimes the notes, with which his pockets were stuffed – some green, some yellow, some smelling of scent, some of vinegar, incense, or blubber – amounted to about seventy roubles. When he had accumulated several hundred, he took them to the Mutual Credit Society and paid them into his current account.

During the entire four years following Yekaterina's departure he had been only twice at the Turkins', at the invitation of Mrs Turkin, who was still being treated for migraine. Yekaterina came to stay with her parents every summer, but he never saw her; somehow it just did not happen.

But the four years had passed, and one still, warm morning a letter was brought to the hospital. Mrs Turkin wrote that she missed Dr Startsev very much and she begged him to come and see her and alleviate her sufferings, particularly as it happened to be her birthday. At the bottom was a postscript: 'I join in Mother's request. K.'

Startsev thought it over and in the evening went to see the Turkins.

'Ah, good evening, how are you, please?' Mr Turkin greeted him, smiling with his eyes only. '*Bonjour* to you.'

Mrs Turkin, greatly aged and her hair gone grey, pressed Startsev's hand and sighed affectedly.

'Doctor,' she said, 'you don't want to flirt with me. You never come to see us, I suppose I must be getting too old for you.

But the young one has come back now and perhaps she'll be luckier.'

And Kitty? She had grown thinner, paler, more beautiful, and more graceful, but it was Yekaterina Ivanovna and not the old Kitty: her former freshness and the expression of childlike naïveté had gone. There was something new in her glance and manner, something timid and guilty, as though she no longer felt at home here in the Turkin house.

'It's ages since we met,' she said, holding out her hand to Startsev, and one could see that her heart was pounding uneasily; and looking intently and with curiosity at his face, she added: 'How stout you've grown! You're sunburnt and you've grown more mature, but on the whole you haven't changed much.'

Now, too, he found her attractive, very attractive, but something seemed to be missing in her now, though he could not say what it was, except that it was something that prevented him from feeling as he had felt before. He did not like her pallor, her new expression, her weak smile, her voice, and a few moments later he did not like her dress, the armchair in which she sat; there was something he disliked in the past when he had nearly married her. He remembered his love, the dreams and hopes that had agitated him years before, and he felt uncomfortable.

They had tea and jam tart. Then Mrs Turkin read her novel describing things that never happened in life. Startsev listened, looked at her beautiful grey head, and waited for her to finish.

'It isn't the person who can't write stories who is third-rate,' he thought, 'but the person who writes them and cannot conceal the fact.'

'Not so horridiferous,' said Mr Turkin.

Then Yekaterina played the piano, noisily and long, and when she had finished everyone thanked her for a long time and expressed their admiration of her.

'It's a jolly good thing I didn't marry her,' thought Startsev.

She looked at him, evidently expecting him to ask her to go into the garden, but he said nothing.

'Come, let's have a talk,' she said, walking up to him. 'How are you getting on? Has anything happened? How are things in general? I've been thinking of you all these days,' she went on nervously. 'I wanted to write to you, to go and see you in Dyalizh; and I was almost on the point of going, but I changed my mind – goodness only knows what you feel about me now. I felt so excited waiting for you today. Please, come into the garden.'

They went into the garden and sat down on the seat under the old maple tree, as they had done four years before. It was dark.

'How are you?' asked Yekaterina.

'I'm quite all right, thank you,' replied Startsev.

He could not think of anything more to say. Neither of them spoke for a while.

'I'm so excited,' said Yekaterina, covering her face with her hands, 'but take no notice, please. I'm so happy at home, so glad to see everyone, and I can't get used to it. So many memories! I thought you and I would have so many things to talk about that we'd go on talking all night.'

Now he could see her face closely, and her shining eyes, and here in the dark she seemed younger than in the room and even her former childlike expression seemed to have come back. And indeed she gazed at him with naïve curiosity, as though she wished to examine him more closely, so as to be able to understand the man who had loved her so ardently, so tenderly, and so unhappily. Her eyes thanked him for that love. He too remembered everything that had happened, everything to the smallest detail, how he had wandered about the cemetery, how he had gone home in the morning feeling terribly exhausted, and he suddenly felt a sadness and pity for his past. And a little flame was kindled in his soul.

'Do you remember how I gave you a lift to the party at the club?' he said. 'It was raining then, it was dark. . . .'

The flame in his soul was getting bigger, and he was already beginning to feel like talking, like telling her how he regretted the sort of life he led.

'Oh dear,' he said with a sigh, 'you ask me how I live? How do we all live here? We don't. We grow old, put on weight, let ourselves go. The days are flying and passing, life passes drearily, without impressions, without thoughts. . . . During the day you make money, the evenings you spend at the club in the company of card-players, alcoholics, raucous argumentative fellows whom I detest. What's good about such a life?'

'But you have your work, a noble aim in life. You used to like talking about your hospital so much. I was such a funny girl then. I fancied myself a great pianist. Today all young ladies play the piano, and I, too, played it like the rest, and there was nothing special about me. I am as much a pianist as my mother is a novelist. Naturally, I didn't understand you then, but afterwards, in Moscow, I often thought of you. I thought of no one but you. How wonderful to be a rural district doctor, to help sufferers, to serve the people. How wonderful!' repeated Yekaterina, rapturously. 'When I thought of you in Moscow, you seemed to me to be such a perfect, such an ideal person. . . .'

Startsev remembered the banknotes he took out of his pockets with such a feeling of satisfaction every evening, and the flame in his soul went out.

He got up to go back to the house. She took his arm.

'You're the best person I have ever known,' she went on. 'We'll see one another and talk, won't we? Promise! I am not a concert pianist. I am no longer under any illusions about myself and I won't play or talk about music when you are there.'

When they went into the house and in the light of the lamps Startsev saw her face and her sad, grateful, searching eyes looking at him, he felt uncomfortable and thought again :

'What a jolly good thing I didn't marry her!'

He got up to take his leave.

'You have no right under Roman law to leave before supper,' said Mr Turkin, as he saw him off. 'It's highly perpendicular on your part. Now then,' he said, turning to Pava in the hall, 'perform!'

Pava, no longer a boy but a young man with a moustache, struck a pose and declaimed in a tragic voice:

'Die, unhappy woman!'

All this irritated Startsev. Getting into his carriage and looking at the dark house and garden, which had once been so dear and precious to him, everything came back to him in a flash – Mrs Turkin's story, Kitty's noisy playing, Mr Turkin's witticisms, and Pava's tragic pose; and he could not help thinking that if the most talented people in the town were such mediocrities, then what could be expected of the town as a whole?

Three days later Pava brought a letter from Yekaterina.

'You don't come to see us,' she wrote. 'Why not? I am afraid you have changed towards us. I am afraid, and the very thought frightens me. Please, put my mind at rest. Come and tell me that everything is all right. I must talk to you. Yours, Y.T.'

He read the letter, thought it over, and said to Pava:

'Tell them I can't come today, my good fellow. I'm very busy. Tell them I shall probably call in about three days.'

But three days passed, a week passed, and still he did not go. Some time later, driving past the Turkin house, it occurred to him that he really ought to call, if only for a short time; but – he did not call.

He never called on the Turkins again.

V

A few more years passed. Startsev put on more weight, he was very fat and short of breath and had to walk about with his head thrown backwards. When he drove about, red-faced and corpulent, in his carriage drawn by three horses, harness bells jingling, with Panteleimon also red-faced and corpulent sitting on the box, holding his arms straight in front of him as if they were made of wood and shouting 'Keep to the r-r-right!', the overall picture was quite an impressive one and it seemed that it was not a human being but an idol driving past.

He had so large a practice in the town now that he had not a moment for himself; he had a country estate and owned two houses in the town, and had his eyes on a third one that was likely to bring in more money. Whenever he heard in the Mutual Credit Society of a house for sale at a public auction, he would enter it without ceremony and, passing through all the rooms and paying no attention to the half-dressed women and children, who looked at him with astonishment and alarm, would jab the door with his stick and say, breathing heavily and mopping the perspiration from his brow, 'Is this the study? Is this the bedroom? And what room is this?'

He had a great many things to take care of, but he still did not give up his rural district job: his greed had got the better of him and he wanted to get as much as he could in Dyalizh as well as in the town. In both places he was now known simply by his patronymic of Ionych. 'Where's Ionych off to?' or 'Shouldn't we call in Ionych for a consultation?'

Possibly because his throat had grown so fat, his voice had changed and become shrill and harsh. His character too had changed: he had become irritable and hard to get on with. In receiving patients he would get cross, bang his stick on the floor impatiently, and shout in his unpleasant voice:

'Please answer my questions! Don't chatter!'

He has remained a bachelor. His life is dull, nothing interests him.

During the whole of his life in Dyalizh his love for Kitty has been his only and, perhaps, his last joy. In the evenings he plays cards at the club and then sits all by himself at a big table and has supper. Ivan, the oldest and most respected of the club's servants, waits on him. He usually has Lafitte 17 at his meals, and everyone in the club, from the manager to the chef and the footman, knows his likes and dislikes and tries hard to please him, for otherwise he might fly into a rage and start banging his stick on the floor.

When having his supper, he sometimes turns round and joins in some conversation.

'Who is it you're talking about? Oh, I see.'

And when at some nearby table the conversation happens to turn on the Turkins, he asks:

'What Turkins are you talking about? You mean those whose daughter plays the piano?'

That is all there is to say about him.

And the Turkins? Mr Turkin has not aged or changed in any way and he still goes on cracking his jokes and telling his funny stories. Mrs Turkin still reads her novels to her visitors as readily as ever and with the same heartfelt simplicity. Kitty plays the piano for about four hours every day. She has grown perceptibly older, is ailing, and goes to the Crimea every autumn with her mother. Seeing them off, Mr Turkin wipes away his tears as the train draws out of the station, and shouts:

'Good-bye, please!'

And waves his handkerchief.

The Darling

OLGA, the daughter of the retired middle-grade civil servant Plemyannikov, was sitting on the steps of her house leading to the yard, lost in thought. It was a hot day. The flies were making an awful nuisance of themselves, and it was pleasant to think that evening was not far off. Dark rain-clouds were gathering in the east, and from time to time there came a breath of moisture in the air from that direction.

Kukin, manager and proprietor of the amusement park Tivoli, who lived in a wing of the house, was standing in the middle of it and looking at the sky.

'Again!' he cried in despair. 'It's going to rain again! Every day it rains, every day, as though on purpose! It's the end! It's ruin! Terrible losses every day!'

He threw up his hands in despair, and turning to Olga he went on:

'That's what my life is like, my dear Olga. Enough to make you weep. You work, you do your best, you wear yourself out, you lie awake at night, always thinking how to improve things – and what happens? On the one hand, the public – ignorant savages. I give them the best musical comedies, dramatized fairy stories, first-class comics, but do you think they want it? Do they appreciate it? All they want is sideshows! All they ask for is vulgarity! On the other hand, look at the weather! Almost every day it rains. It started coming down in buckets on the tenth of May and it rained the whole of May and June. It's simply awful! No business, but I have to pay the rent just the same, haven't I? Paying the actors, aren't I?'

The next evening the clouds gathered again, and Kukin cried, laughing hysterically:

'Well, what do I care? Let it rain! Let it flood the park, damn me! Damn my luck in this world and the next! Let the actors sue me! I don't mind going to court. I don't mind going to prison! To Siberia! To the scaffold! Ha, ha, ha!'

The next day the same thing. . . .

Olga listened to Kukin in silence. She looked serious, and sometimes tears started in her eyes. In the end Kukin's misfortunes touched her and she fell in love with him. He was small and thin, with a yellow face, his curly hair combed back at the temples; he spoke in a thin falsetto, and when he talked his mouth became twisted; his face always wore an expression of profound despair; and yet he aroused a deep and genuine feeling in her. She was always in love with someone and could not live without it. When she was a young girl she had loved her daddy, who now sat in a darkened room in an invalid chair, gasping for breath; she had loved her auntie, who sometimes used to come to visit them twice a year from Bryansk; earlier still, as a schoolgirl, she had been in love with her French master. She was a quiet, good-natured, compassionate girl, with gentle, soft eyes and excellent health. Looking at her full rosy cheeks, her soft white neck with a dark mole on it, her kind, naïve smile, which came into her face when she listened to anything pleasant, men thought 'Yes, you'll do!' and also smiled, while women visitors could not restrain themselves from catching hold of her hand suddenly in the middle of a conversation and declaring in a transport of delight:

'Oh, you darling!'

The house in which she had lived since she was born and which was left to her in her father's will was on the outskirts of the town in Gipsy Lane, not far from the Tivoli; in the evenings and at night she could hear the band playing in the park, the hissing and banging of the fireworks, and she could not help thinking that it was Kukin fighting with his fate and taking his chief enemy – the public – by storm; her heart thrilled at the thought, she did not feel like sleeping at all, and when he came back home early in the morning, she tapped softly at her bedroom window and, showing him only her face and one shoulder through the curtains, smiled tenderly at him. . . .

He proposed to her and they were married. And when he had had a good look at her neck and her robust, plump shoulders, he threw up his hands and said:

'Oh, you darling!'

He was happy, but as it never stopped raining on his wedding day and on his wedding night, the expression of despair never left his face.

They lived well after their wedding. She sat in the box-office, saw that everything in the park was in excellent order, kept an account of the expenses, and paid the wages. Her rosy cheeks and her charming, naïve, radiant smile could be seen now at the box-office window, now behind the scenes, now in the refreshment bar. And already she was telling her friends that the theatre was the most remarkable, the most important, and the most necessary thing in the world, and that it was only in the theatre that one could obtain true enjoyment and become truly educated and humane.

'But,' she added, 'do you think the public realizes this? All they want is a sideshow! Yesterday we gave *Faust Inside Out*, and almost all the boxes were empty. But if Vanya and I had put on some vulgar rubbish, then, I assure you, the theatre would have been packed. Tomorrow Vanya and I are putting on *Orpheus in Hell*. Do come.'

Whatever Kukin said about the theatre and the actors she repeated. Like him, she despised the public for their ignorance and indifference to art, interfered at the rehearsals, corrected the actors, looked after the good behaviour of the musicians; and when a bad notice appeared in the local paper, she cried and then went to the editorial office to demand an explanation.

The actors were fond of her and nicknamed her 'Vanya and I' and 'darling'; she was sorry for them, lent them small sums of money, and if they happened to deceive her she did not complain to her husband but only shed a few tears in secret.

In winter too they lived well. They rented the theatre in the town for the winter season and let it for short periods to a Ukrainian company, to a conjurer, or to local amateurs. Olga was growing stouter and was always beaming with pleasure, while Kukin grew thinner and yellower and complained of their terrible losses, although they had not done at all badly all the winter. He coughed at night, and she made him drink hot raspberry tea and lime-flower water, rubbed him with eau-de-Cologne and wrapped him in her soft shawls.

'Oh, my sweet,' she used to say with complete sincerity, stroking his hair. 'Oh, my handsome one!'

During Lent he left for Moscow to engage actors, and she could not sleep without him. She sat at the window and gazed at the stars. All that time she compared herself to the hens who also cannot sleep at night and feel uneasy when the cock is not in the hen-house. Kukin had to stay longer in Moscow; he wrote that he would be back at Easter and was already giving instructions in his letters about the Tivoli. But late at night on the Sunday before Easter there was an ominous knocking at the gate. Someone was hammering on the gate as though on a barrel: boom! boom! boom! The sleepy cook ran to open the gate, splashing through the puddles with her bare feet.

'Open up, please,' someone was saying in a hollow voice. 'There's a telegram for you.'

Olga was used to getting telegrams from her husband, but this time for some reason she was paralysed with fear. With shaking hands she opened the telegram, and read as follows: 'Kukin died suddenly today stop metely awaiting instructions stop guneral tuesday.'

That was how it was actually written in the telegram, 'guneral', and some incomprehensible word, 'metely'. It was signed by the producer of the operetta company.

'Oh, my darling!' Olga sobbed. 'My sweet little Vanya, my darling! Why did I ever meet you? Why did I know you and love you? Who have you left your poor unhappy Olga to?'

Kukin was buried in Moscow on Tuesday. Olga returned home on Wednesday, and as soon as she got into her bedroom she flung herself on the bed and sobbed so loudly that it could be heard in the street and in the neighbouring yards.

'The darling!' the neighbours said, crossing themselves. 'Poor darling, how she does take on!'

Three months later Olga was returning home from mass, heart-broken and in deep mourning. It so happened that one of her neighbours, Vasily Andreyich Pustovalov, who was also returning home from church, walked beside her. Pustovalov, the manager of the merchant Babakayev's timber yard, who wore a straw hat, a white waistcoat, and a gold watch-chain, looked more like a land-owner than a business man.

'Everything,' he said gravely, with a note of compassion in his voice, 'happens according to the natural order of things. If any of your dear ones dies, it is because it is the will of God. In such a case we must be brave and bear our cross without a murmur.'

After seeing Olga to her gate, he said good-bye and walked on. All day afterwards she could hear his grave voice and she had only to shut her eyes to see his dark beard. She liked him very much. And apparently she had made an impression on him too, for a few days later an elderly woman whom she did not know very well came to have a cup of coffee with her, and as soon as she sat down at the table she began talking about Pustovalov. According to her, he was a most excellent man, whom one could depend on and whom any girl would be glad to marry. Three days later Pusto-valov paid her a visit himself. He did not stay long, about ten minutes, and did not say much, but Olga fell in love with him so passionately that she did not sleep a wink all night, tossing about as though in a fever; and in the morning she sent for the elderly woman. Soon they were engaged, and then came the wedding.

After their marriage Pustovalov and Olga lived happily together. He was usually at his office till dinner time, then he went out on business and his place at the office was taken by Olga, who was there till the evening, making out accounts and seeing to the delivery of the goods.

'The price of timber,' she would say to her acquaintances and customers, 'rises twenty per cent every year now. Why, we used to sell local timber, and now every year my Vasily has to go for timber to the Mogilyov province. And the freight!' she cried, covering her cheeks with her hands in horror. 'The freight!'

It seemed to her that she had been in the timber business for years, and that the most important and necessary thing in life was timber; and there was something dearly familiar and touching to her in the sound of the words beam, block, board, balk, plank, slat, scantling, batten, slab. . . . At night, when she was asleep, she dreamt of mountains of planks and boards, long, endless strings of wagons carting timber somewhere far from the town; she dreamt of a whole regiment of six-inch beams, twenty-eight feet high, standing on end and marching on the timber yard; beams, logs, and boards knocking against each other with the resounding crash of dry wood, falling and getting up again and piling themselves on each other. Olga cried out in her sleep, and Pustovalov said to her tenderly:

'What's the matter, Olga darling? Cross yourself, my dear.'

Her husband's ideas were her ideas. If he thought the room was too hot or business was slack, she thought the same. Her husband did not care for any diversions and spent the holidays at home. She did the same.

'Why are you always at home or at the office?' her friends asked her. 'Why don't you go to the theatre, darling, or to the circus?'

'Vasily and I have no time to go to the theatre,' she replied gravely. 'We are working folk. We can't waste time on all sorts of nonsense. What's the good of theatres?'

On Saturdays Pustovalov and Olga used to go to evening service, on holy days to early mass, and they walked side by side on the way back from church, an unctuous expression on their faces. There was a nice smell about both of them, and her silk dress rustled pleasantly. At home they drank tea with buns and various jams, and afterwards they ate pie. Every day at noon there was a lovely smell of beetroot soup and roast mutton or duck in the yard and in the street near the gate, and of fish on fast days, and it was impossible to walk past the gate without feeling hungry. At the office the samovar was always on the boil, and customers were treated to tea and ring-shaped rolls. Once a week husband and wife went to the baths and returned side by side, both red in the face.

'Oh, we're very happy, thank God,' Olga used to say to her acquaintances. 'God grant everyone such a life!'

When Pustovalov was away buying timber in the Mogilyov province, Olga missed him very much and lay awake at night and cried. A young army veterinary surgeon called Smirnin, who rented the cottage in the yard, sometimes came to see her in the evenings. He used to tell her all sorts of stories and played cards with her, and this used to divert her. His stories of his private life were particularly interesting; he was married and had a son, but was separated from his wife, who had been unfaithful to him, and now he hated her and sent her forty roubles a month for the maintenance of their son. Hearing this, Olga sighed and shook her head. She was sorry for him.

'Well, God preserve you,' she used to say, seeing him off to the stairs with a lighted candle. 'Thank you for helping me to while away the time, and may the Lord and the Mother of God keep you in good health.'

And she always expressed herself with the utmost gravity and soberness, in imitation of her husband. Before the veterinary surgeon disappeared downstairs behind the door, she used to say:

'I think you really ought to make it up with your wife, Mr Smirnin. You ought to forgive her, if only for the sake of your son. I suppose the poor little boy understands everything.'

When Pustovalov came back, she told him in a low voice all about the veterinary surgeon and his unhappy family life, and both of them, owing to some strange association of ideas, went down on their knees before the icons, prostrating themselves and praying that God should give them children.

The Pustovalovs lived like that in peace and quiet, in love and complete concord, for six years. But one winter day, after drinking hot tea at the office, Vasily went out into the yard without his cap to see to the loading of some timber, caught a cold, and was taken ill. He was attended by the best doctors, but his illness did not respond to treatment and he died after having been ill for four months. And Olga was once more a widow.

'Who have you left me to, my darling?' she sobbed, after burying her husband. 'How can I live without you, unhappy wretch that I am! Take pity on me, good people, left with no one in the world to care for me!'

She went about in a black dress with long *pleureuses*, and gave up wearing a hat and gloves for good. She seldom went out of the house, except to go to church or to pay a visit to her husband's grave, leading the secluded life of a nun. It was not till six months later that she took off the *pleureuses* and opened the shutters of the windows. Sometimes she could even be seen in the morning, but how she lived and what went on in her house no one really knew. People did surmise something from the fact that they could see her, for instance, having tea in her garden with the veterinary surgeon, who read the newspaper to her, and also from the fact that on meeting a woman she knew at the post office she said:

'We haven't any proper veterinary inspection in our town, and that's why there are so many illnesses about. One is always hearing of people falling ill from drinking milk or catching some illness from horses and cows. One really ought to take as much care of the health of animals as of the health of people.'

She was repeating the veterinary surgeon's ideas and now she was of the same opinion as he about everything. It was clear that she could not live a single year without some attachment and that she had found new happiness in the wing of her own house. Anyone else would have been condemned for that, but no one could think ill of Olga, for everything about her was so natural. Neither she nor the veterinary surgeon said anything to anyone about the change in their relationship. They tried to conceal it, but without success, for Olga could not keep a secret. When she handed round tea or served supper to his visitors, fellow-officers of his regiment, she would begin talking about foot-and-mouth disease or tuberculosis among the cattle, or about the municipal slaughter-houses, while he looked terribly embarrassed; and after the visitors had gone he would seize her by the arm and hiss angrily:

'I've told you a hundred times not to talk about something you don't understand. When we vets are talking among ourselves, please don't interfere. Why, it's just silly!'

She would look at him with astonishment. 'But what am I to talk about, darling?' she would ask him in dismay.

And she would embrace him with tears in her eyes, imploring him not to be angry with her, and they were both happy.

This happiness, however, did not last long. The veterinary surgeon left with his regiment, left for good, for the regiment had been transferred somewhere very far away, almost as far as Siberia; and poor Olga was left alone.

Now she was absolutely alone. Her father had long been dead, and his armchair lay in the loft covered with dust and minus one leg. She grew thinner and not so good-looking, and people meeting her in the street no longer gazed at her as before and did not smile at her; her best years were apparently over, left behind her, and now a new kind of life was beginning, an inscrutable kind of life that did not bear thinking about. In the evening poor Olga sat on the front steps and she could hear the music in the Tivoli gardens and the banging of fireworks, but this no longer stirred up any thoughts in her mind. She gazed apathetically at her empty yard, thinking of nothing, desiring nothing, and afterwards, after nightfall, she went to bed and saw nothing but her empty yard in her dreams. She ate and drank as though against her will.

But the main thing, and what was worst of all, was that she had no opinions of any kind. She saw all sorts of things around her and she understood everything that was happening around, but she could form no opinions about anything and did not know what to talk about. Oh, how dreadful it is not to have any opinions! You see a bottle, for instance, or the rain, or a peasant, and you cannot say what they are there for, and you could not say it even for a thousand roubles. When married to Kukin or to Pustovalov, or when living with the vet, Olga could have explained everything and would have expressed an opinion about anything you like, but there was the same emptiness in her thoughts and in her heart as in her yard. And it was as frightening and as bitter as if she had supped on wormwood.

The town was gradually spreading in all directions. Gipsy Lane was already called a street, and where the Tivoli and the timber yard had been there were houses and a whole row of side-streets. How quickly time flies! Olga's house grew dingy, its roof got rusty, the shed rickety, and the whole yard was overgrown with weeds and stinging-nettles. Olga herself had aged terribly and had lost her good looks; in summer she sat on the steps, and as before she felt empty and bored and there was a bitter taste in her mouth; and in winter she sat at the window and looked at the snow. When spring was in the air or when the sound of church bells came floating on the wind, she would be suddenly overwhelmed by memories of her past, a delightful thrill would shoot through her heart and a flood of tears gush out of her eyes; but that lasted only for a short time, and then there was the same feeling of emptiness and again she wondered what she was living for. Her black cat Bryska rubbed against her, purring softly, but Olga remained unmoved by these feline caresses. It was something else she wanted. What she wanted was a love that would seize her whole being, her whole mind and soul, that would give her ideas, an aim in life, and would warm her ageing blood. And she would shake the cat off her skirt and say with vexation:

'Go away, go away . . . I don't want you!'

And so it went on, day after day, year after year – no joy of any kind and nothing to express an opinion about. Whatever her cook Mavra said was all right with her.

Late in the afternoon one hot July day, just as the herd of cattle was being driven along the street and the whole yard was full of dust, someone suddenly knocked at the gate. Olga went to open it herself, and she gazed thunderstruck at the visitor; it was Smirnin, the veterinary surgeon. His hair had gone quite grey and he wore civilian clothes. She suddenly remembered everything and, unable to restrain herself, burst into tears and put her head on his chest without uttering a word; and in her great excitement she never noticed how they both went into the house or how they sat down to tea.

'Oh, my dear,' she murmured, trembling with joy, 'what has brought you here?'

'I'd like to settle here for good,' said the vet. 'I've resigned from the army, and I've come to try my luck as my own master and open a practice of my own. Besides, it's time for my son to go to a secondary school. He's a big boy now. I've made it up with my wife, you know.'

'Where is she?' asked Olga.

'She's at the hotel with our son. I'm looking for a flat.'

'But, good heavens, why not take my house? It's a good enough place to live in. I won't charge you any rent!' cried Olga excitedly and burst into tears again. 'You can live here, the cottage will do nicely for me. Oh dear, I'm so happy!'

Next day the roof was already being painted and the walls whitewashed and Olga, arms akimbo, was walking about the yard giving orders. Her face lit up with her old smile, she brightened up and looked younger, as though she had awakened from a long sleep. The vet's wife arrived – a thin, plain woman with short hair and a capricious expression. With her was her little boy,

Sasha, small for his age (he was nine years old), with bright blue eyes, chubby, and with dimples in his cheeks. As soon as the boy walked into the yard he ran after the cat, and immediately the place resounded with his gay, joyful laughter.

'Is that your cat, auntie?' he asked Olga. 'When she has kittens, let's have one, please. Mummy is terribly afraid of mice.'

Olga had a long talk with him, gave him tea, and her heart suddenly went out to him just as though he were her own son. And when he sat in the dining-room in the evening doing his homework, she looked at him with great tenderness and pity and whispered:

'My darling, my pretty one. . . . Oh, my sweet child, so clever, and so fair . . .'

'An island,' he read, 'is a piece of land surrounded on all sides by water.'

'An island is a piece of land . . .' she repeated, and this was the first opinion she had expressed with absolute conviction after so many years of silence and complete vacancy of mind.

She already had her own opinions and at supper she talked to Sasha's parents about how difficult children found it at secondary schools, but that a classical education was much better than a technical one for all that, for with a classical education all careers were open to you – you could be a doctor if you wished, or an engineer if you preferred it.

Sasha began going to school. His mother went on a visit to her sister in Kharkov and did not return; his father went off every day somewhere to inspect cattle and was often away from home for three whole days. Olga could not help feeling that the poor boy had been completely abandoned, that no one cared for him, that he was dying of hunger, and so she took him to live with her in the cottage and made him comfortable there in a little room of his own.

For six months Sasha had been living with her in the cottage. Every morning she came into his room and found him fast asleep with his hand under his cheek, breathing inaudibly. She did not feel like waking him.

'Sasha dear,' she would say sadly, 'get up, darling. Time to go to school.'

261

He got up, dressed, said a prayer, then sat down to breakfast, drinking three cups of tea and eating two large buns and half a buttered French loaf. He was only half awake and consequently in a bad mood.

'I don't think you really know your fable by heart, Sasha,' said Olga, looking at him as though she were seeing him off on a long journey. 'You're such a worry to me, dear. You must try and do your lessons well, darling. Obey your teachers.'

'Oh, leave me alone,' Sasha said.

Then he walked down the street to school, a little fellow but in a big cap and with a satchel on his back. Olga followed him noiselessly.

'Sa-a-sha!' she called after him.

He looked round, and she thrust a date or a caramel into his hand. When they turned into the street where his school was he would feel ashamed of being followed by a tall, stout woman.

'You'd better go home, auntie,' he said. 'I can go the rest of the way by myself.'

She would stop and follow him with her unblinking eyes till he had disappeared in the entrance of the school. Oh, how she doted on him! Of all her former attachments not one had been so deep. Never before had her soul submitted so entirely, so selflessly, and with such delight as now, when her maternal instincts were getting a more and more powerful hold on her. For this little boy, to whom she was not related in any way, for the dimples in his cheeks, for his school cap, she would have given her whole life, she would have given it gladly and with tears of tenderness. Why? Who can tell why?

Having seen Sasha off to school, she would return home quietly, contented, at peace with herself, brimming over with love; her face, which had grown younger during the last six months, smiled and shone with pleasure. People who met her in the street could not help feeling pleased.

'Good morning, Olga darling! How are you, darling?'

'They make you work hard at school nowadays,' she would tell them at the market. 'It's no joke! They gave my boy, who is in the first form, a fable to learn by heart, a Latin translation, and a problem. How do they expect a little boy to do all that?'

And she would start talking about the teachers, the lessons, the school books, repeating what Sasha had said about them.

At three o'clock they had their dinner, in the evening they did his homework together and cried. When she put him to bed, she would make the sign of the cross over him for a long time and would whisper a prayer; then, when she went to bed herself, she would dream of the far-away misty future when Sasha, having finished his studies, would become a doctor or an engineer, would have a big house of his own, horses, a carriage, would get married and have children. . . . She would fall asleep, thinking of the same things, and tears would run down her cheeks from her closed eyes. Her black cat lay purring at her side: 'Purr . . . purr . . . purr . . .'

Suddenly there would be a loud knock at the front gate. Olga would wake up, breathless with terror, her heart pounding violently. Half a minute later another knock.

'It's a telegram from Kharkov,' she thought, beginning to tremble all over. 'It must be Sasha's mother sending for him. Oh, dear!' She was in despair. Her head, feet, and hands would turn cold, and she could not help feeling that she was the most unhappy woman in the world. But a minute later she would hear voices: it was the veterinary surgeon coming home from the club.

'Well, thank God!' she would think.

The weight was gradually lifted from her heart and she felt at ease again; she went back to bed, thinking of Sasha, who was sleeping soundly in the next room and crying out in his sleep from time to time:

'I'll give you one! Get out! Don't hit me!'

Lady with Lapdog

I

THE appearance on the front of a new arrival – a lady with a lapdog – became the topic of general conversation. Dmitry Dmitrich Gurov, who had been a fortnight in Yalta and got used to its ways, was also interested in new arrivals. One day, sitting on the terrace of Vernet's restaurant, he saw a young woman walking along the promenade; she was fair, not very tall, and wore a toque; behind her trotted a white pomeranian.

Later he came across her in the park and in the square several times a day. She was always alone, always wearing the same toque, followed by the white pomeranian. No one knew who she was, and she became known simply as the lady with the lapdog.

'If she's here without her husband and without any friends,' thought Gurov, 'it wouldn't be a bad idea to strike up an acquaintance with her.'

He was not yet forty, but he had a twelve-year-old daughter and two schoolboy sons. He had been married off when he was still in his second year at the university, and his wife seemed to him now to be almost twice his age. She was a tall, black-browed woman, erect, dignified, austere, and, as she liked to describe herself, a 'thinking person'. She was a great reader, preferred the new 'advanced' spelling, called her husband by the more formal 'Dimitry' and not the familiar 'Dmitry'; and though he secretly considered her not particularly intelligent, narrow-minded, and inelegant, he was afraid of her and disliked being at home. He had been unfaithful to her for a long time, he was often unfaithful to her, and that was why, perhaps, he almost always spoke ill of women, and when men discussed women in his presence, he described them as *the lower breed*.

. He could not help feeling that he had had enough bitter experience to have the right to call them as he pleased, but all the same without *the lower breed* he could not have existed a couple of days. He was bored and ill at ease among men, with whom he was reticent and cold, but when he was among women he felt at ease, he knew what to talk about with them and how to behave; even when he was silent in their company he experienced no feeling of constraint. There was something attractive, something elusive in his appearance, in his character and his whole person, that women found interesting and irresistible; he was aware of it, and was himself drawn to them by some irresistible force.

Long and indeed bitter experience had taught him that every new affair, which at first relieved the monotony of life so pleasantly and appeared to be such a charming and light adventure, among decent people and especially among Muscovites, who are so irresolute and so hard to rouse, inevitably developed into an extremely complicated problem and finally the whole situation became rather cumbersome. But at every new meeting with an attractive woman he forgot all about this experience, he wanted to enjoy life so badly and it all seemed so simple and amusing.

And so one afternoon, while he was having dinner at a restaurant in the park, the woman in the toque walked in unhurriedly and took a seat at the table next to him. The way she looked, walked, and dressed, wore her hair, told him that she was of good social standing, that she was married, that she was in Yalta for the first time, that she was alone and bored. . . . There was a great deal of exaggeration in the stories about the laxity of morals among the Yalta visitors, and he dismissed them with contempt, for he knew that such stories were mostly made up by people who would gladly have sinned themselves if they had had any idea how to go about it; but when the woman sat down at the table three yards away from him he remembered these stories of easy conquests and excursions to the mountains and the tempting thought of a quick and fleeting affair, an affair with a strange woman whose very name he did not know, suddenly took possession of him.

He tried to attract the attention of the dog by calling softly to it, and when the pomeranian came up to him he shook a finger at it. The pomeranian growled. Gurov again shook a finger at it.

The woman looked up at him and immediately lowered her eyes. 'He doesn't bite,' she said and blushed.

'May I give him a bone?' he asked, and when she nodded, he said amiably: 'Have you been long in Yalta?'

'About five days.'

'And I am just finishing my second week here.'

They said nothing for the next few minutes.

'Time flies,' she said without looking at him, 'and yet it's so boring here.'

'That's what one usually hears people saying here. A man may be living in Belev and Zhizdra or some other God-forsaken hole and he isn't bored, but the moment he comes here all you hear from him is "Oh, it's so boring! Oh, the dust!" You'd think he'd come from Granada!'

She laughed. Then both went on eating in silence, like complete strangers; but after dinner they strolled off together, and they embarked on the light playful conversation of free and contented people who do not care where they go or what they talk about. They walked, and talked about the strange light that fell on the sea; the water was of such a soft and warm lilac, and the moon threw a shaft of gold across it. They talked about how close it was after a hot day. Gurov told her that he lived in Moscow, that he was a graduate in philology but worked in a bank, that he had at one time thought of singing in a private opera company but had given up the idea, that he owned two houses in Moscow. . . . From her he learnt that she had grown up in Petersburg, but had got married in the town of S—, where she had been living for the past two years, that she would stay another month in Yalta, and that her husband, who also needed a rest, might join her. She was quite unable to tell him what her husband's job was, whether he served in the offices of the provincial governor or the rural council, and she found this rather amusing herself. Gurov also found out that her name and patronymic were Anna Sergeyevna.

Later, in his hotel room, he thought about her and felt sure that he would meet her again the next day. It had to be. As he went to bed he remembered that she had only recently left her boarding school, that she had been a schoolgirl like his own daughter; he recalled how much diffidence and angularity there was in her laughter and her conversation with a stranger – it was probably the first time in her life she had found herself alone, in a situation when men followed her, looked at her, and spoke to her with only one secret intention, an intention she could hardly fail to guess. He remembered her slender, weak neck, her beautiful grey eyes.

'There's something pathetic about her, all the same,' he thought as he fell asleep.

II

A week had passed since their first meeting. It was a holiday. It was close indoors, while in the streets a strong wind raised clouds of dust and tore off people's hats. All day long one felt thirsty, and Gurov kept going to the terrace of the restaurant, offering Anna Sergeyevna fruit drinks and ices. There was nowhere to go.

In the evening, when the wind had dropped a little, they went to the pier to watch the arrival of the steamer. There were a great many people taking a walk on the landing pier; some were meeting friends, they had bunches of flowers in their hands. It was there that two peculiarities of the Yalta smart set at once arrested attention: the middle-aged women dressed as if they were still young girls and there was a great number of generals.

Because of the rough sea the steamer arrived late, after the sun had set, and she had to swing backwards and forwards several times before getting alongside the pier. Anna Sergeyevna looked at the steamer and the passengers through her lorgnette, as though trying to make out some friends, and when she turned to Gurov her eyes were sparkling. She talked a lot, asked many abrupt questions, and immediately forgot what it was she had wanted to know; then she lost her lorgnette in the crowd of people.

The smartly dressed crowd dispersed; soon they were all gone, the wind had dropped completely, but Gurov and Anna were still standing there as though waiting to see if someone else would come off the boat. Anna Sergeyevna was no longer talking. She was smelling her flowers without looking at Gurov.

'It's a nice evening,' he said. 'Where shall we go now? Shall we go for a drive?'

She made no answer.

Then he looked keenly at her and suddenly put his arms round her and kissed her on the mouth. He felt the fragrance and dampness of the flowers and immediately looked round him fearfully: had anyone seen them?

'Let's go to your room,' he said softly.

And both walked off quickly.

It was very close in her hotel room, which was full of the smell of the scents she had bought in a Japanese shop. Looking at her now, Gurov thought: 'Life is full of strange encounters!' From his past he preserved the memory of carefree, good-natured women, whom love had made gay and who were grateful to him for the happiness he gave them, however short-lived; and of women like his wife, who made love without sincerity, with unnecessary talk, affectedly, hysterically, with such an expression, as though it were not love or passion, but something much more significant; and of two or three very beautiful, frigid women, whose faces suddenly lit up with a predatory expression, an obstinate desire to take, to snatch from life more than it could give; these were women no longer in their first youth, capricious, unreasoning, despotic, unintelligent women, and when Gurov lost interest in them, their beauty merely aroused hatred in him and the lace trimmings on their négligés looked to him then like the scales of a snake.

But here there was still the same diffidence and angularity of inexperienced youth – an awkward feeling; and there was also the impression of embarrassment, as if someone had just knocked at the door. Anna Sergeyevna, this lady with the lapdog, apparently regarded what had happened in a peculiar sort of way, very seriously, as though she had become a fallen woman – so it seemed to him, and he found it odd and disconcerting. Her features lengthened and drooped, and her long hair hung mournfully on either side of her face; she sank into thought in a despondent pose, like a woman taken in adultery in an old painting.

'It's wrong,' she said. 'You'll be the first not to respect me now.'

There was a water-melon on the table. Gurov cut himself a slice and began to eat it slowly. At least half an hour passed in silence.

Anna Sergeyevna was very touching; there was an air of a pure, decent, naïve woman about her, a woman who had very little experience of life; the solitary candle burning on the table scarcely lighted up her face, but it was obvious that she was unhappy.

'But, darling, why should I stop respecting you?' Gurov asked. 'You don't know yourself what you're saying.'

'May God forgive me,' she said, and her eyes filled with tears. 'It's terrible.'

'You seem to wish to justify yourself.'

'How can I justify myself? I am a bad, despicable creature. I despise myself and have no thought of justifying myself. I haven't deceived my husband, I've deceived myself. And not only now. I've been deceiving myself for a long time. My husband is, I'm sure, a good and honest man, but, you see, he is a flunkey. I don't know what he does at his office, all I know is that he is a flunkey. I was only twenty when I married him, I was eaten up by curiosity, I wanted something better. There surely must be a different kind of life, I said to myself. I wanted to live. To live, to live! I was burning with curiosity. I don't think you know what I am talking about, but I swear I could no longer control myself, something was happening to me, I could not be held back, I told my husband I was ill, and I came here. . . . Here too I was going about as though in a daze, as though I was mad, and now I've become a vulgar worthless woman whom everyone has a right to despise.'

Gurov could not help feeling bored as he listened to her; he was irritated by her naïve tone of voice and her repentance, which was so unexpected and so out of place; but for the tears in her eyes, he might have thought that she was joking or play-acting.

'I don't understand,' he said gently, 'what it is you want.'

She buried her face on his chest and clung close to him.

'Please, please believe me,' she said. 'I love a pure, honest life. I hate immorality. I don't know myself what I am doing. The common people say "the devil led her astray". I too can now say about myself that the devil has led me astray.'

'There, there . . .' he murmured.

He gazed into her staring, frightened eyes, kissed her, spoke gently and affectionately to her, and gradually she calmed down and her cheerfulness returned; both of them were soon laughing.

Later, when they went out, there was not a soul on the promenade, the town with its cypresses looked quite dead, but the sea was still roaring and dashing itself against the shore; a single launch tossed on the waves, its lamp flickering sleepily.

They hailed a cab and drove to Oreanda.

'I've just found out your surname, downstairs in the lobby,' said Gurov. 'Von Diederitz. Is your husband a German?'

'No. I believe his grandfather was German. He is of the Orthodox faith himself.'

In Oreanda they sat on a bench not far from the church, looked down on the sea, and were silent. Yalta could scarcely be seen through the morning mist. White clouds lay motionless on the mountain tops. Not a leaf stirred on the trees, the cicadas chirped, and the monotonous, hollow roar of the sea, coming up from below, spoke of rest, of eternal sleep awaiting us all. The sea had roared like that down below when there was no Yalta or Oreanda, it was roaring now, and it would go on roaring as indifferently and hollowly when we were here no more. And in this constancy, in this complete indifference to the life and death of each one of us, there is perhaps hidden the guarantee of our eternal salvation, the never-ceasing movement of life on earth, the never-ceasing movement towards perfection. Sitting beside a young woman who looked so beautiful at the break of day, soothed and enchanted by the sight of all that fairy-land scenery – the sea, the mountains, the clouds, the wide sky – Gurov reflected that, when you came to think of it, everything in the world was really beautiful, everything but our own thoughts and actions when we lose sight of the higher aims of existence and our dignity as human beings.

Someone walked up to them, a watchman probably, looked at them, and went away. And there seemed to be something mysterious and also beautiful in this fact, too. They could see the Theodosia boat coming towards the pier, lit up by the sunrise, and with no lights.

'There's dew on the grass,' said Anna Sergeyevna, breaking the silence.

'Yes. Time to go home.'

They went back to the town.

After that they met on the front every day at twelve o'clock, had lunch and dinner together, went for walks, admired the sea. She complained of sleeping badly and of her heart beating uneasily, asked the same questions, alternately worried by feelings of jealousy and by fear that he did not respect her sufficiently. And again and again in the park or in the square, when there was no one in sight, he would draw her to him and kiss her passionately. The complete idleness, these kisses in broad daylight, always having to look round for fear of someone watching them, the heat, the smell of the sea, and the constant looming into sight of idle, well-dressed, and well-fed people seemed to have made a new man of him; he told Anna Sergeyevna that she was beautiful, that she was desirable, made passionate love to her, never left her side, while she was often lost in thought and kept asking him to admit that he did not really respect her, that he was not in the least in love with her and only saw in her a vulgar woman. Almost every night they drove out of town, to Oreanda or to the waterfall; the excursion was always a success, and every time their impressions were invariably grand and beautiful.

They kept expecting her husband to arrive. But a letter came from him in which he wrote that he was having trouble with his eyes and implored his wife to return home as soon as possible. Anna Sergeyevna lost no time in getting ready for her journey home.

'It's a good thing I'm going,' she said to Gurov. 'It's fate.'

She took a carriage to the railway station, and he saw her off. The drive took a whole day. When she got into the express train, after the second bell, she said:

'Let me have another look at you. . . . One last look. So.'

She did not cry, but looked sad, just as if she were ill, and her face quivered.

'I'll be thinking of you, remembering you,' she said. 'Good-bye. You're staying, aren't you? Don't think badly of me. We are parting for ever. Yes, it must be so, for we should never have met. Well, good-bye. . . .'

The train moved rapidly out of the station; its lights soon disappeared, and a minute later it could not even be heard, just as though everything had conspired to put a quick end to this sweet trance, this madness. And standing alone on the platform gazing into the dark distance, Gurov listened to the churring of the grass-hoppers and the humming of the telegraph wires with a feeling as though he had just woken up. He told himself that this had been just one more affair in his life, just one more adventure, and that it too was over, leaving nothing but a memory. He was moved and sad, and felt a little penitent that the young woman, whom he would never see again, had not been happy with him; he had been amiable and affectionate with her, but all the same in his behaviour to her, in the tone of his voice and in his caresses, there was a suspicion of light irony, the somewhat coarse arrogance of the successful male, who was, moreover, almost twice her age. All the time she called him good, wonderful, high-minded; evidently she must have taken him to be quite different from what he really was, which meant that he had involuntarily deceived her.

At the railway station there was already a whiff of autumn in the air; the evening was chilly.

'Time I went north too,' thought Gurov, as he walked off the platform. 'High time!'

III

At home in Moscow everything was already like winter: the stoves were heated, and it was still dark in the morning when the children were getting ready to go to school and having breakfast, so that the nurse had to light the lamp for a short time. The frosts had set in. When the first snow falls and the first day one goes out for a ride in a sleigh, one is glad to see the white ground, the white roofs, the air is so soft and wonderful to breathe, and one remembers the days of one's youth. The old lime trees and birches, white with rime, have such a benignant look, they are nearer to one's heart than cypresses and palms, and beside them one no longer wants to think of mountains and the sea.

Gurov had been born and bred in Moscow, and he returned to Moscow on a fine frosty day; and when he put on his fur coat and warm gloves and took a walk down Petrovka Street, and when on Saturday evening he heard the church bells ringing, his recent holiday trip and the places he had visited lost their charm for him. Gradually he became immersed in Moscow life, eagerly reading three newspapers a day and declaring that he never read Moscow papers on principle. Once more he could not resist the attraction of restaurants, clubs, banquets, and anniversary celebrations, and once more he felt flattered that well-known lawyers and actors came to see him and that in the Medical Club he played cards with a professor as his partner. Once again he was capable of eating a whole portion of the Moscow speciality of sour cabbage and meat served in a frying-pan. . . .

Another month and, he thought, nothing but a memory would remain of Anna Sergeyevna; he would remember her as through a haze and only occasionally dream of her with a wistful smile, as he did of the others before her. But over a month passed, winter was at its height, and he remembered her as clearly as though he had only parted from her the day before. His memories haunted him more and more persistently. Every time the voices of his children doing their homework reached him in his study in the stillness of the evening, every time he heard a popular song or some music in a restaurant, every time the wind howled in the chimney — it all came back to him: their walks on the pier, early morning with the mist on the mountains, the Theodosia boat, and the kisses. He kept pacing the room for hours remembering it all and smiling, and then his memories turned into daydreams and the past mingled in his imagination with what was going to happen. He did not dream of Anna Sergeyevna, she accompanied him everywhere like his shadow and followed him wherever he went. Closing his eyes, he saw her as clearly as if she were before him, and she seemed to him lovelier, younger, and tenderer than she had been; and he thought that he too was much better than he had been in Yalta. In the evenings she gazed at him from the bookcase, from the fireplace, from the corner — he heard her breathing, the sweet rustle of her dress. In the street he followed women with his eyes, looking for anyone who resembled her. . . .

He was beginning to be overcome by an overwhelming desire to share his memories with someone. But at home it was impossible to talk of his love, and outside his home there was no one he could talk to. Not the tenants who lived in his house, and certainly not his colleagues in the bank. And what was he to tell them? Had he been in love then? Had there been anything beautiful, poetic, edifying, or even anything interesting about his relations with Anna Sergeyevna? So he had to talk in general terms about love and women, and no one guessed what he was driving at, and his wife merely raised her black eyebrows and said:

'Really, Dimitry, the role of a coxcomb doesn't suit you at all!'

One evening, as he left the Medical Club with his partner, a civil servant, he could not restrain himself, and said:

'If you knew what a fascinating woman I met in Yalta!'

The civil servant got into his sleigh and was about to be driven off, but suddenly he turned round and called out:

'I say!'

'Yes?'

'You were quite right: the sturgeon *was* a bit off.'

These words, so ordinary in themselves, for some reason hurt Gurov's feelings: they seemed to him humiliating and indecent. What savage manners! What faces! What stupid nights! What uninteresting, wasted days! Crazy gambling at cards, gluttony, drunkenness, endless talk about one and the same thing. Business that was of no use to anyone and talk about one and the same thing absorbed the greater part of one's time and energy, and what was left in the end was a sort of dock-tailed, barren life, a sort of nonsensical existence, and it was impossible to escape from it, just as though you were in a lunatic asylum or a convict chain-gang!

Gurov lay awake all night, fretting and fuming, and had a splitting headache the whole of the next day. The following nights too he slept badly, sitting up in bed thinking, or walking up and down his room. He was tired of his children, tired of the bank, he did not feel like going out anywhere or talking about anything.

In December, during the Christmas holidays, he packed his things, told his wife that he was going to Petersburg to get a job for a young man he knew, and set off for the town of S—. Why? He had no very clear idea himself. He wanted to see Anna Sergeyevna, to talk to her, to arrange a meeting, if possible.

He arrived in S— in the morning and took the best room in a hotel, with a fitted carpet of military grey cloth and an inkstand grey with dust on the table, surmounted by a horseman with raised hand and no head. The hall porter supplied him with all the necessary information: Von Diederitz lived in a house of his own in Old Potter's Street, not far from the hotel. He lived well, was rich, kept his own carriage horses, the whole town knew him. The hall-porter pronounced the name: Dridiritz.

Gurov took a leisurely walk down Old Potter's Street and found the house. In front of it was a long grey fence studded with up-turned nails.

'A fence like that would make anyone wish to run away,' thought Gurov, scanning the windows and the fence.

As it was a holiday, he thought, her husband was probably at home. It did not matter either way, though, for he could not very well embarrass her by calling at the house. If he were to send in a note it might fall into the hands of the husband and ruin every-thing. The best thing was to rely on chance. And he kept walking up and down the street and along the fence, waiting for his chance. He watched a beggar enter the gate and the dogs attack him; then, an hour later, he heard the faint indistinct sounds of a piano. That must have been Anna Sergeyevna playing. Suddenly the front door opened and an old woman came out, followed by the familiar white pomeranian. Gurov was about to call to the dog, but his heart began to beat violently and in his excitement he could not remember its name.

He went on walking up and down the street, hating the grey fence more and more, and he was already saying to himself that Anna Sergeyevna had forgotten him and had perhaps been having a good time with someone else, which was indeed quite natural for a young woman who had to look at that damned fence from morn-ing till night. He went back to his hotel room and sat on the sofa for a long time, not knowing what to do, then he had dinner and after dinner a long sleep.

'How stupid and disturbing it all is,' he thought, waking up and staring at the dark windows: it was already evening. 'Well, I've had a good sleep, so what now? What am I going to do tonight?'

He sat on a bed covered by a cheap grey blanket looking exactly like a hospital blanket, and taunted himself in vexation:

'A *lady* with a lapdog! Some adventure, I must say! Serves you right!'

At the railway station that morning he had noticed a poster

announcing in huge letters the first performance of *The Geisha Girl* at the local theatre. He recalled it now, and decided to go to the theatre.

'Quite possibly she goes to first nights,' he thought.

The theatre was full. As in all provincial theatres, there was a mist over the chandeliers and the people in the gallery kept up a noisy and excited conversation; in the first row of the stalls stood the local dandies with their hands crossed behind their backs; here, too, in the front seat of the Governor's box, sat the Governor's daughter, wearing a feather boa, while the Governor himself hid modestly behind the portière so that only his hands were visible; the curtain stirred, the orchestra took a long time tuning up. Gurov scanned the audience eagerly as they filed in and occupied their seats.

Anna Sergeyevna came in too. She took her seat in the third row, and when Gurov glanced at her his heart missed a beat and he realized clearly that there was no one in the world nearer and dearer or more important to him than that little woman with the stupid lorgnette in her hand, who was in no way remarkable. That woman lost in a provincial crowd now filled his whole life, was his misfortune, his joy, and the only happiness that he wished for himself. Listening to the bad orchestra and the wretched violins played by second-rate musicians, he thought how beautiful she was. He thought and dreamed.

A very tall, round-shouldered young man with small whiskers had come in with Anna Sergeyevna and sat down beside her; he nodded at every step he took and seemed to be continually bowing to someone. This was probably her husband, whom in a fit of bitterness at Yalta she had called a flunkey. And indeed there was something of a lackey's obsequiousness in his lank figure, his whiskers, and the little bald spot on the top of his head. He smiled sweetly, and the gleaming insignia of some scientific society which he wore in his buttonhole looked like the number on a waiter's coat.

In the first interval the husband went out to smoke and she was left in her seat. Gurov, who also had a seat in the stalls, went up to her and said in a trembling voice and with a forced smile:

'Good evening!'

She looked up at him and turned pale, then looked at him again in panic, unable to believe her eyes, clenching her fan and lorgnette in her hand and apparently trying hard not to fall into a dead faint. Both were silent. She sat and he stood, frightened by her embarrassment and not daring to sit down beside her. The violinists and the flautist began tuning their instruments, and they suddenly felt terrified, as though they were being watched from all the boxes. But a moment later she got up and walked rapidly towards one of the exits; he followed her, and both of them walked aimlessly along corridors and up and down stairs. Figures in all sorts of uniforms – lawyers, teachers, civil servants, all wearing badges – flashed by them; ladies, fur coats hanging on pegs, the cold draught bringing with it the odour of cigarette-ends. Gurov, whose heart was beating violently, thought:

'Oh Lord, what are all these people, that orchestra, doing here?'

At that moment he suddenly remembered how after seeing Anna Sergeyevna off he had told himself that evening at the station that all was over and that they would never meet again. But how far they still were from the end!

She stopped on a dark, narrow staircase with a notice over it: 'To the Upper Circle.'

'How you frightened me!' she said, breathing heavily, still looking pale and stunned. 'Oh dear, how you frightened me! I'm scarcely alive. Why did you come? Why?'

'But, please, try to understand, Anna,' he murmured hurriedly. 'I beg you, please, try to understand. . . .'

She looked at him with fear, entreaty, love, looked at him intently, so as to fix his features firmly in her mind.

'I've suffered so much,' she went on, without listening to him. 'I've been thinking of you all the time. The thought of you kept me alive. And yet I tried so hard to forget you – why, oh why did you come?'

On the landing above two schoolboys were smoking and looking down, but Gurov did not care. He drew Anna Sergeyevna towards him and began kissing her face, her lips, her hands.

'What are you doing? What are you doing?' she said in horror, pushing him away. 'We've both gone mad. You must go back tonight, this minute. I implore you, by all that's sacred . . . Somebody's coming!'

Somebody was coming up the stairs.

'You must go back,' continued Anna Sergeyevna in a whisper. 'Do you hear? I'll come to you in Moscow. I've never been happy, I'm unhappy now, and I shall never be happy, never! So please don't make me suffer still more. I swear I'll come to you in Moscow. But now we must part. Oh, my sweet, my darling, we must part!'

She pressed his hand and went quickly down the stairs, looking back at him all the time, and he could see from the expression in her eyes that she really was unhappy. Gurov stood listening for a short time, and when all was quiet he went to look for his coat and left the theatre.

IV

Anna Sergeyevna began going to Moscow to see him. Every two or three months she left the town of S—, telling her husband that she was going to consult a Moscow gynaecologist, and her husband believed and did not believe her. In Moscow she stayed at the Slav Bazaar and immediately sent a porter in a red cap to inform Gurov of her arrival. Gurov went to her hotel, and no one in Moscow knew about it.

One winter morning he went to her hotel as usual (the porter had called with his message at his house the evening before, but he had not been in). He had his daughter with him, and he was glad of the opportunity of taking her to school, which was on the way to the hotel. Snow was falling in thick wet flakes.

'It's three degrees above zero,' Gurov was saying to his daughter, 'and yet it's snowing. But then, you see, it's only warm on the earth's surface, in the upper layers of the atmosphere the temperature's quite different.'

'Why isn't there any thunder in winter, Daddy?'

He explained that, too. As he was speaking, he kept thinking that he was going to meet his mistress and not a living soul knew about it. He led a double life: one for all who were interested to see, full of conventional truth and conventional deception, exactly like the lives of his friends and acquaintances; and another which went on in secret. And by a kind of strange concatenation of circumstances, possibly quite by accident, everything that was important, interesting, essential, everything about which he was sincere and did not deceive himself, everything that made up the quintessence of his life, went on in secret, while everything that was a lie, everything that was merely the husk in which he hid himself to conceal the truth, like his work at the bank, for instance, his discussions at the club, his ideas of the lower breed, his going to anniversary functions with his wife – all that happened in the sight of all. He judged others by himself, did not believe what he saw, and was always of the opinion that every man's real and most interesting life went on in secret, under cover of night. The personal, private life of an individual was kept a secret, and perhaps that was partly the reason why civilized man was so anxious that his personal secrets should be respected.

Having seen his daughter off to her school, Gurov went to the Slav Bazaar. He took off his fur coat in the cloakroom, went upstairs, and knocked softly on the door. Anna Sergeyevna, wearing the grey dress he liked most, tired out by her journey and by the suspense of waiting for him, had been expecting him since the evening before; she was pale, looked at him without smiling, but was in his arms the moment he went into the room. Their kiss was long and lingering, as if they had not seen each other for two years.

'Well,' he asked, 'how are you getting on there? Anything new?'

'Wait, I'll tell you in a moment. . . . I can't . . .'

She could not speak because she was crying. She turned away from him and pressed her handkerchief to her eyes.

'Well, let her have her cry,' he thought, sitting down in an armchair. 'I'll wait.'

Then he rang the bell and ordered tea; while he was having his tea, she was still standing there with her face to the window. She wept because she could not control her emotions, because she was bitterly conscious of the fact that their life was so sad: they could only meet in secret, they had to hide from people, like thieves! Was not their life ruined?

'Please, stop crying!' he said.

It was quite clear to him that their love would not come to an end for a long time, if ever. Anna Sergeyevna was getting attached to him more and more strongly, she worshipped him, and it would have been absurd to tell her that all this would have to come to an end one day. She would not have believed it, anyway.

He went up to her and took her by the shoulders, wishing to be nice to her, to make her smile; and at that moment he caught sight of himself in the looking glass.

His hair was already beginning to turn grey. It struck him as strange that he should have aged so much, that he should have lost his good looks in the last few years. The shoulders on which his hands lay were warm and quivering. He felt so sorry for this life, still so warm and beautiful, but probably soon to fade and wilt like his own. Why did she love him so? To women he always seemed different from what he was, and they loved in him not himself, but the man their imagination conjured up and whom they had eagerly been looking for all their lives; and when they discovered their mistake they still loved him. And not one of them had ever been happy with him. Time had passed, he had met women, made love to them, parted from them, but not once had he been in love; there had been everything between them, but no love.

It was only now, when his hair was beginning to turn grey, that he had fallen in love properly, in good earnest – for the first time in his life.

He and Anna Sergeyevna loved each other as people do who are very dear and near, as man and wife or close friends love each other; they could not help feeling that fate itself had intended them for one another, and they were unable to understand why he should have a wife and she a husband; they were like two migrating birds, male and female, who had been caught and forced to live in separate cages. They had forgiven each other what they had been ashamed of in the past, and forgave each other everything in their present, and felt that this love of theirs had changed them both.

Before, when he felt depressed, he had comforted himself by all sorts of arguments that happened to occur to him on the spur of the moment, but now he had more serious things to think of, he felt profound compassion, he longed to be sincere, tender. . . .

'Don't cry, my sweet,' he said. 'That'll do, you've had your cry. . . . Let's talk now, let's think of something.'

Then they had a long talk. They tried to think how they could get rid of the necessity of hiding, telling lies, living in different towns, not seeing one another for so long. How were they to free themselves from their intolerable chains?

'How? How?' he asked himself, clutching at his head. 'How?'

And it seemed to them that in only a few more minutes a solution would be found and a new, beautiful life would begin; but both of them knew very well that the end was still a long, long way away and that the most complicated and difficult part was only just beginning.

MORE ABOUT PENGUINS

Penguinews, which appears every month, contains details of all the new books issued by Penguins as they are published. From time to time it is supplemented by *Penguins in Print* – a complete list of all our available titles. (There are well over three thousand of these.)

A specimen copy of *Penguinews* will be sent to you free on request, and you can become a subscriber for the price of the postage – 4s. for a year's issues (including the complete lists) if you live in the United Kingdom, or 8s. if you live elsewhere. Just write to Dept EP, Penguin Books Ltd, Harmondsworth, Middlesex, enclosing a cheque or postal order, and your name will be added to the mailing list.

Some other Penguin Classics are described on the following pages.

Note: *Penguinews* and *Penguins in Print* are not available in the U.S.A. or Canada

PLAYS

Chekhov

Translated by Elisaveta Fen

One of a generation on the brink of a tremendous social upheaval, Anton Chekhov (1860–1904) paints in his plays an essentially tragic picture of Russian society. The plays in this volume – *Ivanov*, *The Cherry Orchard*, *The Seagull*, *Uncle Vania* and *Three Sisters*, together with three one-act 'jests' – all display Chekhov's overwhelming sense of the tedium and futility of everyday life. Yet his representation of human relationships is infinitely sympathetic, and each play contains at least one character who expresses Chekhov's hope for a brighter future.

TOLSTOY

War and Peace

Translated by Rosemary Edmonds
(in two volumes)

Few would dispute the claim of *War and Peace* to be regarded as the greatest novel in any language. This massive chronicle, to which Leo Tolstoy (1828–1910) devoted five whole years shortly after his marriage, portrays Russian family life during and after the Napoleonic War. Tolstoy's faith in life and his piercing insight lend universality to a work which holds the mirror up to nature as truly as Shakespeare or Homer.

The first volume of Rosemary Edmonds's modern translation takes the story as far as the appearance of the celebrated comet before Napoleon's crossing of the Niemen. The second volume describes Napoleon's Russian campaign of 1812 and the retreat from Moscow.

Anna Karenin

Translated by Rosemary Edmonds

Anna Karenin, which Tolstoy began in 1873, has been called the greatest of all novels – surpassing in humanity even the earlier *War and Peace*. In this tragedy of a fashionable woman who abandons husband, son, and social position for a passionate liaison which finally drives her to suicide, Tolstoy has in addition given us, in the character of Levin, a true reflection of himself and his tortured search for the meaning of life. For the Penguin Classics Rosemary Edmonds has rendered into fluent English Tolstoy's great canvas of contemporary Russian life, with its deep and varied insight into human nature.

Also available
CHILDHOOD, BOYHOOD, YOUTH
RESURRECTION
THE COSSACKS/IVAN ILYICH/HAPPY EVER AFTER

DOSTOYEVSKY

The Brothers Karamazov

Translated by David Magarshack
(in two volumes)

The Brothers Karamazov, the culmination of Dostoyevsky's work, was completed in 1880, shortly before his death. A story of parricide and fraternal jealousy which profoundly involves the questions of anarchism, atheism, and the existence of God.

The first volume in David Magarshack's excellent modern translation introduces Fyodor Karamazov, a mean and disreputable Russian land-owner, and his three legitimate sons: Dmitry, a profligate army officer; Ivan, a writer with revolutionary ideas; and Alexey, a religious novice. They meet to resolve a family dispute in the presence of the monk Zossima. In the second volume Dmitry is apprehended at the height of a wild orgy with his mistress and charged with the murder of his father, who has been robbed and killed by night.

The Idiot

Translated by David Magarshack

The Idiot, Prince Myshkin, is perhaps the most appealing of all Dostoyevsky's heroes. Gentle, saintly, foolish, and kind, Myshkin is on one view the pure idealized Christian: on another he is the catalyst of a bitter criticism of the Russian ruling class. This dual vision marks out for the modern reader *The Idiot* as one of Dostoyevsky's major novels.

Also available
CRIME AND PUNISHMENT
THE DEVILS
THE GAMBLER/BOBOK/A NASTY STORY

THE PENGUIN CLASSICS

The Most Recent Volumes

BEROUL

The Romance of Tristan *Alan S. Fedrick*

PLATO

The Laws *T. J. Saunders*

XENOPHON

Memoirs of Socrates *and* The Symposium *Hugh Tredennick*

ZOLA

L'Assommoir *L. W. Tancock*

BALZAC

A Harlot High and Low *Rayner Heppenstall*

GOETHE

Italian Journey *W. H. Auden* and *Elizabeth Mayer*

MENCIUS

D. C. Lau

THE PILLOW BOOK OF SEI SHŌNAGON*

Ivan Morris

PAUSANIAS

Guide to Greece (2 vols.) *Peter Levi*

TACITUS

The Agricola *and* The Germania *H. Mattingly* and *S. A. Handford*

*Not for sale in the U.S.A.